PENGUIN BOOKS

One
Christmas
Kiss in
Notting Hill

Mandy Baggot is an international bestselling
and award-winning romance writer.

The winner of the Innovation in Romantic Fiction
award at the UK's Festival of Romance, her novel,
One Wish in Manhattan, was also shortlisted for the
Romantic Novelists' Association Romantic Comedy
Novel of the Year award in 2016. In 2024, Mandy's novel,
Desperately Seeking Summer became a Hallmark Original
Movie entitled *A Greek Recipe for Romance*.

Mandy loves the Greek island of Corfu where she
has a home. She also loves wine, cheese, Netflix, handbags
and horse racing. Also a singer, she has taken part in
ITV's *Who Dares, Sings!* and *The X Factor*.

Mandy is a member of the Society of Authors and splits her
time between living in Wiltshire, UK and Corfu, Greece.

Find out more about Mandy on her website
www.mandybaggot.com

One
Christmas
Kiss in
Notting Hill

Mandy Baggot

PENGUIN BOOKS

PENGUIN BOOKS

UK | USA | Canada | Ireland | Australia
India | New Zealand | South Africa

Penguin Books is part of the Penguin Random House group of companies
whose addresses can be found at global.penguinrandomhouse.com

Penguin Random House UK,
One Embassy Gardens, 8 Viaduct Gardens, London SW11 7BW

penguin.co.uk

Penguin
Random House
UK

First published by Ebury Press 2017
Published in Penguin Books 2025
001

Printed and bound in Great Britain by Clays Ltd, Elcograf S.p.A.

The authorised representative in the EEA is Penguin Random House Ireland,
Morrison Chambers, 32 Nassau Street, Dublin D02 YH68

A CIP catalogue record for this book is available from the British Library

ISBN: 978–1–804–96157–5

One

Beaumont Square,
Notting Hill, London

BANG! CRASH! RATTLE!

Isla Winters' eyes snapped open and she fought to push the sheaves of auburn bed-hair off her face. It was still dark, no light at all coming from behind the curtains ... and there were noises coming from downstairs. Shuffling and drawer-opening and ... was that the fridge door being thumped shut? What time was it? What day was it? She opened her eyes wider, hoping it would somehow help her hear better. Pieces of glitter fell from her hair and on to her face, then the pillow, then the sheets ... those do-it-yourself Christmas cards had a lot to answer for.

Swinging her legs out of bed, she then groped about on the chair beside her dressing table for the long cherry-red jumper she had taken off last night. It was freezing and she shivered, pulling the wool item over her chemise-clad body. She liked winter, she needed to remind herself of that. It was the season to be jolly, it snowed (well, sometimes), the shops were stacked with festive chocs and novelty present suggestions that should never have been invented. It was party season! Life sparkled! But she did prefer it when the central heating had kicked in and she was wrapped up and two macchiatos down.

She caught sight of the alarm clock on her nightstand: 5 a.m. Hannah was never up at 5 a.m.

Drawers were *definitely* being opened downstairs. But she wasn't going to panic. It *had* to be Hannah, didn't it? Although she hadn't heard her disabled sister's stairlift. She *always* heard the stairlift. Sometimes she even woke because she *thought* she'd heard the stairlift. No one had told her subconscious to stop being overprotective.

Creeping out on to the landing, Isla tip-toed as ballet-dancer elegant and mouse-like quiet as she could manage on the chilly wood floor towards Hannah's room and gently pushed the door. It opened a crack, but not enough to confirm an occupant in the bed. Isla pushed a little more forcefully, and the hinges let out the kind of noise you would expect to emanate from a hyena trapped in the mouth of a lion.

'What's happened? Isla?'

Hannah tried to sit bolt upright. It took her three or four moves, arms hitting the string of fairy lights and Christmas-themed bunting she had tied above her bed. By the time she'd managed to make it to a sitting position Isla was inside the room, her fingers to her lips.

'Sshh.'

Hannah smiled, sleep-coated eyes blinking, short crop of light brown hair looking the same as when she had gone to bed. 'Is it Christmas yet? Is Father Christmas here?' The joke had been started around mid-November.

'No,' Isla replied. 'But someone is.'

'What?' Hannah asked, more responsive now. 'Someone's downstairs? What time is it?'

'Five o'clock,' Isla reached for the phone on her sister's bedside table, knocking off a pile of loom bands and baubles in her haste. 'I'm calling the police.'

'Wait,' Hannah said, hand reaching out and catching Isla's. 'Don't do that.'

'Hannah! Someone is in our kitchen!'

'I know,' Hannah said. 'But Mrs Edwards hasn't been sleeping lately and she'll be awake and that means she'll see the police coming and the last time the police came they were here for *Mr* Edwards ... you know ... when they thought he'd died in suspicious circumstances.' Hannah raised her eyes. 'With the pestle and mortar.'

'Hannah, right now, Mrs Edwards' disposition isn't at the forefront of my mind. Didn't you hear me? There's someone in our kitchen!'

'Okay,' Hannah said, breathing deeply. 'Give me a second to get in the chair ... or help me down on to the floor and I'll crawl to the stairlift. Crawling will take less time and be much quieter.' She sniffed. 'We should have hung those really loud jangly old Christmas bells of Mum and Dad's over all the doors. They're perfect burglar alarms, you know.'

Isla raised her eyes. 'The bells wake us up every year if there's even a draught. And you know I absolutely *hate* you crawling.'

'Pah!' Hannah said, waving a hand in front of her face. 'It's the twenty-first century, get over the feeling-sorry-for-people-who-can't-walk vibe, already.' She grinned. 'Actually, crawling is surprisingly liberating. You get to feel a deep empathy for snails and, last time, I found a little black top under my bed I thought I'd left at Creepy Neil's.'

A crash from downstairs had them both refocusing. *Now* was the time to panic. What was immediately to hand that she could wallop an intruder with? Isla swapped the phone she held for a pottery Hugh Grant that one of Hannah's regular customers at the florists had thrown for her. It was twelve inches tall, solid as a brick and Hugh's nose could definitely be used to gouge out an eye if necessary.

'What are you doing with Hugh?' Hannah exclaimed.

'I thought it might scare away whoever's downstairs.'

'It's actually a very good likeness, and don't be so mean about Valerie's artistic skills. She's still waiting for her carpal tunnel operation, you know.' Hannah shifted closer to the edge of the bed and put on a pathetic-looking face. 'Help me get down and crawl.'

'No,' Isla said, turning towards the door. 'You stay in bed and ... if I don't say I'm okay within five minutes, you call the police, whether it's going to upset Mrs Edwards or not. Got it?'

Hannah nodded. 'Got it.' She sniffed. 'Isla ...'

'Yes.'

'Be careful. I don't know what I'd do without ... Hugh.' She stifled a laugh against her bird-print bedspread.

Isla shook her head and made for the landing. Sometimes she wondered if Hannah's spine wasn't the only thing that had been injured in the accident. She seemed to be completely blasé about the possibility of an intruder in their home. Okay, so whoever it was was not being very ninja in their style and, to her, that ruled out serial killer. But she was worried that by the time she got downstairs the would-be thief could be gone with her MacBook ... or, if it was a surprise makeover team, the whole kitchen could be painted the colour of liver.

Holding her breath, Isla slid each bare foot down on to the oriental-patterned carpet runner that tracked up the centre of the stairs. Avoiding the creaky seventh step from the top, Isla strained to listen to where the noises were coming from. Crockery chinked, cutlery rattled. Was that the coffee machine? Who broke into someone's home and made an espresso?

Feeling slightly less afraid of a robber with a taste for her Krups, the weighty Hugh Grant gripped in her left hand, Isla moved softly down the hall towards the kitchen at the back of the house.

She paused at the door and looked into the dark. The blue illuminated ring on top of the coffee machine provided the only light. Someone *was* there. Someone her height, wearing what looked like a cap and a thick coat. What to do? Speak? Let Hugh Grant do the talking? *She could put on the lights.* If she quietly stuck out her right hand she could reach the switch on the wall just inside the kitchen door. She inched forward, the clay model raised, other hand snaking across the wall and then, she hit the button …

BAM! The spotlights in the ceiling flooded the room with brightness and, adrenalin pumping, Isla lunged with Hugh Grant like she was holding a sabre.

'Waaaaa!'

'Argggh! Don't shoot! Don't shoot! It's me! It's just me, bro!'

Heart racing like Mo Farah on the home straight, Isla stopped, staring into the face – well, the hands across the face – of twenty-something Raj, their postman. He nudged the kitchen cupboard door with his elbow and two Christmas cards Isla had stuck on last night fell to the worktop.

'Raj!' Isla exclaimed. 'What are you doing here?' She slid Hugh Grant on to the kitchen worktop, a hand clutching her chest, determined to keep her heart where it should be.

'Just making coffee … just coffee,' he stammered, blowing out terrified breaths. 'Hannah, she said it would be all right. She gave me a key, innit.'

Isla leant her body against the countertop. Her sister had given their postman a key to their house … and not said a word. She shook her head then stopped. That *was* typical of Hannah.

'She didn't tell you,' Raj guessed, holding his hands up. 'I'm sorry. I was just moaning 'bout the coffee at the sorting office last week and how I's got to start even earlier now it's December, you know – cards, parcels, all that stuff Yodel can't do for Amazon – and Hannah said, if I had time … if I was this way, I could, like, come in your crib and make a coffee before I start my round.'

Total Hannah. Despite being the one that everyone wanted to protect, her sister had a penchant for taking people under her wing. Sometimes it was endearing, other times it was annoying, like now, when their postman had trodden dirty slush from the last snowfall over the kitchen tiles and woken them up.

'I'll go,' Raj said, taking a step towards the back door, hands pulling his cap further down over his head. 'I'll get coffee from that new café. It's Moroccan, innit, infused with orange blossom … and that's no bad shit, man.'

'Raj …' Isla began, now feeling a little mean.

'It's okay, we're sweet, bro,' Raj said, backing away, eyes on the pottery statue, hands held up in surrender.

'Raj! Don't you go anywhere!' It was Hannah's voice at full volume. 'I'm coming down!'

'I should go,' Raj said, directing the statement to Isla.

'No,' she sighed. 'Honestly, it's fine.' And she would never hear the end of it from Hannah if she let him leave now. She could hear the whirr of the stairlift which meant her sister had crawled to the top of the stairs, dragged herself into the seat and was on her way down.

'Let's put some more water in the coffee machine, shall we?' Isla suggested.

Two

'I don't think they is gonna last.'

'No? But they've only been here about a month. I haven't even had a chance to invite them over for dinner yet.'

'I wouldn't waste your pasta, Hannah. Always going at it, innit.'

'Going at it? Like arguing?'

'You is feeling me.'

While Isla put on her shoes in the lounge she watched Raj and her sister sitting in the cushioned area of the bay window that looked out over Beaumont Square, their little piece of Notting Hill. The soft plum chenille fabric seating with pearl-coloured fluffy cushions was the only place Hannah insisted on getting out of her wheelchair to relax on. It was her outside from the inside, an opportunity not to miss a thing that went on. Currently, the pair were scrutinising number eleven, whose new residents – a couple in their thirties – had only just moved into the street. So much for Raj starting his rounds early. It was almost seven thirty now and he had had three cups of coffee.

'What does he do for a job do you think?' Hannah asked, sipping from her mug.

'Insurance, innit,' came Raj's reply.

'How do you know that?' Hannah asked, with a giggle.

'It's the three-piece whistle.'

'I know what that means!' Hannah exclaimed in delight. 'Whistle and flute – suit.'

'You is bangin' it now, girl.'

'I is gettin' your East End vibe.'

'Hannah,' Isla said. 'Don't you have to get ready for work?'

'Yeah, yeah,' Hannah responded. 'In a bit.'

Isla checked her watch again. Seven thirty-four. She needed to leave soon to avoid the everyday Tube mayhem and get to the Breekers' offices on time. Plus, there was a little shop on her walk to the station that had the most gorgeous white, feather and diamante Christmas tree in the window display. They had barely started on Christmas in the house, hadn't got a Christmas tree yet and, even though this one was artificial, she loved it … and she knew Hannah was going to love it too. She would look at it again this morning, then maybe put a deposit down tonight and pick it up at the weekend. As clichéd as it might sound, the Winters Sisters did love this season!

'Han, it's just I have to go in a minute,' Isla began. 'I've got a client coming in at nine and then I'm spending all day trying to keep on top of the organisation of the big party.'

Now Hannah paid attention, her head snapping away from the window. 'Can you tell me the theme yet?'

Isla smiled. 'I can't. It's top secret, like always, until a week before, you know that.'

Hannah did in fact know that, but that didn't stop her asking for insider information about Breekers Construction London's Christmas party every single year.

'James Bond?' Hannah guessed.

'We did that two years ago.'

'*Titanic*?'

'No.' But that wasn't a bad idea for next time. They could easily make a function room into a mock-up of the deck of the stricken vessel. Isla could already envisage a huge ice-coated wheelhouse for photo opportunities and vintage dress.

Definitely one for the ideas mood board she'd created on Pinterest.

Hannah turned back to Raj. 'Ooo, *West Side Story* with an East End twist … what's the name of that gang you told me about the other day?'

'FX Crew? Or the Needle Boys?'

Isla closed her eyes. Now it was like the lounge had just turned into the clubhouse in *Sons of Anarchy*. Any second now Raj was going to be talking about 'packing a piece' or 'icing' someone … and she knew enough 'street' to know that that kind of icing had nothing to do with *Titanic*.

'Han … if you need some help then—'

'I don't need help,' Hannah stated flippantly.

'But, you need to get ready for work and—'

'Ronnie Kray is right here.' Hannah punched out a fist and hit the wheelchair's arm.

'Is that what you call that thing, though?' Raj asked, smiling widely. 'Wicked.'

'I know,' Isla began. 'But—'

'Raj can help me into Ronnie. Raj can help me into the stairlift. I can crawl the rest.'

'Han, what about getting dressed?'

'Don't!' Hannah exclaimed. 'I'll manage! I *can* manage! I don't need you watching over me all the time.'

Isla swallowed, hearing the desperation in her sister's voice.

'Listen, I'd better go, yeah?' Raj said, standing up and looking around for somewhere to place his coffee mug. 'These letters and Christmas stuff ain't gonna deliver themselves.'

'You don't have to go yet,' Hannah said through wounded pride.

'I will see yous later, sweets,' Raj said, grinning at Hannah. 'I might even drop into the flower place.'

'Bye, Raj,' Isla said as the postman made a move for the door. 'Sorry about … the misunderstanding … and Hugh Grant.'

'We're cool,' he replied, doffing the peak of his cap. 'It's all good, innit.'

There was utter silence as Raj left the room until the front door slammed shut. Isla was well aware what was coming next.

'Why do you do that?' Hannah yelled. 'You always sodding do that!'

'Sorry,' Isla began. 'I just … have to get to work but I wanted you to know that I had time to help … if you needed help.'

'If I want help I will ask for it,' Hannah retorted. 'My voice didn't get severed in the accident.'

Isla swallowed. Even after five years, it didn't get any easier. Losing their parents in the car crash was one thing, but to have Hannah left permanently unable to walk was almost worse. Isla had been twenty, looking to leave home and start her own life adventure and then everything had been turned on its head. She was suddenly a guardian in charge of a fifteen-year-old trying to cope with being paralysed. Yet, somehow, through it all, her fun-loving sister was still able to be her fun-loving sister, just minus the ability to dance on her toes or rollerblade.

'Well, we need to discuss who you give keys to the house to,' Isla said, almost changing the subject.

'Raj is my friend.'

'Friends don't automatically get keys to our front door.'

'It was the back door, actually.'

Isla shook her head and sighed.

'What?' Hannah asked, cocking her head to the left a little. 'Still surprised how irritating I can be without full use of limbs?'

'Don't, Han,' Isla begged. 'I'm just trying to … do the right thing here.'

Hannah sniffed hard and turned her head to face the glass again, a sure sign there was emotion flowing. Isla was caught between staying where she was, picking up her work bag and beating a hasty retreat or going to her sister and trying to resolve this now.

'Hannah—'

Hannah interrupted. 'What do you think of the couple at number eleven?'

'I don't know,' Isla replied, moving towards Hannah, standing close, but not too close and looking out on to the still-winter-dark street. 'I've said one hello, I think.'

'They have a cat,' Hannah continued. 'Well, they did have. It arrived the day they moved in, in a basket like the big hampers Fortnum and Mason do, and it had a pink and diamante collar. Haven't seen it since then.'

'Maybe it's an indoor person,' Isla suggested.

'Like me, you mean?'

Isla smiled at her sister, putting a hand on her shoulder. 'Hannah Winters, no one could ever call you an indoor person. You're out more than I am!'

'Always with a chaperone in case I fall out of Ronnie into traffic ... or wheel myself *into* traffic and become the reason for delay in the Capital FM travel news.'

This was a disagreement they had quite often. Isla just didn't feel comfortable with Hannah going out completely alone. She knew her sister craved her independence, needed it, but she was so vulnerable. A young woman on her own in the city was bad enough before the sun came up or after it had gone down, but a young woman on her own, in a wheelchair, unable to defend herself against, well, anything that might happen ...

She patted Hannah's shoulder. 'Let's get you upstairs and ready for when Poppy gets here.'

'I do wonder what your job really is at Breekers,' Hannah remarked, shifting in her seat as Isla got ready to aid her into Ronnie. 'Because the conversation avoidance techniques you've got going on are so on point.'

'On point? Not *bangin' bro*?' Isla asked, thickening her tone with all of Raj's would-be gangster.

'Don't *ever* speak like that again,' Hannah said, looking as if she was doing her very best not to laugh. 'You sound like Keith Lemon attempting Snoop Dogg.'

'Ready?' Isla asked, positioning herself to lift her sister.

'If I must be,' Hannah said, sighing.

'Wicked, though,' Isla said, grinning.

'Arrggh! Stop, I said!'

Three

The Royale, Hyde Park, London

Chase Bryan stepped out of the black cab and immediately felt the need to blow into his hands. God, it was cold. It was actually *New York* cold, despite The Weather Channel's promise that London temperatures would be above freezing on their arrival. He ran a hand through his crop of tawny hair and took in his surroundings. Here they were. London. Hyde Park.

In some ways, Hyde Park was like Central Park in New York – a wide expanse of snow-coated greenery in the midst of the grey of the city. But it was also completely different, completely *British*. It was prettier in its design. Thick, sweeping pathways and tree-lined avenues, benches alongside the banks of the Serpentine. The last time he had been here there had been boats on the river, people enjoying the sunshine, lazing on the grass or in striped deckchairs with picnics, horses trotting past. It was no less awesome now, just covered in a dusting of white, joggers and commuters alike buzzing past the lion and unicorn on the Queen Elizabeth Gate.

Chase looked back to the hotel he was standing outside, lights bright against the dawn sky. The fascia of this building was either authentic nineteenth century or just downright tired. A bit like him – the tired reference. He was blaming the red-eye flight over from JFK as the reason he was feeling ill-humoured and the fact it was so goddamn cold wasn't helping.

'I'm dying ... Daddy ... I'm dying!'

Chase turned back to the taxi and quickly held a hand out to his younger daughter, nine-year-old Maddie. Her fingers felt like ice as he helped pull her down from the cab to join him on the pavement.

'London taxis are cold,' Maddie stated through juddering lips. 'England is cold.'

He smiled, brushing a stray strand of tawny-coloured hair off her face, the rest of it carefully pinned into place and topped with a JoJo Siwa rainbow bow. 'Hey, where's my New York girl? We have colder winters than this at home.'

Maddie wrinkled her nose. 'Am I still a New Yorker?' she queried.

'Who told you different?' Chase asked.

'Well, how about the fact that we don't live in New York any more?'

The interjection came from his eldest daughter. Thirteen-year-old Brooke stepped out of the taxi with teenage nonchalance and angst all wrapped up in one looking-way-older-than-she-should package. Wavy dark brown hair sat on her shoulders, yesterday's make-up just about having survived the flight, and a fresh slick of lip gloss on her mouth. She was the image of her mother.

'Did Mom say you weren't New Yorkers any more?' Chase asked. He instantly regretted it. This wasn't meant to be a fight any more. The divorce was done. They had promised to concentrate on being better parents to their children. Although, unlike him, Leanna didn't have the billion-dollar business counting on him and taking up the majority of his time. But she did have

Colt and the new house in Montgomery. *That ... guy!* Anger and bitterness fizzed up his spine before he could stop it.

'It's always Mom's fault, isn't it?' Brooke said, hair flicking first left and then right, iPhone in her hand ready to take a selfie at a moment's notice.

'I don't know if I want to be a Montgomery-er,' Maddie continued. 'It doesn't sound the same.'

'Because it's not the same,' Brooke replied.

'I want things to be the same,' Maddie snapped back.

'Never. Gonna. Happen,' Brooke said coolly.

'Okay,' Chase jumped in. 'That's enough.'

'I don't want to be in London,' Brooke said. 'Why did we have to come with you?'

The cab driver was putting their cases on the street now and the temperature seemed to be dropping even further. Traffic flowed past them, not quite like the yellow taxis and horn-blowing of Manhattan but there were plenty of vehicles including those London icons, the red double-decker buses. Christmas was here in earnest too. Whole fir trees hung from business premises, speckled with golden lights, signs flashing in multicoloured LEDs stating 'Hark the Herald' and 'Merry Christmas'.

'You know why,' Chase said with a sigh. 'For two reasons. Mom had to look after Mawmaw while she gets over her operation and—'

'I don't know why Pawpaw couldn't do it.' This came from Brooke.

'Because Pawpaw isn't that well either.'

'He has a bad leg, Brooke,' Maddie reminded her sister. 'From the war.'

'How could we forget about Vietnam?' Brooke retorted. 'It's all he talks about.' She snorted then and picked up her rucksack with one hand and her suitcase with the other. 'There'd better be a big suite … and they better have a great room service menu.'

'Brooke, wait,' Chase said as the teenager began to move towards the hotel entrance. The second reason they were here was because he *wanted* to have them with him. It had been so long since he had been able to spend quality time with the girls. This job had taken over his life lately and he had had to let it. This was his new start. Another one. He had had so many new starts he was starting to wonder how many reset buttons he was going to be allowed to press. He squeezed his nails into the palm of his hand. He was still here. He was okay. Life was good. He had his children for the holidays and as soon as he had got the ball rolling on this new project it was going to be all about them. In truth, everything he had ever done, every decision he had ever made had always been about protecting them.

'Mom says it's best to leave her when she's like this,' Maddie said, teeth chattering together.

'When she's like what?' Chase asked. 'How she is every day?'

Maddie shrugged. 'Shall I carry my suitcase, Daddy?'

'No, Pumpkin, it's too heavy for you … but thank you.' He put his fingers out to Maddie's coat, drawing the two edges together and fastening the poppers. 'You go inside with your sister and I'll pay for the cab and bring in our bags.'

'Okay, Daddy,' Maddie replied, turning towards the hotel frontage.

He watched her go, then his eyes went across the street to another hotel. Unlike the Royale they were booked into, this one was modern, sleek, with a black frontage that was trying its best to shout 'luxury'. But something about it wasn't working for him. *And* it was small. It only made him even more certain that the vision he had sold to Breekers was the right one to take the company forward, to branch out into an exciting new territory. It was going to be a reset for the company and an imperative distraction for him. As soon as he had caught up on some much-needed sleep.

Four

Notting Hill, London

'You see,' Hannah began, hands working at the wheels of Ronnie Kray. 'This is a classic example of someone *with* the use of two legs falling foul of London life.'

She was referring to Poppy from the Life Start Community Centre who hadn't turned up to walk Hannah to work. Hannah went to the centre a couple of evenings a week to meet with friends who suffered from similar life challenges. It was a run-down building that still had original, dog-eared versions of Trivial Pursuit and Twister (which was ironic as most of the attendees were in wheelchairs) and a CD/cassette combi to provide the music. Hannah had hated it when she'd first gone there at fifteen, fuelled by hatred for the position she found herself in, but Gabby – a very loud but gorgeously hilarious girl with spina bifida – had asked in no uncertain terms if Hannah thought she was too good for the group, and somehow a friendship had been forged.

Isla paid Poppy to walk Hannah the few streets to her job at Portobello Flowers. However, this morning, on the phone, Poppy had cited a gas main rupture on her street, but as soon as she started elaborating about pipe work and smart meters, Isla suspected she was reading the information from the British Gas website and was instead tucked up under a thirteen tog with a Warburton's Giant Crumpet.

'You don't have to walk me all the way there,' Hannah continued.

'It's okay,' Isla replied. 'Most of it is on my way.' She checked her watch. She was going to be hard pushed to make it to the offices before nine.

'Stop!' Hannah said, wheeling to a sit-still.

'What is it?' Isla asked, one foot skidding on slush.

'There,' Hannah said.

Hannah was pointing to one of the benches on this section of street, opposite the black railings of the park. Sitting on the bench were a couple who only had eyes for each other. Life was going on around them – cyclists navigating around static cars, joggers navigating around static postboxes, people on their phones, people carrying briefcases/tote bags/dogs – but they were completely oblivious. And then it happened. Isla couldn't tell who had moved first, but smoothly, slowly, the couple had become one, lips locked together in a perfect movie scene-stealing kiss.

'And that's the first one of the season,' Hannah said with a sigh. 'Mark it on the advent calendar and eat the chocolate.'

'Oh, Han,' Isla said. 'I think this has to stop.'

'Really? Another thing to add to the list of things I can't do?' Hannah asked, pushing herself forward again. 'I can't help it if I'm surrounded by people having a much better love life than me ... actually, make that *any* sort of love life at all.' She sniffed. 'Apart from you.'

'It will happen, Han, when it's supposed to.'

'Speaks the woman who could have any man she wanted.'

'Why would you say that?' Isla exclaimed. She hadn't had a date in a year. Her last date was someone Hannah had set her up with. His name was Ptolemy and it had been Hannah who fancied him! Except because she was almost permanently in a sitting position, she thought that he wouldn't be interested. And he wasn't. Not because Hannah wasn't amazing, but because he was obviously shallow and blind with no personality and therefore not worthy of her sister.

'Because it's true.'

'My last date was Ptolemy.'

'It wasn't.'

'Han, it was.'

'God! Was it really?'

'Yes! And I only did that for you.'

'And he was a right loser.'

'Agreed.'

Hannah bumped herself down over the kerb and sped across the junction to the next pavement drop. 'It shouldn't be too much to ask though, should it? One perfect movie-moment kiss in Notting Hill. Just one. Just like when Julia Roberts kisses Hugh Grant for the first time.' Hannah sighed, before her eyes opened wide. 'Maybe I could pay someone to do it … like someone really, really, hot … like …'

'Gerard Butler?'

'Eww! Are you still going through your liking older actors stage?'

'Danny Dyer then?'

'I do like Danny Dyer … but even *he's* forty. Come on, Isla, fit men in their twenties. Go!'

'Taylor Lautner.'

'Too teethy.'

'Liam Hemsworth.'

'Chris is hotter.'

'I think someone is a little picky … and, by the way, that's a good thing.' Isla moved out of the way for a delivery man carrying a large box. 'You know as well as I do that if you pay for your kiss, or grab some random stranger for your kiss, that it won't be a perfect kiss in Notting Hill, it will be an awkward kiss in Notting Hill and no one wants that.' She put a hand on her sister's shoulder. 'What makes it perfect is the two special people who mean everything to each other and the amazing moment of connection.' She swallowed. Just where was she getting this from? It wasn't like she dreamed of a movie-moment kiss of her own …

'I may as well give up now,' Hannah said, grumpily. She shifted her chair to deliberately run over an empty McDonald's coffee cup.

'Han, what's wrong?' Isla asked. 'It's December. It's our favourite month, our favourite season. Christmas is just around the corner and we've got so much going on. You're busy at the florists, you've got the Life Start party, we've got the Breekers' party, we've got the Beaumont Square Residents Wine and Cheese Night …'

'I like Raj.'

Isla swallowed, shaking her head and half-hoping her sister's words had been sucked in by the passing bin lorry, scrunched up by the claws and delivered back out in a different guise. Suddenly she was craving another caffeine hit … maybe even a triple shot.

'And *there's* the silence,' Hannah said, pushing on harder.

'No,' Isla said quickly. 'No, silence. Just …' What was she 'just' doing? *Processing?* That sounded way too negative. 'So, you like Raj.' Repeating the statement. Wow.

'What's funny about that?' Hannah asked.

'Nothing. I didn't realise I had … made it sound that way.' Had she? 'When did you … start to think that you might like him.'

Hannah shrugged. 'He's funny. He makes me laugh. He's good-looking.'

Isla looked at her sister then, saw a blush pinking up her cheeks. Hannah really *liked* Raj. *Really* liked him. This hadn't happened before. Well, if it *had* happened before, she definitely hadn't told Isla about it.

'Do you think he's good-looking?' Hannah queried, pulling her wheelchair to a halt.

'Well … I …' What to say? What to say? 'He has nice eyes.'

'I know,' Hannah said, dreamily. 'So dark and mysterious.'

In truth, Isla hadn't looked at Raj's eyes. She didn't remember seeing much of his face at all as it was always half-hidden by a cap. He didn't smell bad. Was that really all she could conjure up? There was no way she was saying that!

'You can leave now,' Hannah said, swinging Ronnie around and lining the wheelchair up with the ramp into Portobello Flowers.

Isla ignored the slight and instead breathed in the heady scent of the blooms in buckets on the pavement ready for a day of sales. White lilies sat next to plump yellow roses and deliciously fragrant red, pink and purple freesias spilled out of a large pewter urn. Subtle pastel carnations, bright gerberas and tiny pine cones were all wrapped up in Christmas-themed paper waiting to entice shoppers looking for something to festive-up their living space.

'These are so lovely,' Isla said, still sniffing. 'Maybe I should get some for my office.'

'You don't have to buy flowers from here just because I work here,' Hannah reminded her like she did every time Isla felt the urge to purchase. 'Just get some cheap ones from Tesco.'

'I like Claudia's flowers,' Isla protested. 'And they last longer.'

Hannah was already halfway up the ramp. Her sister was here, at work, safe. Now Isla had to sprint for the Tube and hope there were no delays. She would have to look at the feather Christmas tree later, on the route back.

'See you tonight,' Isla called. 'I'm going to make lasagne.'

'Maybe we can invite the couple at number eleven,' Hannah called back. 'If Raj is right about them arguing all the time, perhaps a dinner with new friends might help.'

Isla smiled. 'We'll go over there. Introduce ourselves.'

'See you later,' Hannah said as Claudia opened the front door for her.

'Bye!'

Five

Breekers London, Canary Wharf

It was ten past nine. *Ten past nine!* Isla was late, and on the Tube she had been pressed up against multiple people she wouldn't usually have got within a hundred metres of, given the option. Despite the wind-shear factor rivalling anything the Arctic could throw up, she was now sweaty, with chapped lips and hair that needed Toni *and* Guy. Whisking through the glass doors of Breekers London she steamed toward the lifts, mentally going through the fundamental points of the Ridgepoint Hospital project she had been supposed to be starting to talk about at nine. This project was big – as important as the very first client she had handled. That first success had helped forge her path to the top at Breekers, going from personal assistant to department manager in a few quick years. She had come so far and grown so much from that desperate, yet hopeful, twenty-year-old, fresh out of college and suddenly a carer to her sister. *9.13.*

'Morning, Isla.'

'Good morning, Denise.' She greeted her favourite receptionist, then took a much-needed breath. 'I don't suppose Robert Dunbar's running late, is he? Apparently there's a gas main causing all sorts of problems out there.' She hadn't believed Poppy for a minute but it was worth a shot.

'Robert was in at eight,' Denise answered, pushing her glasses up her nose.

'Of course he was,' Isla muttered under her breath. You could set Big Ben by Robert's punctuality. She made to stride off, perhaps run up all the stairs and get fit while she tried to beat the lift. Oh, there was a Christmas tree now. When did that arrive? She slowed her pace a little. It was beautiful and *real*. She inhaled the pine, spruce scent and it seemed to immediately lower her heart rate and inject her with a calming antidote to the rush and tear of crossing the city …

'So,' Denise began. '*He's* coming here.' The last part of the sentence was whispered like a government secret was being passed over and it had something to do with the Pope.

'He?' Isla asked, her interest piqued enough to turn away from the Christmas tree. 'Santa? … Richard Branson again?'

'More infamous than both of those,' Denise said.

'Batman?'

Denise leaned forward over her granite and sparkle reception desk. 'Chase Bryan.'

Was she supposed to immediately know who that was? If it hadn't been fifty-something Denise starting this conversation she might have thought it was one of the twenty-something hot actors Hannah was wanting to talk about. It still could be. Hadn't Denise had a month-long obsession with Zac Efron last year?

'Um … is he in *La La Land*?' 9.17.

'Almost,' Denise breathed. 'New York.'

Isla racked her brain for film titles. 'Um … *Miracle on the Hudson*?'

'He's your boss. And my boss. And virtually the boss of the whole world.'

'I thought that was Stephen Hawking.'

'Chase Bryan is the new CEO of Breekers International.'

What? When did the company get a new CEO? Wasn't it still 'Big' Bill Wartner? Big Bill with his thick, reassuring beard and pearly white smile, hair like salt and pepper candyfloss. He spoke like he had just stepped off the set of a Western and she had always imagined him in a leather waistcoat and chaps on a Dress Down Friday. Had he retired?

But instead of asking where Big Bill was Isla blurted out 'When?' and 'Why?' Was he going to be here for the Christmas party? What if he thought she had spent too much on the food this year? Was she going to have to switch lobster for crab at short notice? The caterers had gone suspiciously quiet lately. Perhaps she needed to drop them another email today ...

'I thought you would have known, being one of the top brass and all,' Denise stated. 'No one I've spoken to seems to know why. I didn't know he was coming until this morning when Carrie heard something from Liz on the fourth floor ... and then we got the email.'

Had Denise said 'top brass'? Was she 'top brass'? Ideally, Robert's job would make her feel like she had *really* arrived but she knew the sort of hours he worked and she had Hannah.

'So, they didn't tell you then ... before the email,' Denise continued.

Isla looked at her watch again. 'I've no idea about anything except that I'm very late and by the sound of it I need to check my emails,' Isla said, turning away from the desk.

'Oh,' Denise said. '*Strange.*'

She stopped in her tracks. Something in Denise's tone was off. Facing the receptionist again she asked, 'Denise ... what should I have needed to know before this email?'

'Well, that's why I'm surprised you didn't know any of this.' *9.20.*

'Denise!' Isla exclaimed. 'What do I need to know?'

'Well ...' Denise breathed. 'You're going to be Chase Bryan's go-to girl.'

What? What had she just said? She swallowed. 'His what?' she asked out loud.

'It said that any messages or calls or anything for the CEO had to be filtered via you while he's over here.'

What?! She was going to be a *secretary* to someone she didn't even know was in the company at all? How did that happen? Denise had just said she was 'top brass'! Why couldn't one of the actual personal assistants assist? And, surely you informed someone they were about to have a job role change before you announced it to the entire firm! She didn't know what to say. And what exactly did being a 'go-to' girl entail? Going back to taking minutes and typing? Answering his mobile phone?

'I need to go upstairs,' Isla said, looking at her watch again. *9.22*. She suddenly felt queasy and the lovely spruce aroma was somehow smelling a little too much like Olbas oil.

'Do you know what time Chase Bryan gets here?' Denise asked. 'Because I might be able to squeeze in a hair appointment in my lunch break if it's not until this afternoon.'

Isla closed her eyes as she headed to the elevator. Up until ten minutes ago she didn't even know who the guy was. Now it seemed like he was about to take over her December.

Six

The Royale, Hyde Park

Chase felt like he'd been hit by a 4x4 driven by an angry business rival – or his ex-wife – that had then reversed back over him several times. And there was noise. A buzzing and a bleeping and something else that sounded like an Adam Levine high-note. He raised his head off the pillow ... it felt like someone had swapped it out with a giant marshmallow.

'Maddie, you're not doing it right.'

'I'm pressing as hard as I can.'

'You're not doing it right. Let me do it.'

'That's not fair. I wanna play.'

'But you can't play it right.'

'Can so.'

'Maddie, just give up already.'

'No ... gimme the controller back!'

The bickering was like a bucket of cold water to the face. Chase drew back the covers, grabbed his T-shirt, pulling it over his head before walking to the doors of their suite.

'Give it back!' Maddie screamed. 'If you break it then we're gonna get in trouble.'

'If I break it I'll say you did it,' Brooke retorted.

'Hey!' Chase yelled, seeing enough. He stepped into the living area and looked at his daughters. Both of them had stopped at the sound of his voice. Brooke had an Xbox controller in her right hand, her left hand over Maddie's, trying to tear away the other. Maddie looked pale-faced, exhausted and ready to cry. The bleeping was from the TV where cars and what looked like Smurfs were bouncing around on the screen in a computer animation.

'What's going on here?' he asked.

Neither of them spoke or moved.

He sighed. 'I thought we were catching up on some sleep.'

Now Brooke dropped her hand from Maddie's and settled for folding her arms across her chest and adopting a chin-stuck-out obstinate stance.

'It's too light outside,' Maddie replied. 'And it's the day.'

'I know it's the day and we're all trying to work out our time zones, but we're all dog-tired.'

'I'm not tired,' Brooke announced.

'Me neither,' Maddie said.

So, it was just him who felt like someone had removed all his internal organs on the flight over here and put them all back in in the wrong order.

'Okay, so what do we do?' he asked, moving towards the full-length window that overlooked the street outside. It was busy, the streets buzzing with working-day life, yet there was also a laid-back vibe he never seemed to feel in the thick of Manhattan. God, there were people down there with steaming cups of take-out in their hands. He would just about kill for a caramel latte right now.

'We could go to McDonald's,' Maddie suggested.

'Are you kidding me?' Chase asked, looking to her.

'I like McDonald's,' Maddie protested.

'The burgers suck, Maddie. Seriously suck,' Brooke stated.

'We're not gonna come all the way across the pond to eat crap we can eat at home,' he said. Apart from a one-minute visit to Starbucks. But that was coffee. Coffee had a whole different set of rules.

'Daddy!' Maddie exclaimed. 'You said the C-R-A-P word.'

Brooke sniggered. It was the closest thing he had seen to a smile since they'd left JFK.

'Sorry, Maddie.' He cleared his throat. 'I just mean, if you wanna go eat, let's go eat something British.'

'What sort of thing do they eat?' Maddie asked.

'I know they drink a lot of tea,' Brooke informed. 'Tyler has a cousin who lives somewhere called Leighton Buzzard.'

'Sweet tea? Like Mawmaw makes?' Maddie queried.

'No, it's not sweet and you add milk,' Chase told them.

'Can we try it?'

'Sure,' Chase agreed, as his mind still served him images of froth and Arabica beans. 'Listen, I'll go get dressed and we'll take in the town and drink tea.'

'Cool,' Maddie said excitedly.

'Can we go somewhere with WiFi?' Brooke asked with a sigh.

'Sure,' Chase answered. 'I'll be a minute.'

The controllers for the game station were dropped to the chaise and Maddie went scuttling off to her bedroom while Brooke sunk down on to the sofa with another pout. Chase turned back towards his room and once inside, closed the doors behind him. Taking a deep breath, he leaned his entire weight on the oak doorframe and shut his eyes. This wasn't just fatigue or jetlag he was feeling, this was fear. He needed this job to work more than he had ever needed anything before, but maybe he wasn't up to it. How did you come out and be the man with a vision and all the business answers when really you were running on empty? And there was no way he could go back to that dark place, not again. The current solution was to try and do what he had been doing since the day Leanna had told him she was leaving him … dig deep, dig *deeper* and pretend. The trouble was he had been doing a lot of pretending for so long …

'This is a golden opportunity,' he whispered to himself. 'Don't mess it up.' He opened his eyes and blinked at his reflection in the mirror on the wall above the bed. 'There is no such thing as a bad decision,' he repeated. 'A decision is only bad because you let success escape you.' He breathed out: 'O-Y-F.' He focused his inner self. 'Own your future.'

Seven

Breekers London, Canary Wharf

'So, picture the scene.'

Isla's colleague Aaron moved his hands in the air like he was painting the shape of a rainbow and edged closer to her desk.

'Somehow, I end up at a country music night at this club in Soho. Don't ask. And ... Sugar. Honey. Ice Tea. There's this hotter than hell guy I've been eye-flirting with at the bar all night ... and he's wearing the tightest pair of jeans – and I mean *the* tightest pair of jeans – and I think to myself, as I've drunk more bottles of Sol than Mexico produces in a month, that I am the luckiest guy right now and then ...' He performed a dramatic pause. 'Guess what happens?'

Aaron still smelt of those bottles of Sol and nothing like the sweet fragrance of the sugar, honey or ice tea words he always said super-fast when he didn't want to say shit. Isla sat back in her chair to both look at him and inch further away from his breath.

'I don't know what happens,' she replied. 'But I'm hoping those tight jeans stayed on, at least until you were out of the club and in a hotel room.'

'He kisses a *girl*!' Aaron exclaimed like Mr Tight Jeans had committed mass murder.

'Oh,' Isla stated.

'Oh?' Aaron said, sliding his bum on to her desk and looking shocked. 'The guy is gay! He's gayer than gay. Gayer than Ian McKellen gay ... and obviously hotter, a bit Matt Bomer if I had to pin him down to something, and ...' He sighed. 'I really thought I was going to get to do that but—'

'Aaron,' Isla said. 'Is there a point to this story or is it something we can pick up another time? Maybe at a bar when I'm not trying to work out why I don't seem to have arranged enough blinis for the Christmas party or why the caterers aren't responding to my emails?' She was completely ignoring this dropping-to-secretary level thing. Ignoring it! She had more important things to manage ... and blinis were important when it was already December!

Aaron stood up, his dark head nudging one of the glittery, supposedly Christmas, pompoms Ethel the cleaner had made and hung from the ceiling at random points around the office. He took a step back and fastened the button of his jacket. Now he looked a bit miffed and Isla felt instantly guilty for not listening properly. The girl-kissing-alleged-gay-guy scenario was obviously more to Aaron than an anecdote they were going to share for years to come.

'I get it,' Aaron said. 'You're the "Go-To Girl" now. Super-important. Uber-busy.'

The Go-To Girl. She was hating that phrase already.

'It really isn't my new job description,' she said quickly. Although theoretically it was, as of this morning, when she had stumbled late, dazed and confused, into what was supposed to be a meeting about the new hospital development. Instead it had turned into a meeting about how she was going to be the contact point for all things Chase Bryan while he was in town. And either no one knew how long he was going to be in London or they were all remaining pretty tight-lipped about it. She had quickly made a suggestion that one of the admin staff take on the role but Robert had looked at her a little like she had just offered up the services of a monkey who couldn't even peel a banana. Isla had always found the typists and assistants very competent, but when she had opened her mouth to elaborate on this the conversation had been moved on and she knew she had no immediate choice. She was clinging to the word 'immediate'. A cooling-off few hours, perhaps a day, and she was almost sure there would be some wiggle room on the role.

'Well, I've heard he's hot,' Aaron remarked, his tone a little softer.

'And gay?' Isla asked.

'Sadly not … well, if you can believe Denise's third-hand gaydar. She hasn't actually seen him yet, says it's like a clairvoyance. He's divorced, two children. Wanted to be an astronaut but ended up playing ice hockey, so I'm envisaging tight pants and buttocks like two of Harry Hill's heads down his trousers.' Aaron sighed like a thespian in *Othello*. 'Then after hockey he relaunched himself as a business coach.'

Ugh! Business coach/life coach. She hated those sorts of people. In her opinion, they seemed to get paid an awful lot of money for boosting people's egos and doling out plain old common sense. *Believe in yourself. Make your own destiny. Anything is possible.* Chase also didn't sound like safe, head of industry, Big Bill at all. Where was his experience in construction or even just industry in the broadest sense? She needed to look up Chase Bryan's photo on the website. She moved her fingers to the keyboard.

'I looked him up on the website. No photo yet,' Aaron stated. 'One of those terrible grey "coming soon" images they really should get the tech guys on to.'

She would google him later. There must be some photos of him somewhere on the Internet. You didn't get to be the CEO of a global firm without a history.

'So, when does he get here?' Aaron asked.

'I have no idea.' Isla was more concerned with the rapidly approaching Christmas party than this babysitting task that looked like it was going to take up all the time in her favourite month. She had hoped this December would be like all the others ... full of celebration on what they had achieved in the year, back-to-back parties with all the clients she had helped, mince pies, prosecco and a little Michael Bublé on the sound system. Although she was still busy with her clients, December was special. It wasn't about being anyone's Go-To Girl. She felt tension creep into her shoulders. She would just have to keep ahead of the game. Take some of the party organisation home with her – maybe Hannah could help with things she didn't need to know the theme for. Although Isla had never been good at delegating.

'I don't envy you,' Aaron began. 'That hospital project is enough of a hot potato without Mr U.S. of A. popping over the pond.' He stretched his arms over his head, getting his watch caught in the string of a suspended pompom and struggling to get it out. 'And ... you have the Christmas party ... no pressure ... argh, help! Get me out of this thing!'

Aaron flapped his arm around like he was a large bird trying to take flight. Isla stood up, going to his aid and taking hold of the wool. Then she dropped her hands to her side and stamped her feet.

'It's no good. I'm so annoyed!' She sounded like a child but she didn't care. Only Aaron was listening and she needed to vent.

'Why do *I* have to be the one looking after him? I am "top brass", Denise even said so, and I have enough to do in

December.' All the lovely, glittery, sparkly things she enjoyed so much. 'Robert knows that.'

'Maybe it wasn't his decision,' Aaron suggested, looking at her with concern.

'Well, whose decision would it have been? And why didn't I know he was coming until he was imminently coming?'

'I thought that about one of my exes.'

Isla closed her eyes and took a deep breath. This wasn't just about Chase Bryan. This was about Hannah … *liking* Raj. She knew she shouldn't be worried. She knew she was totally overprotective of her perfectly capable sister but …

'Perhaps,' Aaron began, 'he asked for the hottest Go-To Girl in the building.' He pointed a finger as if he had just come up with an Einstein-worthy theory. 'Maybe he perused *your* photo on the website … you still have the one that makes you look like Drew Barrymore during her auburn stage, don't you?'

'This is ridiculous,' Isla said. 'And I don't have to do it, do I?' She felt her shoulders relax a little at the thought of absolutely shirking this new responsibility. 'I can just say I don't have the time.' She nodded. 'I really *don't* have the time … I'm going to The Matthews Corporation party on Friday and there's the big meeting with Cleggs coming up … and the … blini situation.' She was making the canapé issue sound like it was right up there with world poverty. But the workforce could get a little antsy if they were hangry.

'Well … I would just be a little careful if I were you,' Aaron said.

Isla caught the note of warning in his tone. What did that mean? 'Careful?'

'I'm just saying, you remember Karen Kinsey?'

Karen Kinsey had left last year. Isla remembered only that there had been talk of a relocation to another Breekers office.

'We all thought she went to Breekers Frankfurt, yes?'

'She didn't?' Isla queried with a swallow.

Aaron sniffed. 'Nothing wrong with it but ...' He looked over his shoulder as if expecting to be hauled into an interrogation room. 'You'll find her in the M&S Simply Food at Waterloo.'

'No!' Isla exclaimed. Karen Kinsey had been far more experienced than her, had seemed destined to beat Isla to the role of Robert's right-hand woman. 'But ... why would she have been sacked?'

'Not sacked, darling, they're far too clever for that. Let's just call it a parting of ways.' His eyes shifted sideways. 'Rumour is ... she was paid to leave.'

'But why?'

'Well, don't take it as gospel but ... I heard she *passed* on a client Robert wanted her to take on. Something to do with ethical reasons ... maybe they wanted the bricks to be made out of the wrong type of shale ... anyway, all I know is she made a stand and her stand got her ...' He looked over his shoulder again. 'Relieved of her duties here to take up stacking sushi and wasabi peas for commuters.'

'You think I should do it,' Isla guessed. 'Be this Go-To Girl.'

'I don't want to see you with your hands on all things raw day in and day out.'

'It won't be for long, will it?' she asked. 'A week tops, do you think?'

'And he might be hot,' Aaron added.

'And he's not a postman with mysterious eyes,' Isla murmured.

'What?' Aaron queried. 'Now that sounds intriguing. I do love a guy in shorts. They do still wear shorts whatever the weather, don't they?'

'Sorry, ignore me … just thinking out loud.'

Aaron shook his head. 'You and Ed Sheeran, eh?' He sucked in a breath, his torso stretching. 'Now, there's a guy I'd like to get to know better. Guitarists,' he mused. 'Always know exactly what to do with their fingers.'

Eight

Westbourne Grove, Notting Hill

This was it. Chase had his feet on the ground where change was going to happen. He looked around, taking in the houses, independent shops and parkland, and seeing buildings almost as dilapidated as he felt. If ever there was an area in desperate need of rejuvenation it was this one. He had never been one for history. One man's prized antiques was another man's worn-out old crap. The plans weren't final yet. This was one of the three proposed sites, but it was the one he was gunning for, the one that was getting him super-excited. And, when the builders moved in and Breekers' first super-hotel and entertainment village in the UK was constructed, everyone was going to be talking about it ... and wanting to stay in it.

He looked across the street at Sugar High, the mocha-painted coffee shop he had left Maddie and Brooke in. It was cutesy, with two decorated fir trees in pots outside the door, strings of silver tinsel and gold baubles hung inside from the window frames. The girls had gone crazy over the cakes and were happy to be left with hot chocolates and two large cupcakes decorated in all manner of spun-sugar craziness he never understood the attraction of. They had eaten British pies with mashed potatoes, vegetables and gravy for lunch, washed down with tea – a rather un-fancy plain white coffee for him – and, finally,

Brooke's ill-humour about being in London seemed to be breaking.

In the pocket of his jeans his phone rumbled. Another message and he could guess right away who it would be from. *Leanna.* He had had five messages since they had arrived in London. *If it's cold make sure Maddie wears a hat. You can try with Brooke but good luck with it.* Followed by: *Have you landed? Call me.* Then: *Why haven't you called me? Don't do this, Chase. We promised to be adult and I'm keeping my side of the bargain.* And finally: *I asked to talk to YOU. An emoji of the British flag from Brooke is not telling me anything!!!*

He pulled the phone out of his pocket and looked at the latest message. *Colt says if you don't communicate with me during this trip you will be in breach of the terms of the court arrangement.*

Colt. His teeth were gritting together already. Colt was the whole fucking problem. He should have kicked his ass a long time ago. He had just about messed up his life and taken everything from him ... except this one thing, this new opportunity at Breekers. The chance to put the new improved him to the test. He was going to show his children that a boy with a dream to walk on the moon could still reach it in a different way no matter what struggles there had been in the past. That sacrificing everything you always wanted wasn't the end of dreaming big, it was just the beginning of a new path. He swallowed. After the way everything had turned out for him with his family? So many Square Ones. Did he believe that mantra? He had to. There was no other way.

'O-Y-F,' he spoke out loud. 'Own your future.'

Nine

Sugar High, Westbourne Grove, Notting Hill

'Oh! I so need this!'

Hannah's exclamation as she sunk her teeth into what café owner Vicky had christened the Mulled Christmas Muffin, was so loud Mrs Smith's little brown terrier, Rolo, let out a bark.

Isla needed it too. She had skipped lunch, instead resolving to solve the missing blini mystery – still no reply from the catering firm – and making a start on the finer details of the 'hot-potato' Ridgepoint Hospital project. Deadlines for submitting for planning were getting tight if the building was going to be sticking to the original proposed timescale. Now it was almost six o'clock and she had abandoned the thought of buying the feather Christmas tree in favour of taking her sister here for sustenance.

'What's in this, Vicky?' Hannah asked through a mouthful of crumbs.

'Oh, Hannah, you know I can't tell you that,' brown-haired, forty-something Vicky answered, squeezing between tables with a full tray of drinks and more cakes in her hands. 'I've heard on the grapevine that that new coffee shop – you know the one that seems to be adding orange blossom to everything – has been sending spies here to see how we do things at Sugar High.'

'You know I wouldn't tell,' Hannah insisted, filling her mouth again. 'And I'm not a spy,' she added. 'Pretty hard to go incognito in a wheelchair.'

'Oh, I don't know,' Vicky replied. 'It's always the ones in plain sight you have to watch.' She ducked her head closer as she got to their table. 'My money's on Rolo.'

Hannah laughed out loud and the little dog barked again. 'Shall I give him some of my muffin?'

'No!' Isla said quickly. 'Remember what Mrs Smith said last week? He's on a special diet after he got pancreatitis from that overdose of leftover Chinese chicken balls she gave him.'

'I'm not sure you can overdose on chicken balls, can you?'

'That wasn't supposed to be the start of a food dare so don't go getting any ideas,' Isla said, wiping her lips with a napkin.

'So,' Hannah said, leaning over the table and talking in hushed tones. 'Who do we think the stranger is?'

Isla knew exactly who her sister was talking about. They came to Sugar High so much they knew almost everyone who regularly frequented the place. And today, sitting in one of the window seats, was a brown-haired teenage girl.

'Tourist,' Isla responded. 'Visiting student. Maybe Polish.' The girl had an iPhone in her hand and seemed to be mouthing some words as her eyes looked at the screen.

'Alone though?' Hannah asked. 'She doesn't really look old enough to be completely on her own.'

Isla shook her head. 'Speaks the girl who demanded to walk to the postbox at the far end of our street on her own when she was six.'

'I was mature for my age.'

'And stubborn.'

'You say that like it's a bad thing.' She grinned. 'It's actually on my CV as a positive.' Hannah gasped suddenly, her eyes back on the girl. 'Two plates and cups. Phew! She's waiting for someone.'

Hannah was right. And now the girl was looking wistfully out of the window. Was she waiting for someone? Maybe a mum or a gran …

'So, are we going to invite the couple at number eleven over for dinner?' Hannah asked, sipping her hot chocolate.

Isla had forgotten all about that crusade after everything that had happened at work. She looked back to Hannah. 'Oh … well …'

'Isla! You said we could!'

'We can,' Isla responded. 'Just, maybe not tonight. I've got a lot on and …' She had planned to run a steaming hot bath, light some cinnamon-and-apple-scented candles, pour a glass of prosecco and not think too hard about what tomorrow might bring at Breekers. Plus, she really ought to think about making their traditional Christmas baked fayre to freeze for the big day. Their mum had always made thick, shortcrust sausage rolls and deep-filled mince pies with little holly leaves of pastry on top.

'Everything is going okay with the party-planning?'

'Mmm,' Isla said through a mouthful of muffin. She wasn't committing to anything when she felt this much out of control. And the news of Karen Kinsey's current employment had scarily niggled away at her all day.

'That wasn't convincing,' Hannah replied. 'Please don't tell me you've had to scrimp on the shrimp.'

Isla swallowed. She was still half-expecting Chase Bryan to be coming over here solely to discuss her budget for the annual festivities. However, in her new role as his 'Go-To Girl' she could easily become economical with the sharing of under-ling information. He was surely far too important to worry about catering.

The bell above the coffee shop door chimed and Isla looked up from her plate.

'Bloody hell!' Hannah announced, the end of the muffin dropping out of her fingers and hitting the plate.

She didn't need to ask why Hannah was practically sali-vating. It had nothing to do with the contents of Vicky's Christmas muffin, it was all down to the man who had just come into the café.

Tall, well-built, with an athletic vibe going on. Tawny hair sort of muzzed into a style, stubble on his jaw and wearing jeans that flattered every inch of him. He wore a T-shirt declaring NY Jets under a tan brown leather bomber jacket that couldn't possibly be warm enough for the temperature outside ... but visually it was pretty much perfect.

'Tourist,' Isla said, without even realising. She seemed to be making everyone in London a tourist today.

'A fucking hot-as-shit tourist,' Hannah stated way too loudly.

'Han!' Isla exclaimed.

'Well! Look. At. Him.'

Isla couldn't deny this was an attractive guy, but now he seemed to be heading towards the teenage girl. Now her danger senses were being poked. What if the girl was meeting this man after chatting to him on the Internet? Maybe he had courted her for months, telling her he liked Justin Bieber and was in Year 7.

'That's him,' Hannah breathed. 'That's who I have to have my kiss with.'

'What?!' Isla exclaimed. 'No! No ... because ... what about ... you said ... you like Raj.'

'I know.' Hannah breathed a sigh. 'But ...'

'But your head's been turned in five seconds.' She was torn between admonishing her sister and keeping an eye on what was going on a few tables away. The girl was smiling at the guy. She was almost waiting for him to get a packet of sweeties out of his pocket.

'And you're the one who's still looking at him,' Hannah remarked.

Yes, she was. Because she was thinking he was a paedophile about to hit on an innocent girl who didn't know any better, not because she wanted some Disney-style kiss with him.

The man put his hand on the younger girl's shoulder then kissed the top of her head, slipping an arm around her shoulders. Right, that was it ...

Ten

'I think you need to leave. Right now.'

Chase wondered if that question was directed at him. It was a woman's voice and she sounded annoyed. He turned around and there she was, right at his shoulder. Auburn hair sat on her shoulders and her wide blue eyes were sparkling. But their beauty was off-set by her angry expression.

'Excuse me?' he answered, all the while racking his brain as to what British etiquette he had fouled up to get her so riled.

'I know what you're doing,' she snarled. 'And you either leave, right now, or I'm going to make a citizen's arrest.'

'A what now?' Who was this woman? The last time he was in London he was pretty sure there hadn't been sheriffs. He stood his ground and folded his arms across his chest.

'Hannah,' the woman said, eyes shooting to the left then quickly resting back with him. 'You need to call the police.'

'What?'

Another woman had spoken now. She was three tables away, in a wheelchair.

'Ma'am, I think there's been some sort of misunderstanding,' he began.

'Don't ma'am me!' Isla ordered. 'I'm not an innocent, naïve teenager who falls for chat about Shawn Mendes and … *Pretty Little Liars*.'

'No?' he asked. 'I actually quite like that show.'

'Oh, I just bet you say that to all the vulnerable kids you stalk on social media,' she erupted.

'What?!' Now he was starting to get a little mad himself. What was this?

'Hannah, have you called the police?' the woman questioned loudly.

'Um ... did you really mean that?' came the reply.

'Listen,' he began. 'I don't know what you think I've done but—'

'Daddy,' Maddie interrupted as she came back to the table. 'Are we in trouble?'

Daddy.

Isla turned around to see another girl standing just behind her, younger with fair hair. She was brushing her hands together and looking at the man with wide, confused eyes.

Oh God. She wanted the floor of Vicky's café to turn into sticky Christmas pudding so she could sink right into it and drown in brandy-infused sultanas. What had she done?

'No, Pumpkin, we're not in trouble,' the American guy answered the younger girl who was slipping into a seat at the table. He then looked back to her. 'We're not, are we?'

Her cheeks were giving off more heat now than the Guy Fawkes bonfire she and Hannah had almost melted at last month. Why had her first thought been *pervert* and not *father*? She shook her head at him. 'No ... I'm sorry ... I thought ...' What did she say next? That she'd pitched him into the Jimmy Savile bracket without so much as a second thought? It was also likely he wouldn't even know who Jimmy Savile was. That was a blessing.

'I got it all on video,' the older-looking girl announced. '"Cray-cray woman in London" might just go viral on YouTube.'

'Brooke,' the man said. 'You will delete that right now.'

'It's gonna cost ya,' Brooke answered. 'Or maybe ... cost her.'

God, she was now about to be fleeced by a girl she had thought she was trying to protect from a molester.

'She won't be posting anything,' the man said sincerely. 'And, I guess, if you were thinking along the lines of what I'm now realising you were thinking ... I should be thanking you for looking out for my daughter.'

She shook her head again, willing her cheeks to stop heating up like they could broil the Christmas turkey. 'No, I should apologise. For accusing you like that and for assuming the worst.' She swallowed. 'I'm very sorry.' She cleared her throat. 'What must you think of the British?' She tested out an attempt at humour and hoped he might think her charming enough to never remember the moment again.

'I think the British are cool,' he told her. 'Confident and ultimately never afraid to say they're sorry.'

Wow. That was a great answer. And she had to tell Hannah, up close, he had the deepest chestnut-coloured eyes.

She smiled. 'We're also very good at making tea and know one hundred and one different ways to use an umbrella.'

The girl he'd called Maddie giggled. 'We had lots of English tea at lunch.' She smiled. 'And pie.'

'Then you're basically almost British yourselves,' Isla replied. 'Listen, I'm very sorry for the misunderstanding—'

'Forget about it,' the man answered. 'Like I said. You were just looking out for my girl and I appreciate that.' He smiled. 'And I'm also very happy I didn't get to see any of those umbrella uses ... because that might have scared me a little.' He held out his hand to her. 'Chase Bryan, nice to meet you.'

And now Isla's face lit up like it could power all the Christmas lights on Oxford Street. She had to leave. Right now. Rude or not.

'Nice to meet you too,' she answered, shaking his hand and internally wincing.

What was she doing? She had just accused the head of Breekers International of being a letch and tomorrow morning he was going to find out exactly who she was. His stupid Go-To Girl. As she backed away, making more apologies, she began to wonder if Karen Kinsey could swing her a job at Waterloo.

Eleven

Beaumont Square, Notting Hill

'Slow down, Isla! I know I suggested trying out for the Paralympics one year but I was only kidding.' Hannah blew out a breath as she worked the wheels of Ronnie Kray along the road into their square. 'And after a Christmas muffin, my core is a bit lax.'

Why had this had to happen? Why had the figurehead of the company, the guy she was going to be right-hand woman to, been in Sugar High? It wasn't fair! Why was this December turning into a curse? She slowed a little, letting her sister catch her up.

'I know what it is,' Hannah said with deep authority, her breath hot mist in the chilly evening air. 'You liked him too, didn't you?'

'What?' She shook her head. Then added, 'Who?'

'The guy you accused of being a paedophile. You know, the *really* hot one, who looks like a cross between Ryan Philippe and Charlie Hunnam … wow, can you actually imagine that hybrid?'

'Why don't we go and knock on the door of number eleven and see if they want to share some lasagne?' Isla changed the subject. Her sister didn't need to know the full extent of how much more embarrassing this situation actually was.

'Well, just you remember,' Hannah started, expertly rolling the wheelchair off the kerb. 'I saw him first … and I work nearer to Sugar High than you. I might start popping in there for a Christmas muffin every day. You know … casually stalk him.'

'He has two children,' Isla reminded her.

'So?'

'So … number eleven,' Isla said, pushing open the black wrought-iron gate that opened into the sections of grass and bark-chipped borders in the middle of the square. It housed two benches, one at either end, both dedicated to former residents who 'loved this place', plus the late Mr Edwards' rose bush, and was the focal point of local activities – weekly choir, camp-o-thon in the summer and the other Beaumont Square seasonal activities like the Christmas wine-and-cheese evening. Their corner of London was far removed from the high-pace of city living you might expect from the English capital. In fact, it was far more *Gilmore Girls*' Stars Hollow than anything else. And Isla loved it that way. She might not join in with group activities as much as Hannah did, but living here had always been predominantly about Hannah. It was what Hannah had always known, what they had *both* always known, and when you had lost your parents, clinging on to a tight-knit and comfortable familiarity had meant everything.

'And I saw him first,' Hannah continued as they made their way through the park to the other side of the square. 'I've got dibs.'

She almost wanted to suggest Hannah thought more seriously about Raj than have her mooning over Chase Bryan. She settled for not commenting on either one and took a breath as they stopped on the pavement outside the steps to number eleven. 'What are they called?'

'He said his name was Chase, didn't he?' Hannah breathed in, closing her eyes. 'Chase is a very sexy name, isn't it? Makes you think of … fast moves and heavy breathing …'

'I meant the couple at number eleven,' Isla interrupted.

'Oh. Oh, I've no idea,' Hannah replied. 'You'll have to do the knocking.'

Hannah was referring to the ten steps that led up to the front door, the same with all the houses on the square, except theirs. One of the first modifications they had had done after Hannah's accident was to do away with the steps and create a ramp.

Isla climbed the steps, moving towards the light shining through the frosted glass in the front door. Hopefully it signified that someone was home. A red-berried Christmas garland hung over the door knocker and Isla took hold of the brass and rapped lightly. Then she looked back to Hannah, waiting on the pavement, blowing on to her fingers. It was cold tonight and snow was forecast to fall, just as the short flurry from last week was starting to clear up. She loved snow but, right now, everything she usually welcomed with open arms about December, seemed to feel a little off. All her routines were as up in the air as Santa's sleigh.

The door opened a crack, stopping on a chain, and one eye and a section of blonde hair appeared in the few inches of gap.

'Hello,' Isla greeted. 'I'm Isla and … down there, is my sister, Hannah and—'

There was a rough and frustrated sigh. 'Which charity is it?'

'Oh … oh no, we're not—' Isla began.

'Of course you're not,' the woman replied sharply. 'That's what they all say at first. Then you'll be wanting me to sign up to a standing order for some lucky draw every month.'

'No, honestly, we live here, in the square and—' Isla tried again.

'Playing the local angle now?' the woman laughed, face still half-hidden by the blue doorframe. 'Well, that won't work.

We've only just moved in and we're only going to be here a few more weeks at most.'

'Oh, well, that doesn't matter, we can still—'

'So, local *doesn't* matter now?' The woman laughed. 'As long as you have my bank details, right?'

Isla had had enough of this. 'I don't want your bank details,' she yelled. 'We live across the square and we *had* wondered if you and your husband wanted to come over for dinner.' She sighed. 'But, to be honest, I'm not sure I want to extend the invitation any more.' She looked back down the steps to Hannah who was watching every moment. This was for her. She always wanted to extend the hand of friendship, make people feel welcome in Beaumont Square.

She heard the chain on the door come away and then the woman revealed herself, looking a little contrite.

'I'm sorry,' she began. 'I just ... where we lived before I was forever having people cold-calling on the doorstep.' She smiled, stepping out into the porch. 'Everything from the air ambulance to the Jehovahs Witnesses and, well, you can't give to everyone.'

'I understand,' Isla answered a little stiffly. 'I'm Isla.'

'Verity,' she replied, extending a hand.

'And I'm Hannah!' Hannah had put her hands either side of her mouth to make her voice carry.

'It's nice to meet you both,' Verity said. 'And I'm sorry I was a bit ... shall we say offish? That sounds so much better than rude.'

'Don't worry,' Isla replied. 'So, do you and ... what's your husband called?'

'John.'

'Do you like lasagne? It's just we always make too much and then we try and eat it all and—'

'It goes to Isla's hips!' Hannah called again. 'Help us eat it, please!'

'I would love to,' Verity answered. 'But John and I are going out tonight … in about half an hour, actually.'

'Oh, that's a shame,' Isla said. 'Another time then? Maybe next week?' She pointed over the road. 'We're just there, number sixteen.'

'I'll check my diary and we'll fix something up. Definitely,' she replied, nodding.

'Okay,' Isla said. 'Well, it was nice to meet you.'

'You too.'

Isla turned, then made her way back down the steps towards Hannah. She looked back to wave to Verity but the woman was already back inside and closing the door.

'So, what was she like?' Hannah asked.

'I'm not sure,' Isla admitted.

'Do you think they'll come over for dinner next week?'

'I don't know,' Isla said, sighing. 'Some people just prefer to keep themselves to themselves, Han.'

'Not in Beaumont Square.'

'Come on,' Isla said, putting her hands to Hannah's chair. 'Let's make this lasagne and try and eat it all. I think my hips can handle one last blow-out before I squeeze myself into my Christmas party dress.'

Twelve

The Royale, Hyde Park

The bourbon in Chase's hand almost slipped from his grasp as his eyes closed. Jerking himself awake, he steadied the glass, putting it down on the table he was sitting at in the master bedroom of his suite. The chairs were so uncomfortable he was unsure how he had managed to even drop off for a second. Although perhaps jetlag was kicking in early, like it had with Maddie. His youngest daughter had eaten spaghetti and meatballs from room service and drunk a glass of milk before her eyes had started to droop and he'd taken her to bed. Brooke had called her sister 'lame' and declared she was staying up all night. Before his eyelids had betrayed him, Brooke had still been on the sofa in the lounge area, earbuds in, connected to the entire world and no one, all at once.

Chase was taking advantage of Brooke's preoccupation and going over the plans before he went to the office in the morning. He wanted to make sure he had everything perfectly clear in his head when he met with the London team. He needed to be able to head off any questions with immediate answers and solutions. That's why he had been given this project ... simply because it had the potential to produce almighty conflict. And that's what he did. That's what he had retrained to do. He was managing his own conflicts by sorting out other people's. And that's why Breekers had hired him. He helped businesses step out of their comfort zones, take risks. He helped guide them through the business-world minefield with no compass. It was all about allowing yourself to be pulled into a different direction businesswise by gaining the confidence to choose an unnatural, sometimes uncomfortable path.

He smoothed his hands out over the maps and schematics and blinked, trying to force a little moisture over the surface of his eyes. He could have suggested the easy choice, the large, almost pool-table-flat parcel of land to the north of the city, or even the choice to the south that would limit their size but would be easier to implement. Instead, he was going for maximum impact. If you were going to create something of this magnitude, something that was going to turn the industry on its head, then you needed to be all in. Breekers was changing tack. It had its sights set on something more than construction and there was going to be no compromising if this was going to globally succeed.

In his mind, for this to really make the ultimate splash, location was key. And that's why he was going to turn up the charm and pull out all the stops to see this work in his favour. And, after he had laid this vision on the line at the UK company headquarters, he was going to continue to grease the wheels and meet with the Head of Planning and Building Control in Kensington and Chelsea who he'd been courting on social media for weeks now. Rod Striker loved a single malt almost as much as he loved golf. His wife was called Shirley and he had two sons (Benjamin and Jeremy) who already looked like they could advertise for the perils of fast-food living. Like with most men he had encountered in business, Rod's motivation was money and power. Money was an easy fix, power would come with strings attached: he hadn't worked through the finer details yet. But he would get there. Failure just wasn't an option.

His cell phone lit up and shifting his eyes to look at the screen, he saw it was Leanna's mother. He swallowed, caught between snatching it up and letting it go to voicemail. Why would Fay be calling him? She was supposed to be resting after her operation. Unless something had happened to Ralph ... or Leanna.

Now worried, he picked up the phone and pressed to accept the call.

'Chase Bryan,' he greeted on instinct.

There was an expiration of air from the other end of the line and then ... 'So, you knew it was Mom's phone number and you answered like that.'

Leanna. He'd been duped and so damn easily. It pinched at his ego. So much for being the big man of business he had just mentally pitched himself as.

Another breath left his ex-wife and crossed the pond via cell. 'What's wrong with you, Chase?'

He suddenly became aware he hadn't actually said anything yet, apart from his name, and somehow that had intensely annoyed her.

'It's late here,' he said. 'So, if you're calling to talk to the girls I'm afraid they're in bed.'

He hadn't meant to sound quite so short. Where was the 'being adult' they had promised?

'Really?' Leanna asked curtly.

'Really, what?' he responded.

'The girls are in bed.'

'Yeah,' he answered, a slight lack of conviction creeping in to his tone. 'It's past eleven.'

'And Brooke posted on Instagram three minutes ago,' Leanna informed. 'A video where she eats an entire sachet of salt.'

Now he was listening. 'What?' He was moving quickly, through his room, out through the double doors to the lounge area, eyes searching for his eldest daughter who was now not on the sofa where she had seemed content to scowl and pout and pose. He had neglected her and now she had done something really, really dumb, close to dangerously dumb, on his watch … because he had neglected her.

'You know how bad salt is, Chase, right? You know you can actually die from something like that?'

He couldn't really hear his ex-wife now, every ounce of spare energy he had left was focussed on finding Brooke in this obviously too-damn-big suite. He rushed out of the lounge area to the twin room his daughters were sharing. He saw Maddie first, mouth open, one hand making a fist around the bedspread then there was Brooke, fully clothed, not unconscious, eyes on the ceiling, earphones in.

'She's good,' Chase hissed into the phone. 'I'm ending the call now to inform her of the dangers of salt.'

'Wait! Don't you end the call! I'm not done!' Leanna shrieked. 'We need a conversation!'

He tossed his cell on to the dressing table by the door then stalked towards his elder daughter's bed. He waved a hand in front of her face and then, when that had no effect, he tugged at the sleeve of her long-sleeved top.

'What the hell are you doing?' Brooke shrieked, ripping her buds from her ears then shooting her stretched legs back in, folding her arms around her knees as if trying to make herself small.

'I could ask you the same thing,' Chase snapped out a reply. 'Give me your cell.'

'What?' Brooke exclaimed. 'No way.'

'Give it to me, Brooke.'

'I won't. It's an invasion. You can't take what's mine.'

'As I bought it, and I pay the charge on it, I think that legally makes it mine.'

'No way!' Brooke repeated her mantra and tried to surreptitiously hide the cell phone behind her back.

This tactic wasn't working. She was stubborn and hormonal – not that he pretended to know all there was to know about that – but he needed to think of it like business. Just say the right things to get what he needed. He started with a change in stance. He dropped his body down, lowering to sit on the edge of her bed.

'Truce?' he suggested in softer tones.

'Seriously?' Brooke queried, darkly pencilled eyebrows raising. 'You can't have a truce at the *start* of an argument.'

'Were we having an argument?' he queried, blinking his grainy, sleep-deprived eyes.

She tutted and shook her head, eyes moving away from him as if finding the patterned wallpaper far more interesting. Disinterest, he'd long since decided, was better than hissing and scratching.

'Listen, Brooke ... now, I'm sure this isn't true but ... your mom is concerned.' He took a deep breath. 'Just tell me, reassure me, that you didn't eat a sachet of salt live on Instagram.'

He had worded that all wrong. He hadn't followed his own carefully built plan. He had made it sound like her licking sodium was oddball behaviour. He should have come at it from a more understanding angle. Perhaps all was not lost if he jumped in again quickly.

'I mean ... if you did then, okay, but you need to know that salt isn't good for you, honey.'

'What are you now? Some sort of health advisory service?'

'Brooke—'

'For God's sake it was a tiny sachet. There was this new hashtag called #freakyeating and I figured I'd just join in.' She huffed a sigh. 'There was no need for Mom to have a haemorrhage over it or to call you.'

'No?' Chase asked. 'We're good here?'

'I don't wanna be here, but you know that already.'

Yes, Brooke had been making that quite clear from the moment Leanna had said she had to look after Fay.

'I know it's not home …' He swallowed. *Home.* Home had been turned upside down for them. They were no longer in New York, had to change schools, fly to almost the other end of the country, leave friends. They didn't even know which way was up, let alone where home was. 'I know it's not … where you're used to but … it's London.' He nudged Brooke's knee with his elbow. 'London's cool, right? Let me think … who do you like over here?' He racked his brain, trying to work out who was 'sick' in his daughter's world right now. 'I know. How about Kate Middleton … great hair, right?'

'So, the only cool thing you can think of is a princess?' She shook her head. 'I'm not Maddie.'

'Chelsea Football Club. Now, they're pretty neat.'

'Not. A. Boy.'

'Wow, Brooke, are you turning into a teenage girl stereotype right in front of me?'

'No!'

'Come on then,' he teased good-naturedly. 'Who's cool in London right now?'

She shrugged. 'I don't know.'

He sighed. 'Listen, I know hanging out here wasn't in your holiday plans but we're here. I love it that you're here with me and we need to make the most of it and—'

'Not do anything to make Mom pissed?'

He opened his mouth to reprimand her for her language then thought better of it. 'She loves you and Maddie and you're a whole ocean away. She's gonna worry and … that wasn't what I was gonna say. I was gonna say we need to get along. The three of us.'

'Happy families,' Brooke sighed out.

'It can be,' Chase said.

'But you have to work.'

Yeah, he did. For most of their trip. But that was the nature of things. Especially if Brooke wanted to keep that iPhone and all the Netflix, Spotify and countless other subscriptions that came with it, not to mention the new home in Montgomery.

'Yeah, I have to work,' he admitted. 'But, they'll give me someone to help out while I'm here. Maybe even a team of people. And you can tell them exactly what you wanna do and where you wanna go and they'll take you.'

Brooke reached for her earphones. 'Great.'

'Come on, Brooke, it won't be the whole time. I'll find us somewhere really great to eat tomorrow night, I promise.'

His time was up. The earbuds were back in and Brooke's eyes were back on the ceiling. He would make it up to them both once the new plans were going firmly forward and he could take his foot off the gas a little. He stood, scooping his phone up from the dressing table and checking the display. Five missed calls from Leanna's mom's phone and two missed calls from Leanna's own cell. Well, she was just going to have to wait too.

Thirteen

Beaumont Square, Notting Hill

'Isla! Isla, wake up!'

Isla's eyes snapped open and she sat up, immediately coming-to like there was imminent danger. 'Hannah?' She searched the half-light for sign of her sister.

'I'm down here,' Hannah puffed, hand reaching out to grab hold of the bed.

'You crawled again! You have to stop crawling!'

'Er, not so breaking news, I can't walk. And Ronnie's downstairs. We forgot to bring him up last night.'

The doorbell sounded. Three light presses.

'And that noise is why I'm here,' Hannah said. 'Someone's at the door.' She dragged herself up, arms working overtime to swing her body on to Isla's bed.

'Come on,' Isla said, immediately getting out of bed and helping Hannah up. 'Let me help.'

'I've got this,' Hannah insisted, voice straining. 'Go and see who's at the door.'

'What time is it?' Isla asked.

'Not Christmas yet,' Hannah offered. 'And too cold to be out of duck feathers.' She dragged Isla's duvet over her.

Isla checked her watch. Five o'clock again! Was she ever going to get a full night's sleep? Most of what she *had* been able to get had been interspersed with nightmares about Chase Bryan and the embarrassment she was going to have to face later. *So, Mr Bryan, let me introduce your personal assistant for the duration of your stay. She's professional, competent, capable and ... practically accused you of being a child molester in front of your daughters.*

'Stay there,' Isla ordered. 'Do not move off that bed until I get back up here.'

'Understood,' Hannah answered. 'No moving unless you call out for a SWAT team.'

She hurriedly pulled on her jumper as she left the room, rushed down six steps and skipped the seventh. The doorbell rang again, somehow sounding both urgent and hesitant.

'I'm coming.' Isla tried to latch the security chain. She was all fingers and thumbs this early and there seemed to be a string of gold tinsel around the latch that definitely wasn't there when she went to bed. Finally, she managed to slip the chain on and open the door to ...

'Did I wake yous up, though?'

It was Raj and alongside him was ... was that Mrs Edwards and ... a cat? Isla blinked and blinked again, desperately trying to encourage her eyes to work better.

'Raj.' She unlatched the chain and opened the door a little wider.

'I didn't wanna use the key again after scaring yous yesterday but Mrs E ... she's locked out of her house, though, and I thought, while we're waiting for the lock guys to arrive she could like, come in for tea.' He blew out a long breath, visible in the early morning air. 'I'm freezing my nads off out here and Mrs E ...' Raj lowered his voice. 'She only got one of them thin old-lady nightdress things on under my coat, innit.'

It was only then that Isla noticed Raj was wearing just a Royal Mail polo shirt – thankfully trousers not shorts – and Mrs Edwards was wearing his thick uniform jacket. She looked a little pale, her grey shampoo-and-set hair unusually wild, her gnarled hands holding on to the cat for dear life.

'Come in quick!' Isla ordered. She understood enough about old people to know that you did not, under any circumstances, let a pensioner get too cold or too hot. Too hot usually meant fainting and too cold could lead to pneumonia … in minutes.

'Do I need to call the SWAT team?' Hannah's voice carried down the stairs.

Isla touched Raj's bare arm, her fingers retreating from the icy-to-the-touch sensation. 'Take Mrs Edwards into the living room and get the kettle on. I'll turn the heating on and go and get Hannah.'

'Sweet,' Raj replied, teeth juddering a little.

Isla pulled Hannah's purple, fluffy fleece off the wooden pegs on the wall of the entrance way. 'And put this on before you get hyperthermia.'

'Do you think she's going gaga?' Hannah whispered, pushing the sugar pot into the gap between her leg and the side of her wheelchair for transportation purposes.

'I don't know,' Isla replied. 'You know her better than me. How was she before?' She paused. 'You know, before her husband died?'

'Happier,' Hannah admitted. 'And not turning up on people's doorsteps at five in the morning cuddling someone else's cat.'

'What?' Isla exclaimed. 'It isn't hers?'

'No, it's the cat that arrived in the basket like a Christmas hamper. I'm almost sure of it. The one that belongs to Verity and John at number eleven.'

'Almost sure?' Isla queried.

'Well, I'm pretty sure Mrs Edwards doesn't have a cat.'

'Pretty sure?' Isla poured boiling water into the multi-coloured spotty teapot Hannah had bought her for Christmas last year. 'Maybe she got one after ... her husband passed.'

'No,' Raj interrupted, appearing at the kitchen door. 'She don't have a cat. She used to have a dog. It hated me. Barked all high and yappy and did shits that looked like them Chelsea bun cake things.'

'O ... kay ...' Isla said, popping the lid on the teapot and passing Hannah the jug of milk.

She didn't know why they stuffed things in the wheelchair when there was a tray she was perfectly capable of carrying through to the lounge. Except she knew Hannah liked to help and presumed it was for the same stubborn, independent reasons as the fact her sister refused to have an electric wheelchair. When she once brought up the idea, Hannah had made it sound like if she had a motorised chair she would turn twenty-five stone overnight and develop a passion for KFC. She hadn't mentioned it again.

'It's number eleven's cat, isn't it?' Hannah said to Raj, wheeling up to him.

'I dunno. I deliver their post and get off their steps as soon as, innit. Always shouting about paperwork and deadlines.' He sniffed. 'If I was their cat I would go and live with Mrs E.'

'Come on,' Hannah said, passing the teapot to Raj. 'Let's make sure she drinks a hot cup of tea.' She looked back to Isla. 'There's some tuna in the cupboard. I'm pretty sure the cat will be hungry.'

Isla checked her watch again. Almost 5.40 a.m. As much as she wanted to ensure her neighbour was safe and well she could not afford to be late today.

'Have you seen them?' Mrs Edwards asked, in between loud sipping of tea, the cup shaking a little in her hand.

'Seen who, Mrs E?' Hannah replied, petting the cat, who had fallen asleep on the old woman's lap after having its fill of tuna.

'The people with their measuring sticks and their cameras.'

'The tourists?' Raj asked. 'I don't think they is measuring sticks, Mrs E. They is selfie sticks. You hold them up in the air and get your whole family in it, innit.' He held his arm out and mimicked the pose.

'No,' Mrs Edwards said, getting a little agitated. 'Not the Japanese.' She shook her head. 'Here, in the square, not Pearl Harbor.'

Isla shared a look with Hannah. This sounded more like dementia than grief-fuelled depression. Perhaps they needed to find Mrs Edwards' family. Did she even have any family?

'Number eleven,' Mrs Edwards blurted out. 'The spies.'

'Spies?' Raj said, moving to the edge of his seat in the armchair and tugging at the sleeves of Hannah's fleece that stopped halfway up his forearm. 'Like MI5?'

'I don't know what they're up to,' Mrs Edwards breathed. 'But I don't trust them. If it *is* a *them*. Everyone says *them* but I've only seen a woman.'

'Oh, Mrs Edwards, I met Verity last night,' Isla began, putting her cup on the coffee table. 'She was a little closed when Hannah and I invited her over for dinner, but she said she had a bad experience with cold callers where she lived before.'

Mrs Edwards tutted. 'And you believed that one?'

Isla looked to Hannah who was hanging on Mrs Edwards' every word, her dark, wide eyes drinking it all in like it was the beginnings of a Poirot mystery.

'They do get a lot of brown envelopes,' Raj informed.

'Do they?' Hannah exclaimed.

'Something isn't right,' Mrs Edwards continued, nodding her head, tea sloshing into her saucer as she did so. 'And ... I've never actually seen the man.'

Isla swallowed. Was this for real? She cleared her throat. 'His name is John.'

'Have *you* seen him?' Mrs Edwards inquired, eyes startled.

'Well, no, but ...' Isla turned to Raj. 'Raj has. Haven't you, Raj?'

'No,' Raj answered. 'I ain't seen him.'

'No, but you said you heard them arguing.'

'True dat.'

'But that's the oldest trick in the book,' Hannah pointed out. 'Remember *Home Alone*? Kevin using a recording of the TV to fool people?'

'Now, hold on, this is crazy,' Isla began. 'Just because they—'

'Didn't want to come to dinner,' Hannah stated, beginning to count on her fingers. 'Fake argue with voice recording software ... not a sniff of Christmas in the windows of their house ...'

'They have a garland on the door,' Isla said.

'They have measuring sticks,' Mrs Edwards joined in.

'And a cat they don't love enough.'

'No,' Isla said. 'This is ridiculous. They're new to the square and you're turning two, probably perfectly nice, people into ... into ... something from *The Bourne Identity*.'

She looked at her watch. It was well past six now. She needed to shower and put on something special to wear. Not wedding special but one of her two good, expensive suits. Perhaps the pant suit that Hannah always said made her look like she was about to kick professional arse. And she needed to help Hannah get ready before Poppy arrived.

'I don't trust them,' Mrs Edwards announced. 'Strangers. Newcomers. Things changing.'

'I know,' Hannah said with a sigh. 'I don't like change either, Mrs E, but sometimes you just have to go with the flow.' She patted the woman's hand. 'Change usually happens whether you want it to or not.'

Isla swallowed a lump in her throat. Her sister had been force-fed a whole lot of change in her twenty years. She smiled at Mrs Edwards and Hannah. 'I'll chase up the locksmith's, see if we can't get you back home. That should make you feel a bit more comfortable.'

'Yes, dear,' Mrs Edwards replied. 'Because the view here …' she shifted in her seat, eyes being drawn to the bay window. 'Isn't quite so extensive, and I don't want to miss anything.'

'Don't you worry yourself, Mrs E. I will keep yous informed,' Raj promised. 'We can be like information ninjas.'

And on that note Isla made for the telephone. As soon as she settled her neighbour and saw to Hannah she could start preparing for the world of embarrassment she was about to endure at work.

Fourteen

En-route to Canary Wharf

'This is your idea of a good time, is it?'

It was snowing. Thick, white flakes dashing through the air and settling on everything in the city. Chase was freezing and all Brooke had done since the moment she opened her eyes was be all Pink angst. He stopped walking and turned to face his daughter. Now blocking the London streets, they were being walked around, commuters rushing, steaming takeout coffees in their gloved hands, laptop bags slung across their bodies. Just to their left the sound of 'Silver Bells' was emanating from a store selling all manner of Christmas wrapping paper, bows and bags adorned with Santa Claus. Happy sounds and shimmery, glowing fayre that didn't match anyone's mood in the Bryan family.

'Don't be like this, Brooke,' Chase said.

'Like what?' she challenged.

'Daddy, look at that snowman!' Maddie exclaimed, tugging at his sleeve.

Brooke sighed. 'Grow up! That's not a snowman. It's just some guy in a stupid costume.'

'Hey!' Chase ordered his older daughter. 'That's enough.'

'Why?' Brooke asked. 'Because you have to get to work? I just can't wait for eight or nine hours of super-dull building talk.'

'You mean you were actually gonna take your headphones off today?' he snapped back.

'Not if the whole day is gonna to be about concrete and iron.'

'Quit it!' Maddie begged. 'I hate when you fight.'

He looked to his younger daughter then and wondered what the hell he was doing. There were tears in her tired-looking eyes and here he was arguing in the middle of the street. He had known this wasn't going to be easy. Compromising with a teenager was near-on impossible but here he was.

'Listen,' he began, in his calmest voice. 'I know the situation isn't ideal ...'

That comment earned him a tut and a hair flick from Brooke.

'But, I promise, cross my heart ...' He made the necessary sign. 'We are gonna go out tonight, somewhere real special ...'

'Can we see a show?'

He watched Maddie's eyes light up like a dozen heavenly angels had just descended.

'Well, I ...' Chase began. He'd been thinking more of a fancy dinner – early – because there would be much work to be done after today.

'Oh, Daddy, the West End is like Broadway. Ellie went last summer with her aunt and uncle to see *Charlie and the Chocolate Factory*! Maybe we could see that too!' Maddie clapped her gloved hands together and span around in a circle, her mouse-brown hair flying out from under her hat, catching snowflakes in the air.

'I ...' He couldn't promise a show. He didn't even know if you could get tickets for a show here on the same day. 'I'll try my best.'

'Yay!' Maddie answered, a little like he had just committed.

'Okay. So ...' He looked to Brooke. 'We're good? Or can we at least make a move up the street before we get taken down by the fake snowman?'

She refused to make eye contact. He guessed it was a step up from biting his head off.

'Oh, Daddy, look at those pretty lights!' Maddie said, pointing at the buildings in front of them displaying glowing Christmas trees and trumpeting angels. 'I like London. It's all sparkly.'

He smiled and took hold of Maddie's hand. Externally, Christmas was all around, but within their family there appeared to be a lot of thawing still to do.

Fifteen

Breekers London, Canary Wharf

Signallng problems on the Central line again!! Won't be able to make it to walk Hannah. Sorry! Poppy x

Poppy's text message had just arrived on Isla's phone seconds before she was about to phone the girl to ask where she was. But, despite knowing she couldn't be late for work a second time this week, Isla didn't panic. She flew into an organisation whirlwind like a festive Mary Poppins under the influence of Red Bull. Hannah was helped to dress, her sister's day bag packed and hung on Ronnie, make-up wafted over her own face, non-laddered tights pulled on under the pantsuit that was hopefully going to make Chase Bryan forget all about the insanity of the previous day. Then she'd power-walked Hannah to work and sprinted to the Tube, off the Tube and up too many steps to count.

And now she was here. Rosy-cheeked, her red hair stuck to her face in a snow and icy wind combo, with precisely eleven minutes to cool down, calm down and mentally prepare. Inhaling oxygen mixed with the scent of peppermint, fir trees and businessmen, she pushed open the door to the building.

'And here she is!'

It was Aaron, standing in reception, as if he was waiting for her. Isla checked her watch again. It was working, wasn't it? She was *early*, wasn't she?

'Hello,' Isla began tentatively, stepping into the area.

Denise was leaning over her reception desk, fully made-up like she was about to enter a Miss World pageant, or work on the beauty counter at Debenhams. Even the Christmas tree looked somehow slightly sparklier.

'He's here!' Aaron breathed, all gaspy the way he had been when they'd employed a young, firm postboy with a look of Brandon Flowers. 'Chase Bryan.'

'He's gorgeous,' Denise added. 'Drop. Dead. Gorgeous.' She put her hands to her heart and inhaled. 'If I was still young enough to have babies I would want them to be his ... in fact, I might just adopt his kids because they're gorgeous too.'

Oh no! This was even worse. His girls were here. The same girls who had witnessed her display of ridiculousness at Sugar High.

'Sugar. Honey. Ice Tea. Did you not put on make-up today?'

The question came from Aaron and suddenly he was scrutinising her like she had developed crow's feet overnight.

'What's wrong with you two?' Isla asked. 'Haven't you got work to do?' She needed to ignore this mad display of fuss over the New York newcomer who, she had decided, had obviously ousted the lovely Big Bill. She had a hospital project to oversee and the Christmas party to finalise – although using the word *finalise* was slightly ambitious. But she would be brazen. She would head to her desk, figure out the lay of the land, and then she would face this head on. It was sounding so easy in her head but the thought of facing this man again and overcoming ultra-embarrassment was making her legs wobble a bit.

Aaron followed her to the lifts. 'His suit is made-to-measure and I mean, made-to-fucking-measure.' He sucked in a breath. 'Thighs like two large hams and an arse like—'

She wasn't sure she could handle another butt simile. 'Aaron, where is Mr Bryan right now?' She pressed for the lift.

'Robert took him up to our floor. Gave him the whole royal treatment just like when we had Richard Branson in here.'

Isla shook her head. 'He didn't get out that horrible red carpet, did he?'

Aaron laughed. 'No, darling, thank God!' He used the stainless steel of the lift door to check his reflection and began straightening his tie. 'But it was all handshakes and back-patting and business speak. You know, *hymn sheet, blue sky, same page, teamwork, the best version of yourself* – that last one is a personal favourite.'

Isla rolled her eyes. Big Bill had never visited the London office and she now felt aggrieved on his behalf for not having this kind of special treatment. As the doors opened she steeled herself. She had to remember a couple of things before she was face-to-face with Chase Bryan again. One: she desperately needed to keep this job. And two: his elder daughter had a video she had been all too keen to upload to YouTube last night. And, seeing as there was a lot of movement – hair whipping, finger-pointing and shouting – it had the potential to go more viral than the best amateur attempt at JuJu on that Beat.

Sixteen

Chase's jetlag was hitting him full force. Right now. At the most inconvenient point when all these people – he'd had to estimate at sixteen – were talking at him. And the boardroom chairs were easily the most uncomfortable things he had ever sat in. Worse than the chair in his suite.

While one of the men went through a slideshow of projects the London company had delivered on, he took a sideways glance at his daughters. They had hastily been found temporary chairs in the corner of the room next to the heater. Maddie had set her gloves and hat on top of it to dry and now had her eyes closed, mouth open, seemingly asleep. Brooke was on her phone, eyes on the screen, until she saw him looking, then she delivered a killer glance of disdain.

'We cannot tell you how wonderful it is to have you here and we are so looking forward to hearing all about the new project we're going to be collaborating on.'

Everyone at the table started to clap and Chase wasn't sure how to respond. Boy, they did things differently this side of the Atlantic. He smiled, trying hard to make it look authentic. It wasn't that he wasn't excited about the super-hotel, he was, it was just his body was still on that jumbo jet and his head was swimming with thoughts of the girls, his ex-wife, Colt …

Bristling over that last thought, he stood up. There was only one way forward. Dive in. Take control. No thinking back.

'Thank you,' he started, once the applause had died down. 'Thank you all so much for this *splendid* welcome.' He smiled. 'I'm already getting there with the language, right?' The titters of amusement that followed pleased him. He was striking the right chord. 'Now, today I was going to set a time for announcing the new Breekers International plans as I know y'all are going to be super-hyped – that is ...' He cleared his throat and made an adjustment to his collar. '*Jolly excited* about what we have in store. So ...' He looked at his watch, more as a chance to pause and think what he was going to do with the children. 'How does this afternoon sound? Say, 2 p.m.?'

There was a general sound of concurrence and then the guy who had pumped his hand to death in the lobby and seemed to be in charge around here – he really should have paid more attention to his background file on the plane – stood up.

'Excellent, Mr Bryan. Two o'clock it is.'

'Please,' Chase interjected. 'Call me Chase.'

'Very good, sir,' the man answered. 'So, now, why don't I introduce you to the lady who is going to be your personal assistant during your stay. She's one of our brightest employees, has worked her way up through the company and is now in charge of people management, troubleshooting and special projects—'

'Actually,' he interrupted. 'Could I have the room right now?'

'Have the room?' the guy asked, looking a little confused.

'Just for a minute ...' Chase lowered his voice. 'With my daughters.'

'But of course! My apologies.' He began to back away, almost bowing like Chase was a member of a Saudi Arabian royal family.

As soon as the door was closed Chase turned to Maddie and Brooke. Maddie was definitely asleep and Brooke had her buckle-covered booted foot up on the windowsill, eyes on the outside. He took steps towards them, looking out the window at the London skyline. Through the driving snow there were office towers like in Manhattan but on a much smaller scale. And while the architecture of the Chrysler Building and the Empire State was certainly iconic, London's Shard and Gherkin had their own unique vibe going on. London also had history, stacks of it, and interspersed between the high-rises and the modern were the ancient and historic. That's what he needed to factor in with this hotel. Somehow, he needed to make it contemporary *and* historic. A singular, idiosyncratic flagship.

'Can we get out of here?'

Brooke's question drew him back into the room and he turned to face her. 'Honey, I'm going to be here the whole day, you know that.'

'So, what are we meant to do? Just sit here like freaking jerks?'

Gone were the days when they would both be content with paper and crayons. And he didn't have an answer. Why hadn't he considered a nanny? Yes, that was it. He would look up an agency online and get someone over here. She – or he – could take them out someplace.

'No,' he said. 'I'm right on it.' He took his phone out of his pants and began to google.

'Finding someone you can pay to mind us?' Brooke guessed. Her foot came down from the windowsill, knocking into Maddie's chair and roughly waking her up.

There was a knock on the door.

Isla couldn't think of a more embarrassing scenario. Not even the time she had got a ring stuck on her finger at one of the many little antique jewellery shops in Portobello Road when she was eleven and her mum had told her not to touch anything.

Through the partially opaque glass of the boardroom door she could see Chase Bryan and his two daughters across the room and her stomach started making motions like it was trying to break down a particularly spicy jalfrezi. This was about to be the moment. The moment he realised he was going to be pushed towards an assistant who had verbally abused him and the moment he demanded someone more suitable, told Robert everything that had gone down over Christmas muffins, and she was fired. A professional life looking at the arrivals and departures board at Waterloo …

As Robert pushed at the door she thought about the white, feathery, stupidly expensive Christmas tree in the shop window she had desperately wanted to buy for Hannah. She needed to get back to being the realist she usually was, because the moment you took your eye off the ball, you insulted the head of your company in the worst possible way.

'Mr Bryan … Chase,' Robert greeted as he stepped into the room. 'This is Isla Winters.'

She shuffled in, using Robert like a human shield, waiting for the explosion. She held her breath … still waiting the onslaught … Why was nothing being said? She inched her head out in an emu-esque fashion, looking beyond Robert's right shoulder. Chase Bryan was eyes down, concentrating on his mobile phone.

'Mr Bryan?' Robert began again.

Chase looked up then and Isla darted behind her boss again, neck retracting – more agile swan this time.

'Let me introduce Isla Winters,' Robert continued. 'She will be on call for you while you're in London.'

There was no hiding now. She had to just face the music ... and with swagger.

Isla sashayed out from behind Robert like she was performing a *Strictly* rumba move. 'Good morning, Mr Bryan.'

What was happening? It was the woman from the café yesterday. The one who had wanted to call the police. The one who had crazy-hot red hair and was wearing a rather appealing pantsuit that was making the very best of her figure. He wasn't quite sure what to say. Jeez, what had happened to him on that flight? It seemed he had lost focus, direction and the ability to make any sense of situations he was usually all over.

'Hey,' he greeted. *Hey?* Was he back on the ice rink? 'Good morning, Ms ...'

'Miss,' Isla corrected. 'Miss Winters. Isla.'

'Chase,' he said, holding out his hand. 'But, you already knew that.'

He watched her cheeks colour up a little, clashing with that hair. And that accent, now she was talking rather than shouting, was adorable.

'Right, I will leave you two to get acquainted then.' The guy whose name he couldn't remember headed towards the door. 'Let me know if you need anything. Anything at all.'

'I sure will,' Chase answered, waving a hand.

The door closed and they were left alone, apart from his two girls staring at them from the corner of the room.

He looked directly at Isla. 'Look, as I already know you've got my kids' best interests at heart, how do you feel about spending some more time with them?'

Seventeen

He wanted her to be a nanny. Isla should have guessed that from the moment she'd known he had children accompanying him. She was a woman. She was his Go-To Girl for everything while he was in the UK. It stood to reason that was all he thought her capable of. The only help she would be qualified for giving him, while he was overseeing whatever project he had been sent here to direct, would involve entertaining juveniles.

'I think we need to start with a clean slate,' Isla said, putting the leather-bound executive folder she was carrying on the boardroom table.

'A what now?' Chase inquired.

She breathed deeply. 'I know that yesterday will have blighted your opinion of me, but I want you to know how deeply I regret my actions, my inference, or any defamation of your character that may have occurred.'

'Daddy? What's defecation?' Maddie piped up.

Isla's hands went to her mouth in horror. She hadn't said that, had she? Shit! Yes, that exactly. Was everything involving this American set to go down this way?

'Miss Winters said "*defamation*", Maddie,' Chase answered. 'It means saying things about someone that aren't true and ruining their reputation.'

Yes. Yes it did. And that's what she had done. Maybe she should just suck up the nanny duties and be glad that he still needed her at the company at all … for now.

'Like when everyone in the news said that Donald Trump liked to squeeze women's—'

'Kinda,' Chase interrupted quickly. 'Kinda like that.' He cleared his throat. 'And it's just not nice to say things about other people like that.'

'Unless the rumours are true and you can use it to your advantage,' Isla added. 'Then it might be the difference between getting a contract or missing out to a competitor.'

There. That should prove there was more to her than child-minding. Chase turned then, ridiculously chocolate-coloured eyes scrutinising her and her bluster was squashed slightly. She had to remember that as irritating as it was for her schedule to be disrupted this close to Christmas, he was the CEO of the whole company. If there was one person you had to suck up to it was him, and she had got off to the very worst beginning.

'What projects are you currently working on?' he asked her.

'Yadda, yadda, yadda,' Brooke broke in. 'One step away from talking about mortar and girders.' She put both her feet on the windowsill.

'Ridgepoint Hospital on the outskirts of north London,' Isla began. 'A shopping centre, provisionally called Sovereign Gate on the site of an old seventies building that's set to be demolished and ... the Breekers London Christmas party.'

'Okay,' Chase answered, nodding. 'And exactly what is it that you do?' He pulled out a chair and she found herself gravitating towards it. She consciously stopped herself from moving. He was trying to 'coach' her into sitting in it. That's what these people did. Led you into decisions you thought you'd made yourself.

'I think Robert told you what I do.' If he had actually been listening while he was looking at his phone. She swallowed. It was best to keep that thought in her brain rather than letting it leave her lips.

'I heard him say something about "people management" and "trouble-shooting".' He leaned against the table, the movement causing the suit trousers to tighten on his thighs. Damn Aaron and his comments about large hams. They did look exceedingly muscular.

'And that's what I do,' Isla answered.

'So,' he said on an out-breath. 'You're a secretary.'

He was testing her. As her blood temperature began to heat up to the level of perfection for Campbell's soup she maintained the smile on her face. She needed the salary to pay bills and to cover Christmas ... the beautiful tree, the baking ingredients, presents for everyone who had helped Hannah at Life Start.

'I'm just playing with you,' Chase said, clapping his hands together. 'There's nothing wrong with being a secretary. And where would we be without Xeroxing, right?'

She held on to the smile, secretly wishing she could punch those stupidly full lips no matter how attractive. 'Oh, I'd say probably stuck in the eighties.'

'Touché,' he replied.

There was a hint of a smile on that mouth now and those eyes seemed to be warming. There was no way her sister was going to get anywhere near him again. This was not the man Hannah would be sharing her perfect Notting Hill kiss with. This man was a cad.

'Still here,' Brooke announced. 'Still bored.'

'Okay,' Chase said, slipping back off the table. 'Let's all get out of here.'

'Really?' Maddie exclaimed, jumping off her chair and snatching up her hat and gloves.

'Going into another boardroom?' Brooke inquired. 'As in b-o-r-e-d room?'

'No,' Chase said. 'Miss Winters is gonna show us around.' He stretched his arms above his head and gave a yawn. 'I want to get a real feel for some of the places.'

'And cake,' Maddie said excitedly. 'We need more cake.'

'I ... can't go out,' Isla announced. She had work to do. She had thought he would maybe give her some tasks, phone calls, emails. She could tick them off while minding his children, if that was part of the remit, then she would be free to get on with her own business. Projects she had started and intended to finish. The beautiful party that wouldn't be beautiful if she didn't constantly primp it.

'Sure you can,' Chase answered. 'I thought the guy – what was his name again?'

'Robert.'

'I'm sure Robert said you were at my disposal.'

'I feel confident he meant for business tasks not ... cake ... as inviting as that sounds.' She swallowed, looking at Maddie's expectant face.

'Say "inviting" again,' Chase asked her.

Her British stiff demeanour suddenly turned into jelly. 'Don't be absurd.'

'We like the British accents,' Maddie informed. '*Jolly holiday*,' she said in full English pronunciation.

'I might even call you Mary,' Chase added, his accent a perfect imitation of Dick Van Dyke.

Isla didn't know whether to laugh or cry. There was no escaping this. The sooner she took them out the sooner she could get back. As she watched his daughters ready themselves – Maddie stretching the fingers of damp gloves, Brooke checking out a pouty expression in the reflection of the full-length windows – she knew there was no way she was going to get to the bottom of her blini issue today. Christmas preparation was cancelled as suddenly as the Central line at rush hour.

Eighteen

Portobello Market, Notting Hill

As they stepped into the crowded streets that flowed through the market stalls, the snow began to fall in earnest. This was no blizzard but, with a keen wind, it was enough for Brooke – the only one without a coat – to start trying to fold her body inwards against the elements.

Isla opened her mouth to make a coat-buying suggestion but then:

'Brooke, where's your coat?' Chase asked her.

'She doesn't have one,' Maddie answered.

'What?!' Chase exclaimed.

'I mean, she does have one,' Maddie elaborated. 'One from Saks that Mommy got her, it's blue—'

'Shut up!' Brooke hissed at her sister.

'She doesn't wear it,' Maddie carried on. 'Like ever.'

'Shut up, brat!' Brooke roared.

My God! Even when Hannah had been fifteen with no parents and no working lower limbs, her sister hadn't ever made noises like a furious, venomous cobra. And how was the CEO of Breekers going to sort out this kind of anarchy in the ranks? Isla got her answer to this question when he pulled his mobile phone out of his pocket and stared at it like it held all the answers. So much for being Aaron's hot King of Industry!

'This,' Isla exclaimed, her voice rising above the hubbub of the market, 'is Portobello Market.' She cleared her throat, feeling she should have an umbrella and a clipboard like the numerous London tour guides around the city. 'It's one of the most iconic and well-known markets in the whole of London and was, once, just a lone winding country path known as Green Lane.'

She looked over at the ornate sign on the side of number 177 declaring 'The World Famous Portobello Market' decorated in pale blue with red and gold writing. Inside were trinkets – magnets depicting local sites, old-fashioned prints of famous posters including Moulin Rouge, the J Howard Miller wartime picture of the woman in a red-and-white spotted headscarf declaring 'We Can Do It' and a canvas of Charlie Chaplin. There were hooks holding leather bags and signs saying 'Banksys this way'. But outside, further along the street, were the traditional market stalls, which people came from across the world to browse around.

'The country?' Maddie queried. 'In the city?'

'Well,' Isla said, turning her attention to the younger girl as they walked side-by-side, snowflakes collecting on their hair. 'Everywhere was countryside to begin with.' She sighed. 'Until people started to build.'

'Like the company you and Daddy work for,' Maddie added.

'Yes, Pumpkin,' Chase replied, the phone going back into his pocket. 'And now people need infrastructure more than ever. Houses, businesses, industry … it's what makes the world go round.'

Ugh. Someone had obviously been reading the company manual. Isla remembered the thick document – if PDFs could be thick – she had been emailed when she had accepted the job. Even in her most junior starting position she had been expected to be up-to-the-minute with the company's vision and mission statement. But, if she was honest, although she knew her job inside out, construction didn't fill her with joy the way walking around this area of London did. There was something special here. Not that she couldn't be passionate about construction when it came to winning a client or pushing through a difficult planning situation, but the reason behind her performance was personal motivation, pure and simple. She enjoyed her job because she was good at it and it suited her. She didn't get excited about the price of cement or the degree of curve on glass. Chase Bryan obviously did. Maybe his cute talk about breeze blocks was what made the board hire him ... and get rid of Big Bill, who was starting to feel like an old friend she should have tried to reach out to a little more ...

'Well, things are a little different in this area of Notting Hill,' Isla informed the children. She took an inward sniff, side-stepping a street artist on a unicycle who was juggling Christmas baubles. 'Tell me. What do you smell?' She stopped walking then, feeling the rush of air as pedestrians edged past her, eager to get on their way to their chosen destination.

'Boredom,' Brooke answered quickly. 'Total freakin' boredom. I never knew you could actually smell it before today.'

Isla opened one eye and saw the girl shiver. Her hoodie was looking pretty damp and her hair hung in two dripping sections down her chest. How had her father let her leave wherever they were staying without a coat in minus temperatures?

'I smell ...' Maddie began, 'sugar ... and caramel ... and gingerbread and ... trees!'

'Yes,' Isla said, opening her eyes fully now. 'Me too. And chocolate ... from that little bright blue shop just over there.'

She pointed, watching her companions' eyes follow her lead. 'And that's why Notting Hill is one of the most interesting places in London.' Isla breathed in, taking in the row of quirky, multicoloured shops that ran the length of this street. 'Because you never know quite what you're going to find.'

'Daddy, can we get chocolate from the little blue shop, please?' Maddie begged, tugging at Chase's arm.

'Sure,' he answered. 'I just need to make a phone call.' He was already reaching towards his pocket.

'Daddy!' Maddie exclaimed in frustration.

'Give me some dollars and I'll take her,' Brooke said, huffing a sigh.

Isla sensed that her immediate show of helpfulness was just because she wanted to get out of the cold. 'It's pounds,' Isla said. 'You're in England now.' She offered a smile.

'Will a fifty do?' Chase asked, pulling the note from his wallet.

'Gosh!' Isla exclaimed. She couldn't remember seeing a fifty-pound note since she'd found a stash of cash in a shoebox under their parents' bed after their deaths. 'Haven't you got anything smaller?'

Brooke snatched the note from her father's hand, took Maddie's hand, and began making strides towards the shop before anything more could be said.

'Kids, huh?' Chase offered, putting the phone to his ear.

'I'm sorry,' Isla began. 'I don't mean to be rude but … what exactly is the purpose of me being here showing you around Notting Hill?'

On the Tube she had suggested the children might like to see some of the famous London landmarks – Buckingham Palace, the Houses of Parliament, the London Eye – but

Chase had seemed set that they come here, so close to her own home.

'To see the quirky little stores,' he answered, a grin on his mouth.

Was that sarcasm? God, if he wasn't the head of the whole company she would deliver an equal measure back.

'You don't like them?' she offered. 'Because people from all over the globe flock here in their thousands to visit this area, in particular, *this* market.'

She loved this market. Hannah loved this market. Today, on a weekday, it was slightly less manic than the shopping frenzy of a Saturday. But there was still so much to see, something for everyone. From fruit and vegetables – traditional parsnips and swede to pak choy and choy sum – antiques – plates, Toby jugs, gold watches and rings with diamonds so big you could almost eat snacks off them – and clothing – everything from vintage chic from the sixties to knock-offs of whatever Kylie Jenner was currently wearing. Add in the Christmas stalls – fragranced candles, warm almond and exotic spice; wooden, hand-crafted Nativity scenes – providing every sort of present you could wish for: silk scarves, woollen hats, stuffed guinea pig toys. Actually, on closer inspection, the guinea pig toys were a little creepy.

'I didn't say I didn't like the market but the stores …' Chase began, phone coming away from his ear.

'Shops,' Isla corrected.

'Do I need to say "ye olde" in front of that too?'

'Perhaps just "historic",' she offered.

She watched him smile at her comment, then his cocoa-coloured eyes went from her to further up the street where Brooke and Maddie were just about to enter the chocolate shop. 'To be honest with you,' Chase began. 'It looks like time stopped here in about 1950.'

Isla suddenly felt like a mother lioness who had just been told that her first-born was overweight and too slow to catch prey. She felt her teeth touch her lip and stifled the urge to growl. He was the boss. Even if he was proving to be an irritating pain in the arse. She didn't have the time or inclination for sightseeing when he wasn't even appreciating the seeing of the sights. And her head definitely wasn't turned by the cut of his suit ... although Aaron was right about the made-to-measureness of it.

'You said that like it's a bad thing,' she countered.

'Isn't it?' Chase asked. He was looking directly at her now.

'I don't think so,' Isla replied. 'Surely London, the world, would be a very boring place if everything was the same.' She stretched out her arms. 'Imagine if this road was nothing but sleek steel and skyscrapers like Canary Wharf? No "quirky little stores" or market traders.'

Chase felt his heart quicken a little at her words. He had thought about that. He had thought of nothing else over the last six months – divorce issues aside. But not in the same way Isla had thought about it. He was *Mr* Sleek and Steel now. He had to be. This project had to be the making of him. He didn't know what he was going to do if it wasn't.

'You work for an international construction company,' he pointed out.

'I do,' Isla answered.

'Then your whole life is spent managing redevelopment.'

'My whole life,' Isla repeated.

Jeez, when she said it, it sounded way more dramatic than how he'd meant it.

'That's what you do, right?' He cleared his throat. 'Trouble-shooting, wasn't it? People management?'

'Yes,' she answered. 'I'm more about the problem-solving and smoothing out creases than I am about the actual proposals.'

So was he. Good. This was good. He had somehow landed someone who was going to be a real asset in getting Breekers London completely on board with the US office's plans. He was expecting a little surprise, a bit of hesitance and doubt, but that was to be anticipated. It was a brand-new project. Untried, untested. But great things didn't happen without a degree of risk.

'Not that I don't know my way around plans and proposals.' She sniffed. 'I've worked in just about every department.'

'So, you know everybody, right?' he asked.

'Most people.'

'All their little habits … and secrets?'

'All their "quirks"?' she offered.

'Nice,' he answered with a smile. 'You're thinking way ahead of me, Miss Winters.'

'I hope you're not asking me to be some sort of spy,' she asked. 'Because I would be quite uncomfortable with that.'

Those wide blue eyes were studying him now and then she put her hands to that Titian hair, brushing flakes of snow from it, her breath hot in the freezing air.

'And,' she continued, 'although I've worked in every department of Breekers, espionage wasn't part of my training.'

'Really?' Chase asked. 'In New York that's covered on Day One.'

Just as he thought, it took a second for the sentence to hit home and for her to then realise it was a wisecrack. He watched her cheeks go crimson.

'Daddy!'

His eyes went across the street to Maddie, jumping up and down struggling to hold a giant foil-covered Santa, almost as big as her. Brooke had a smile on her face that told him he was getting no change from the note he'd given her.

'Jeez!' he remarked. 'Is that chocolate? If she eats all that she's gonna be sick.'

'I hate to tell you, Mr Bryan,' Isla stated. 'If she eats even *half* of that she's going to be sick. You see, nothing's hollow in Notting Hill.' She smiled. 'And that Father Christmas is no different.' She drew in an icy breath. 'It's solid, right the way through.'

His eyes went to Maddie, eagerly tearing at the wrapping.

Nineteen

Breekers London, Canary Wharf

'Ladies and gentleman, nine minutes. I repeat, nine minutes.' Aaron bit his nails as he hovered close to Isla's desk. It was a horrible habit he had started since he stopped smoking six months ago. Isla had suggested vaping as an alternative because she had always been rather jealous of Aaron's previously perfectly rounded nails he'd taken mani-pride in. But apparently trading nicotine for an untested, probably-found-to-be-poisonous liquid wasn't a goer. And Aaron had said Mr Wong from his local Chinese went through more vaping cartridges than he made chop-suey.

'Isla,' Aaron said, picking up her stapler. 'Nine minutes.'

'I heard you,' Isla answered, eyes still on her screen. There was a structural issue with the hospital design, according to the latest civil engineer. She'd had an email thirty minutes ago, just after she'd got back to her desk from cleaning chocolate Father Christmas off her fingers. Maddie had only managed the head section before she started to feel nauseous and Isla had carried the headless Santa on her lap all the way back on the Tube.

'Then … Sugar. Honey. Ice Tea … why aren't you getting ready?' Aaron questioned. 'Putting on a bit of Sexy-Mother-Pucker or tousling that gorgeous hair?'

She still didn't look away. She needed to call up the latest plans. 'Because I'm not auditioning for a film?'

Aaron slid his arse on to her desk, fingernails still being gnawed. 'Where did he take you?'

Where were these plans? She couldn't seem to find them in the file they were supposed to be in. She clicked open a second folder and hoped Aaron would leave her alone for what was left of the eight point five minutes.

'You're the envy of the office you know.' He moved even closer. 'The women *and* the gay men.'

It was no good. She couldn't find what she was looking for and Aaron was apparently going nowhere. 'If you really must know *I* took *him* and his children to Portobello Market.'

Aaron began to cough like he'd swallowed a rather large, sharp thumbnail that had managed to puncture a lung.

'Sorry.' He tried to catch his breath. 'For a second there I thought you said you took the CEO of Breekers International to a market.'

'A world-renowned market,' Isla responded. 'Yes, I did.'

'Well, Isla, why would you do that?' Aaron exclaimed. 'Look at him! Look *the fuck* at him!'

He twisted and jerked his head in the direction of the boardroom just visible from Isla's desk. She looked. Inside Chase was leaning over papers on the desk and tapping at a keyboard. Yes, he was attractive. Tall and broad-shouldered and Hannah wasn't wrong about the pin-up status. But he was interfering with her carefully constructed December.

'The guy is luxury, Isla. All the way.' Aaron sighed. 'I would have taken him up the Shard.' Another breath left him. 'Whizzed him thirty-two floors to the Oblix and wowed him with the whole sophisticated dining experience.'

'We had his children with us,' Isla reminded him. 'And he actually *asked* to go to that particular area of London.'

Aaron looked like he'd swallowed a golf ball as well as those fingernails. 'He did?' He shook his head. 'Seriously?'

Isla nodded, wheeling her chair away from her desk. Where was her leather portfolio containing her iPad? She might need to take notes in this meeting. Wasn't that what Go-To Girls were expected to do? 'And, as you should know by now, I think it's the best part of London and I live there.'

'Antiques!' Aaron exclaimed. 'Of course! That will be it.' He smoothed down his tie. 'Men like that will have started a collection of some sort for investment purposes.' He sighed, his attention on the windows of the meeting room. 'I always fancied half a dozen Banksys myself.'

'How many minutes now?' Isla queried, standing up and opening one of her drawers.

Aaron checked his watch. 'Seven, no, wait, six and fifty-nine seconds ... fifty-eight ... fifty—'

'Good,' Isla answered. 'I've got time for a coffee.' She moved to leave.

'No!' Aaron exclaimed, sliding off her desk. 'You definitely haven't. And you don't want espresso breath for the meeting, do you?'

Isla stopped walking. 'At least I don't smell of Mexican beer.'

'Do I?' Aaron asked, cupping a hand over his mouth and blowing into his fingers then inhaling.

'Not today,' she answered. 'And *I* don't need a breath mint or any hair products.'

She held Aaron's gaze and something about his look was off. She kept her eyes steady, using an expression she had perfected when scrutinising unscrupulous councillors until ...

'All right! It was Denise's idea,' Aaron spat out.

'What was Denise's idea?'

'Well, you being Chase Bryan's Go-To Girl and everything, Denise deciding that in reality, as much as she hated it, he was never going to look her way unless he was into women from an era when the Mini Cooper first came out—'

'You're rambling, Aaron and now I feel like I need *two* macchiatos.'

'It's time you got back on the horse, isn't it?' he blurted out.

'What?'

'No offence, but Denise and I aren't really sure what happened to the last horse.' He swallowed. 'Or if there even was one.'

She swallowed down the embarrassment about this topic of conversation as much as she could. She didn't talk about her love life at work like Aaron did, and he knew that. Plus she was always busy and … she had Hannah.

'I can't believe you're discussing my …' She lowered her voice to a virtual whisper. 'Lack of equines with Denise. You know she's the biggest gossip at Breekers.'

Aaron pointed a finger. 'She's also the most caring, slightly man-obsessed sweetie too.'

'And she makes you cakes.'

He nodded. 'And she makes me cakes … Hang on, we were talking about you and stallions, not me and a chocolate and walnut.'

Isla smiled. 'I don't need a stallion.'

'We all need a stallion, sweetheart.'

'Not me,' Isla answered. 'Too busy. Perfectly satisfied with my life and certainly not interested in *my boss* from the States.'

'But those thighs …' Aaron sighed. 'And those eyes …'

'Five minutes,' Isla stated. 'You'd better be quick at making my coffee.'

Twenty

Chase was nervous. This was crazy. All the multi-million dollar deals he had led in New York in a whirlwind six months and he was getting stressed over a boardroom in London that was half the size of his office. Why was that? The guys here were going to be thrilled that Breekers International had decided to choose London as the site of the super-hotel, weren't they? Although it was going to be a joint project, the London office was going to be very much in charge. It was ground-breaking. A purpose-built village in the heart of the city encompassing everything the discerning traveller could need ... This was better. He needed to just stick to the script he'd written. There would be questions but none he wasn't going to be prepared for. Prior preparation prevents poor performance. He was strong again. He was going to remain strong.

'O-Y-F,' he whispered to himself. 'Own Your Future.'

His cell phone erupted from its position on the table. Maddie's face flashed on the screen: her sweet smile, her brown hair spilling over her shoulders and a princess crown on her head. He checked his watch. In a couple of minutes he would have the movers and shakers of the London office in here needing his complete attention. Had the receptionist he'd left the kids with until the hired childminder turned up got a problem?

'Maddie?' he greeted.

'No,' came Brooke's sharp reply. 'The other daughter. The not so smiley, cooler one with much better hair.'

'Brooke, I'm kinda busy right now.'

'Yeah, I know, like every freakin' day.'

'Listen, for real, I need to go.' He breathed in hard, trying to temper down the moths that were emerging from a multitude of cocoons in his abdomen. 'I'm just about to get going on a real important meeting and—'

'The chick you hired to come sit with us isn't coming.'

Shit. This was all he needed. He took a second to adjust. This was Brooke on Maddie's phone, not the receptionist who would have taken the call from the agency.

'Are you for real, Brooke?' he queried.

'What?'

'Is this another one of your pranks or something?' he asked. 'Have you got me on webcam for some hilarious jerk-around-with-your-dad sketch you're gonna upload later?'

'You don't believe me?'

Brooke's tone now was both scalding and hurt. He quickly reminded himself she was vulnerable, both his daughters were, and he needed to tread carefully.

'I just—'

'You just what? Thought I'd call you and make something up?' Now the tone was verging on vicious. 'Maddie's still throwing up, by the way. I told her not to but she ate from Santa's shoulder down to his big ol' belt buckle.'

Chase closed his eyes. Any second now the door of the room was going to open up and a dozen employees were going to waltz in expecting to be wowed. Could he wow? He used to wow when he had his own business. Back when things in his life were a whole lot less complicated. Back when he had a solid marriage – or so he'd thought. His gaze went to the windows of the room and the flame-coloured hair of Isla. She was standing at her desk, sipping from a cup, its saucer in her other hand. How quintessentially British and somehow ... erotic. He swallowed and turned away, refocussing on his conversation with his elder daughter.

'Is the receptionist okay?' he asked. 'To stay with you a minute?'

'She wears way too much make-up and I don't think her eyebrows are real.'

He turned back to the door. There were people gathering at the entrance. 'Brooke, I promise, just sit tight for an hour or so and I'll treat you to something.'

'The new iPhone?'

Jeez. How was he still getting this all so wrong after all these years? Offer something and the kids reach for the moon. What did he say? He was in a spot. He swallowed. 'Remember Christmas is right around the corner.' He ended the call and slipped the phone into his pocket as the Breekers London team descended.

Twenty-One

'Thank you everyone for coming today at short notice. I know how extremely busy you are.'

Isla sat back in her chair and got ready to watch Chase in action. In the four minutes it had taken to make macchiato, Aaron had informed her that Chase was something of a phenomenon when it came to motivational speaking. As if the business coach thing wasn't enough! *Dream big! Walk tall!* She had always thought they were made-up phrases to give solace to people whose lives were on a downward spiral. Since Hannah's accident she was more of the 'roll your sleeves up', 'keep calm and carry on' mindset. What were you ever really in control of apart from that? And she wasn't sure how Chase's background and philosophy was going to work with a construction firm.

Chase continued. 'So, I guess y'all wondering why the CEO of Breekers is spending December here in London.'

There was no murmuring, hardly a breath, even from Robert who was usually a clearing-the-throat kind of man.

'Well …' Chase sucked in a long, slow breath. 'Right now, I would like you to just … close your eyes for a second.'

Oh no. This might work in America where they were used to all things weird and wonderful on every street corner, but the British were different. If he had self-affirmations chanting in mind then this was about to get very uncomfortable. And she wasn't closing her eyes. She had long since come to the conclusion that anyone who asked you to close your eyes was either going to do something inappropriate or steal your handbag.

'Come on, guys,' Chase stated. 'Work with the crazy Yank here.'

No, she was not shutting her eyes. Isla turned her head to look to Aaron. His eyes were shut tight and he had his arms outstretched, palms up. Robert had one eye closed, the other still not quite committing. How had she not noticed until now that he was wearing the most awful red, green and white striped Christmas tie covered in motifs of candy canes? She looked back to Chase.

'Don't make me hypnotise you,' Chase said in a tone that was somewhere between sinister and playful.

God, she hated hypnotists too. Another load of made-up waffle taking advantage of vulnerable people.

'Miss Winters,' Chase addressed her. 'Your eyes need to be closed right now.'

Isla jerked her head in a one-eighty to find that everyone else around the room had their eyes shut. She didn't have any choice, but she still thought it was all twaddle, and stunts didn't go down well with Brits unless it involved fire or dancing dogs. Poor, poor Pudsey.

'Okay, so, now I want you to imagine ... luxury,' Chase said.

Why had he started whispering? Isla felt the need to sit forward slightly. Did he say 'luxury'? How did you imagine 'luxury'? Wasn't that the word Aaron had used about him earlier?

'Relax ... into ... it ... and ... think ... about ... what ... that ... word ... means ... to ... you?'

He was talking super-slow now. She knew this trick. She had seen it on some Royal Variety Performance or something

Hannah had been glued to because The Vamps were on it. Right now she was supposed to be feeling tricked into becoming tired and relaxed.

'Does … it … mean … power?'

Ha! That was a man's perception of luxury if ever there was one. She was still definitely not feeling tired.

'Does … it … mean … money?'

Ugh. He really was Mr Corporate. And her eyes were not getting gritty. She stifled a yawn.

'Or … does … it … mean … quality? Quality space … quality time … quality business?'

Actually, a short nap right now wouldn't go amiss. If Raj was going to keep waking them all up before the milk was delivered.

'Now …' Chase whispered. 'Open your eyes!'

The last command was shouted so loudly the baubles on the Christmas tree in the corner shook and, as Isla snapped to alert, two toy soldiers fell off a branch and hit the carpet.

'Feels good, yes?' Chase asked, nodding to his audience.

It didn't feel good. Everyone was looking at each other as if they were survivors from a monsoon, disorientated with their surroundings, possibly in need of therapy.

'Remember how it felt to think of luxury and quality?' Chase inquired.

No. All Isla remembered was being lulled into a false sense of security with her eyes shut and then being yelled at to come-to sooner than she would have liked.

'Quality time. Quality space. Quality design.' He pressed the clicker in his hand to display the Breekers logo on the screen in front of them. 'Ladies and gentleman, it is my pleasure to show you all Breekers' new vision.' There was another click and then ... 'Breekers London. A super-hotel and entertainment village right in the heart of the capital.'

Isla felt sick, her eyes hurting as she stared at the screen. It was a mock-up of a giant, black glass and chrome hotel that looked like someone had built an enormous scary building emulating Darth Vader.

'What's that?' It was a second before she realised she had spoken aloud.

'This is Breekers' new arm of the business.' He smiled. Arm? It looked more like a whole body ... a giant Sumo wrestler's body.

'Hotel complexes,' Chase added.

She was certain she had fallen into a parallel universe. Any minute now she was going to walk into *Wayward Pines* and know it was a nightmare. She shook her head, blinked and blinked again but the Darth Vader towering monster remained.

'Hotel complexes,' she repeated. There was now murmuring among the troops around the boardroom table. Aaron was looking aghast too but he was a little too far away for her to ascertain whether it was horrified aghast or aghast awe. He did like hotels. But ... Breekers was a construction company. Who were they building this mammoth thing for? They definitely needed to know that. Was this a new company or an existing client? Who would build such a grotesque thing? She opened her mouth to speak—

'I know what you're thinking,' Chase pre-empted her. 'Breekers is an international construction firm. We help design and build and then we move on to the next project. Well, this time we're going to complete the construction ... and then we're going to run the hotel. It's going to mix what we excel at with what we can *become* exceptional at.'

They were building it *and* running it. Breekers were about to try and rival Hilton and Holiday Inn? How had this happened without anyone getting a sniff of it?

'Breekers London is going to be the *first* super-hotel and village but it's something, if successful, we're hoping to build in every major city in the world.' Chase began to hand out brochures. 'There is going to be everything the discerning traveller needs in the village. From state-of-the-art gyms to someone who will walk your dog, shine your shoes, clean your golf clubs, go get your favourite food at any time of the night ...'

'How many rooms?' The question came from Robert.

'Three thousand,' Chase answered.

There was a collective sharp intake of breath.

Chase's palms were sweating as he finished handing out the brochures. The London office hadn't reacted quite how he had hoped. It was also nothing like the response he had had in New York. There it had been high fives and back-patting, guys saying it was just what the company needed to boost its revenue and create new energy. Isla's mouth was hanging open as his slideshow began to move, showing the virtual reality of the planned village. Why could no one see what he could see? Thousands of jobs created. A visionary flagship for the company to be proud of.

'Is that a circus big top?' Isla asked.

She had leant her head to the left and was looking at the panoramic shot on the screen.

'Yes,' Chase answered. 'The super-hotel will have its own circus and zoo as well as three nightclubs, two casinos and a shopping mall full of all the brand names you can think of.'

The hubbub was waning. As soon as he'd said the word 'zoo' eyes were on him and a chilly feel was invading the room.

Had someone opened a window? His eyes went to the snow battering the glass outside. No, definitely no fresh air seeping in. He needed to turn this around and quickly. And that was, theoretically, what he did best now.

'Guys, I feel a little reticence and resistance right now and I get that, seriously, I do,' Chase began. 'This is a brand-new project, it's a big swerve from what Breekers has traditionally been all about, but it hasn't been implemented without a lot of thought.' He kept his voice calm and measured. 'This has been in the planning stages for ...' He stopped talking. How many months did he have to say to get the British to feel secure? 'Almost eighteen months.' It was actually a little over four but they didn't need to know that. He had found 'almost' covered virtually anything.

'I'm sorry,' Isla began. 'But wouldn't something like this be more at home in the States? Like maybe Las Vegas?'

He looked directly at her then. 'Miss Winters, have you ever been to Las Vegas?'

He knew the answer already. From the way she had talked about Portobello Market and Notting Hill in general he had her pegged as a home bird who hadn't ever flown very far from the nest.

'Yes, of course I have,' Isla replied. 'It's full of places just like this. Loud, brash, giant complexes just as you've described.'

Wow. That was a surprise. For a moment he wondered where else in America she'd visited. Had she ever been to New York? What would she think of the area of the city he hung out in? Slick, contemporary eateries where your order was never remembered even if you ate there weekly and had the same dish. You could be anonymous there, and he liked that. It wasn't a fluffy, cupcake town with extra sprinkles, like Notting Hill. It served a purpose and didn't ask any questions.

'I don't think you really meant "brash", Isla.'

It was Robert who had spoken now and Chase sensed a shift. Robert had realised who was in charge here, that this had gone way beyond a decision-making process. They were now well on their way to implementation.

'I think I did,' Isla retorted.

'A knee-jerk reaction perhaps?' Robert was now nodding his head like he was trying to send Isla subliminal messages.

Chase leapt in. 'Everyone is entitled to their opinion, of course.' He smiled at Isla. 'But we're hoping to get started in a few months' time.'

Murmuring began again.

'It's an exciting time for Breekers and for you here in London. You are going to own the first super-hotel,' Chase announced.

Isla looked like she was trying to speak above the nudging and chatter, the employees all beginning to flick through the brochures he had handed out. She put her hand in the air like she was addressing a teacher.

'Yes, Miss Winters.'

'So, where exactly are you planning to put this super-hotel? Because, just in case you aren't up to speed with things in London, space is limited and I'm not sure there's anywhere in the city large enough to accommodate *that*.'

Ah. Location. He didn't want to spill his desire about that just yet. He had hoped to address it in a few days' time when he had made contact with Rod Striker. When he had the agreement in principal he was *sure* he was going to get.

Isla was studying him, waiting for a response and so, it seemed, were a number of others around the table.

Suddenly there was a shrill wail that had him reaching for his ears. He clamped his hands to the side of his head, while the noise continued and everybody in front of him got to their feet and started making for the door.

'What's going on?' he shouted above the din, directing his question towards Isla.

'It's the fire alarm,' she answered. 'You need to follow me.'

Twenty-Two

'I need to find my daughters,' Chase stated as the whole work-force began to filter out of the building heading towards fire exit signs.

'Where are they?' Isla asked. 'I thought someone was taking them out for the afternoon.'

'There was a change of plan. They were staying in reception with … the woman on reception.'

'Which one?'

'I don't know.'

'You don't know!'

'I mean, I *do* know. She has quite a lot of make-up and … fake eyebrows.'

Isla watched him swallow as he came to the end of the sentence. She got the impression that childcare still wasn't something he had perfected yet. Just how new was his divorce? She was guessing the children didn't live with him full-time or, if they did, it was still very much a learning curve.

'Her name is Denise,' Isla informed. 'And she is well versed in the fire evacuation procedures. She will get them out.'

'Okay,' Chase answered with a nod.

He looked worried. A complete contrast to the gung-ho, let's-all-build-a-mammoth-complex-and-call-it-a-village indi-vidual he'd been in the boardroom.

'It's a false alarm.' It was Aaron sidling up to them as Isla power-walked toward the doors to the staircase. 'Hello, Mr Bryan, it's a pleasure to meet you. I'm Aaron Kincaid.'

'Aaron, we're shifting out of a burning building here,' Isla pointed out.

'I told you, it's a false alarm.' Aaron smiled at Chase, nudging a little close into personal space. 'Denise called me on my mobile. Of course, we all follow strict protocol here. File out. Wait for the guys with the big hoses to tell us its safe.'

'Well,' Isla breathed. 'That's a relief.' She slowed pace a little, then considered how Denise could be so sure it was a false alarm.

'Wonderful hotel,' Aaron continued now he had a captive audience. 'Or should I say *super-hotel*.'

'Thank you,' Chase replied. 'I'm glad you like it.'

'*I* don't like it,' Isla said bluntly. *Bugger*. She really hadn't meant to say that out loud. She needed to remember that the guy next to her was the head of the whole company and she did not want to be working in M&S Food this time next week. 'I mean ... I just think it's a little large and ... not in keeping with London's unique ... personality.'

'You hate it,' Chase responded. 'It's okay. I totally got that vibe back there in the boardroom.'

Isla pushed open the door to the back stairs and took a breath. She was going to be fired, the feather Christmas tree would never be Hannah's and if she didn't find something as equally well paid they might have to move house, something smaller ... in Crawley.

'I don't know enough about it yet, that's all. And I think we were all a little shocked to learn that Breekers are moving from construction to the hotelier business.'

'It's not as big a leap as you might think,' Chase stated.

'I agree,' Aaron replied, keeping pace as Isla hurried down the steps. 'I think it's a smart move.'

'We build the hotels for other big chains and then we hand the product over for them to make millions of dollars out of something we ultimately helped to design and create.'

'Yes, but those chains have been running hotels for decades, very successfully. And you're planning to start competing with some of our best clients,' Isla protested.

'Are you afraid of a little competition, Miss Winters?' Chase inquired.

She didn't need to look at him to know how his eyes and mouth would be set. Those cinnamon eyes would be resting on her, inviting her to engage, his full lips set to amused. She carried on down the next flight of steps. It was both annoying and irritatingly sexy. Had she really just thought that?

'I'm afraid that this super-hotel is going to suck a whole lot of the profit away from all the other highly successful global projects the company has been working on over the last twenty-five years and, while Breekers is busy breaking into shoe shines, concierge management and trim trails, Blox Limited are going to steal the lion's share of the construction contracts.' She took a breath. 'And if the super-hotel isn't so super ...'

She was astute. Although Chase hadn't really doubted it. He had looked her up earlier, wanting to know a little more about the Go-To Girl who had held Maddie's hand and had wet wipes to dab at her lips when the chocolate Santa had been overindulged in. Isla Winters had been involved in most of the high-profile deals Breekers London had been part of. And, if the client testimonials were all fact, she was highly thought of by pretty much everyone. He suspected she didn't have the killer instinct like some of the women he worked alongside in NYC, but sometimes it took a softer approach to get the job done and he was getting to thinking that this was where Miss Winters came into her own. Perhaps she reeled people in with that smile and then sucker-punched them when they weren't looking. He found that idea strangely alluring.

'Trust me,' Chase said, his mouth close to her ear and tendrils of that red hair. 'It's going to be more than super.'

An icy snow flurry hit him as they stepped on to the street. God, it was cold and he'd left his jacket in the boardroom.

'Daddy!'

It was Maddie's voice but he couldn't see her. His heart kicked up a gear as he searched the throng ahead of him. Where was she? Was she okay? Had this really been a false alarm? Why wasn't Brooke with her?

'She's over there,' Isla's voice cut through the background moans and groans about having to go out in the cold.

'Where?'

Isla pointed and then he saw his younger daughter. Hat on her head, jumping up and down and making her hair flash about, snowflakes taking hold. The receptionist was with her. There was no sign of Brooke.

'Hey,' Chase greeted Maddie as she ran into him, arms clinging and squeezing tight. 'Were you scared, Pumpkin?'

Maddie looked up at him, immediately shaking her head. 'No.'

'That's good,' Chase answered, putting a hand to her hat and trying to shield her from the weather with his body.

'We don't think there's a fire,' Isla explained. 'So, there's nothing to worry about. We just have to stay warm.' She nudged Aaron. 'Have you got any sweets?'

Aaron shook his head and looked bemused. 'No.'

'Aaron, I know you carry a packet of fruit pastilles around to eat when you're not chewing on your nails,' Isla replied.

'We're good here,' Chase said. 'Given the whole chocolate Santa episode I think Maddie's gonna be just fine for sugar.'

Aaron dug his hand into his trouser pocket and pulled out a tube. 'Fruit pastille?' He offered it to Isla then retracted a little. 'Or maybe a pony?'

'A pony?!' Maddie exclaimed excitedly. 'Do you have ponies at Breekers London?'

Chase watched the exchange of expressions between the pair.

Isla could have gladly throttled Aaron right about now with his horse references. The only horse she was interested in was the one currently in her bedroom that had the job of drying all the clothes before the weekend. They could really do with a tumble drier in the winter. Perhaps it should be a present to themselves if they could find a good deal in the sales.

And then something caught her attention, driving away the thought of warm clothes. There, right in front of her, across the path, seemingly uncaring that office workers were rushing from the skyscraper in chaos, was another perfect couple locked at the lips under the snow-laden boughs of one of the trees next to the Canary Wharf station entrance. She sighed. She would have to tell Hannah … or maybe not. Maybe all this Christmas love in the air was best forgotten.

She quickly regrouped. 'Take no notice of this silly man, Maddie,' Isla said. 'This is my friend Aaron and he seems to be a little horse mad at the moment.'

'Just stallions, actually,' Aaron responded. 'With either Mexican or Cuban in their lineage.'

'T.M.I.,' Isla whispered through gritted teeth. This was not the sort of conversation you wanted to have in front of your boss and your boss's young daughter.

Maddie looked up at Chase. 'Don't be mad at Brooke, Daddy.'

'Why would I be mad at Brooke?' Chase paused, then: 'What has she done now?'

'Well, she got antsy when Denise wouldn't let her go on her computer for YouTube,' Maddie began. 'And then we thought we would move some of the garlands on the Christmas tree, but Denise didn't like that either so—'

'So …' Chase interjected.

'I don't think Brooke *meant* to set off the fire alarm but—'

Isla watched the colour fall from Chase's face as the realisation that his teenage girl had caused this commotion became implanted on his psyche.

'She said she just wanted to see how tough the tough glass really was and … well, then the glass smashed and the noise started.'

'Where is she?' Chase questioned. Colour, vibrant colour was returning to his face.

'I'm afraid she's with security, Mr Bryan.' It was Denise. She really had overdone the eyeliner and blusher today.

Isla's gaze went back to the CEO of Breekers. He was biting his bottom lip in an obvious attempt at regrouping. She couldn't help but wonder whether controlling his unruly daughter was harder work than being the figurehead of a global company.

'Show me where she is,' Chase ordered. 'Miss Winters, you'll come with me.'

'I will?'

'You will,' Aaron said, giving her a shove then mouthing the word 'pony' and working his hips like he was writhing to the *Magic Mike* soundtrack.

Isla took steps towards Chase, following Denise, just as the first fire engine turned up.

Twenty-Three

'Can I ask a question?'

Isla had been wanting to ask this particular question for the last thirty minutes. She had been in the boardroom with Chase for the past hour helping him with contact details for people he wanted to get in touch with about the super-hotel. She hated that name. It reminded her of that ridiculous computer on *Ant and Dec's Saturday Night Takeaway*. What she really wanted to be doing was gazing out of the window at the beautifully festive London streets noting down ideas for the decoration for the Breekers' Christmas party. She needed something vintage, traditional, cosy ... warm, glowing lights alongside cool, silver sparkle ...

'You're not going to put your hand up again like you did earlier?'

Mind back in the room Isla realised Chase hadn't even raised his head from his laptop. She looked over to the other side of the room where a still-moody Brooke and Maddie were gathered around the big screen, headphones on, watching *Elf*.

'So, what's the question?' Chase had looked up and was looking at her. She swallowed. Risk of unemployment for Christmas aside, she needed to know.

'Why London?'

'For the super-hotel?' he queried.

How she hated that word. Super-hotel. It wasn't even a proper word. She managed a nod. 'Why not New York ... or Tokyo? I think it would go down so well in Tokyo.'

'Have you been there as well as Las Vegas?' Chase queried.

She shook her head. She hadn't really been to Las Vegas. She'd fibbed to get herself off the spot in the meeting earlier. But she'd seen plenty of photos that told a tale – several tales – with more than enough Elvises.

'No, but they love everything big over there. I just think they would be exactly the type of city to fully embrace your circus and your zoo and your ...'

'Nine-hole golf course?'

'It has a golf course as well?'

He nodded. 'We thought about a water park too but decided the climate wasn't quite right, so we went for an ice rink/bowling/cinema combination.'

'You did?' The more she heard about this project the more it frightened the life out of her. This wasn't just a hotel, super-sized or not, this was a city in itself. Where did London have the capacity for this? It wasn't that long ago since they developed Olympic Park.

'Have you not read the brochure?'

She hadn't. He had been keeping her busy and, in truth, she wasn't sure she wanted to see it. Perhaps, as soon as Chase had gone back to America, she could sidestep away from the project completely, as she was sure Aaron would be more than keen to take a lead role. Then she could get back to the clients she loved working for, helping them with buildings that didn't look like they were capable of leading an alien invasion. And the Christmas party ... it was coming up so fast.

She cleared her throat. 'We've been talking planning and committees for the past—'

'You really do hate it, don't you?' Chase said. He closed the lid of his laptop. 'Can I ask why?'

She swallowed as he paid her his full attention, turning in his chair a little, those firm thighs appearing from under the desk.

'I told you,' she answered. 'I'm not sure something that big fits with London.'

He nodded, eyes still trained on her. 'Okay, well, how about instead you think about whether London fits with something that big?'

She almost laughed. 'I don't mean to be rude, given you're the CEO, but answering a question with a question has never worked for me and actually neither has someone turning my sentences around to suit their own remit.'

He smiled. 'Okay, Miss Winters. Duly noted.'

He had put on that British accent again and as patronisingly unfunny as it was, it was also a little bit sexy. God, why had she thought that? It was official. She was morphing into her sister. Any more Christmas kisses and she was completely done for. She would be sobbing into a box of man-size tissues to the soundtrack of *The Snowman* before Christmas Eve Eve.

'So,' Isla said. 'Do I get an answer? Why London?'

He sat back in his seat, stretching his arms over his head and elongating his spine, his shirt pulling tight over a well-defined chest.

'Well, what you said about Tokyo is kinda right. The super-village would work well for them, but only because they *already have* habitation and vacation parks like this over there—'

'A "habitation and vacation park"? Is that what you're calling it?' How on earth were they going to soften that for branding purposes? It sounded almost clinical.

'Here in London it's gonna make a mark,' Chase continued. 'It's gonna be new, be even bigger than anything in Shanghai and the States. It's gonna stand out.'

'Like a sore thumb,' Isla replied.

'Like a what now?'

'A sore thumb ... something that looks completely opposed to its surroundings.'

'So, like the Shard?' Chase offered. 'Bigger than anything around it.' He smiled again. 'Iconic.'

How exceedingly irritating. He did have a point. She had hated the Shard too, until she got used to it and everyone said how utterly amazing the views were. Then she had seen it for herself. Getting Hannah comfortable in the lift had been a bit of a task but it had been worth it for the sights from the very top. She had thought about going again now it was Christmas. The festive lights were hung all over the city and with a layer of snowfall on roofs it would be quite the sight. London did look beautiful in the winter.

'You and the rest of Breekers London need to trust the New York decision-makers,' Chase told her. 'And trust *me*.'

'We don't have much to do with the New York office,' Isla responded. 'And we don't know you yet.' Her mind went to Big Bill. She hadn't really known much about him either.

'I'm hoping to put that right,' Chase answered, adding another dazzling smile.

'Well, I think you've scared people.' Good one, Isla. Nothing like being blunt to the CEO. She could almost feel the Marks & Spencer uniform creeping over her shoulders.

'Scared people?' he queried.

Now he looked confused. She needed to elaborate.

'Pardon my frankness but ... you've been here a day and you've come in and told the team that Breekers is going to start running hotels. That's a big shock in itself,' she told him. 'Then you've sprung it on them that this office is going to be in charge of building this giant vacation and ... and ...'

'Habitation,' Chase filled in.

'Yes, that. And they don't know what to think right away or what to do.' She sighed, pushing her hair back off her face. 'These are people skilled in construction, so arranging the building isn't a problem, but they're seeing the shopping malls and the casinos and they're wondering how they are going to fit in to it all.'

Again, Isla had made an excellent point. He had steamed in like a snowplough in fifth gear expecting a little hesitance and surprise but not really having considered the bigger picture for the staff. They were going to have to adapt in their roles. This development was going to be the main focus for this office for the foreseeable future. It *had* to be successful, so it needed their full attention and cooperation.

'You're right,' he said with a nod.

'I am,' Isla said with a nod and no hint of questioning.

'I've come straight off the plane and blustered in here like the ass of a Yank you probably all think I am.'

'Well ...'

She seemed to deliberately leave the sentence hanging and he smiled. She wasn't someone who was going to let him have his own way without questioning him. He could do with a dose of that type of honesty in the New York office. Most people seemed to think keeping their heads down and their enthusiasm up – be it real or fake – was enough. Isla's take on this project was interesting and refreshing ... even if he was going to end up getting his own way in the long run. Her inquisitiveness could help him iron out any creases. She could be like his business satnav, reliably showing the optimum route while he explored off-course options.

'Let's go out to dinner,' he said.

'Dinner,' Isla repeated. She moved in her chair, wheeling it slightly backwards.

'Yeah. I promised the girls I would take them somewhere real nice. You could show us some place fancy and join us.' He could really use a nice cold beer right about now, in a warm, cosy, British restaurant, with a roaring fire on the go. He was on vacation. Kind of. He could do cute and kitsch instead of sleek and contemporary for once. Take a time-out.

'I can't,' Isla stated. 'I have to leave soon to get my sister.'

'Your sister?'

'Yes. Hannah. We live together. You actually saw her, the other day, in the café. In Sugar High when I ... when we first met,' she finished with a slight cough.

The girl in the wheelchair. The girl in the wheelchair was her sister.

Isla started to pack up her laptop and iPad portfolio. It had been a long day. A really long day. And she was convinced she was going to be seeing mocked-up shoe shiners in their candy-striped aprons, circus lion tamers and roulette wheels in her sleep. All she wanted to do was get home and tell Hannah the disaster that was this super-hotel-stroke-village-stroke-habitation-vacation-whatever-it-was. Except she couldn't do that, could she? It was all confidential and had to remain so.

'She could come too,' Chase said.

'No, I ... thank you but ...' Hannah would be a hundred per cent more effervescent than anything fizzy and alcoholic that was served up. And that wasn't always a good thing. She was already wondering who to sit her next to at the Christmas party after last year's fiasco, which she had spent doing tequila shots with Laura from accounts' fiancé.

'But?' Chase queried.

'We've actually made a lasagne for tonight so ...'

'God, I love lasagne,' Chase remarked, fingers rubbing his eyes. 'There's this restaurant in New York that does the best lasagne.'

She swallowed. What to do? She had turned down his dinner invitation and divulged that she and Hannah were going to be wolfing down his very favourite dish. This was awkward.

'Well, you enjoy every béchamel-sauce-covered inch of it,' he said.

Argh! She hated her conscience and, right now, she hated it was the season of goodwill to all men. There was only one option.

'You could ... come and help us eat it, if you wanted?' How wooden and insincere had that invitation sounded? Perhaps it was a good thing. He was now bound to say no. Or think she had asked him on a date! Her cheeks flushing furiously she blurted out: 'You and the girls ... obviously.' She added an eye roll.

'Hey, when I said I loved lasagne I wasn't hitting on you ... on the meal ...' He swallowed. 'I mean ... the food.'

Now *he* looked a little awkward. She had overstepped the mark. What had she been thinking inviting him to dinner? She hated being his Go-To Girl. She loathed the super-hotel.

She really needed to spend tonight fingertip-deep in Christmas party planning.

Isla spoke quickly. 'It's probably not as good as the one they serve up in New York but—'

'Well, if you're sure it wouldn't be a problem.' He smiled. 'My girls are lasagne lovers too.'

No, she wasn't sure. But she had made the offer and there was no going back on it. And now her sister was going to have the current man of her big Notting Hill Christmas kiss dreams in their house. At least they had two children as chaperones. Perhaps she should find out where Raj lived and invite him too.

'Yes,' she breathed. 'Quite sure.'

'Great,' Chase answered, closing down his laptop.

'You're ready now?' Isla asked.

'You have to get your sister, right?' Chase said, getting to his feet.

Yes, she did. But not before she called Hannah and warned her they had guests for dinner. Her sister was either going to love her or hate her and the worrying thing was that could all be dependent on how many bouquets of flowers she'd sold today.

Twenty-Four

Beaumont Square, Notting Hill

'Do you have pets at home? Maddie, you look like a doggy person to me and Brooke, you look like—' Hannah began.

'She wants to look like Bella Thorne but Mom won't let her dye her hair red.'

'Shut up, brat!' Brooke bit back.

Isla closed her eyes and tried to concentrate on how good this lasagne was rather than the bickering that was going on at their makeshift dinner table. Their small table for eating at had been extended by propping up their coffee table on hardback books and an ottoman. Hannah had wheeled around adding glittery fir cones and red taper candles to the table settings and had selected a Christmas playlist from Spotify. Currently Justin Bieber was rapping about the Little Drummer Boy. She wasn't sure it quite worked.

Maddie was sitting on Isla's dressing table stool and Chase was in the office chair. Ordinarily, the only time they had to cater for more than two was when it was their turn to host the Beaumont Square Food Night. Everyone in the square made a plate and one house hosted the night and the community descended to eat the communal feast.

'Brooke, watch your manners. We are guests tonight. Show some respect,' Chase ordered.

Maddie made faces at Brooke, poking out her tongue in a taunt.

'And you, Maddie,' Chase chastised. He looked to Isla. 'I apologise for my daughters. They seem to have forgotten how to behave.'

'That's okay,' Hannah answered. 'You should see me and Isla when we get going.' She ate a forkful of food then turned back to Maddie. 'So, do you have a dog?'

'No,' the young girl replied. 'We had a cat but we had to give her to our neighbour when we left New York.'

'You don't live in New York any more?' Hannah queried.

'No,' Chase interrupted. 'That is, I do still live in New York but the girls, they live with my wife, my ex-wife, in Montgomery, Alabama ... near her parents.'

'Is that far away?' Hannah asked.

'Yeah,' Brooke answered. 'Like the other side of the freakin' country far.'

'But I bet you have a cool new school and new boyfriends?' Hannah suggested quickly.

'Hannah,' Isla said, warningly.

Hannah grinned then whispered, 'Don't worry, you can tell me later when your dad isn't listening.'

'The lasagne is superb,' Chase said.

He'd directed the remark to Isla and she could already feel her cheeks blushing at the compliment. She knew she didn't get it quite as perfect as her mother had, but just trying to make it the same way seemed to have therapeutic qualities.

'Thank you,' Isla responded.

'I like the garlic bread too,' Maddie said, munching down on a slice in her hand.

'I'm surprised you can eat at all after that Father Christmas,' Isla said.

'What Father Christmas?' Hannah queried.

'Maddie bought one of the huge Santas from the Little Blue Chocolate Shop.'

'You're kidding!' Hannah exclaimed. 'You didn't eat it all, did you?'

'Thankfully not,' Isla said.

'I was sick,' Maddie admitted.

'Which we don't need to talk about at dinner,' Chase stated.

'What did *you* buy, Brooke?' Hannah asked her.

Isla raised her head. Brooke had hardly touched her food and looked like she would rather be absolutely anywhere than eating Italian food in Notting Hill.

'I don't have any money,' Brooke responded. 'And Dad's taken away my phone.' She shot Chase a hard glance.

'She set off the fire alarm at the office,' Chase informed.

'Really!' Hannah exclaimed. 'Cool. I bet there were a lot of really cold, really stiff business types moaning into their laptops and artisan coffees.'

Isla opened her mouth to berate her sister until she saw Brooke smirk. 'So, what happened with you today?' Isla asked Hannah.

'Oh, nothing much. You know, a few displays for funerals, a couple of husbands who've done the dirty and think a bunch of flowers is going to fix things. But someone did come in to plan their wedding flowers. That was nice.'

'Hannah works in a florists,' Isla told the group.

'You can do that?' Maddie asked. 'In a wheelchair?'

'Maddie!' Chase exclaimed, his fork hitting his plate.

Hannah laughed. 'Yes, I can sell flowers in a wheelchair.' She lowered her voice to a whisper. 'Sometimes I set the buckets of roses up and do a slalom when no one's looking.' She winked at Maddie. 'My best time is eleven seconds. That's spiralling around six buckets and tagging the birds of paradise at the far end of the shop.' She grinned. 'That fastest time I was up on one wheel at one point.'

Isla was horrified. 'You're not serious.'

Hannah shrugged her shoulders. 'She worries like a *mom*.'

Both Brooke and Maddie laughed at Hannah's attempt at an American accent.

'Would you like another beer?' Isla offered. Chase had gone to the off-licence while she had collected Hannah. He had bought a six pack of beer she had never heard of and two bottles of wine. The wine was a smooth, yet spicy Merlot that went ridiculously well with the lasagne. She was on her second glass and feeling a little light-headed.

'I think I would,' Chase replied. 'But I can get it if you show me where.' He got to his feet.

'Can I have another Coke, Dad?' Maddie asked.

'Me too,' Brooke mumbled, finally picking up some cutlery and digging into her meal.

'It's just through … I'll come with you,' Isla said, standing up too. She had left the kitchen in a state. If she got there first she could sling some tea towels over the full washing-up bowl and the bin whose lid didn't shut properly.

Chase followed her out of the room, through the hall and into the kitchen. This place was cute. It was traditional, yet somehow unorthodox and very, very English. It was a home, filled with cushions and easy chairs and scraps of paper pinned to boards. He'd almost forgotten what that was like. Living on his own he had his e-calendar and little else. Before the move he'd had drawings from Maddie slipped into his messenger bag, the odd Barbie shoe or, one time, Ken and a pink Jeep. He might tell himself daily he didn't miss the chaos, repeat the mantra as part of his self-affirmation routine before he left for the office, but, in down time, it was as far from the truth as you could get.

'So, what are your plans for Breekers tomorrow?' Isla asked, opening the fridge, retrieving the beer bottle and reaching for the bottle opener.

'Do you mind if we don't talk about work?' Chase asked, leaning against the worktop.

Isla flipped off the top of the bottle and it hit a cloth that seemed to be draped over pans and plates in the sink.

'Oh.' She sounded surprised.

He smiled. 'I guess you pegged me as someone who never switches off.' He *had been* that someone. Completely. But he also remembered what had happened when he had not let anything else into his life. He had lost his wife and he had almost lost himself. And he wasn't going to go back there. Also, this new super-hotel was super-secret. The very last thing he wanted was for Brooke to go posting about it on social media. He knew that sooner or later he was going to have to give her back her phone. There was only so much sulking and heavy sighing he could cope with under the misery of jetlag.

'Well, I'm not quick to judge anyone but—'

He laughed. 'Miss Winters, that was almost genuine.' He smirked. 'Almost, but not quite.'

She thrust a beer into his hands and looked a little contrite. It was cute … and hot. God, how long had it been since he had even noticed if someone was cute or hot? Sometimes that was the cause of a marriage break-up, but in his case he wasn't sure he had ever had a chance.

'If you must know, speaking as someone who invited you for dinner, and hoping it won't be held against me on a professional level ... I'm struggling a little with the whole Go-To Girl scenario.'

'You are?' He was intrigued.

'It's just, Christmas at Breekers London, it's always very, very busy. I have client meetings—'

'You mean parties,' Chase interrupted.

'So, some of them may be along the lines of a meeting in the evening, with perhaps some wine but—'

'A party.'

'It's more to it than that,' she said, sounding flustered. 'I have the Ridgepoint Hospital project at a very difficult stage and—'

'You don't have time for me, Miss Winters?' Chase asked. 'Is that what you're saying.'

'No ... I—'

'You don't have time for the CEO of Breekers International?'

'I wasn't *exactly* saying that.'

'Hey, I know all about multi-tasking. I'm the guy who turned up here with two kids and no one to look after them.'

'So, you understand my dilemma?'

He watched her pour herself another glass of wine.

'Absolutely,' he agreed with a nod. 'That's why we're both gonna delegate.'

'We are?'

'Sure,' he said. 'I'm gonna find someone to mind my kids from tomorrow and you're gonna delegate your hospital project to the guy I met earlier. What was his name? Aaron?'

Chase had said Aaron with soft 'A's. And right now Isla wasn't of the mind to correct him. She wasn't just about to hand her hospital project over. She had spent months building a relationship with the NHS trust involved. She prided herself on her personal service. That's what got her recommendations and referrals and clients requesting to work with her. She was going to tell him, right now, that this was not how it was going to go.

'I need you working with me on the super-hotel project,' Chase said. 'I have a lot of work to do in only a couple weeks. I need the best Breekers London has and I've heard that's you.'

Had he heard that? Her first thought was to plump up like a turkey being fattened for Christmas, feathers erect, wattle shaking. Then she came to. He was skilled in getting people to do what he wanted. He was a business coach. This was cheap flattery.

'You mentioned Aaron,' Isla began, taking a sip from her wineglass. 'He's very good too. And he did love the whole entertainment habitual vacation concept.'

'I want you,' Chase reiterated.

Had he deliberately made his voice provocative then? If he had it was working and she utterly hated that fact. And the way his dark eyelashes were framing those deep russet eyes …

'I know you're not one hundred per cent on board with this yet, but I think I can bring you around,' Chase said, swigging back his beer. 'And, like I said, I want *you* for this. You know all the people around here, they like you.' He smiled. 'Liking someone goes a long way, even in the hard, crazy world of the construction business.'

She suddenly stood up straight, body reacting to a niggling feeling in response to his words. 'They like me because I'm good at my job and because I tell them the truth. Not because I wear a dress and heels and can throw a party.'

'I thought nothing else,' he responded.

She needed to calm down a little. Think logically. Perhaps she *could* give something to this venture. Maybe, if she *did* work alongside him in this, she could even get him to scale it down. Perhaps she could make him see that Breekers' first foray into the hotel business might be best done with baby steps not footprints the size of a triceratops.

'So, what do you say?' Chase asked. 'Before we end work talk.' His eyes met hers. 'Are we gonna work together?'

She swallowed. Did she really have a choice? She suspected not if she wanted to keep her job. But at least she had voiced her concerns and he seemed to realise she was a little more than a secretary-cum-childminder.

'Okay,' Isla replied, moving towards the hallway.

'Okay?' Chase asked. 'We're good?' He stepped in behind her.

'I'll speak to Aaron about taking on a little of the hospital project tomorrow.'

'Atta girl,' Chase said, patting her shoulder. 'If I'm honest, I find it hard to delegate too. It's a pretty much constant learning curve.'

His thumb and forefinger grazed her collarbone and she realised then it was the first time a man had touched skin since the impasse with Ptolemy. Perhaps she did need a horse … or maybe the couple at number eleven's neglected cat.

Twenty-Five

Maddie put a playing card down. 'Lightning bolt!'

'Carrot!' Hannah called.

'Ice cube!' Another card went down.

'Question mark!'

'Spider!' Chase leapt in. He pressed his card to the pack on the cleared coffee table, back to its original position, and revealed it was his last.

'Oh, Daddy!' Maddie squealed. 'How can you win on your first try?'

'I can't believe you've never played Dobble before,' Hannah remarked, picking up the cards.

'It's a bit lame,' Brooke announced.

Isla smiled. Brooke had joined in as soon as she had seen how much fun the card game was and had even won a couple of rounds.

It had been a light-hearted evening. Here they were, an eclectic mix, being brought together by lasagne, red wine – of which Isla had had four glasses now – an addictive children's card game and a super-hotel. But it had been relaxing. Chase had been true to his word and not spoken any more about work and Hannah and Maddie had chatted at breakneck pace, with Brooke chipping in with the occasional retort or eye-roll, but in an almost non-combative way.

Isla watched Chase look at his mobile phone and then he got to his feet. 'We should go.'

'Aww!' wailed Maddie. 'One more game!'

'It's late,' Chase said. 'And your mom's called a few times. We ought to FaceTime before you go to bed.'

'Ugh!' Brooke groaned, standing up and flicking her hair back. 'She's gonna moan about something I posted on Twitter. I swear she's cloned my phone.'

'What did you post on Twitter?' Chase queried, his tone a little concerned. He patted his trouser pocket. 'Did you take your phone back?' He looked at his daughter. 'Brooke.'

'It had nothing to do with salt,' Brooke retorted.

'You could always delete the tweet,' Hannah suggested. 'Even if she's seen it, it might help if it's not there any more.'

'Believe me,' Brooke said, facing Hannah. 'My mom will have screenshotted it.'

Isla got up and passed Maddie her coat, gloves and scarf. 'Here we are. I think they're just about dry before you go out into the snow again.'

'Thank you,' Maddie said, taking the items. 'And thank you for dinner. It was awesome.'

'Wow,' Isla said. 'Awesome. That's quite a compliment.'

'What I think Maddie meant to say was "frightfully nice",' Chase said with a grin.

'You are way too good at the British accent,' Hannah commented, wheeling herself into Chase's space. 'You should really do something with that.'

'Pur-lease don't encourage him,' Brooke begged.

'I will see you tomorrow, Miss Winters,' Chase said. 'Thank you for dinner. It *was* awesome.'

Isla led the way down the hall to the front door and opened it. Outside, the snow was falling, but gently, covering the rooftops and the garden area of the square with a fine, white blanket. The sky was clear, stars visible despite the glow from the city.

'So, if you turn left the Tube station is about a five-minute walk …' Isla reminded him.

'It's okay,' Chase replied. 'I've called an Uber.'

'Okay, good. Well, I'll see you tomorrow.'

'Bye!' Maddie replied, waving a gloved hand as she descended the ramp.

'See ya,' Brooke said, scuffing the snow with her boots.

'Hey, one more thing,' Chase said, stopping in his tracks and turning to face Isla. 'What's the dress code for the Matthews' corporation party tomorrow night?'

The Matthews' party. How did he know about the Matthews' party? For a second she was floundering.

'Is it tuxedo? Or business suit? Or … maybe dress up?' Chase asked.

'I … er … you're going to the party?' she queried.

He smiled. 'I got invited earlier. For some people it's a big deal having the CEO of Breekers in town.'

'Yes, of course,' Isla said quickly. 'Of course it is.'

'So, what are we wearing?' Chase queried again.

She swallowed. 'It's black tie.'

'Okay. I can do that.' He waved a hand. 'See you tomorrow.'

Isla watched them reach the pavement and then she back-tracked indoors, closing the door behind her. When she turned around she almost walked straight into Hannah.

'Bloody hell, he's hot!' Hannah remarked. 'I mean fucking scalding!'

'Hannah! He's my boss, the head of the whole company and …' And she was concerned Hannah had said the sentence so loudly Chase and his daughters might still be in earshot.

'I wanted to be that slice of garlic bread he licked his lips all over at one point.' Hannah narrowed her eyes at her. 'Did you deliberately sit me furthest away from him? So I couldn't accidentally-on-purpose brush my wheels against his leg?'

'Don't be silly.'

'So, is he on the market? He mentioned his ex-wife. Do you think that was deliberate? Was it me or did he *really* accentuate the word "ex"?'

'Hannah, I thought you were head over wheels with Raj.'

'I am … I was … I thought I was.'

'Well, what's changed?' Isla moved around behind her sister's wheelchair and turned her around, heading for the lounge.

'I can move myself you know! Get off!'

'Sorry,' Isla said, taking a step back.

Hannah sighed, hands pushing herself forward and shifting down the hall. 'Raj didn't come to see me today. I thought he might because he usually has a chicken sub from the deli opposite and then makes out they gave him something by mistake – like chocolate cake – and he gives it to me.'

'Oh,' Isla said. 'Well maybe he had something to do today. Maybe, with it being close to Christmas, he had extra deliveries. He did say he was busy this morning.' This morning felt like so long ago.

'Or maybe we're just destined to forever stay in the friends' zone.'

'You don't know that.'

'He's known me for ten months now and he's not made a move or asked me out.' Hannah reached out and pushed at the lounge door then moved around it.

'Well, maybe he's shy.'

'Shy? Raj?!' Hannah exclaimed. 'This is the guy who lets himself into our house in the early hours of the morning.'

'Point taken,' Isla said. 'Well, there's one way to find out if he's interested or not.' She really didn't know why she was suggesting this when she wasn't sure how she felt about her sister and a relationship.

'Take all my clothes off and see what he does?' Hannah suggested. 'I'm not sure that's going to work when I need someone to help me get my knickers on and off.'

'I was going to suggest *you* asking *him* out.'

'Because *that's* romantic.'

'Hannah,' Isla said. 'You're a twenty-first-century woman.'

'Who has no problem sharing restaurant bills or picking up heavy buckets of dahlias or holding open doors – Ronnie allowing.' She punched the side of her wheelchair. 'But when it comes to romance I just think ...'

Isla swallowed, watching her sister's eyes mist over like they always did when it came to 'that' scene in chick flicks where the hero sweeps the heroine off her feet at the end. Corny, perhaps, but also utterly satisfying, especially when accompanied by a Terry's Chocolate Orange and a tube of Pringles.

'I want someone to do the running for me,' Hannah stated. 'No pun intended.'

'I know,' Isla replied with a sigh. 'I know you do. And it's no more than you deserve. But ...'

'But?'

'Life isn't like the movies.'

'Well, it bloody well should be,' Hannah moaned, spinning her wheelchair in the direction of the hall again. 'And why don't we have a Christmas tree yet? We always have a Christmas tree before the second week of December.'

'I know we do, I've just been so busy and—'

'I'm going to bed,' Hannah said. 'To dream about men who aren't afraid to ask a girl out.' She wheeled at pace, across the room and through the door to the hall.

Isla waited. There were still some things Hannah did without thinking it through. And rather than stop her in the moment she always found it was better for Hannah to make these discoveries herself. It was a matter of pride.

'Isla,' Hannah called.

'Yes?'

'Can you help me into the stairlift so I can storm off to bed?'

'Coming.'

Twenty-Six

There were feathers, floating down around Isla like a warm rain of snow and she was dancing in a dress that looked way too expensive for her to actually own. It was silver, with tiny mother-of-pearl beads sewn into it and the music was ... a Michael Bublé tribute act? And there was Chase, smiling at her, coming out of some sort of smoke machine cloud to the strains of 'Holly Jolly Christmas'. What else could she hear? Heavy breathing and ... purring ...

'I've seen the man.'

Isla was wrenched from sleep and her dream by a voice right in her ear canal. She sat bolt upright, eyes wide but not working, clutching her bedspread in fear. She blew away the tendrils of hair on her lips and thought about screaming until she saw who was standing next to her bed.

'Mrs Edwards? What are you doing here?'

Mrs Edwards plumped herself down on the bed, settling the cat in her arms on to her lap. 'I've seen the man.'

'What man?' Isla exclaimed. 'A man in the house?'

'Yes,' the old lady replied. 'But not that man.'

'Mrs Edwards, is there a man in my house?' Isla pulled back her covers and felt around for the switch on her bedside lamp. The clock said it was five o'clock. These early awakenings with her neighbours in the property had to stop.

'Yes, dear. He's making coffee.' Mrs Edwards stroked the cat a little like a Bond villain. 'But he isn't the one we have to watch.'

Raj. It had to be Raj making coffee, didn't it?

'Isla,' came Hannah's sleepy voice. 'Do I need to call a SWAT team?'

'Mrs Edwards,' Isla said, getting to her feet and reaching for her jumper to conceal the 'Cover me in Christmas' T-shirt she was wearing. 'Is Raj downstairs?' She looked at her neighbour. 'The postman.'

'Yes, dear, he's making coffee. I thought I told you that.' Mrs Edwards shook her head as if it was Isla who was having trouble comprehending the conversation.

The cat jumped down from Mrs Edwards' lap and began winding its body around Isla's legs. Paying attention to its ginger tail, Isla noticed Mrs Edwards was still wearing her slippers.

'I saw the other man,' Mrs Edwards said, standing up and reaching out to adjust the too-long sleeves of Isla's jumper.

'Why don't we go downstairs and get you some coffee?' Isla suggested. 'Or perhaps a camomile tea.' She touched Mrs Edwards's shoulder. 'Have you locked yourself out again?'

'No,' the woman answered a little gruffly. 'I didn't lock myself out yesterday either. I told Raj that.' She tutted. 'I went out to fetch Purdy and the door slammed shut.'

'Purdy?' Isla queried.

'My cat, dear,' Mrs Edwards stated. 'The cat ... just here. Is there something wrong with your eyes?'

'Do yous think she's proper ill?'

Raj slurped at his coffee, dark eyes looking first to Hannah and then Isla as the three of them sat in the living room, talking in whispered tones as they watched Mrs Edwards curtain-twitching at the bay window.

'I don't want to think that,' Hannah immediately responded.

'But it's a consideration,' Isla replied. 'And I don't necessarily think any of us are equipped to deal with it.'

'You've lost me, innit,' Raj answered.

'Isla thinks we might have to contact Mrs E's doctor,' Hannah translated.

'I hate doctors, man.' Raj sucked in a breath that suggested he would rather face the wrath of number fourteen's Alsatian than walk into a GP's surgery. 'You go in wiv nothing wrong wiv you and you walk out with months to live. It's wrong, bro.'

'See! Look!' Mrs Edwards called from her window position. 'There's the man!'

Both Raj and Isla bolted out of their seats, Hannah wheeling after them, to gather around the old woman to see what she was pointing at.

'Leaving in the half-light,' Mrs Edwards whispered. 'Thinking no one can see him.' She tutted. 'Well, I saw him last night. Talking to a group of strangers with hats and now, this morning, sneaking through the snow with that case of secrets.'

Isla narrowed her eyes, her fingers inching the curtain open a little more. A figure was coming out of number eleven. A dark-haired man, dressed in a business suit, the snow making it almost impossible to distinguish his features, except he was wearing glasses and carrying a briefcase. She watched him by the light of the Christmas fairy lights that had been interwoven around the iron railings of the square's garden, until he disappeared from sight.

'Do we think this is Verity's husband John?' Isla asked.

'Who knows who he is?' Mrs Edwards responded. 'I just sense there's something not quite right there.'

'You sense?' Hannah queried. 'You mean like a *sixth* sense? As if you have a feeling of unease about him and you can't explain why?'

'Yes, dear,' Mrs Edwards said. 'Exactly like that.'

'You think that house is haunted, like?' Raj asked.

'Okay, I think that's enough talk of sixth senses and ghosts,' Isla said. 'All I see is a man who might be up a little earlier than most in Beaumont Square, but who's just making his way to work like countless others in the city.'

'With a briefcase full of secrets?' Hannah asked, hitching her head towards Mrs Edwards.

'And that is nothing but conjecture. Come on,' Isla said. 'It's time everyone went to where they're supposed to be.' She pulled the sleeve of Raj's coat. 'You need to get to the sorting office and Mrs Edwards, you need to get home and tuck yourself back in bed.'

'Bed?' Mrs Edwards asked. 'It's morning, dear, not night time.'

'Come on, Mrs E, I will take yous and Purdy back home, innit,' Raj said. 'Put a bit of the Challenge channel on. You know you love you some *Supermarket Sweep*.'

'So,' Hannah began. Isla watched her sister wheel herself into the postman's sightline. 'Are you going to be over my way today, Raj?'

Isla pretended not to listen and scooped up the cat who was finding amusement poking its paw at the Christmas cards set around the original Victorian fireplace filled with fir cones and silver and red and green tartan bows.

'Your way?' Raj asked.

'You know, near the florists,' Hannah continued. 'Maybe at the sandwich shop?'

'Goodfillers?' Raj questioned.

Hannah nodded and Isla just wished she would be slightly more straightforward. Not that she was one to talk about asking men out or being direct. Men she fancied just never seemed to be in her orbit. She swallowed, burying her face in the cat's fur as her dream about Chase and the Michael Bublé tribute came back to mind.

'I dunno today,' Raj replied. 'I might have to work through.'

'Oh,' Hannah answered. 'Oh well.'

'Maybe tomorrow?' Isla jumped in.

'Tomorrow?' Raj queried.

'Maybe you'll be near the florists tomorrow?' Isla asked.

'Isla,' Hannah hissed.

'Only,' Isla started, 'I've heard the sandwich shop is very good and I was thinking of trying it myself.' She really did need to learn when to stop interfering.

'It is good,' Raj agreed. 'I like the chicken.'

Isla could feel her sister's eyes burning a hole in the back of her head all the way to the front door.

Twenty-Seven

The Royale, Hyde Park

Music. Loud music. It slapped Chase into consciousness and instinctively he reached for his phone on the nightstand, thinking he was somehow responsible for setting an alarm that was playing this thumping bassline. With gritty eyes he unlocked the screen, but still the noise continued. It was then he realised it was coming from the lounge room. After the six beers of the night before he needed to make it stop and quickly.

'Hey! Hey! What's going on?' He strode into the room.

Brooke was the architect behind the noise, pointing the remote at the large TV and making the volume increase.

'Give me that,' Chase ordered, grabbing the controller and lowering the sound. 'What the hell are you doing, Brooke? You're gonna wake up the whole hotel.'

'Well, you asked,' Brooke stated nonchalantly.

'I what?'

'You asked me who in London was cool,' Brooke reminded her dad. 'He's cool.' She motioned to the television screen.

Goddamn it, this was an opportunity. She was giving him an in to what she was thinking, what was important to her, and he was not prepared for it. Why had he drunk all six of those beers last night? He wanted to puke. He swallowed down that feeling and sat on the edge of the sofa with a nod.

'He's cool,' he said, nodding his head in time to the beat. He hoped it was in time. 'Does he have a name?'

'Rag 'n' Bone Man,' Brooke responded.

'Wow ... seriously, that's his name?'

'Yeah?' Brooke asked, hand on hip.

'Very ... British.'

'And cool,' Brooke added. 'So, can we go see him while we're in London?'

'Oh, Brooke, I don't know. I mean—'

The scowl was on her face instantaneously. And there was that fine line. He didn't want to be drawn into spoiling his kids but he also wanted this trip to go perfectly. They deserved a great time. Despite the gadgets and the clothes Leanna insisted were necessities, it had been tough for them recently.

'I knew you weren't freakin' interested,' Brooke said, slumping down on to the couch.

'Brooke, come on, I'm interested,' he insisted. 'I asked you, didn't I?'

Brooke was already putting her earbuds back into her ears, her body language screaming disappointment.

'Daddy!' Maddie's voice screamed from the other room. 'Daddy! I have a rash!'

When was London going to start giving him a break?

'I'm coming,' Chase called, grabbing a shirt from the chair and putting it on. He only hoped that in addition to being well-versed in all things to do with local planning, his Go-To Girl also knew what to do about a kid with spots.

Twenty-Eight

Notting Hill

'I'm going to fire Poppy!' Isla announced as she tramped through the fresh layer of snow, speeding ahead of Hannah. 'Because, correct me if I'm wrong, but I don't think she's turned up at all for at least ten days.'

'It isn't ten days,' Hannah replied, her breath coming out in bursts against the freezing air as she chased her sister along the street towards Portobello Flowers.

'And today's excuse?' Isla said. 'ITV are filming a segment for *This Morning* in her street and she can't get past without getting up close and personal with Alison Hammond!'

Isla stopped speeding and turned a little to look at her sister. It appeared she was musing on what Isla had just said. 'Oh, Hannah, come on!'

'Well, it isn't *that* unbelievable.' Hannah sniffed. 'And you're just grumpy because Mrs E woke you up with her pussy.'

'Han, please don't repeat that to anyone today.'

Hannah laughed then quickly stopped. 'No, I'm not laughing. I'm still cross with you.'

Isla came to an abrupt halt outside the shop with the feather Christmas tree in the window. It was beautiful and now had some mirror-ball baubles on it, together with black and rainbow tinsel. She didn't want Hannah to see it. She wanted to be buying it as a surprise. She took hold of Ronnie and span her sister a little, almost making her collide with a newspaper seller dressed as Santa.

'Whoa! Watch out! I almost ended up on Father Christmas's knee then!' Hannah gripped the side of her chair. 'And *I'm* the one who's cross.'

'Why are you cross?' Isla asked, recommencing her walk at a more sedate place.

'Like you don't know.'

'I don't know.'

'Raj and Goodfillers?'

'A Bollywood take on the Robert De Niro epic?'

'I'm not even going to acknowledge that.'

Isla sighed. She knew exactly what her sister was talking about. She had skirted around it, after Mrs Edwards and Raj had left, by making more coffee and talking through every item she was packing in Hannah's day bag.

'I'm sorry I interfered,' Isla stated quickly.

'Could you say that again? Only slower,' Hannah said. 'And with more feeling ... and perhaps add "and I promise never to interfere again" on the end.'

'I was just trying to help you,' Isla said. 'You know, so you didn't have to do the asking out.'

'Because my sister organising a date is so much cooler.'

Isla checked her watch. She needed to brief Aaron fully about the hospital project before she relinquished it ... a little.

'And now you're not even listening!' Hannah snapped. She pushed her wheelchair faster, tyres flicking up snow as she moved.

'I am listening! Hannah, wait!'

Isla's phone began to ring and running, pursuing her sister, she unzipped her bag and attempted to remove it. She managed to take it out and answer just before the junction. She put a finger in her free ear to dull the sound of traffic and the choir of school children who were singing 'Good King Wenceslas' on the corner. They all looked freezing. The front row all had blue lips. It was heart-warming though. She did love carols and if she hadn't been on a mission to catch her sister she would stop and listen. The phone rang louder.

'Hello, Isla Winters.'

'Chase Bryan,' the formal reply came. 'Sorry … it's Chase,' he breathed. 'I'm stuck between modes here.'

'Oh, really, that sounds … painful.' Her eyes went to Hannah, about to cross the road ahead of her. She needed to catch up. The way her sister was manhandling Ronnie she was liable to run over a pedestrian or find herself stuck on the bull bars of a 4 × 4. She started to move, looking left and right to dodge the traffic.

'So, she has no fever but she has these spots all over her abdomen.'

'Spots? Sorry, I'm not with you.' And she wasn't with Hannah either. The giant junction with four different intersections was coming up. She wasn't going to let Hannah cross that on her own. Ever.

'Maddie has a rash,' Chase stated.

'Oh! Oh no!' Her attention was back with the phone call. 'Well, have you pressed a glass against it?'

'A what now?'

'She doesn't have a temperature?'

'The temperature? I've got the heating on low. I guess it's a little over sixty-five.'

'*Her* temperature.'

'She's not hot,' Chase replied. 'Or cold.'

'That's good,' she said. 'But get a glass tumbler and press it to the spots.'

'What's gonna happen?'

'Hopefully the spots will disappear when you press the glass to them.'

'And that's it?' Chase asked. 'That's some magic British cure for a rash? If it works I will be floored.'

'It's not a cure. The spots will still be there when you remove the glass, but if they don't disappear *at all* when you press the glass to them then you need to get her to the hospital.'

'I'm getting a glass right now.'

'Call me back ...'

'Can you stay on the line?'

She looked for Hannah. She couldn't see her. There was a growing crowd of commuters ahead and her sister wasn't in sight at all. Cars were beeping their horns, a red double-decker bus was motoring along. She needed to hurry. She quickened her pace, holding her elbow into her body as much as she could while still pressing the phone to her ear.

'I'm still here,' she answered Chase.

There was no response.

'Chase?'

She was right at the edge of the street, about to tip into the traffic, to be propelled over the junction with no idea where her sister was. Suddenly something caught her arm and dragged her into the pole that housed the box you pressed for safe crossing.

'Hannah!' she exclaimed. 'I was so worried. I thought ...'

'I could have crossed it on my own,' Hannah replied. 'But I knew you wouldn't like it.' She looked a little sheepish and all Isla wanted to do was hug her.

'The spots disappeared, Miss Winters,' Chase's voice came through the phone.

Isla breathed a second sigh of relief and rolled her eyes at Hannah. 'Good. It's probably an allergic reaction to something.'

She took a breath of icy air infused with the beginnings of sleet. 'Perhaps you could tell her it's chocolate.'

'That's a very good idea,' he replied. 'So, what do I do now?'

'I'll get some cream on my way to the office.'

'Thank you, Miss Winters.'

Isla ended the call and slipped her phone back into her bag.

'That was Chase, wasn't it?' Hannah remarked, edging her wheelchair back towards the kerb.

'Maddie has spots,' Isla informed.

'Hmm,' Hannah said. 'And you have flushed cheeks that I don't think are coming from the cold weather or chasing your sister through London.'

'What?' Isla asked, instinctively putting her cold fingers to her face.

'I don't think I'm the only one with a crush on him,' Hannah stated.

'That's poppycock!'

'God, Isla, you say that to him, all Kate Winslet, and he might want to marry you.' Hannah let out a laugh. 'Come on. Or I'll be late for work.' She made to move off and then stopped. 'Oh yes, yes karma, that's just what I need right now.'

Isla let her eyes move to her sister's sightline and there were two gorgeous guys, passionately locked in an embrace, one clinging on to the rail of the bus as he prepared to leave. Their parting looking like it could be eternal.

'Another perfect Christmas kiss in Notting Hill I'm not on the receiving end of,' Hannah sighed.

'Christmas isn't here yet,' Isla told her softly. 'There's still time.' She smiled. 'Come on, if we're quick we've got time for an espresso before I have to buy rash cream from Boots.'

Twenty-Nine

Breekers London, Canary Wharf

'You look like something out of *Doctor Who*,' Brooke commented.

They were in a boardroom that Chase had commandeered as his office and Isla was dabbing cream on Maddie's neck and torso. It looked like a heat rash to her and she wondered just how high the Americans had needed to have the heating in their hotel room to feel warm in the UK.

'What's *Doctor Who*?' Maddie queried.

'Well,' Isla began, '*Doctor Who* is just about one of the most famous British television shows. It features a "doctor" who goes backwards and forwards through time saving the world from alien things and some creepy-looking robots called Daleks. The latest doctor is a woman. And, for some reason, that caused quite a stir.'

'You look like one of the alien things,' Brooke remarked. 'I've taken three photos and sent them to all my friends on Snapchat.'

'Brooke!'

'Try to keep still, Maddie, I'm almost finished,' Isla said, liberally applying the Sudocrem.

'It smells.'

'Like a baby having its diaper changed,' Brooke added.

'Stop it!'

'Listen,' Isla said, popping the top back on the cream pot. 'I'm sure if you two are really well behaved this morning then your dad will take you out somewhere this afternoon.' That was her hope anyway. Despite agreeing to free up some of her tasks, she still had the Breekers party on her mind. A couple of hours of freedom from this titanic of an assignment, enjoying ordering the prosecco and making a final decision on canapés, if the blinis she'd wanted were really off the table. She was thinking hot turkey and cranberry on skewers with a take on Christmas pudding and brandy sauce in some sort of edible cone. There had been no response about that and when she'd phoned she'd got an answer machine.

'Wanna bet?' Brooke said with a heavy sigh. 'All he does is work.' She levelled her boot at one of the chairs. 'He works every day, every night and every freakin' vacation.'

'This is the first time we've seen Daddy since the end of the summer.'

'What?' Isla exclaimed. She had no right to be shocked at that. She had no right to be opinionated over any of this. His business was not her business.

'He's in New York,' Brooke pointed out. 'And we're not.'

'I realise that but—'

'Mommy likes us to be with her and Colt,' Maddie added.

Who was Colt? Their mother's boyfriend? It was natural to be curious, wasn't it? Perhaps Chase had someone else too. Why wouldn't he? Just how long *had* they been separated?

'It's okay,' Maddie carried on. 'But I miss Daddy.'

'And I hate Colt,' Brooke added.

The boardroom door opened and Chase re-entered, with Melanie, Isla's secretary, following him carrying a tray of drinks. Chase was on the phone.

'I appreciate that, Rod. I know you're a busy man ...' Chase spoke into the phone at his ear. 'Absolutely. I will do. Bye.'

Melanie put the drinks on the table and headed back out of the room.

Chase put his phone down and clapped his hands together. 'Good news, Miss Winters. That was Rod Striker returning my call. He's agreed to have an informal chat about the super-hotel tonight at the Matthews' party.'

Why had Chase plumped for that charlatan? Rod Striker was one of the most obnoxious men in planning she knew. And she didn't remember putting his name on the list of people Chase should contact while he was here. She opened her mouth to say something along those lines but stopped herself. Her gaze met not Chase but his two children, one with her headphones stuck in her ears and a moody look and the other smeared with white cream like she was a ghost at Halloween. They needed to get out of this stuffy office.

'Listen, Chase—'

'So, this morning I thought we could look over the plans of the structure. I want to get your take on how we've initially done with meeting UK regulations. I want it to be perfect when we present to planning. I don't want to give them any excuse for turning us down.'

'Okay,' Isla agreed with a nod. 'But maybe we could take it out of the office.'

'Out of the office?' he queried.

She hitched her head to the left. Maddie was looking forlorn, playing with the fingers of her gloves in her hands and gazing out of the window at the snow falling. Brooke was nodding her head to something Isla could almost hear the lyrics to.

'I take it the nanny agency wouldn't take Maddie because of the rash and you didn't want Brooke looked after on her own.'

No, the truth was the nanny agency had told Chase that they no longer had space for two children because someone was sick and it was December. They had said the word December like it was ridiculous to even think of getting *any* service, let alone *good* service in this month at late notice.

'They need to get out of here,' Isla told him. 'All day cooped up in an office when the whole of London is out there waiting to be explored.' She sighed. 'They must be going stir-crazy.' She sniffed. 'And it's almost Christmas. You know, bright, twinkling lights, everything covered in glitter, singing songs about silent nights and eating mince pies.'

God, Christmas. He was trying to do his best to forget it was on its way. He didn't know where he would be spending it. He had presumed Leanna would have the girls and he would ... what? Spend it alone? FaceTime Brooke and Maddie and pretend that was okay? And there Colt would be. Living the life he used to have. The life he had worked hard for, fought for, was still fighting for, to some degree.

'We have work to do,' he reminded her. 'That's the whole reason I'm in the UK.'

'I know that. I just ...' He watched her swallow, as if she was getting ready to temper her words, withhold what she really wanted to say because he was her boss. He was used to that. It's what happened all the time in New York. But, even only knowing her a day, he knew he didn't want that from her. He'd already found her honesty endearing, and obviously a necessity to enable him to move along smoothly with this assignment.

'Don't start soft-soaping me, Isla,' he interrupted. 'I told you. I don't want you on this project for that.'

She pushed back her flame-coloured hair, keeping her eyes on him. 'Okay.' She took a breath. 'Let's take the plans to … the Tower of London.'

'The Tower of London,' he repeated.

'The girls can see the Crown Jewels and the yeoman tour and get some fresh air and we can talk about the plans as we go round. Maddie will love it.' She smiled. 'Then maybe we could head over to Madame Tussauds. I'm sure there will be all the celebrities Brooke knows and loves there.'

'Rag 'n' Bone Man?' Chase queried.

'What?'

He waved her reply away. 'I'm not sure he's real.'

'I'm sorry if I've overstepped the mark but—'

'I asked you to,' Chase said. 'And, let there be no doubt, I want marks overstepped. I want honesty.'

'We might not be able to carry around foolscap plans but we can take an iPad or a laptop and work around that.'

She was right. His daughters. His beautiful daughters were here in London with him and he was virtually ignoring them. Not because he wanted to. Because he had to. For the business and, in a little way, for his own sanity. But they didn't deserve this. They had done nothing wrong. The divorce was on him and Leanna.

'We can do that,' Chase answered.

'We can?' Isla asked.

'Yeah,' he said. 'Let's go.' He smiled. 'Girls,' he called, getting their attention. 'Let's go see the Queen of England's bling.'

Thirty

The Tower of London

'Wow!' Maddie exclaimed.

She had said 'wow' three times now. The first had been in reaction to a speedboat they had seen zipping up the freezing-looking Thames, the second to all the big black horses outside the London Underwriting Centre and this third time in response to the Tower of London itself.

It was majestic. A large, foreboding castle wall surrounding four tall towers with domed roofs, all flying the Queen's standard from each pinnacle. Every part of it was coated in snow, making it look a little like Hogwarts. Despite the trickle of wintry flakes falling from the sky, the sun was out, warming enough to render hats and gloves unnecessary. Isla led the way through the entrance, remembering the first time she and Hannah had visited. She had been seven, Hannah only two and they had held hands and chased the ravens around. There had been blossom on the trees then and they'd eaten a picnic of scotch eggs and homemade chocolate cake. For a second she was stung with a memory of her parents ... and Hannah before the wheelchair. How different would life be now if that accident had never happened?

'Is this where the Queen lives?' Maddie queried.

'She lives in Buckingham Palace, idiot,' quipped Brooke.

'Hey!' Chase exclaimed. 'Remember what I said about behaviour.'

'Oh yes,' Isla said. 'You can't be naughty here or the Beefeaters will lock you up in the White Tower.'

She watched as Maddie's eyes went from their group to the turrets above them. She stuttered out: 'Beefeaters?'

'Is that what they call the guards?' Brooke questioned.

'Yes,' Isla stated. 'Apparently, they're called that because in years gone by, right up until the nineteenth century, part of the salary of the yeoman was paid in chunks of beef right from the king's table.'

'You're kidding, right?' This came from Chase. 'This is just a British story to kid the dumb American tourists.'

She laughed, shaking her head. 'I swear it's in the guidebook.'

'I need one of those guidebooks, Miss Winters.' He tutted. 'And to think you promised me honesty.' He shook his head. 'How gullible am I right now?'

'It's true! Honestly!'

'Come on, girls, we can't trust anything this guide tells us.' He linked arms with Maddie. 'Let's go find us a real yeoman to show us around.'

'Fire exits,' Isla whispered to Chase. She was holding an iPad in one hand, pressing the screen with her other.

'There are currently six routes.'

'You might have to revisit that.' She zoomed in on the schematics. 'And all the doors should be a minimum of one thousand and fifty millimetres, going up at five millimetres per person after a capacity of two hundred and twenty.'

'Sshh!'

It was Brooke who had shushed them. They were being shown around the tower by a real-life yeoman who had accidentally loomed large over Maddie at the start of the tour and had her quivering with fear. Now she was staring at him, hanging on his every word, as he described the imprisonment, execution and torture that had taken place in this monument over the years. It was probably close to being a 12A rating.

'Sorry,' Isla whispered. 'But it had just been playing on my mind since your presentation yesterday. That many rooms. That many people. Fire escapes are going to be looked at very closely.' She took a breath. 'And, after what happened at Grenfell, Breekers really need to be thinking about the very best there is with regard to sprinkler systems.'

'I know that,' Chase responded. 'And with something that large, safety is always going to be paramount.'

She was glad they were on the same page about something. 'So,' she began, lowering her voice a little, 'how many proposed sites do you have? And which one is the favourite?' she asked. 'I mean, judging on the scale of the project, I'm thinking only the very north of the city is going to have capacity.'

'Did he just say how many people were beheaded here?' Chase asked, appearing to tune into the guide.

'I'm not sure,' Isla admitted. So much for berating Chase about his only interest being work, she was just as bad. And she had suggested this outing in a bid to entertain his children. Perhaps, while he was occupied, she should click on to the caterer's website for the Christmas party. See if there was a second phone number. She perhaps should have used the same company as last year but this one had a sparklier website … and was slightly cheaper, meaning she had more in the budget for props, and with the theme this year, props were vital.

'This is good stuff, Miss Winters,' he said. 'Brooke has even taken her earbuds out.'

She looked up from the device. She had noticed that earlier. Also, as they had walked around the castle, Brooke had been pointing things out to her younger sister, making sure she didn't miss anything.

Suddenly, there was a bang and a crash and Maddie leapt in the air as the yeoman stomped a staff to the flagstone floor. Isla instinctively pulled the girl towards her, iPad clasped under her armpit, hands on Maddie's shoulders protectively as the other members of the tour all clapped their hands together in applause.

'That was awesome,' Maddie said through juddering lips. 'Scary but awesome.'

Chase watched his daughters rushing up to the next exhibit of jewels. They were actually talking to one another. No sniping, just agreeably chatting, remarking on what they were seeing. It was nice. It was a welcome change and he didn't really know why he had needed his British assistant to point out to him something that should have been obvious.

And the jewels themselves were astounding. Diamonds as big as walnuts – rubies, emeralds, sapphires – you name it, it was here in gargantuan form.

'Wow!' Maddie exclaimed. 'This one is huge!'

'Ah,' Isla said, hurrying forward. 'They've found the Imperial State Crown.'

'Miss Winters, do you know everything there is to know about this place?' Chase asked, keeping pace with her.

'Not everything,' Isla said. 'I've just been here a few times.'

'How many?' he inquired. 'Because I've been to the Statue of Liberty a score of times but I couldn't tell you any of the dates or numbers.'

'I like it here,' she admitted.

'Because of the diamonds?'

'No,' she answered. 'Because of the history.' She let out a breath. 'For me it's the history that makes London special. The stories, hundreds and thousands of years old, the people who have walked the same paths, seen the same sights ...'

'History has its place, of course, but every day we're making a bit of new history, aren't we?' Chase asked.

'Well, yes ... but if it isn't special why do millions of Americans come over to Britain to visit each year?' She didn't wait for him to answer. 'It's because we have what you don't have.'

'Quaint little cottages, fish and chips and teapots?' Chase teased in his best British voice.

'Relics,' Isla informed him. 'Real, ancient relics and one-of-a-kind experiences.'

'And visitors will have the best of both worlds when Breekers opens the super-hotel.' He drew in a breath. 'Stay in the latest leisure village and go visit the monuments, knowing you're coming back to duck-down covers and free, high-speed Internet.'

She shook her head, a smile on her lips. 'No wonder they gave you the job as CEO. You really do have an answer for everything.'

Her reply hit him hard. But only because it was true. That was the sum strength of his employment. Being able to get him and the company out of a corner and knowing just what to say. That was his only talent these days but it had saved him in so many ways. Except, right now, when she'd asked him about the proposed sites he had had no words. After last night, finding out exactly where Isla and her sister lived, he was getting concerned about the final boundaries for the Notting Hill area plan. He needed to look at the map again as soon as he could, because on his walk to the corner of Beaumont Square to wait for the Uber, he'd seen Hogarth Lane ... and he was pretty sure that was a street name he recognised.

Thirty-One

Madame Tussauds

'Maddie, look! Here's the Queen! You'd better bow.'

Brooke laughed as her sister ran up to her and gawped at the waxwork in front of them.

'Now that *is* life-like,' Chase commented as he and Isla joined the children in front of Elizabeth II, the model dressed in white and silver lace, a bright blue sash over one shoulder.

'There are fifty-three thousand crystals in that dress,' Isla informed them.

'Miss Winters, seriously? How do you know this stuff?' Chase asked.

She fluttered the guidebook at him. 'It's in here.' She smiled. 'I've always been more of a counting escape routes girl rather than a Swarovski girl.'

'But you like the details,' Chase said as they moved along to Prince Philip. 'And details are important.'

Yes, he was right. Despite her role at Breekers being predominantly for the money, she did enjoy the planning, organisation and fine-checking. It was what she had always been best at. No stone was left unturned on her projects. If you could pre-empt catastrophe then catastrophe never had room to breathe. It was a similar story at home with Hannah. She was always prepared. Like the very best girl scout.

'You know, when these plans were drawn up,' Chase began, 'and I mean more an artist's impression rather than the detailed versions we have today, not one person asked about exits.'

'And they were the first things I thought of,' she replied. 'How dull must you think I am? Not to be wowed by the casino or the cordon bleu restaurant.'

'Not dull,' he answered. 'Practical.'

'I'm not sure that's a step up from dull.'

'It was a compliment, Miss Winters. Take it.'

She looked at him, found those eyes dreams were made of and felt her cheeks heating up like a Madame Tussauds model next to a woodburner. This was all Hannah's fault and her comments about crushes this morning.

'Daddy!' Maddie called. 'Take a photo of me and Prince Harry!'

Chase stepped towards Maddie who was posing next to the model of the young prince dressed in Army fatigues. 'Okay, smile and say "Let's go eat lunch soon".'

'Let's go eat lunch soon,' Maddie said, showing teeth.

'Lame,' Brooke mumbled, shaking her head.

Chase snapped the photo then turned to his elder daughter.

'Brooke, you want me to take a photo of you with someone?' he asked. 'Maybe sat on Will.i.am's lap on those chairs from *The Voice*?'

Brooke shook her head.

'Or Adele?' Chase asked.

'Can we eat already?' Brooke asked, poking her earbuds back in.

Chase turned to Isla. 'Miss Winters, where's the best place to eat around here?'

'Well ...' Isla began.

'Can we go to the cake shop again? I really wanna Christmas muffin and hot chocolate.'

'The cake shop?' Chase queried.

'In Notting Hill,' Maddie quipped. 'It was called something with sugar.'

'Sugar High,' Isla informed. 'You know that's only a few streets from my house.'

'You are so lucky to live so close to somewhere that does cake that good,' Maddie answered, practically licking her lips.

His stomach was turning again and not in a suggestion of hunger. He might not remember the exact final coordinates of the proposed boundary for the super-village, but one thing he did know was that the street where Sugar High was located was definitely in line to be demolished. That's why they had been in Notting Hill that very first day. So he could envisage how the land was going to look, levelled and prepared for construction. And he was absolutely not going to start thinking emotionally about that. So, his kids liked cake? Cake could pretty much be found anywhere.

'We can find a cake shop a little closer,' Chase suggested. 'Miss Winters ...'

'Well, we could go to Selfridges. They are very famous for their afternoon teas and—' Isla began.

'I really, really wanna go to Sugar High, Daddy,' Maddie said, pulling on Chase's arm.

This was ridiculous. Of course they could go there. Why shouldn't they? He was getting too sentimental and losing his focus. He blamed Christmas. There was tinsel just about everywhere here – hanging from Michael Jackson and Benedict Cumberbatch – a tree with flashing silver lights and golden bells next to Rafael Nadal. There was nothing wrong with making memories in London, especially if the area would be different this time next Christmas. Good times, then moving on to a new history, just like he'd told Isla earlier.

'Sure,' he replied to Maddie. 'We can go to Sugar High.'

O-Y-F. Own Your Future. This project being a success was all that mattered. It was going to set him and his children up for life and prove to Leanna and Colt that hurting him had not destroyed him. That he was, and would remain, strong.

He smiled at Isla. 'Let's go.'

Thirty-Two

Notting Hill

Seeing the part of the city she had grown up in through Maddie's eyes made Isla fall in love with it a little bit more. On leaving the Tube station she had deliberately walked them south, knowing how much the nine-year-old was going to adore everything on their way to Portobello Road.

'Oh, Brooke, you know I've always wanted a pink house. Look at all the houses!'

Maddie's eyes went to the townhouses painted in every colour imaginable. Bright red, canary yellow and Greek flag blue, all nestled together, their tiled roofs clad in thick, white snow. There were holly wreaths on doors, flickering electric candles in the bay windows, lines of fairy lights across the eaves ... she really did need to pep up her and Hannah's decorations this year.

'I'm surprised they could paint them like that,' Chase remarked. 'Isn't there some British bylaw that states they've gotta be "in keeping" with their surroundings.'

'Speaks the man proposing a super-hotel.'

Isla knew Chase wouldn't like it here. It wasn't clinical lines and chrome fixtures and fittings like his proposals. It was different and Bohemian with a new scene around every corner.

'It *is* in keeping with the surroundings,' she continued. 'Perhaps if only *one* person had painted their house and the others were all white but ...'

She didn't need to finish her sentence. She breathed in, stepping on through the snow and heading for Portobello Road.

'Are we going to the market again?' Maddie queried, linking her arm through Isla's. 'I liked the market. I even liked the weird toy hamsters with the googly eyes.' She lowered her voice. 'I was thinking of getting Brooke one for Christmas.'

'They were guinea pigs,' Isla told her in whispered tones. 'Like a hamster, only bigger, with no tail.'

'I don't think I've ever seen a real one.'

'I had one when I was little. He was called Fudge,' Isla told her.

'What happened to him?'

'Oh, he died.'

'That's so sad!' Maddie exclaimed, rubbing at the spots on her face with her free hand.

'Not too sad,' Isla said. 'He *was* five. That's a good age for a guinea pig.'

'OMG,' Brooke erupted, earphone being tugged from her ears. 'Can I smell Asian food?'

'Asian, Greek, Spanish, Portuguese ... there's everything here.'

'Maddie, come on, we don't want muffins when there's Asian!' Brooke exclaimed. 'When was the last time we had Asian?'

Maddie was practically dribbling in anticipation. 'I really can't remember.'

'There's a street food café called Diwali just fifty yards along here, run by my friends Geeta and Iqbal. They do the most amazing *laal maas*.'

'What's that?' Maddie asked.

'It's jungle red lamb,' Isla informed. 'It's quite spicy.'

'I want that,' Maddie stated. 'Can we go there, Daddy?'

'I don't know. I was kind of sold on cake now,' Chase said.

'Dad!' Brooke exclaimed. 'You love Asian food! You and Mom had Asian food for every wedding anniversary!'

Everything suddenly went quiet apart from the hubbub from the street. Brooke's cheeks began to pink up, her fingers went to her mouth, and she started chewing on the nails.

'I do love Asian food,' Chase jumped in. 'And who says it has to be for a special occasion, huh? It's almost Christmas and I'm freaking starving.'

Maddie cheered, let go of Isla's arm and instead clasped hold of her sister, pulling her into the buzzing melee of shoppers, commuters and tourists, enjoying the mad mix of sunshine and snow showers.

'I apologise,' Isla said, matching Chase's pace as they followed the children.

'You're apologising for making my kids crazy happy at the thought of Indian food in a multicoloured building?'

She smiled at his attempt at humour. 'No, I mean, getting them caught up in the Notting Hill vibe here. I'm afraid it does that to people.'

'I guess that's why they set the film here, right?' Chase answered.

'And the film is the reason my sister has Hugh Grant by her bed every night.'

'He really lives around here?' Chase asked.

She laughed, shaking her head. 'Not the real one. Hannah's is twelve inches of solid plaster. Sometimes she carries it in her handbag and one thing I've learned is that you must never underestimate a paraplegic's upper body strength.'

'I don't know how you deal with that, Miss Winters,' Chase said.

'Deal with what?' Isla asked.

God, he was an idiot. That had come out completely wrong and there was no getting out of it.

'I just ... Hannah being in a wheelchair ... I can't imagine how hard that must be.'

'Hard for me?' Isla queried. 'Well, yes, because she's a complete opinionated pain in the arse and still refuses to stop watching *Big Brother*.' She sighed. 'Actually it's harder for her, you know, not being able to walk.'

He nodded. 'Yeah, I get that ... I mean, I guess I don't actually get that, but ...' He was making a complete mess of this. 'How did it happen?'

'A car accident,' Isla responded quickly. 'Our parents were killed and Hannah ... ended up not being able to walk.'

'Hey. I shouldn't have asked.'

She shrugged like it didn't matter and a gnawing in his gut told him he ought to do something, reach out to her somehow. He took a hand out of the pocket of his trousers ...

'It could have been worse,' Isla said, a smile on her lips. 'And as annoying as she is, she does get us the best seats at concerts.'

He swallowed, retracting his hand before she could notice.

'That was a joke,' Isla told him. 'Hannah loves wheelchair humour.' She took a breath. 'And that's the most amazing thing about my sister. She might get frustrated sometimes, currently with our postman, but she never really wastes any time feeling sorry for herself. And I admire that so much.' She smiled. 'I admire *her*.'

Chase watched her expression go from sad to contemplative to happy like a fast-forward of the changing seasons. His

Go-To Girl was gorgeous as well as intuitive, they were all about to eat Asian food and he was going to deliver on his promise to Breekers. Suddenly, here in London, life was better than it had been for some time.

'I think I'd like to try this jungle red lamb,' Chase told her. 'And you can talk me through who's gonna be at the Matthews' party tonight.'

'Okay,' Isla said. 'Actually, you can see the venue from Diwali.'

'You can?' Chase queried. 'It has views of Canary Wharf from here?' He found that hard to believe.

'No,' Isla laughed. 'The Matthews' party isn't in the city. This year it's at the Electric Cinema.'

'The what now?'

'It's here,' she smiled. 'Right in Notting Hill. On this street.'

He steeled himself, forcing a smile on to his lips. Of course it was. Because right now, somehow, Notting Hill was the epicentre of everything.

Thirty-Three

Diwali

Somehow, breaking her no-alcohol-at-lunchtime rule didn't seem so bad when Isla was doing it with the CEO of the company. And it *was* December. December had different rules. Geeta's homemade sweet apple white wine infused with notes of spice was slipping down nicely and the warmth of the cosy burgundy-and-chocolate-painted interior was making her feel like Mumbai in the autumn, not the UK in winter. There were no traditional Christmas decorations here but, as every year, Geeta had hung Indian garlands and bright pink bunting with gold tassels across the ceiling and around the window frames.

Maddie and Brooke had declared they were too full for dessert after poppadoms, patties, and mouth-watering lamb but were now digging their spoons into chocolate *kulfis*.

'My God, Miss Winters, I have to give it to you,' Chase said, sitting back in his chair. 'That was the best food I've ever tasted.'

'Better than cake,' Maddie commented, ice cream on her nose.

'My goodness! Better than cake?' Isla said with a smile. 'I don't believe it.'

'You come here a lot?' Chase asked, taking a sip of wine.

'Probably at least once a fortnight,' Isla replied. 'Hannah loves the mushroom balti. She would actually probably eat it every day if we could afford it.'

Oh dear. The wine was loosening her tongue. Had she just sounded like she was angling for a pay rise? It wouldn't go amiss, but bluntly dropping hints into conversation was more Aaron's style, not hers. She quickly continued. 'And, you know, Indian food all the time isn't that good for you ... the spices and the ... ghee.'

He smiled at her. 'Gotta love the ghee.'

'So, what's the Asian food in America like?'

'Not anything like this,' Chase admitted. 'Apart from this one little place we used to get takeout. It was in Brooklyn, run by this Indian couple who looked about a hundred years old—'

'The poppadoms crackled and popped in your mouth,' Maddie butted in.

'Their naan bread was the best,' Brooke added.

'What happened?' Isla asked. 'Did it close?'

'What?'

'You said it was where you *used* to get takeaway,' Isla said. 'Did it shut down?'

Yeah, Chase *had* said that and his perceptive assistant had straight off picked up on it. What should he do? Did he spin her something like he would ordinarily do to anyone asking him something personal? Or did he tell her the truth? She had been open when he'd inquired about Hannah's accident. She'd been pretty open about everything ...

He started. 'I ... we ...'

Then his cell phone erupted into life and Leanna's face flashed on to the screen for everyone to see.

'It's Mommy!' Maddie exclaimed, sounding highly delighted.

Chase's gaze went to Brooke. 'So, before I pick up, give me the heads up: is there anything inappropriate you've posted on Instagram?'

'Oh, so right away you think I've done something!' Brooke exclaimed.

'Well, no, I—'

'I've been with you all day hearing about the Traitors' Gate and the Bloody Tower and having my photo taken with King Kong! When would I have time to post anything on Insta?'

'Is everything okay with the food?'

It was the sweet, tiny Asian woman who had served them their exquisite feast. And his phone was still ringing.

'Yes, thank you, Geeta, it was delicious as always,' Isla answered. 'How is Iqbal? We never see him now he's full-time in that kitchen.'

'What can I say?' the woman replied. 'Times are tight. We cannot afford to employ any extra help on week days.'

This could be an intriguing conversation. As lovely as this restaurant was, if the owners were struggling to make ends meet … Breekers planned to offer residents a not insignificant sum of money to leave their premises. Money was always welcome and he was sure they would see it as an opportunity. A chance to start again somewhere else in the city maybe? Perhaps the unusual, off-beat independents weren't having it so good after all. Maybe, if he did manage to nail down this area as the final site for the village, it would come as somewhat of a relief to business owners who were struggling. As cosy and eclectic as it all was, perhaps everyone was missing the point, deluded by kitsch and not taking into account the real point of business: profitability. And if you weren't profitable, couldn't make a decent living, what was the point of clinging on? It was time for some of that new history. Just like they'd been talking about.

'Are you not gonna answer Mommy?' Maddie asked.

'Yes,' Chase answered. 'Sure.' He stood then, picking up the cell and moving away from the table before he answered. 'Hey.'

'Hey?' came the reply. 'I've called you six times today. We agreed you would check in, Chase. That was the basis of our arrangement. The reason I let you take the girls to London.'

'I had no idea you'd called.' He hadn't really looked at his phone since … was it really since they had left Breekers' offices? 'We've been—'

'You don't have to tell me where you've been. I know where you've been.' She drew in a breath. 'This is from Brooke's Twitter last night … *So freakin' bored.* And yesterday *Seen one office, seen them all #London.*'

Chase closed his eyes.

'You're working all day and all night again, aren't you?' Leanna yelled. 'This isn't a vacation for them, is it? There's something going on over there that's taking up all your time and you're neglecting them.' She huffed an irritated sigh. 'You know what happens if you let work take over, Chase.'

He pushed open the door to the outside. He needed the air, even if the temperature was in negative degrees and it was snowing a little heavier than when they were at the Tower. He knew what he had to do. He had had months of re-programming and reading *Men are From Mars, Women Are From Venus*. That book had been a particular eye-opener. But even its insightful take on why men and women behave the way they do hadn't been enough to save his marriage. And for that he didn't blame himself or even Leanna … he blamed Colt. Because as much as Colt had been absent he had always been right there in the background, lingering like a bad smell.

But, right now, swallowing his immediate emotional response that was the elephant in the conversation, he was going to listen to Leanna's concerns, not criticise, not bite back, but validate her issues. Because, whether he liked it or not, she did have a point and he needed to reassure her.

Jamaican music filled the air, the smell of jerk chicken emanating from a food truck with a line of people waiting for the wrapped spiced meat they were selling. To his left a brass band played, their Santa-hat wearing conductor flashing a baton and keeping them in time to 'We Three Kings'. It was a crazy mix of sense stimuli but, somehow, it all worked.

'Chase! Where are Brooke and Maddie right now?' Leanna screamed.

'Leanna, I hear what you're saying and I understand,' he began, bringing his mind back to that conference in New York that had helped shaped his new path. *You are invincible. But you are human. And humans always have the capability to be better than they are. You can change. Anything is possible, you just have to manage it right. Own Your Future.*

'You do, do you?' She didn't sound convinced.

'Of course,' he answered. 'You feel like you're an ocean away ...'

'Because I *am* an ocean away!'

'But the girls are right here at the end of a cell.'

'If anybody ever answers them!'

'Leanna, the girls are fine,' Chase reassured. 'I'm fine.' He took a breath. 'And we've been out today.'

'Out?'

'Yeah, we went to the Tower of London. They heard all about the murder and treachery against the monarchy, saw the Crown Jewels – God, they were these giant gemstones on crowns and sceptres, bigger than anything they've got on sale at Tiffany's – and then we went to Madame Tussauds.' He laughed. 'Maddie stood next to Prince Harry and One Direction.'

'She did?' Leanna replied, her tone a little softer. 'I'd really like to see that.'

'I'll send you some photos,' Chase said. He scuffed his shoe in the snow on the pavement. 'So, how's your mom doing?'

'She's okay,' she answered. 'Healing as well as can be expected.'

'And your dad?'

'Dad's ... well, you know how he is. Down. Thinks life is pointless. No one can do anything right for him.'

'Stick with him,' Chase said. 'He'll come around.'

'Well,' Leanna sighed. 'He's been like it for almost forty years ...'

'People can change, Leanna,' he reminded her. 'No matter how long it might take.'

'Like you?' she queried.

'Yeah,' he answered. 'Exactly like that.'

'Maybe you had more in common with my dad than we ever realised,' Leanna suggested.

'Maybe,' he answered. 'Listen, I've gotta shoot. Maddie and Brooke are devouring Asian food like there's gonna be Armageddon sometime soon.'

'You're having Asian?' Leanna said. Was that a note of wistfulness in her voice?

'Yeah, Isla took us to this cute little Indian restaurant with brightly coloured scarfs and miniature Taj Mahals everywhere and we ate this amazing lamb.' His eyes went to the scene around him. 'And I'm actually stood outside in the snow here smelling Jamaican chicken, sweet orange and the strongest, richest coffee ... London is crazy. And it's December. Everywhere is lit up. Lights on all the buildings, the London Eye, Piccadilly Circus ...' He stopped himself. He was reacting emotionally. He didn't do that. He was regressing.

'Chase,' Leanna broke in.

'Yeah?'

'Who's Isla?'

Thirty-Four

Beaumont Square, Notting Hill

'Are you sure you're going to be okay?' Isla had lost count of how many times she had asked that question of her sister and Hannah had started to get antsy after the first query and thrown a stuffed reindeer at her.

'You know we watched that programme on Channel 5 called *Women Who Kill*?'

'Yes.'

'I'm thinking of auditioning for the next series if you dare to ask me if I'm going to be okay one more time.' Hannah lifted up the black refuse sack that was sitting on her lap. 'I have Christmas decorations to sort and put up and—'

'But you won't try and put them anywhere high, will you?' Isla asked. 'And don't do any crawling, Hannah, promise me.' She turned away from the mirror above the fireplace and looked at her sister.

'Angel Gabrielle,' Hannah said. She was addressing the girl angel with the lopsided blonde head that wobbled more each year in her hands. 'Please pray for me.' She looked at the model with sincerity. 'And pray for my sister, who seems to think leaving a perfectly capable woman on her own on a week night is akin to abandonment.'

'Should I call Poppy?' Isla suggested.

Hannah laughed. 'You haven't fired her yet then?' She grinned. 'I knew you couldn't be that mean this close to Christmas.'

'Shall I call her?'

'She won't come,' Hannah stated. 'She texted me earlier. She's started watching the box set of *Game of Thrones*.'

'Was that what she was doing this morning when she told me she was with the crew from *This Morning*?'

'I have no idea,' Hannah replied. 'But she can't walk me to work tomorrow because her gran has a hospital appointment.'

'Another one!'

'She's a good granddaughter,' Hannah answered.

Isla let out a breath and turned to face her sister. 'How do I look?'

'Oh,' Hannah said, her expression matching the tone of her voice.

'That wasn't really the reaction I was hoping for,' Isla said. 'This is Colin Matthews' big Christmas extravaganza. It's one of my favourite parties of the season. It's at the Electric Cinema,' Isla reminded her sister. She brushed her hands over her smart little black dress she'd been alternating between parties for at least the last five years. She really did need a little trip to H&M. Last time they went she had picked up some festive party gems.

'I know, you said,' Hannah said, wheeling forward a little. 'And I'm jealous but …'

'But?'

'Well, I know Colin Matthews is a client of Breekers and everything, but the dress isn't saying "Christmas extravaganza".'

'What is it saying?' Isla asked.

'It looks like you're going to work,' Hannah said. 'No offence.'

The 'no offence' comment couldn't have been more tongue in cheek. Isla checked her watch. She had twenty minutes before Chase arrived to pick her up. She had insisted being collected wasn't necessary, that she could walk, but while he was sweet-talking Denise to mind Brooke and Maddie for the evening, he had organised a company car and a driver.

'Well,' Isla began. 'What should I wear? Bearing in mind I've done my hair and there isn't a lot else in my wardrobe.'

Hannah coughed and hitched her head towards the door of the living room. Isla's attention was drawn to a navy-blue suit carrier hanging over the door. Her first thought was how come she hadn't noticed it earlier and her second thought was what position had her sister had to get herself into to hang it on the top of the doorframe.

'I know what you're thinking,' Hannah stated. 'And I did not hang it up there. Claudia brought it round when you were in the bath.'

'Well,' Isla said, approaching the package with a degree of caution. 'What is it?'

'It's something I was thinking of wearing to the Breekers' Christmas party but, well, Claudia helped me try it on and it just didn't look right.' She sniffed. 'Plus, I don't know the theme yet and it might not be appropriate … Argh! Just open it already!' Hannah ordered.

Isla reached up and took the hanger from the doorframe before unzipping the carrier and looking at what was inside. She recognised it instantly.

'Mum's favourite dress,' she breathed.

'Remember when she wore it to watch *The Phantom of the Opera* and Dad even dressed up in a shirt and tie. I thought she looked like one of those beautiful actresses from the old movies; Deanna Durbin with the same auburn hair.'

Isla touched the black diamantés forming tiny roses on the jade green dress. This was the only item of clothing of their mother's they had kept. It hadn't felt right to give it to charity with the rest, not when both women had such fond memories of the times their mother had worn it. Family meals. Parties. That one trip to the West End to celebrate a wedding anniversary.

'I can't wear this,' Isla stated, emotion welling up. 'It's too special. What if I drop hog roast down it?'

'Are you having hog roast? Now I really *am* jealous!'

Isla's eyes were still on the beautiful dress. She knew it wouldn't have come from one of the very expensive boutiques, perhaps it had even belonged to someone else before their mother, but it was such a gorgeous reminder of the perfect person she had been. Loving, kind, a shoulder to cry on and a keen listening ear …

'How do you think Mum would feel knowing we kept her favourite dress but that it never saw the light of day?' Hannah's question broke into Isla's reverie. She made to answer but Hannah hadn't finished.

'I'll tell you what she would think. She would think what a waste of sequins to be shut in a musty cupboard never to sparkle again. And so what if you spill hog roast down it? We'll get it dry-cleaned. I don't remember pig being high up on the list of stains that never come out … and Claudia is forever telling me what washing miracles you can perform with a squeeze of Fairy Liquid.' Hannah sniffed. 'And she has sons, remember? Sons who play rugby.'

'Okay, okay,' Isla conceded. 'I'll get changed.' She made for the door, knowing time was pressing.

'Wait!' Hannah ordered.

Isla stopped in her tracks, turning back to face her sister.

'So, I've been thinking and ...' She sighed. 'I know I said I had dibs on the hot New Yorker but ... if you feel like you might want to pull his Christmas cracker then I won't sit in your way.'

Isla felt herself flush from the tips of her toes right up to the ends of her red hair – or that's what it felt like. This is what happened after too much wine at lunchtime. She hadn't dared tell her sister they had gone sightseeing and to her favourite Indian restaurant. She would make it up to her. They would go Diwali at the weekend and eat until they couldn't move.

'And I'm pretty sure he likes you,' Hannah stated.

'What?!' Isla exclaimed. 'Don't be ridiculous.'

'What's ridiculous about it? He's single. You're single. You're both crazy obsessed with the architectural merits of homes, hospitals and hotels.'

'He's the head of the company,' Isla pointed out.

'Hot *and* powerful,' Hannah said.

And he was funny, Isla thought to herself. Funny and intelligent but equally frustrating and opinionated. She shivered and quickly tried to mentally balance out his eyes the colour of a rich, deep mocha with the fact he had dreamt up an ogre of a super-structure.

'He has Maddie and Brooke to concentrate on and I'm not looking for a man,' Isla said stiffly, the dress getting a little heavy balanced over her arm.

'Please, Isla, now I know Ptolemy really was your last date I feel ridiculously guilty. You need to get back ...'

'Do not, under any circumstances, say the word "horse" right now,' Isla begged.

'I was going to say "in the dating arena".'

'Wait a second,' Isla said. 'Just last night you were shaping up to lunge at Chase in a bid to make him the star in your Notting Hill kiss scenario. What's changed?'

She eyed her sister who was now paying much more attention to the collection of Christmas items in her lap rather than her.

'Hannah,' Isla said softly.

Hannah looked up, the hint of a smile of her face, her cheeks a little reddened. 'Well,' she began. 'I know I didn't like you mentioning Goodfillers to Raj yesterday but ...'

Isla felt the beginnings of a smile lifting the corners of her mouth, waiting for what Hannah was about to say next.

'He came in today,' Hannah burst forth. 'And he hadn't even been to the deli. He said he was just passing ... and he brought me a whole box of mince pies!'

Her sister's eyes were shining so brightly you would have thought Raj had presented her with rubies the size of something in the Crown Jewels.

'He said they were going spare at the sorting office but ... he knows how much I like them and ... he brought them to me.'

Isla smiled at Hannah's excitement. This was good. This was not something to worry herself about. Despite his street talk, Raj was nice, kind, he had steady employment and he lived with his gran. You couldn't have too many concerns about someone who lived with their gran.

'And,' Hannah said. 'He said he might—' She stopped a little abruptly. 'Now, if I tell you, you have to promise not to be over-the-top or worried or in any way apprehensive.'

Isla felt all of those immediately, her stomach churning in anticipation of what was to come.

'Isla,' Hannah said. 'Promise!'

Isla coughed. 'Mmm.'

'Was that a promise?'

'It's as good as you're going to get right now.' Her eyes went to the clock on the wall above the television. She had ten minutes to get changed!

'Raj said he might pop over tonight,' Hannah blurted out. 'He has *Logan* on DVD.'

Isla felt immediately sick. So much for leaving her sister to her own devices for the evening. She was now potentially about to leave her in the clutches of a suitor. They would be free to get up to who-knew-what? She took a breath, trying not to let her thoughts seep into her expression. She had to remember that Hannah was twenty. That her wheelchair didn't make her different to any other twenty-year-old looking for love. And it could be worse. They were planning to watch *Logan* not *Fifty Shades Darker*.

'Okay.' Isla forced the letters from her lips.

'Okay?' Hannah checked.

Isla nodded quickly. 'Just remember one thing,' she said, halfway out of the door. 'If he does anything, and I mean *anything* to upset you ...'

'Yes?'

'It might be me who's auditioning for *Women Who Kill*.'

Hannah grinned. 'Okay,' she replied. 'Now hurry up and get changed!'

Thirty-Five

The Royale, Hyde Park

Chase slipped a pill into his mouth and swallowed. Colt had messaged him. Directly. A text that simply said. *Let's talk*. He didn't want that. Why would he want to talk to the man who had his wife and his children 24/7? Their relationship had been over the second Colt had chosen to re-enter their lives and destroy everything Chase had worked so hard for. Colt was the reason he'd fallen off the edge of the highest precipice he'd ever faced. Colt had always been the reason things turned sour. And he wasn't ready to revisit those feelings. He wasn't sure he ever would be. He knew his marriage was over; knew, despite everything, it had been a risk from the outset, but he was done with having his face rubbed in it. And Colt had to accept that. What was done was done and Chase's moving on was only going to be achieved by moving away from Colt.

'Daddy! You look hot!' Maddie remarked, spinning into his bedroom and looking him up and down.

The concierge had conjured up a tuxedo that was almost made-to-measure. He looked ready for business and that was what he was going to focus his efforts on: wowing Rod Striker and sounding him out about the prospect of bringing Breekers' new venture to his part of London.

'You can't tell him he looks hot,' Brooke interrupted. 'He's your dad!'

'How about saying I look "splendid"?' Chase suggested.

'Splendid,' Maddie said in her best British accent.

'What time does the woman with fake eyebrows get here?' Brooke asked, yawning and stretching and almost knocking her earbuds out of her ears.

'Any second now,' Chase responded, looking at his watch. 'And, Brooke, no fire alarms, in fact, no fires period, no smart-mouthing Denise and no worrying your mom to death on social media.'

'Jeez!' Brooke exclaimed. 'What the hell *can* I do?!'

'We could watch *Elena of Avalor* on Disney Channel,' Maddie suggested.

'That's for babies,' Brooke answered.

'How about a movie?' Chase countered, walking into the lounge area and looking for his wallet.

'*Saw*?' Brooke suggested.

'No freaking way,' Chase said.

'*You're Next*?'

'Nothing higher than a G rating.'

'G! Come on!' Brooke exclaimed. 'PG-13.'

'Brooke, your sister's only nine,' he reminded, strapping on his watch.

'She's mature for her age.'

'I'm not sure *I'm* mature enough to watch someone being cut up by a jigsaw,' Chase said.

'A jigsaw?' Maddie asked, looking a little confused. 'How do you cut someone with a jigsaw?'

'Let's watch it and find out,' Brooke suggested, leaning into her sister's face.

'Listen, stop,' Chase said, taking hold of Brooke's arm. 'Let's work a compromise here.'

'I'm listening,' Brooke answered, taking control of her arm back and folding them both across her chest.

'PG rating and that's my final offer.' He really hoped the PG classification hadn't been altered too much since he'd last watched one.

'Colt let me watch an NC-17,' Brooke blurted out.

'He what now?' Chase responded. Fury was bubbling up in the pit of his stomach.

'Devon came for a sleepover and Colt let us watch *Friday the 13th*.'

He was going to call Leanna as soon as he got out of his hotel room. How could Colt be so stupid? He knew the answer to that. Because he *was* stupid. He had a whole, long track record for stupid.

'The music was loud and creepy,' Maddie informed with a scowl. 'I had to put my headphones on to drown it out.'

God, he couldn't hear any more. 'PG rating,' he emphasised. 'And I'll be checking with Denise.'

Brooke smiled. 'If she hasn't succumbed to the chloroform by then.'

He pointed a finger at his elder daughter. 'That is not funny.' He sighed. 'I know it sucks that I have to go out and I can't take you two with me but it's—'

'Work. We know, Daddy,' Maddie answered with a heavy sigh.

'And I'm doing it for you, right?' he said, looking to Brooke. 'So you can have the Apple devices and the grungy boots.' His gaze went to Maddie. 'And the cute rainbow bows.' Chase touched the bow in Maddie's hair and she giggled.

There was a rap on the door of the suite and Chase checked his watch. Shit, he was late for his car and for collecting Isla.

'That'll be Denise,' he said, making strides to answer it.

'Just preparing the anaesthetic,' Brooke answered.

Chase opened the door and swallowed. Denise was wearing a figure-hugging red dress that didn't hide an inch of her and she had bright lipstick to match. High stilettos were on her feet and his first thought was, if she had to escape the suite for flood, fire or an act of God, she wouldn't be able to run. He opened his mouth to say something and settled for 'Come in.'

'Don't you look gorgeous?' Denise frothed, reaching out to brush manicured nails over the lapels of his tuxedo.

'As do you,' he responded, backing away slightly.

'Isla is a lucky, lucky girl,' Denise said, wagging a finger playfully. 'A Christmas date with the handsome New York boss.'

'Is it a date, Daddy?' Maddie chimed, eyes growing larger.

'No,' Chase said quickly. 'It's not a date. It's work. I told you.'

'Isla is real pretty,' Maddie said.

Yes, he agreed with that wholeheartedly. The red hair and the blue eyes were an appealing combination ... and she made him laugh. It had been a long time since someone had made him laugh. He swallowed, suddenly aware he hadn't given his younger daughter a response. He went to reply ...

'And she likes buildings like you do,' Maddie continued. 'And Asian food, and cake and—'

'And she rides the subway without having to read the signs,' Brooke added. 'That's pretty cool.'

She *had* done that on the Tube. Even though he had navigated his way around New York for years he still felt compelled to look, to check he was on the right platform, heading in the right direction. Isla just instinctively glided on and off the trains like it was the easiest skill in the world. In fact, she kinda glided through everything like life was easy ... and with a disabled sister he knew that couldn't really be true. She was just doing so much better than him.

Maddie pulled at his jacket sleeve, drawing him down to her height. 'It could be a date, Daddy,' she whispered. 'Mommy has Colt now. You could have Isla.'

He smiled at his nine-year-old. 'Are you kidding, Pumpkin? When would I fit in a date? I work too much and every spare second I have I want to spend with you.'

He reached out and tickled her ribs until she squealed for mercy. He straightened up, adjusting the sleeves of his jacket and preparing to leave. 'Besides, I'm sure Miss Winters has a guy already.'

'She doesn't,' Denise jumped in quickly, large red patent leather bag dropping down off her shoulder spilling curling tongs, pantyliners and a grubby teddy bear keyring on to the carpet. 'Sorry,' she said, bending to gather up the mess. 'Isla is single. Has been since way before Andy Murray won Wimbledon.' Items back in her bag Denise sighed. 'Such a lovely girl. Intelligent, kind, never a gossip ...'

So she was single. But why would knowing that change anything? She was a colleague he had to keep sweet and off the scent of Notting Hill being the prime location for his project, that was all. And he still hadn't checked the plans concerning Beaumont Square ...

'Okay, I'm gonna go out to the car now.' He kissed Maddie's head. 'Be good for Denise.' Brooke was already nodding her head to whatever track she was listening to through her headphones. He was going to get nothing more from her. He turned his attention to Denise. 'Denise, if there's a problem, any problem at all, just call my cell and I will head right back.'

Denise shook her head. 'We'll be fine,' she answered. 'I took note of all the extinguishers and fire blankets on my way up from the lobby.'

He forced a tentative smile until Denise began to laugh. 'Don't worry, Mr Bryan, I have enough snacks and scary movies in this handbag to keep even the worst delinquents entertained. You go and have a nice time … with Isla.'

A deliberate wink was offered and, as he rushed through the door, he no longer had time to worry if all manner of Freddy Kruegers were in her purse.

Thirty-Six

Beaumont Square, Notting Hill

Isla parted the curtains and looked out of the window. White flakes were dashing past the pane and doing their best to obstruct her view of the street. Chase was behind time and that meant they would be late to the party. She didn't like being late to parties. She liked to get there early, walk in perusing the people who had somehow got there before her, then position herself with a great view of the entrance so she could see exactly who would be in her orbit. If you were late, everyone who wasn't late had the upper hand.

'He will be here soon, won't he?' Hannah commented from her position by the fireplace, trying to attach a rather vile-looking wooden rocking horse bauble to a string of festiveness she was creating.

'I hope so,' Isla responded.

'Because I wouldn't want Raj turning up when you're still here.'

'Why not?' Isla asked, looking away from the window. 'I thought it was just a movie.'

'It is ... it might be ... it's just I wanted to do the whole opening the door, showing him in, bringing in the bottle of Vimto and glasses I've put on a tray ready.'

'Vimto?' Isla queried, a smirk on her lips.

'What's funny? Raj doesn't drink. You know that.'

The doorbell rang and Isla jumped at the sound. She hadn't seen a car pull up. She checked the street outside. Still nothing.

'Is it Raj?' Hannah asked in a fluster. 'Does my hair look okay?'

'You look lovely,' Isla told her. Hannah was wearing a midnight-blue top she had helped her change into earlier and she was pretty sure it was new. Claudia was a great one for shutting shop when she fancied a trip to TK Maxx.

'Don't say anything,' Hannah said, wheeling her way to the door. 'Actually, no, yes, say you're just on your way out … but don't ask him about his day or his nan because they are *my* conversation starters.'

'Okay,' Isla replied. She made sure Hannah had got Ronnie through the doorframe before she slipped out her phone to check for any message. There was one. *On my way, Miss Winters* and an emoji of a snowflake. At least he hadn't forgotten.

She suddenly realised she couldn't hear Raj's deep baritone but a higher voice. One she recognised. She headed out into the hallway.

'Mrs Edwards,' Isla greeted her neighbour. 'Is everything all right?'

'No, dear,' Mrs Edwards responded. 'No, it isn't all right.'

Isla looked to Hannah. Purdy was on a lead by the old lady's feet.

'She's seen Verity from number eleven in the square,' Hannah said.

'And that's unusual because …' Isla said.

'She was wearing a bright yellow hat and she was carrying a computer and she was measuring.'

Isla shook her head. What was Mrs Edwards' obsession with measuring? Perhaps she had been watching too much

Homes Under the Hammer. Weren't they obsessed with square meterage?

'Well, perhaps yellow is in this Christmas season,' Isla offered.

Mrs Edwards looked at her like she had scored minus figures in *Mastermind*. 'It wasn't a bonnet, dear,' Mrs Edwards said severely. 'It was a hat like you have on in that photo on your mantelpiece.' She took a breath. 'A hard hat.'

Really? Well, Isla hadn't had Verity pegged as the hard-hat-wearing kind but she herself wasn't really, only on site when it was required. The photo Mrs Edwards was referring to was the one when she had met Lord Sugar. Hannah had got it framed for her and written #SisterApprentice on the back.

'I think they're going to do a dig,' Mrs Edwards stated. 'For television.' She closed her eyes as if recalling something. 'What's the name of that programme with the scruffy ginger man who wears that green felt hat?'

'*Time Team*,' Hannah announced. 'I quite like that show. If my history lessons had been more about digging up treasure I might have done better at it.' Hannah stroked Purdy who had jumped up and pressed two paws to her lap.

'My Tommy loved that programme. It reminded him of his days as a museum curator.' She sighed. 'There were evenings his kippers went cold because he spent too much time with Neanderthal man.'

'Didn't you ask her what she was doing, Mrs E?'

'I did,' Mrs Edwards stated. 'Because she was sniffing around the rose bush I planted for Tommy after he passed.' There were tears forming in the old lady's eyes.

'Well, what did she say?' Hannah inquired.

'She told me to mind my own business and then ... she said I'd find out soon enough, at the proper time, through the proper channels.' Mrs Edwards shook her head. 'So secretive. It's not right.'

'She told you to mind your own business!' Hannah exclaimed in horror. 'Who says that in Beaumont Square? How dare she?' Hannah wheeled herself towards the still open door. 'I'm going over there.'

'Hannah, wait,' Isla said, grabbing her sister's shoulder and steadying her. 'Don't do that. Not now.' She may as well have said 'not when I'm going out and leaving you alone'.

'I wanted to welcome them to the square,' Hannah stated. 'I wanted to share Mum's special recipe lasagne with them, and they tell Mrs E to mind her own business!'

'Don't get upset, dear. I've faced-off worse than her back in the day.' Mrs Edwards sighed. 'I just want to know what's going on.'

Mrs Edwards using the phrase 'faced-off' would normally have made Isla share a smirk with Hannah, but her sister was all for wheeling across the street with all guns blazing and stopping her before Chase turned up was her only priority.

'I'll find out what's going on,' Isla blurted out.

'You will?' Mrs Edwards exclaimed, sounding nothing short of joyful.

She would? Why had she said that? Hannah was looking at her sceptically. She needed to reassure them both so she could enjoy Colin Matthews' party without worrying about Hannah getting into a fight with their new neighbour or Mrs Edwards researching medieval coinage.

'Yes,' Isla said as a black Mercedes pulled to the kerb. 'I'm going to go over there tomorrow and get to the bottom of whatever needs to be got to the bottom of. I promise.' She smiled at them both then stepped back to scoop up her clutch bag from the console in the hall. 'Enjoy your film, Hannah, and ... don't grill anything if you think you might fall asleep. I'll see you later.' She waved a hand. Skipping past Purdy's attempt to claw at her not-worn-more-than-twice high sheen fifteen denier stockings she descended the snow-covered ramp, praying to Angel Gabrielle that Colin was serving his home-made mulled wine tonight. Because she really need a big, fat vat of it.

Thirty-Seven

Electric Cinema, Portobello Road, Notting Hill

His Go-To Girl looked incredible. Wearing a green and black dress, like nothing he had seen before, she had slid into the backseat next to him looking every inch catwalk ready … but somehow even better. There was nothing over-the-top about Isla, everything was just natural and … perfect. Her make-up was light, her hair not lacquered into place and those auburn waves touched her shoulders, snowflakes like tiny diamond droplets intermingling with its bronze hue. For a second he hadn't known how to even greet her. His well-practised business bravado had left him the moment she had smiled and reminded him he was late and they ought to get going. And she had said 'ought to' not 'oughtta'.

What followed was a lesson in all things Notting Hill. There was the bookstore they had used for the film. There was Mo's Restaurant, an apparently eclectic cross of food popular in the UK in the eighties – fondue and faggots – and food from the Deep South of the US – fried chicken, catfish and grits. Isla described how her parents had loved the restaurant from its bare board floors to its bright red walls and portraits of owner Mo's grandparents on each lavatory door. Hannah had thought the eyes of the paintings moved. Isla had eaten chicken drumsticks and giant knicker-bocker glories.

And with each anecdote he had laughed, really laughed, as Isla told him more and more about this corner of London. But with every story came the realisation that what he was planning to do would take all that away. Sentimentality truly sucked for him. So, instead, he had quickly reverted back to business mode and changed the conversation, talking about her other Breekers projects until the driver pulled the car to a halt.

'We're here,' Isla was already reaching for the handle of the door.

'Hey,' Chase said, leaning over and putting his hand on hers. 'The driver is paid to open the door for you.' He smiled as he took in her expression. 'Don't tell me you've never used Breekers cars before.'

'Well … I live in London,' she reminded him. 'I go most places on the Tube. And I like the Tube.'

He shook his head. 'You are an enigma, Miss Winters.'

'And along with the comment about my practicalities I am also going to take enigma status as a compliment too,' she answered.

It was then he realised his hand was still on hers and he suddenly felt the need to apologise. 'Sorry. I should let you …' Where was the driver to do his door-opening job?

'Food and drinks are going to be in the Electric Diner next to the cinema,' Isla informed, moving both her hands to her clutch purse.

'Diner?' Chase queried. 'Are we talking hotdogs and fries and … hey d'you think there'll be grits?' Chase inquired. 'My stomach got kinda excited when you mentioned those.'

Isla shook her head. 'No, it's a hog roast and traditional Christmas fayre.' She smiled. 'I'm really hoping Colin has his homemade mulled wine. It's exquisite.'

Her saying 'exquisite' in that beautiful British accent sent a shiver down his spine. This was all Maddie's fault for mentioning the word 'date'. He straightened up in his seat. He was going to fire off a message to Colt when he visited the men's room. If he wanted to talk then he could start by explaining what he was doing letting Brooke watch an NC-17 movie.

The door was whipped open and a blast of freezing air flowed into the car. Isla let out a gasp, then accepted the driver's hand as she stepped out on to the pavement. Chase followed her lead, shoes hitting snow. Then he straightened up and took in the building in front of them.

The bright red Electric Cinema sign shone underneath the arched eaves of a white stone building glowing in lamplight. There were white double doors – holly wreaths at their centre – below an old-school cinema sign declaring 'Matthews Corporation Christmas Extravaganza'.

'It's so beautiful, isn't it?' Isla remarked, her eyes seeming to suck in everything she had no doubt seen a million times before.

'It's very ... charming,' Chase answered. He immediately hated himself for making the word 'charming' sound like he was dropping the F-bomb.

'The diner is just here,' Isla informed. 'Next door.'

He looked to where she was indicating. This building had a mainly glass frontage with a dark wood façade, and black and white tiles on the floor where he suspected tables and chairs would be set out in warmer weather. Right now there were Christmas trees in terracotta pots, golden lights spiralling around the branches, matching the radiance coming from the inside. It wasn't like anything anywhere in New York.

He noticed Isla shiver then and realised she wasn't wearing a coat, just that delicate-looking gossamer shawl over her shoulders.

'Let's go in,' he said, stepping a little closer to her. 'Introduce me to everybody.'

Thirty-Eight

'Isla Smiler! You are looking gorgeous, my darling! Gorgeous!'

Isla couldn't help but let salt-and-pepper-haired Colin Matthews sweep her right off her feet into a spinning bear hug that almost took the breath from her. He finally put her down and she struggled to maintain balance, one hand clutching the wooden diner-style table on her right, filled with festive food from shortcrust pastry turkey and cranberry pies to spiced beef, sage and onion skewers and fat tureens of liver pâté. The scent was heavy with cinnamon, orange and sweet mincemeat.

'Hello, Colin,' Isla greeted. 'How are you?'

'Wonderfully more than fair to middling, my darling. How about you?'

'I'm very well,' Isla replied. 'And you've excelled yourself this year.' She indicated their surroundings. The wooden tables and the bare brick walls usually gave the feel of an airy Manhattan loft but tonight icy white lights dropped down from the wooden ceiling, real spruce trees decorated with frosted silver baubles framed the room and on each table stood a solitary illuminated sparkling star.

'David thinks I've gone a little too *The Lion, The Witch and the Wardrobe*,' Colin laughed. 'I said you can never have too much glitter and fur. Have you seen Lady Sylvie Lau?' He put his arm around Isla and drew her close, focusing her gaze across the room full of people to the eccentric local dignitary.

'Gosh!' Isla said, taking in the full-length leopard-print fur and sparkling tiara on the woman's beehived head.

'David thinks it's jaguar,' Colin whispered.

'I sincerely hope he's wrong,' Isla said.

A not-so-subtle cough broke her concentration and she realised quickly that Chase was beside her and she hadn't introduced him. Great start to impressing the boss with her networking skills.

'Oh, Colin, please, let me introduce you to the CEO of Breekers International, Chase ...' Isla began.

'Chase Bryan,' Colin said, shooting his hand forward. 'I know exactly who you are. I've watched some of your motivational videos on YouTube. Very inspirational.'

'Well, I don't know what to say,' Chase replied. He sounded genuinely surprised. 'Thank you.'

'I think Breekers have finally realised that even though they work with bricks and mortar it's all about the people.' Colin pumped Chase's hand up and down before finally releasing it. 'Self-improvement for all.' He looked to her. 'Isn't that right, Isla?'

Isla gave Colin a smile and nodded. 'Yes.' She turned slightly to Chase. 'Colin's charity part-funds affordable housing. Breekers built a small new community in the East End,' Isla informed.

'And I couldn't have done it without this wonderful lady,' Colin said, slipping an arm around Isla's shoulders and squeezing her into him. 'There were things the architect just hadn't taken into account that this young lady spotted straightaway.'

'Well,' Isla said. 'That's my job.'

'And you do it beautifully,' Colin said. 'Oh, excuse me, David is flagging me down like a member of Village People doing semaphore.' He stepped away from their group and pointed out the trays of food on the tables. 'Make sure you eat all these Christmas delights because there's a hog roast ready any minute.' He turned away then quickly turned back. 'Oh, and I've put you two at the very front of the cinema on one of the lovely double beds.' He grinned. 'Tonight we're cosying up with a Christmas classic ... *It's a Wonderful Life.*'

It's a Wonderful Life. Isla did love that film. But had he said one of the double beds? They were along the front row, large, long, cushioned chaises plenty big enough for two, but still, it meant ... being prostrate with your boss.

She opened her mouth to call Colin back but he was already sidling through the throng of guests to his beckoning partner.

'So, a double bed,' Chase commented, picking up a skewer.

'So,' Isla replied. 'Motivational videos.'

'Okay,' Chase replied. 'I'm happy to talk about those but first I think we both need a drink. Where is this mulled wine you told me about?'

'So,' Isla began, 'the videos.'

Chase sipped at the delicious nectar that was Colin Matthews' alcoholic Christmas speciality. The spiced fruits rolled over his tongue, then began warming his throat on the way down to his stomach. It was good stuff.

'You really want to know about that?'

'Of course. If Colin's watched them, and he is a busy, busy man, then they must be good.'

'I don't know about that.' Why had he said that? What motivational speaker stopped sounding confident about his motivational-speaking capabilities?

'Is it more closing your eyes and deep breathing and imagining your happy place like you did in the Breekers boardroom?' she asked.

'Ouch,' Chase replied, looking suitability offended. 'You hated that too.'

'I'm not sure self-improvement comes from someone *telling* you how you should feel.'

Whoa. This was new. He knew, as with everything, there was a degree of dubiety about altering the way you inherently think and respond to problems, but usually he was able to win others' opinions over easily. And he was ready with his answer.

'It's more about trying to get you to be more truthful to yourself.' She made no reply so he continued. 'Is the world going to end if I make this decision or that decision? Unless you're in charge of the nuclear football the answer is almost always no.'

'You can't possibly know that on an individual level,' Isla countered.

'True,' he admitted. 'And the videos have to be for a broad spectrum. But, no matter what the nature of your business, the hurdles faced are the same.'

'But the people aren't,' Isla said.

He watched her take a long, slow sip of her drink, those full lips touching the glass, her blue eyes fixed on him. He was both hating and enjoying this conversation. Being questioned wasn't usually a problem but his confidence had been kicked again tonight by Colt's text, and it seemed like almost everyone was waiting for him to crash.

'So how did you get into it?' Isla asked, finally bringing the glass away from her mouth. 'Aaron tells me you wanted to be an astronaut.'

He took a breath as his insides were pulled tight. It had been a while since anyone had mentioned that but it hurt just as much now as when he had to give up that dream. 'Someone's been on Google.' He managed a nod. 'But yeah, I did.'

'But you're here,' she said. 'Not lost in space.'

'Very observant, Miss Winters,' he concluded.

'Did you not pass the G-Force test?' she asked.

He smiled. 'I've never had a problem with anything starting with G.'

He'd made his reply evasive and deliberately provocative to move the conversation on, to get it back on his terms. He watched her blush, then he responded, 'What happened was the New York Rangers made me an offer I couldn't refuse. But, there's only so many games you can be beaten up on before it takes a toll on your body.' He reached up to the collar of his shirt and pulled it, and the bow tie, away. On his neck was a two-inch-long slim scar. 'Blades can be a bitch on the skin.'

'Wow,' Isla said.

'After that it was time for a fresh challenge.' Skipping the few years in between came almost naturally now.

'But you had your own business-coaching company. Why move into construction?'

He smiled at her as, around them, piped festive music was turned up in volume. 'Why *not* move into construction?'

She shook her head, a slight smile on her lips. 'Answering a question with a question again, Mr Bryan.'

He was about to make a reply when the sound of a rather large bell broke the music and the excited chatter.

'The pig is now ready! Form a disorderly throng, my darlings! Talk, laugh, feast … good-natured scuffles are encouraged and the feature film will commence in sixty minutes at nine o'clock.'

Chase looked to Isla. 'Okay, as much as I'd love to tell you my whole life story I think it would bore you so ... how about we find Rod Striker and you can introduce me.'

She smiled. 'Of course.'

Thirty-Nine

Isla was going to sip her second glass of mulled wine a lot more slowly than the first one. Within three mouthfuls she had been practically interrogating her boss. *He was here, not lost in space?* What was she thinking? Hannah would be dying of shame if she had heard. She could, of course, blame her outburst on the knowledge that some sort of double lounging system was about to come their way soon and it was *that* that had thrown her. Okay, so they would be watching a film but what position would she have to get herself into to see the screen? She shivered and took a micro-sip of her drink.

Chase and Rod Striker looked to be bosom-buddies already. She had made the initial introductions, Rod had practically licked her whole hand when he'd doffed lips to skin, and she had retreated citing another guest she needed to catch. In reality, she didn't like the councillor. He was a type she had experienced a lot of in her time at Breekers. There were *some* people left with a strong moral compass, but she had found they were few and far between in the planning departments of councils. And she really wished Chase was talking to someone she'd listed rather than this racketeer.

Rod was laughing wholeheartedly at something Chase had said now, his large, round, beachballesque face reddening with every guffaw. Was Chase Bryan like one of those rogue councillors? She wasn't sure yet. He had brought this inflated, fabricated town and hotel to the table, but was he going to make sure it was all done the right way? The genuine way. The not-lining-the-pockets-of-the-decision-makers-in-an-underhand way? She wanted to believe he spoke from the heart – that he really did care about her fire doors and escape routes as much as he seemed to care about his children – but he was a businessman and his keenness to meet Rod Striker was a little troubling. She had told him she thought the place for this new venture was north London and, if he agreed with that, the person he needed to be speaking with was not Rod Striker but Vincent Fallon. Vincent 'By The Book' Fallon.

However, motives unclear or not, there was no denying the CEO of Breekers did cut a fine figure in his tuxedo. She watched him talking animatedly, a piece of pie between his fingers, the suit jacket open, revealing that clinging-in-all-the-right-places, bright, white shirt, shiny cummerbund showing off his obviously athletic frame. She sighed. If he was just a guy, just a guest here – perhaps one of David's actor friends – would she be interested? Would she be relishing the thought of watching this film on a bed with him? Would she be allowing her stomach to fizz with a combination of the creamy and delicious pâté and … attraction. Maybe. Just maybe she would be open to conversation and a little flirtation but, as it was, he was the top dog of the whole business. *Does it matter?* She imagined Hannah's voice like it was her conscience on her shoulder dressed in the Devil's robes. Of course it mattered. *Why? He'll be back in New York in a week or so.* She didn't do casual. *You don't do anything. Live a little.* She took a huge gulp of the mulled wine and quickly moved across the room towards a bank manager she knew well.

'Hey, Rod, so, the reason I wanted to hook up with you tonight is two-fold,' Chase began, plucking another glass of steaming mulled wine from a passing waiter and handing it to the councillor.

'I'm intrigued,' Rod replied, gnashing pastry between his teeth. 'Go on.'

Chase lowered his voice. 'Well, firstly, I've been told you're the best there is.'

He watched Rod lap up the compliment like it was cream on top of a Christmas pudding.

'But, this needs to stay completely between us. I mean, absolutely under wraps until everything is in place and the company is ready for the big reveal.'

Rod touched his finger to his nose. 'Chase, I haven't got to where I am today by not being able to keep a secret.'

Chase smiled. 'As I thought.' It was his hope that as soon as the councillor heard about Breekers' plan and the potential kick-back for him personally, he was going to do everything he could to *insist* the super-complex was built in his area.

'So, I'm telling *you*, the best there is, that Breekers want to build something,' Chase carried on as people began to file out of the room, pork-filled rolls in their hands.

'That is what you guys do,' Rod answered with a chuckle. He wiped his mouth on the sleeve of his tuxedo.

'It's big,' Chase stated.

Rod leant forward a little. 'How big?'

'Six hundred acres big.'

He watched the councillor's eyes bulge out of his head and he then began to cough. Chase took his arm, encouraging the mulled wine glass nearer his lips. He waited for him to take a swig of the drink before continuing. The guy didn't need to know the finer details tonight. Chase just had to lay down the groundwork.

'In my zone?' Rod queried. 'It's impossible.'

Chase shook his head. 'Oh, Rod, you're a businessman. The word "impossible" shouldn't exist in our world.'

'Tell that to the other members of the planning committee and the tree-huggers.' He sighed. 'You touch the wrong blade of grass around here you've got to pay compensation and plant a whole football pitch.'

'If this project were to go through,' Chase said, pitching his tone just right. 'There would be a significant thank you to the man who made it happen.'

He had Rod's full attention now; the councillor's eyes were not saying 'impossible' they were asking 'how much'. He struck while the iron was in the fire.

'I'm sure Jeremy and Ben would love their father to be able to drive them to school in a Ferrari, no?'

The man was literally panting now, pastry falling from the fingers of one hand, the other barely gripping hold of the glass.

'Let's arrange to meet next week, yes?' Chase said. 'Go through all the details.' He didn't wait around to hear an affirmative. As he nodded his goodbye and slipped back into the crowd heading for the cinema, he knew whatever he was going to ask of Rod Striker, his support was a given.

'I'll get my secretary to arrange it,' Rod called after him.

And there it was. Chase didn't look back but held up his hand. O-Y-F. Own Your Future.

Forty

Isla sighed with pleasure as she looked down into the auditorium of the Electric Cinema. It was just beautiful. From its rounded ceiling and painted décor reminiscent of its Edwardian roots, to its red leather seats complete with footstools and individual side tables with glowing table lamps. There was no need for additional Christmas cosy here, it was already awash with winter ambience and starting to fill with merry men (and women) high on Colin Matthews' hospitality – and mulled wine.

'Is it wrong to secretly be wishing for a showing of something like *Gravity*?'

Chase's voice was close to her ear and an involuntary shiver made Isla tighten her grip on the glass she was holding. She turned to face him. 'Still hankering after that life in a rocket?'

He grinned. 'No,' he answered. 'I just have a soft spot for Sandra Bullock.'

Isla returned his grin and whispered. 'Me too.'

'Whoa, Miss Winters, the puck hit the back of the net right there.'

She led the way down the aisle towards the front of the theatre where the big screen was displaying the Electric Cinema logo, seemingly waiting for everyone to be seated. 'Is that ice hockey terminology you're quoting? It's not a sport I'm overly familiar with.'

'I guess not,' Chase replied. 'You Brits are more into soccer …'

'That would be football,' Isla corrected.

'And tennis on grass of course.'

'It's the only way to play.'

'I have to say,' Chase said, following her, 'this is one of the craziest Christmas parties I've ever been to.'

'Really?' she asked. 'I'm not sure I believe things aren't crazy in New York.'

'Have you come over to New York?' Chase asked.

'No,' she replied. 'I haven't.'

'Well, it's no Vegas,' he answered.

She cringed. Why had she lied about going to Nevada? She was going to have to look it up, drop some hotels and casino names into conversation ... or just confess. Admit she was twenty-five and had been completely landlocked.

'It's cool though,' Chase said. 'And it's ... home.'

She turned her head to look at him, sensing the slight hesitation before his final word.

'And this looks like us,' Chase said, stopping in front of an enormous red velveteen sofa-bed.

Isla swallowed. Despite its size it looked ... intimate. There were bolsters separating each bed with sumptuous cushions at the back and ... were they cashmere blankets?

'This is so cool,' Chase said, seeming to take everything in. 'We can network with whoever is either side of us. Who can we expect? I'm hoping for someone from the entertainment sector who could be a brand ambassador for the village.' He had lowered his voice to a whisper.

'Brand ambassador,' Isla stated. 'Don't you think you're jumping the gun a little? I mean there's a lot of work to do and—'

'Positive thinking, Miss Winters. Maybe you need to watch a few more of my motivational videos.' Chase jumped right on to the bed, crawling up the upholstery and wasting no time in making himself comfortable. She was concerned about pulling a sequin off her mother's dress and, as she watched Chase spread himself out, she wondered just how much smaller the giant couch was going to feel once they were both on it.

'Come on up,' Chase said, patting the fabric next to him.

Most other people she knew were seated in the respectable chairs. She looked at them, their drinks next to the golden table lamps, with envy in her eyes.

'Am I guessing you're a cinema sofa-virgin too?' Chase said all too loudly. 'Is this somewhere in London you *can't* tell me the history about?'

She moved then, putting her knee on to the velveteen and crawling almost combat-style up the length of the bed. 'Oh no,' she breathed, pulling herself up. 'I can tell you some of the history.' She tried to turn and position her bottom elegantly but instead her elbow slipped off the bolster just as she pivoted and she landed slightly more on Chase's side of the bed than hers, cradling her glass in the attempt not to spill a drop. She shimmied quickly and settled herself down. Conversation – and quickly. 'One of the theories is that it opened on Christmas Eve in 1910.'

'One of the theories?' Chase queried. He handed her a cushion.

'Records were sketchy back then,' Isla said. 'But I do know the first film to be shown was *Henry VIII*.'

'Wow,' Chase said. 'You really do know your stuff.'

She chanced a glance at him: one ankle was crossed over the other, hands behind his head, relaxing into the cushions at his back. He caught her eyes and smiled.

'What?' he questioned. 'Do you think we should take off our shoes?'

'What?' Isla exclaimed. 'Our shoes ...?'

'Yeah, I mean, these velvet covers and these expensive-looking throws.' He was already bringing his shoe up to untie the laces. 'And I hired these with the suit and they're a little tight. I'm never quite sure on the British sizes.'

Was he really going to take his shoes off? What was her problem with him taking his shoes off? They were practically laying on a bed. It did make sense.

'What's the problem, Miss Winters?'

'Nothing, I just—'

'Are we going to violate a dress code?' he queried, pulling off his second shoe.

'It's highly likely.'

'But,' he whispered, 'in a few seconds, everything is gonna go dark.' He smiled. 'And no one is gonna know.'

There was a mischievous look on his face now and she couldn't help but smile back. This whole scenario was a little ridiculous.

'Come on, Miss Winters, unbuckle the heels.'

He was right: if her heel snagged the cashmere blanket she might have to pay for a replacement she couldn't afford. She leant forward, fingers going to the straps on her shoes and peeled them off her feet.

'I'll take those,' Chase said, snatching them from her hands.

'Well, what are you going to do?' Isla questioned, eyes wide.

'Did Google not tell you I was also pretty hot at basketball?'

With that said, he launched one of her shoes up and over the length of the sofa-bed so it dropped down on to the floor. Then, much to the amusement of the couples either side of them, he did it with her other shoe and then his.

'So,' he said, settling back into the cushions. 'What d'you think the chance is of them coming around with popcorn?

Forty-One

'Where have you lived besides London?'

Chase loved movies but the concept of sitting — or lying — still for two hours and not communicating wasn't one he had ever been able to easily buy into. He knew it had cost him a few girlfriends in high school and after that he'd never suggested the movies for anything date-related. The last movie he'd seen was *Despicable Me 2* with Brooke and Maddie at a kids' screening where talking was almost encouraged. And that had suited him more than his girls who had kept telling him to shush.

'Sshh,' Isla responded, eyes glued to the screen.

He had seen this movie — once a few years ago — stuffed from Christmas lunch and not really paying attention while the girls got sugared up and Leanna cried into a box of Kleenex.

'Have you not seen this before?' Chase continued.

Isla turned her head then, her features shrouded by the darkness. 'Of course. It's a classic.'

'So, talk to me.'

'We're at a movie night,' Isla whispered. 'And everyone is watching the film.'

'No, they're not,' he answered. 'They're getting drunk on mulled wine and I'm convinced the group on the back couch are all making out.'

'What?' Isla immediately sat bolt upright and turned her head.

He couldn't help but grin. 'Hey, I was kidding.' A laugh escaped his lips. 'But I really want to know what you were going to do about it.'

Now she looked Britishly affronted. That wasn't going to get him conversation. He moved a little closer to her. 'Okay, so, I'm no good at the whole movie thing.'

'The whole movie thing?'

'Sitting still. Being quiet.'

'It's a picture house.'

'It's a what now?'

'That's what they used to call it.'

'Is it that "ye olde" thing again?'

She was smiling now. There was a laugh brewing, he just knew it.

'You can mock our heritage on this side of the Atlantic but I know it comes from nothing but deep-rooted envy.'

'Come on, Isla. Have a conversation with me,' he said. 'Tell me the places you've lived and I'll buy you the DVD of the movie and you can play it over and over in the Christmas break.'

He watched her take a breath, then adjust her position next to him, turning a little on her side, face pressing into one of her cushions as she looked to get comfortable.

'London,' she said.

'Yes.' He waited for her to continue.

'That's it,' she answered. 'Just London.'

'Okay,' he breathed out. 'So, what parts?'

'This part,' she answered. 'Notting Hill.'

He was halfway to opening his mouth to ask her about the other parts when he stopped himself, instinctively knowing there were no other parts. 'Okay, cool.'

'A shorter conversation than you expected?'

'No ... I just—'

'Well, how about you?' Isla inquired. 'Where have you lived?' She smiled. 'Or will you still be telling me after the film has ended?'

He smiled. 'New York.'

'Obviously.'

'Oregon.'

'I'm sensing California is coming.'

He grinned then. 'I might have spent one summer there on Spring Break.'

'What was your favourite place?' Isla asked.

What *had* been his favourite place? Anywhere but Illinois, if he was honest. Illinois just messed everything up for everybody.

'They were all pretty different.' That was well avoided. And he had been the one to start this conversation. If it slipped into uncomfortable territory it was on no one but him.

'But you feel at home in New York,' Isla stated.

Did he? He had used to. When it was him, Leanna, Brooke and Maddie, closeted in the family unit he believed was strong and unbreakable. In reality, now he stayed in New York because he didn't know what else to do. It was keeping all their heads above water and it was where he had help if he needed it.

'Yes,' he answered. 'Yes I do.' He smiled. 'And you've told me and shown me all of the hot spots around *your* home.'

'Not all of them,' Isla exclaimed. 'It's packed full of great places. We've only just touched the surface.'

He swallowed. 'But don't you ever feel like moving some-place else? Finding other great places?'

'I did once,' she answered.

Her tone was subdued and she glanced back at the cinema screen before looking back to him. 'I was once going to pack a rucksack with my toothbrush, a hairbrush, two T-shirts, a pair of shorts and some mosquito spray and ... fly to Guatemala.'

'Searching for ancient Incas?' he inquired.

'I don't think I cared what I was searching for.' She sighed. 'I just wanted to search. I wanted to reach out and see what I could catch.'

'What happened?' he asked.

She looked straight at him then. 'The truck on the motorway that took my parents happened.'

The expression on her face chilled him to the bone. So much pain, so much desperation, so much enduring strength. Right now he felt like the smallest, most insignificant son-of-a-bitch on the planet. And something in him shifted. He wanted to hold her hand. He wanted to make her feel better, just in this moment if nothing else.

Her hand was right there, resting on the velveteen, nails painted clear. He inched his fingers towards hers ...

'I'm sorry,' she said, hand moving to brush her hair from her face. 'It's this film. It always makes me so sentimental, apparently even when I'm only half paying attention.' She smiled then and shifted back from him slightly. 'So, I didn't go to Guatemala ... and I suppose the Incas' loss is Breekers' gain.'

The moment for contact had gone. 'I very much concur, Miss Winters,' he replied, all British.

'So, Chase,' she said, looking to him again.

'Yeah.'

'Can I ask *you* something?'

'Sure,' he whispered in response. 'Shoot.'

'Who's Colt?'

Her sweet voice speaking the name of the one man he loved and loathed in equal measure hit him full force, and he knew that was something he was going to be unable to disguise. He used all the techniques he taught and *had been* taught to deal with the moment in a level-headed, unemotional way. He took a breath and rolled his tongue along the roof of his mouth, just pausing. And all the time Isla was just looking at him, waiting for a reply he had no choice but to give.

'Who's Colt?' Answering a question with a question. He cleared his throat, and waited for the initial fear and anger to subside. 'Colt is ...' Almost there. O-Y-F. O-Y-F. 'Colt's my brother.'

Forty-Two

Colt was his brother. Even though they had moved on to a discussion about who Chase wanted to speak to when the movie ended, Isla couldn't get that fact out of her mind. She had to be mistaken about what Maddie and Brooke had said. Chase's ex-wife couldn't have moved on with his own brother. Could she?

'I will see you at the Breekers' Christmas Party, Chase. We are very much looking forward to it. Isla always throws the most amazing Christmas party.'

Isla smiled at Jennifer White from the Enterprise Group as they stood in the foyer of the cinema and another sliver of unease for a very different reason rolled through her. She was pretty sure the catering company were deliberately avoiding her attempts to contact them. 'Thank you, Jennifer. See you soon.'

'It was really great to meet you,' Chase replied, shaking the woman's hand.

'You too. My chariot awaits, I'm afraid. Bye.' Jennifer waved a hand and headed towards the doors.

'She was nice,' Chase remarked.

'Yes, she's very nice and a *very* good businesswoman.'

'You said "very" *very* heavily.'

'She would eat you for breakfast.'

'O … kay … got it.' He checked his watch. 'Our car should be here in a few minutes.'

'If it's all the same to you I think I'd like to walk,' Isla told him. She began to tie her shawl around her shoulders.

'Great idea,' Chase replied. 'Shall we?'

He'd offered her his arm like a black-and-white movie idol and she couldn't help but smile.

'Lead the way, Miss Winters. Let's scratch more of that surface.'

She took his arm and they headed out into the night behind all the other guests making their way home or on to other places.

It was freezing and as much as she craved the fresh air and the walk she was really beginning to wish she had brought a coat. She tightened her hold on Chase's arm in a bid to stop herself from shivering.

'I know what you're thinking,' Chase said as they strolled along Portobello Road past the bistros with their glowing interiors, the scent of red wine, garlic and sweet toffee puddings in the air. The eclectic mix of shops were all closed, their shutters pulled down, the quirky pastel-painted houses like chunks of Battenberg against the night sky.

'That I wish I had brought a coat?' Isla stated through chattering teeth.

'Hey, are you that cold?' Chase asked. 'Here,' he said, shaking his body out of his jacket and taking of off. 'Put this on.'

'Thank you, but I can't leave you in just a shirt ... it's freezing.'

'And what sort of asshole would I be if I let you turn into an ice sculpture. Come on,' he said, putting the jacket around her body. 'Put it on. No arguments.' He grinned. 'Call it an order from head office.'

She smiled then and complied readily, slipping her arms into the sleeves of the jacket.

'Better?' he asked once she was buttoned up.

'You?' she queried. The snow was falling steadily, just a light constant flurry but it was going to wet his shirt in no time. Maybe they should have just waited for the car ...

'Seriously, I'm good.' He offered her his arm again. 'You don't spend a couple years of your life on a hockey rink without being able to suck up a little snow.'

'I suppose not.'

'So,' Chase began, 'now we've dealt with the coat ... next you were thinking why my ex-wife is living with my brother, right?'

'I ... well ... it's really none of my business.'

'I know,' he said. 'But, strange as it might seem, I really think I wanna tell you.'

Chase felt sick and scared and invigorated all at once. Was he really going to do this? Could he let it all out somewhere other than the doctor's office? It would be a huge leap forward. It would be getting close to closure, wouldn't it?

'Maybe not. Wow. God, I'm sorry,' Chase said suddenly stopping and putting his hands to his head. 'You did not sign up to this when you agreed to come to this party with me.'

'I don't think we really signed up to a strict guideline of how the night would go,' Isla replied.

The tone of her voice was totally businesslike but her expression was completely open, genuine, no pressure. He just had to take that first step ...

'So, Illinois,' he breathed. 'We talked about Illinois and ... I really hated Illinois.' He fell into step again.

'I only know Chicago,' Isla admitted, taking his arm as she dodged pools of slush on the pavement.

'Yeah, that's where we were. Twelve miserable months in high school where almost everyone brought a weapon to class.' It had been one thing to get into fights with the resident jocks, it had been quite another when they were all tooled up. 'But Colt thought it was like paradise. He's two years older than me, he was a whole lot cooler than me and everyone thought he was like some kind of god.' He sighed.

'Why did you move to Chicago?' Isla asked.

'My dad worked for this new chain of stores called So-Market and whenever they opened in a new city he would go there for six months, a year, and oversee the implementation of everything in the stores in that state.' At first, maybe when he was too young to think about it, he had liked the travelling, but when he hit high school it was harder and harder to start again somewhere else, catching up on work and making new friends.

'Colt met Leanna and I spent nine months or so working my ass off to improve my grades so, when the time came, I had every chance of being that astronaut.'

'Colt met Leanna,' Isla queried.

'Yeah, she was in love with my brother back then.' He let a breath go. 'Just like right now.'

'I don't understand,' Isla said.

'It's a pretty messed-up situation, right?'

'I wouldn't say …'

'Oh, I would,' Chase replied. 'I definitely would.' Was he going to tell her? If he did it had to be quick. No emotion, just the truth. Rip it off like a Band Aid.

'So … back then, fresh out of school, Colt went to prison for armed robbery,' he stated.

He heard Isla's intake of breath. Yeah, it was shocking. He was shocked every time he thought about it. His parents had never really recovered, were still touched by the stigma now.

'And now he's back,' Chase said. 'Picking up right where he left off. Like nothing's changed.'

Forty-Three

Isla didn't know what to say. What could you say? She wanted to ask a hundred questions but also nothing at all. Maybe that was what he needed, for her to say nothing, just to listen.

'God, would you listen to me?' Chase asked. 'What was in that hot wine?'

'Mulled,' Isla responded. 'Warmed, not boiled.'

'It's given me some sort of contagion,' Chase insisted. 'I'm going to start coming out in lesions like Maddie.'

'Because you're being honest?' Isla queried.

He stopped walking and looked at her. 'Yeah.'

'Honesty shouldn't be something you're afraid of,' Isla said. 'You told me you like honesty and … life isn't a perfect, cosy tinsel ball, even at Christmas.'

'I … don't know how I feel about you telling me that,' Chase admitted. 'You're the girl who loves Christmas. The girl with all the stars and glowing references and—'

'A photo with Lord Sugar on my mantelpiece.'

'I have no idea who that is,' he said.

'I think,' Isla began. 'I'm just trying to say that if you're not honest … if you try to hide things, even from yourself, it doesn't ever make it go away. The truth is always still there. The good truth … and the bad truth.'

'I know.'

'Life isn't perfect but it's ours. And I believe we have to make the most of it,' Isla said. 'And it *is* beautiful and sparkly even if sometimes it's hard.'

Right at that moment Chase thought Isla Winters was the most beautiful woman he had ever set eyes on … and talked to. He suddenly felt that if the world ended right then and there his two regrets would be not hugging his daughters enough and not pressing his lips to Isla's. Was he ready to move on? To feel something for someone else? Or was this just emotion railroading him …

'Mr Bryan, I would very much like to show you something.'

'Is it the one hundred and first use of an umbrella?' Chase asked, recovering his composure a little. 'Because that might come in useful right about now.'

'And I thought you said you could suck up a little snow,' she replied with a grin, walking away from him.

They had walked another half mile or so and were now outside an ugly building covered in unreadable graffiti. Even with its roof capped with snow it didn't look like somewhere anyone with any sense would want to hang out.

'Remind you of Chicago?' Isla questioned, taking a deep breath.

'What is this? And what the hell happened here? Did whoever owned it die?' Chase inquired.

'No,' she sighed. 'This is Life Start Community Centre. Where Hannah comes to meet like-wheeled people.'

'No kidding,' Chase stated.

'Yes, this is a little corner of Notting Hill that most people seem to have forgotten about, unless you count the property developer who wanted to knock it down and turn it into luxury apartments.' She turned to him then. 'I know what you're thinking.'

'What?' he asked.

'That perhaps Breekers could have pitched in and built them. Made this into something a lot better than it is.'

'I don't—' Chase began.

'I just wish someone would make it better than it is and want to keep its purpose.' She sniffed. 'Hannah says she hates it because it's full of disabled people but I know that isn't true … that she hates it, I mean. And when she first had her accident and got used to the fact she had Ronnie for good it was a safe place where she could ask questions of people who knew all the answers because they'd been there.'

He looked at this building with the gutter coming away from the brickwork, the safety glass on the front door cracked, and as much as his brain was telling him this road was, without doubt, in the zone for development if the super-village came to Notting Hill, his heart was telling him he wanted it fixed. In fact, the more time he spent in this area of London the more it was slicing into him what he was preparing to do. Isla loved this place. Isla lived here, with her disabled sister. They had never lived anywhere else. It was their comfort zone. And he was planning to destroy it.

'This wasn't all I wanted to show you,' Isla said. She had turned around and was indicating a fenced area across the street. 'Remember that residents' park Will and Anna broke into in the film *Notting Hill*?'

'I remember something about whoops-a-daisy.' He said it as Hugh Grant as he could manage.

'Very good, Mr Bryan.'

'Is this it?' he asked, crossing the road.

'No,' Isla answered. 'This one is better. And I have a key.'

Forty-Four

Larkspur Gardens, Notting Hill

Isla wasn't sure why she had shown Chase the community centre or this park but there had been something different about him since he had told her about his brother. An air of vulnerability. Openness. He had, despite himself, shown her something of the man he was, not just the motivational head of Breekers he appeared to be on paper. And she was a people person, in so far as people mattered to her much more than any blurb written about them. And she was finding Chase's reality rather more intriguing than the synopsis she'd got from Aaron.

She slipped her grandmother's key into the lock and turned, still worrying, still hoping like she did every time she and Hannah came here. It clicked open and that deep sense of relief washed over her.

'Are we breaking in?' Chase inquired, his voice close to her ear.

She smiled, turning to look at him. 'I don't think you can call it breaking in if you have a key.'

'Okay, Miss Winters, let me rephrase.' He cleared his throat. 'Are you meant to have a key?'

'I find sometimes it's best not to ask too many questions.'

He put his hands up in surrender. 'Not asking another damn thing.'

She pushed open the gate and then gasped. They had decorated for the season already. The ancient spruce you could only see the very top of from the outside was strung with glittering gold lanterns and interspersed between its branches were smaller twists of red and green flashing gently on and off. There was a dusting of snow on the grass and the paths through the park and the stark trees were glittering with frost. Then her eyes moved to the small fountain with the marble frog that squirted water from its mouth. It was lit up, but no water was forthcoming. Isla took steps towards it.

'What is this place?' Chase asked. 'It looks like the land that time forgot.'

'Does it?' Isla said, standing in front of the frog. 'Or does it look like a simpler time that everyone wants to remember?' She rubbed at the frog's mouth with her fingers.

'Is this something you do for luck?' Chase inquired, standing next to her.

'No, it should be shooting out water but I guess it's frozen.' She rubbed her fingers over the spout until they started to go numb.

'Let me,' Chase said.

She stepped back and watched as he put his mouth over the frog's like he was resuscitating it. Then he jumped back like he'd been electrocuted and straight away water began jutting out into the frozen pool below.

'God, that was cold,' Chase said, rubbing his fingers to his lips.

'You're completely mad,' Isla said. 'You could have got your lips stuck.'

'But we got the frog working,' Chase said, indicating the now running water. 'I could tell you really wanted the frog working.'

'Yes,' she answered. She looked to the bench, just a few steps away, with the view of pretty much everything here. Her grandmother's bench. The bench held a plaque that said: *Edith Rose Winters. Forever a kiss on the wind.*

'You wanna sit down?' Chase asked her.

'It's freezing,' Isla reminded him. She turned to look at him. His shirt was damp from the snow. She didn't want him getting the look of Jack Dawson in the water after the boat had sunk.

Before she could say anything he had marched up to the bench and started scraping off the layer of snow that covered the wood.

'Ta da,' Chase said, spreading his arms wide. 'One hardly wet bench for you to take in the view.'

'You are certifiably mad,' Isla said, a smile widening her mouth.

'So some people tell me,' he answered with a grin. 'Come on, we'll sit on the jacket and we'll share your poncho.'

'Poncho,' Isla said with a laugh, clutching at her shawl. 'This isn't a Western. And it's actually vintage.'

'As long as it's warm I don't care when it was made.'

His teeth were juddering a little now and she stepped up to him, taking his jacket from her shoulders, laying it on the bench then untying her wrap. She sat down and he joined her. She moved a little closer, passing her shawl around his body until he caught the end with his ice-cold fingers.

'So, this place is special to you,' Chase remarked, his breath a little disjointed as he fought the dropping temperature.

'We're sitting on my grandmother's bench,' Isla informed him. She turned her head to read the plaque again.

'Edith Rose Winters. Forever a kiss on the wind,' Chase read aloud.

Isla smiled. 'That was her catchphrase. Whenever Hannah and I were frightened or being silly over something trivial, she would say "Ah now, don't be afraid, remember there's always a kiss on the wind."' She smiled. 'We didn't really understand it back then but now it comforts me to believe that she's always here, and my mum and dad too. You know, kisses on the wind.'

'That's beautiful,' he replied.

'She lived here, in that house across there.' Isla pointed to a three-storey townhouse with a cat sitting on the wall, licking its paws. 'That's how come I have a key to the gardens.' She sighed. 'She died when I was fifteen. Nothing horrible or spectacular, just fell asleep and didn't wake up.'

'That's not a bad way to go,' Chase admitted.

'And so much better than hyperthermia,' Isla remarked, teeth juddering.

'Don't you go dying of cold on me,' he warned. 'I think I would probably end up losing my job if I killed my Go-To Girl.'

She laughed. 'There's true compassion.'

'Come here,' Chase said. 'Neither of us are dying tonight.'

He put an arm around her and pulled her in tight to him. And immediately her stomach started to move around like a bumper car, waiting for the jolt she knew was going to happen.

'I really needed to know that British winters are just as cold as New York ones,' Chase remarked. 'I might have been more prepared.'

'I love the sky this time of year,' Isla said, breathing in and becoming more and more aware of his firm torso in line with hers. 'On a clear night like this, even in the city, you almost feel like you can see everything. Everything outside of here, you know?'

She looked up, away from the sparkling Christmas tree and the frog whose water spurting was starting to slow, to the thick blanket of night above them.

Then she felt Chase shiver and she looked back to him. 'You're cold,' she said. 'Let's walk to the Tube or call the car.'

'No,' Chase whispered. 'I really don't want to do that.'

There was something in his tone that made Isla turn her head to look at him a little more fully. And when she did, she found those caramel-coloured eyes were studying hers. She caught her breath, held on to it, and tried to beat down the sparks that were zipping through her like excited fireworks. This man, her boss, did something to her and there was absolutely no denying it.

'You don't?' She barely managed to get the words out.

'No,' he whispered. 'Because, I think, if we leave, I'm gonna miss out on seeing the stars.'

She couldn't move. Her heart was pounding. She was looking at him, he was looking back at her and the snow was starting to fall more rapidly around them. She couldn't feel the cold. All she could feel was the warmth radiating from his body, stuck fast to hers, so close but yet not close enough.

There was nothing Chase wanted to do more right now than kiss her lips. He couldn't tear his eyes from hers, but the longer he held the contact the more his emotions were threatening to spill over. That meant losing control and he wasn't so great with losing control.

He reached out a shaking hand, slowly, his fingers grazing her jawline, his thumb resting against her cheek. He watched her close her eyes in reaction to his touch and he knew then he was totally invested in this moment.

'Isla,' he whispered.

Hearing her name made her eyes open again and he moved then, inching his body a little closer to hers, increasing the pressure just a fraction to indicate his intent. He didn't want to mess this up.

Cupping her cheek with his hand, he drew her face towards his, ultra-slowly, giving her every opportunity to back out, subconsciously thinking that was probably what was going to happen and then ... she *did* move and disappointment started to invade until ... she slipped a hand around the nape of his neck and gently edged him nearer.

He kissed her then and she kissed him back, unhurried at first – soft, beautiful, tame – then deeper, darker, with intensity he hadn't experienced or displayed in such a long time. It felt good. She felt so good ...

Her lips left his and she sat back, the shawl dropping off her shoulders. 'I'm sorry,' she gasped.

'No, Isla,' he said softly. 'Don't be sorry.' He took a breath. 'You can feel anything you want to feel about it but please ... please, don't be sorry.' He reached for her hand. '*I'm* not sorry.'

'I don't know what came over me,' she continued. 'Can I blame Colin's mulled wine?' She let go of his hand, claimed back the shawl and got to her feet.

'Isla ...' he began, trying to calm her. He could see she was like a deer caught in the headlights, wide, scared eyes, shaking legs. His kiss had done that to her. That hurt a little. Actually, it hurt a lot.

'We shouldn't have done that,' she said through chattering teeth.

'Why not?' Chase dared to ask.

'Because ...' She appeared to have no answer.

'Because?' he queried, standing too.

'Because ... you're my boss and, officially, we are still meant to be at a networking party and—'

'Okay,' Chase interrupted. 'I get it.' He sighed. 'It's okay.'

'It is?' Isla queried.

'Sure,' he replied. 'No problem. We can forget it ever happened.'

He looked directly at her then, hoping for her to change her mind, longing for her to take a few steps back to him and kiss him again. Instead, she nodded and said, 'We'd better go.'

Forty-Five

Beaumont Square, Notting Hill

The whole ride home in the car Chase had been nothing but polite and Isla had hated every second of responding in exactly the same way. Pretending the kiss hadn't happened wasn't an option because it had changed everything. How was she going to work with him now? What had she been thinking? She had turned into Hannah, seeing movie scene kisses in her head and letting herself get sucked into some alcohol-enhanced dream state where you acted on impulse and temporarily ignored the consequences. That was what teenagers did, not twenty-five-year-old women with responsibilities and a job she needed to hang on to.

Now she was standing outside her own front door, eyes closed, remembering just how it had felt to kiss him. It had been everything, all in one special moment. Passionate, gentle, hot ... her stomach pulsed even now as she recalled how he had tasted – berries, snow, midnight. She opened her eyes slowly, letting the memory disappear gradually until it faded into nothing. It was something so much better than Ptolemy. She couldn't ask for anything more without a whole host of complications. And she just didn't need them. Hannah didn't need them either.

'Isla! If that's you can you just come in?! There's only so long I can hold Hugh Grant in the air! And if it's not Isla, don't come in! Or face twelve inches of ceramic!'

She was late. She needed to get Hannah up to bed. She should have thought more about that earlier instead of reminiscing about her gran and kissing Americans on park benches. She slipped her key in the lock and opened the door.

'It's me,' she called to her sister. Slipping her head around the door first, she saw Hannah in the hallway, Hugh Grant raised above her head.

'What were you doing out there?' Hannah asked, lowering Hugh. 'The light went on ages ago.'

'I was just …' What did she say to this one? She couldn't exactly say she was going over her best kiss ever millisecond by millisecond.

'My God!' Hannah exclaimed, putting Hugh down on the hall console. 'You were snogging someone, weren't you?' Her sister's eyes widened even more. 'You haven't … with Chase Bryan!'

'No!' Isla said quickly. 'No, of course not. I was just … I had … a stone in my shoe and … I had to get it out.'

'Right,' Hannah replied. 'Well, now you're back you need to come in here and look at something.' She began to wheel back towards the door to the living room.

'Well, I was thinking we'd just go to bed,' Isla said, following her sister. 'It's late and—'

'Isla. How's it goin', bro?'

Raj appeared from the living room looking suitably different without his Royal Mail uniform on. In fact he looked almost smart. Box-fresh white trainers, skinny jeans and a bright yellow polo shirt. She almost forgot to speak. 'Hello, Raj. You're still here.'

'Of course he's still here,' Hannah remarked. 'We need to tell you what we found while you were out.' She looked to Raj. 'Could you make some more macchiatos and I'll start the story?' Hannah suggested. 'Don't worry, I'll let you do the bit about breaking in.'

Isla swallowed. What had her sister said? 'Hannah, what have you done?'

Hannah smiled. 'Well,' she said. 'Your heroic sister – that's me, by the way – might just have freaking saved the whole of Notting Hill.'

Forty-Six

The Royale, Hyde Park

'Thank you for watching the girls, Denise,' Chase said. 'I really appreciate it.'

He was tired. He didn't want to talk. He wanted to pour himself a bourbon, drink it slow, and relive every skin-tingling second of his kiss with Isla. She might regret it, but he was going to be remembering every moment of it for the foreseeable future. She had smelled like fondant and ice and ... Christmas ... and her sweet lips had matched his, riding slow at first and then hotter, their tongues rolling latently together. He closed his eyes until—

'Are you all right, Mr Bryan?' Denise questioned.

He came to quickly. 'Yeah ... I apologise ... it's late. I should let you go.'

Denise put her bag over her shoulder and headed for the door. 'We ordered room service. Macaroni and cheese and a couple of burgers. I hope that was all right.'

He nodded. 'Sure.'

'Then Brooke went on about extra salt so ...'

His eyes widened. 'You didn't ...'

'I said she could order some cheesecake so we had that too, and popcorn, and half of a rather large chocolate Father Christmas.'

He sighed. 'I'm wondering if that thing will ever disappear.'

'I ate a whole leg,' Denise informed her boss. 'So he won't stand up any more.'

'Thank you,' Chase answered.

'See you at work tomorrow,' Denise said, opening the door to the suite.

'Goodnight, Denise.' Chase pressed a fifty-pound note into her hand. 'Thank you again.'

'Oh, thank you, Mr Bryan.' She looked at the money then up at him. 'Any time.'

He took a step back and closed the door, leaning heavily against it. Closing his eyes again, he thought about Isla. How she had barely spoken to him on the drive back to her home. She had sat, small, knees bunched together, her body pressed against the door, eyes gazing out into the dark. He'd wanted to talk about it, say something, anything to promote a conversation, but instead he'd said 'So I need to make an appointment to meet with Rod Striker.' And she had responded with: 'I'll call him in the morning.'

'Daddy.' Maddie's voice had him opening his eyes and there was his daughter, too-long pyjama bottoms covering her feet, eyes heavy with sleep.

'Hey, Pumpkin, what are you doing awake? Is it your spots?' he asked, going towards her and putting a hand out to ruffle her hair.

'No. My nose is stuffy.' She sniffed long and hard.

'You want me to get you a Kleenex?'

'Can I have a glass of milk?'

'Sure,' he answered. 'Let's get you back in bed and I'll call room service.' He put his arm around her, shepherding her back toward the bedroom.

Pushing open the door he saw Brooke was asleep. No headphones in her ears, hair brushed, gently breathing. She looked completely different when she wasn't snarling at the world. Younger. Innocent.

He pulled back Maddie's duvet cover and she slipped back into bed. Running the flat of his hand over her hair he tried to encourage her to lie down.

'Did you have a good time with Denise?' he asked.

'We watched *Ratatouille*,' Maddie answered. 'Then a Christmas film with Arnold Schwarzenegger.' She rolled her eyes. 'I think Denise has a crush on him.'

Chase smiled. 'It's the muscles.' He flexed one of his arms strongman style.

'Did you have a good time with Isla?' Maddie inquired.

'Yes,' he breathed. 'We had a good time.'

'Was she wearing a pretty dress?' Maddie continued.

'Yes, she was wearing a very pretty dress.'

'Did it have sparkles?'

It had had sparkles but the ones on the dress hadn't beaten her eyes. He swallowed, smiling at his daughter. 'You need to lie down and I'll go order that milk.'

'I like Isla,' Maddie said, slowly slipping down into a prostrate position. 'She's real pretty and she's clever and she's funny.'

Yeah, his Go-To Girl was all of those things and more. Like super-sexy and opinionated and so damn right about most things. And good. She was so good. He felt like the Devil himself stood alongside her. And maybe that was the crux of the problem. That's why maybe forgetting the kiss was the only thing he *could* do. Because he had been sent here to literally rip up the part of the city that was part of her. God, was that really what he was going to do? He shook his head.

It *was* the right place for the super-village. He had looked at it carefully, the board had looked at it, it was ultimately their decision not his. And he had to do what was right for the company, didn't he? He was fresh in at this job, needing to make it work, so badly. He sat down on his daughter's bed.

'Do you think Isla's funny, Daddy?' Maddie inquired, eyes drooping slightly.

'Yeah, Pumpkin, she's real funny.'

'And pretty,' Maddie continued.

'And pretty.'

'And she likes you.'

He swallowed. 'You think she does?'

'Oh yeah,' Maddie said grinning. 'She totally does that thing that Brooke does when she's trying to catch the attention of a guy.'

'What's that?' He really wanted to know what his teenaged daughter was doing to hook the interest of a boy. He would be looking out for it and putting an immediate stop to it.

'She looks.' Maddie looked at him, all wide eyes with an intense expression. 'She looks away.' She dropped her gaze to the duvet cover. 'Then she looks again.' She hit him with another killer glance that definitely struck a chord, but possibly one in a minor key.

'Wow,' Chase said. 'Brooke does that to attract boys?'

'And Isla does it to you,' Maddie said. 'She did it on the Tube after she had finished wiping up from the Santa explosion.'

'I think that was probably a look that said she wanted to kill me.' He sighed. And after tonight how much more awkward was it going to be?

'But tonight she had a date with you,' Maddie reminded him.

'I told you, Miss Matchmaker, it was a work thing.' He stood up. 'I'll go order that milk.' He stroked her hair again. 'Close your eyes.'

'Daddy,' she said softly.

'Yeah.'

'If I fall asleep, will you drink my milk?' Maddie asked, eyes already closing.

'Sure,' he responded with a smile.

'Promise?'

'I promise, Pumpkin.'

He watched her breathing slow and knew she was going to be asleep before he even put in the order. He closed the door of the bedroom and took a breath. Bourbon for one it was.

Forty-Seven

Beaumont Square, Notting Hill

Hannah had *broken into* number eleven. Isla's wheelchair-bound sister had committed a crime. And it wasn't road rage – which she committed at least twice a day, once during the morning commute and the other on the way home – it was breaking and entering and ... robbery.

Isla was still staring at what was spread out over the coffee table, not able to take any of it in. It couldn't be true, could it? Although it would explain a whole lot of things.

'Well, aren't you going to say anything?' Hannah asked.

'I ... don't know what to say,' Isla said, eyes still flashing over the contents of the coffee table.

Hannah shifted in Ronnie, leaning a little and pointing. 'That's the Breekers logo, isn't it?'

'Yes,' Isla replied.

'And this is a big-arse map of most of Notting Hill and beyond.'

She swallowed. 'Yes.'

'And this,' Hannah continued, 'this other drawing is of some ridiculously crazy big hotel-cum-Milton-Keynes of a thing.'

Yes, the other plan was the same plan she had been looking at with Chase. The nine-hole golf course and the ice rink and the circus ...

'It doesn't take a genius to put two and two together, does it?' Hannah squawked. 'So, tell me … are Breekers going to demolish our town and build *that* on it?'

'I don't know,' Isla responded. What else could she say? She didn't know, not about Notting Hill, and she was bound by her contract not to tell anyone about anything else either.

'Isla! You work there!' Hannah screamed.

'Hannah, it might be that Isla don't work in that department, right?'

Raj had finally said something and Isla was almost grateful. Perhaps she could go with that suggestion for now, until she found out more … until she grabbed Chase by the throat tomorrow and demanded to know what the hell was going on. Could she grab him by the throat? Or was that going to see her destined for Wasabi-peas-ville?

'Crap!' Hannah spat back. 'This is exactly the department she works in. And now we know why the big head of the company is over here right now. He's making plans to seek and destroy.' She turned to Raj. 'Can they do that? I mean there are loads, *hundreds* of historic things here … and the market … and the Ladbroke Estate and it was the whole basis of a movie, for God's sake.'

'I dunno,' Raj replied.

'And our house,' Hannah continued. 'Our *house* is just on the edge of that red line. *Inside* the red line!'

Isla couldn't think properly. Her mind was buzzing and trying to come up with answers and all the while, as she begged her brain to compute what she was seeing and try to rationalise it, all it was doing was sending her images of her and Chase, in the snow in Larkspur Gardens, on her grandmother's bench, kissing like they needed to get a room.

'Isla!' Hannah shouted.

'Sorry,' she said. Her fingers went to the map and she pulled it a little closer to her.

'Our house is on this map,' Hannah continued. 'The whole of Beaumont Square could be turned into a pile of rubble and then something like Donald Trump used to build is put in its place! And why do Verity and John have this stuff in their house anyway?'

That was a very good question and perhaps, for now, until she had a chance to regroup and make sense of this, she should focus on that element of it.

'I can't believe you broke into someone's house, Hannah,' Isla started.

'Actually, though, that was me,' Raj cut in.

'And technically it wasn't really breaking in,' Hannah added. 'We thought we heard a baby crying.'

Isla shook her head at her sister. She had definitely been watching way too many episodes of *Line of Duty*.

'We thought it could be in danger so we had to ...' Hannah began.

'You had to do what?' Isla asked.

'Mrs Edwards was so upset after you left,' Hannah continued. 'We couldn't just sit here and do nothing.'

'And the baby was crying though,' Raj pointed out.

'Are Verity and John going to be calling the police and am I going to have to pay for a broken window to be fixed?' Focus on *this* crime, not the crime that was these plans sitting in front of them.

'No, I have keys,' Raj announced.

'Keys?' Isla queried. 'To number eleven? Have they started inviting you in for coffee too? Or is this a Royal Mail thing?'

'They're skeleton keys,' Hannah interrupted. 'You know ... like locksmiths have.'

'And burglars,' Isla said, one hand on her chest. 'Like burglars have.'

'I borrowed them, innit. From a mate.'

Isla didn't really know what to say.

'So we let ourselves in and there this all was. On the dining table. All these plans and photographs and documents and ...' Hannah's voice was starting to become emotional. 'Did you know about it, Isla? Did you know and not tell me?'

She shook her head furiously. 'No, I didn't know.'

'But you'll do something, won't you? I mean, it can't happen. We won't let it happen, will we? They can't just decide on something like this without meetings and consultations and public opinion, right?'

'Right,' Isla said. Her mind started to recall Chase's animated conversation with Rod Striker. That's why he had been so keen to meet that *particular* councillor. Because Notting Hill was the chosen site ... and she'd shown him almost every street of it.

'The council like meetings though,' Raj added. 'They is always having meetings about the crews near my crib.'

'This isn't about *your* hood though, is it?' Hannah remarked sadly. 'It's about mine.' She sighed. 'I can't believe we invited John and Verity for dinner.'

And Chase, Isla thought. They'd invited him too. And he was the driving force behind this. He had known Notting Hill was where he was going to build his monstrosity and he'd charmed her with his hot accent and his gentleman routine – shrouding her in his jacket, clearing snow off a bench ...

'And John obviously ain't in insurance,' Raj added.

That was a puzzle. Who exactly *were* John and Verity? And why on earth did they have Breekers' supposedly secret schematics?

'I'll get to the bottom of it,' Isla announced suddenly. 'We should return these.' She began to fold up the map and plans.

'Return them!' Hannah exclaimed.

Raj looked concerned. 'I don't think we should be doing that though.'

'How can we keep them?' Isla asked. 'They're not ours.'

'They're evidence,' Hannah stated. 'Evidence that everything Mrs Edwards has been saying is true. Evidence that something's literally going down ... and it's not *Time Team*.' She breathed loud and hard. 'And if we give them back how are we going to explain how we got them in the first place? Say we thought we heard a baby crying so we opened the door with a gang member's keys, discovered there was no baby, and then this huge, random, snow-infused gust of wind just blew everything out of the front door and back here?'

'That's not a bad idea, innit.'

'It's a terrible idea, Raj.'

Isla could see how worried Hannah was and, as always, that was her priority. She needed to ease her concerns, tell her everything was going to be all right. Even if she didn't have all the answers yet, she would get them. God, she would definitely get them. She was seething, quietly so as not to alarm her sister, but inside she was screaming.

'Hannah, you mustn't worry,' Isla spoke calmly. 'If I don't know anything about this then it can't be very far along in the planning state, can it?' She attempted a smile. 'And if Verity or John works for Breekers I would know, wouldn't I?'

'That's what I said,' Raj said proudly.

'But—' Hannah started.

'The likelihood is Breekers are just trialling a few ideas. It happens all the time. It might even be ... an old plan from eons ago that they've ... accidentally on purpose let slip to a competitor ...' This was good. It was vaguely plausible. Sort of. 'Perhaps Verity and John work for Blox Limited.' She swallowed. Had that sounded convincing?

'Do you think so?' Hannah queried.

'It's possible.' She bit down on her tongue. 'And if it isn't then ... well ... it's almost Christmas. Nothing moves very fast at Christmas.'

'But it's an old plan you think?' Hannah continued.

Her conscience just wouldn't let her tell an outright lie. Because if their worst fears ended up being realised, Hannah would never forgive her for it.

'It looks old, doesn't it?' Isla yawned and checked her watch. 'Gosh, is that the time? It's so late.' She stood up, hoping Raj would take the hint.

'I should go, like,' Raj said, getting to his feet.

'I'll show you out,' Isla said, perhaps a little too eagerly.

'I can do that,' Hannah said, wheeling forward. 'He's my guest.'

'Of course,' Isla replied. 'Goodnight, Raj.'

'Night, Isla.'

Isla kept the smile on her face right up until they both left the room. Then she sank down on to the sofa and wondered just who in the universe hated her enough to deal her a little piece of Christmas romance then snatch it back, screw it up into a ball and stomp all over it.

Forty-Eight

Canary Wharf

You're going to ask, aren't you? As soon as you get in ... or sooner. Can't you email someone? Or call Chase? I mean, he shared lasagne with us! How could he share lasagne with us if he was planning to knock down our home!

These were the questions Hannah had thrown at Isla as she had rushed around the house hoping a text from Poppy didn't come in. And it hadn't. Poppy had turned up ... with no mention of her grandmother's hospital visit but limping a little herself. A leg injury didn't bode well for future visits.

Of course they were all things Isla was already thinking herself. And she went from panicked to rational as quickly as the winter wind seemed to change direction that morning. It seemed crazy to think that two people who lived opposite them in Beaumont Square worked for Breekers and she had no idea. Which meant, realistically, if you weren't a believer in all things TV drama, it couldn't possibly be the case. So that left them being employed by a rival, the idea of which she liked just as little, because it meant there was someone at Breekers passing on information and plans. But, whatever was true it still left only one conclusion for the map of Notting Hill: it *was* the desired location for the super-village and Chase had neglected to tell her. Had he really planned to somehow get her on board with this development? Had 'confiding' in her about his marriage and his brother and kissing her been designed to soften the blow? Did he really think she could ever support the destruction of her precious part of London?

She looked up across the street to the Breekers offices, snow flashing faster, the smell of bus fumes mixing with evergreens being sold on the corner. Two trumpeting angels glinted from the façade of the department store next door. Isla had never felt less Christmassy and she hated that. Usually, by now, she would be relishing all the sights, sounds and scents of the season – brass bands and choirs busking carols for charity, chestnuts being roasted in the street over metal barrels, titbits of delicious traditional food being offered to entice you into restaurants. Nothing was evoking joy and happiness. And it was all Chase Bryan's fault. What had she been thinking last night? Kissing him! She shivered as the memory washed over her again. She may have instantly regretted it and Britishly apologised, but she had also hoped to revisit it in her mind sometime, perhaps while eating a box of Lindt and watching *Live and Let Die* over Christmas. Now the whole experience had been tainted. Now all she was going to remember was kissing someone who had lied to her from the moment they had met.

'Coming in or staying out? Ah! You're looking at those angels wondering if they might be something for the Christmas party décor?'

It was Aaron at her shoulder, nudging her arm. And that was something else that wasn't going as seamlessly as it always did – the Christmas party. The highlight of her year, her moment to shine, was, right now, the absolutely last thing on her mind. It was going to be a complete disaster and, at present, she really didn't care.

'No,' she answered. 'I wasn't.' She stepped off the pavement, looking to judge the traffic and attempt to cross.

'Wait a minute. What's up? I thought you went to Colin Matthews' party last night. You love Colin Matthews' parties.' Aaron took hold of her arm.

'I did,' Isla replied. 'It was good.' Again, all she could conjure up was lying on that cinema bed gazing into those hazelnut-coloured eyes. The hazelnut-coloured eyes belonging to the lying back-stabber. She needed to recover before Aaron asked any more questions. 'Are you up to speed with Ridgepoint Hospital yet?'

'Sugar. Honey. Ice Tea. Isla, there *were* six folders to go through,' Aaron stated, one hand of fingernails in between his teeth.

'Eight,' Isla said, stepping on to the road. 'There are eight folders.'

'I only have six,' Aaron answered.

'Well, what have you done with the other two?' Isla questioned, striding forward.

'Nothing, I ... Isla, what's going on?'

She had made the other side of the road but she couldn't seem to shake Aaron's questions. And the worst thing about that was she was stuck between wanting to burst into tears or spit fire. She opened her mouth to reply, not really knowing which one was going to come out.

'I—'

'Yes,' Aaron said.

'I can't tell you,' she blurted out quickly.

'Something happened at the party, didn't it?' Aaron guessed. His eyes then bulged and he opened his mouth wide, palms of his hands slapping his face. 'Something with you and Mr U.S. of A.'

'Absolutely not,' Isla snapped a little too quickly.

'I don't believe you. I know that look,' Aaron continued. 'It's the one I wear when I've had an extremely productive evening at G.A.Y.'

Isla pushed opened the door and stepped into the lobby. She needed to shake Aaron off. The best thing to do was get someone to help. She headed straight for Denise's reception desk.

'So, what happened,' Aaron continued, tracking her. 'You know you want to tell me.'

'Good morning, Denise,' she said, smiling. 'Aaron wants to know all the details of Mr Bryan's hotel suite.' She adjusted the bag on her shoulder. 'How big was the bed? How big was the mini-bar? What's hot and what's not on the room service menu.'

'I ...' Aaron began, looking at Isla.

'Well,' Denise began. 'Let me tell you, that suite is to die for.'

Isla backed away then hurried toward the lifts before Aaron could say anything else.

Forty-Nine

'Give it back, Brooke!'

'Not until you say you're sorry.'

'What for?'

'For treading on my boots!'

'Daddy! She has Cubby!'

'Blah, blah, blah.'

'Daddy!'

And, as he looked at the map, there it was. Chase's very worst fears confirmed. There was Beaumont Square, Isla's home, inside the red line of the Notting Hill plan. He had told himself, no matter what, it wouldn't matter. It was business. He had known there would be some opposition and discomfort. You couldn't get picky about who was affected. But this was feeling so wrong.

'Daddy! She's suffocating him!'

'It's a bear, dummy! You can't suffocate a bear!'

'Stop it!'

'Say sorry!' Brooke ordered.

'All right! Enough!' Chase erupted. 'Just shut the hell up!' He leapt from his seat at the boardroom table and hit out at two ballpoint pens, knocking them to the carpet. He felt sick. He felt emotional. He felt out of control. This wasn't good. This did not bode well. A little disorientated, he tried to regulate his breathing. He was at the window, staring out on to the street. The snow was coming down thick and fast, traffic moved slowly, pedestrians walking with their heads held down against the wind. Was Isla out there somewhere, battling the elements, red hair tousled like it was last night when he'd ached to run his fingers through it …

'Sorry, Daddy.'

Maddie's sweet voice hit him like a train. What was he doing? Shouting at his daughters. Losing it again. He turned back from the window to face his children.

'No,' he said softly. 'No, I'm sorry. I'm real sorry.' He took strides towards them, reaching out to ruffle Maddie's hair. He looked to Brooke but her scowl remained, Maddie's bear still in her hands.

'Is it work, Daddy?' Maddie asked. 'Is it as difficult as my math class?' She slipped a small hand into his.

He shook his head. 'I'm not sure anything could be more difficult than math class.'

'But you're good at math,' Maddie said.

'I was,' he answered.

'It's no excuse for taking your anger issues out on us,' Brooke stated gruffly.

'No,' Chase agreed. 'Like standing on somebody's boots isn't an excuse for kidnapping a bear.'

'I'm sorry for standing on your boots, Brooke,' Maddie said softly.

'Brooke?' Chase asked.

'This thing needs a wash. It smells of every freakin' day of her nine years,' Brooke said. She tossed the toy back to her sister.

'Can we go to Sugar High for lunch, Daddy?' Maddie asked.

'We've only just had breakfast,' Brooke answered, putting her earbuds into her ears.

'I don't know,' Chase responded. He couldn't think past the plan on the table. He needed to do something, but what?

Could he suggest the board looked at reducing the size of the plot somehow? He only needed a couple of hundred yards. Just enough to save Isla and Hannah's home. No, no getting precious and personal. Doing that made a mockery of everything he had been telling people in his motivational videos. Decisions should be led with the head not the heart. Ardent responses were trigger-happy ones. Careful and considered was the only thing that worked. That being the case, the only thing he knew for sure was he had to tell Isla the truth before she heard it from someone else.

Isla stood outside the door. Close but not close enough to be seen. Chase was in the boardroom already and there were plans on the table in front of him. Were they the maps he hadn't shown her? The very plans Hannah and Raj had stolen from her neighbours? Was she going to enter the room and have him jump comedic style and start to try and conceal them? And why was her heart racing just looking at him? Why could she still remember the feel of his body next to hers? Anger, that was the only explanation. And she *was* furious, ready to unleash hellfire. Except, Maddie and Brooke were with him … and it seemed that Ethel had decorated the ceiling with more sparkly woollen pompoms. Could you be furious in a room full of Christmas pompoms? She supposed there was only one way to find out.

She pushed open the door.

'Isla!' Maddie greeted her first and she offered the girl a smile before redirecting her gaze to Chase, expecting him to start flapping around with the paperwork he had seemed so engrossed in. Perhaps these were decoy plans. Maybe the real ones were in his hotel room … or perhaps Verity and John's copy she now had in her handbag was the only one. There was no movement from him apart from his hands going into the pockets of his trousers.

'Good morning,' she greeted brusquely.

'Hey,' Chase replied. 'Do you want coffee? I was gonna order coffee.'

'No thank you,' Isla responded.

'English tea?' he asked.

'I don't want any drink.' She sniffed. 'But I do want to know the location of the super-village.' That was blunt and to the point. 'Right now,' she ended. Now she just had to study his reaction. How was Mr Motivator going to breeze himself out of this one?

'Girls, would you mind giving me and Isla the room for a second?'

He hadn't looked left. She had googled 'the tell of a liar' on the Tube on the way here, and apparently looking left was a sure sign that an untruth was being bleated.

'Can we make coffee?' Brooke asked. 'And have as much sugar as we want?'

'I guess,' Chase replied.

'Maybe have sweetener instead?' Isla found herself suggesting. She swallowed. Someone ready to unleash the hounds of hell shouldn't be concerning herself with a young girl's sugar intake. She needed to toughen up.

'Are you gonna arrange another date?' Maddie asked, smiling.

Isla bit her tongue. Her resolve was not going to crumble. She was not going to keep recalling images of their kiss in the snow. At this moment, she despised Chase. He had lied to her. He had deceived her like the slippery motivational-speaker-slash-hypnotist that he was.

'I told you, Pumpkin,' Chase said. 'Last night was a work thing.'

And there it was. Showing him Hannah's run-down community centre, Larkspur Gardens, her heart and soul, it had all been in a day's work for Chase.

'Come on, Maddie,' Brooke said. 'I'll show you how to make a four-sugar latte.'

'Cool,' Maddie said, cuddling her bear and following her sister.

Isla bit her bottom lip. As soon as that door closed behind them she was going to let rip ...

Chase started talking before the door swung completely shut. 'The location the board has chosen for the super-hotel and village, the location we all felt was the best fit was—'

'Do not even think about lying to me,' Isla blasted. 'If you're thinking of telling me it's on the outskirts of Haringey or Feltham don't bother because—'

'It's Notting Hill,' Chase informed her. Then it seemed to strike him. 'And you already know,' he whispered, shoulders sagging. 'How do you know?'

'So, it's true.' Isla's voice cracked as she caught hold of the back of a chair and attempted to steady herself. 'You've come here, not only to bring this new monstrous idea to fruition, you've come to build it in the middle of one of the most wonderful communities there is. A community I've been sharing with you every day since you got here.'

'Isla,' Chase said, removing his hands from his pockets and taking a step towards her.

'How could you do that? How could you eat cake in Sugar High? How could you let me take you to Diwali, to Portobello Market, to invite you into my home when all the time you knew you were going to plan to tear it apart?'

'It wasn't like that, Isla.'

'No?' she exclaimed. 'Well, what *was* it like? Were you sitting there wondering how much money Breekers were going to have to offer residents for compensation as you tucked into Geeta's curry?'

He shook his head.

'When were you going to ask me what the going rate was for someone's home including some sort of nostalgia bonus?' She gasped theatrically. 'Were you sizing up whether the lion enclosure would fit on mine and Hannah's plot?'

'Isla, please, let me speak.'

'Why?' she exclaimed. 'Why should I let you speak? Because you're the big boss and I have to do what you say if I want to keep my job?' She took a breath. 'Well, Mr Bryan, you should remember you also told me you valued my opinion and my honesty, so this is me being honest.' She pointed a finger at him. 'I will not let you do this. I will not let Breekers do this. There is absolutely no way you are going to get planning permission for this in Notting Hill, no matter how much you grease Rod Striker's palm. And even if by some ugly Christmas miracle you *do* get permission, then I am going to lie down in front of the bulldozers myself.'

She felt sick now, completely sick with tension like she might spew all over the floor at any moment. She wanted to scream and cry and throw herself at him, pummelling her fists on his chest ... and he was just standing there looking so cool and calm, practically emotionless.

'My beautiful sister who had her whole life torn apart in that car accident is now petrified that we are going to have to move. That everything she loves – her job, our square, the shitty little community centre, our friends, their shops and restaurants – it's all going to be turned to rubble, and the company I work for is in charge of that.'

'I understand how you feel,' Chase spoke.

'People only say that when they have completely no bloody idea how you feel!' she screamed. 'I told you how I felt about Notting Hill. I showed you everything I loved about it. I took you to Larkspur Gardens, I—'

He interjected hard. 'Kissed me like no one's ever kissed me before.'

Chase couldn't help it. Looking at her now, soaking up the insults he knew he more than deserved, he couldn't stop thinking about that moment in the private park, with the crazy frog fountain, feeling colder than he'd ever been on the outside and hot as hell on the inside. Then emotion had got the better of him and he wouldn't have changed that moment for anything.

'Don't!' Isla exclaimed. 'Don't talk about that! You lied to me!'

'I didn't lie,' Chase said. 'And you did know I wanted to meet with Rod Striker.'

'I thought that was because he knows everyone and you wanted to know everyone.' She shook her head. 'Was I a joke to you? The naïve little Go-To Girl who didn't have a clue what you were planning?' She swallowed. 'Just some dumb secretary you could hoodwink!'

'I was gonna tell you—'

'So tell me now,' she snapped. 'Tell me why my neighbours, the new people across the street, had this plan in their house.'

He watched her draw a map out of her bag and flap it at him.

'What?' He had no idea what she was talking about now.

'Verity and John, I don't know their last name or names, or even if they're real names, but they either work for you or they work for a competitor. Whichever it is they have all the details, the whole shebang.' She folded her arms across her chest. 'So, which is it?'

He had never heard of these people. No one was working for him. And if a competitor knew what they were planning it would be a disaster. Anxiety was flooding his gut two-fold now. 'I genuinely have no idea.'

'Genuinely?' She scoffed. 'I'm not sure you know the meaning of the word.'

'Isla, please, that isn't fair.'

'Fair? How dare you talk about fair!'

'This is a business decision,' Chase reminded her. God, he hated himself a little right now. 'It's about the best location, the most *central* location, the right place for this project to succeed.' And he needed to succeed. To replenish his daughters' depleted college funds for one thing. Divorce didn't come cheap.

'Don't business-speak me,' Isla ordered. '*I* am a person. And Notting Hill, it's more than a *location* … it's a hub, it's a living, breathing community full of eccentricity you don't get anywhere else. Places like that should be held up and admired and … *saved*. Not swapped for chrome and glass and … shoe-shiners and golf and … *Cirque du Soleil*.'

'Isla, I'm caught between a rock and a hard place,' Chase attempted. Maybe he should tell her, tell her *everything*. Be honest. He'd asked for that from her and she'd given it to him. He had started to open up about Colt, but it wasn't all of it. Perhaps if she knew the whole story, knew exactly what he'd been through and how he was still clawing his way back from the brink. He took a breath. No, that was just selfish and this wasn't about him. This was entirely about her now.

'And what about me?' Her voice cracked just a little and he saw the tears forming in her eyes. 'How am I going to tell Hannah that it's true? That the firm I work for wants to destroy her world? How can I tell her that if I want to pay the bills I am going to have to be complicit in that?'

'Isla.' He reached for her, needing to connect with her. To what? Console her? At this moment there was nothing that he could offer her.

She stepped back. 'I can't work with you today,' she said, swallowing. 'If I'm honest, don't know how I'm going to be able to work with you, or even for this firm, ever again.' She sniffed. 'So perhaps it might be better if you talked to Aaron.'

'Isla, please,' he begged.

She shook her head. 'I'm sorry, there's absolutely nothing left to say.'

Fifty

Portobello Road, Notting Hill

Isla had walked out. She had never walked out of work in her life. In fact, it had been known for her to be forced out of work when the late-night security took over. But here she was, playing truant, AWOL, a Sugar High Christmas muffin in her hand, the hood up on her coat, sitting in Portobello Road and taking in every single nuance as if it was all going to disappear the moment she took her eyes off it.

She watched everyone going about their business, this leading-up-to-the-Christmas-season day just like any other. Except for her it wasn't just an ordinary day. Everything had altered because of that map and the thick red line that said change was coming. And what control did she have over it? What handle did anyone here have on it?

Just a few yards away a delivery driver brought out a large cardboard box from the back of his van and, as he lifted it, a multitude of reindeers spilled out on to the snow. Their noses all started to light up, antlers swaying to the tune of 'Jingle Bell Rock' as he began to gather them back up. She shifted on her seat, preparing to help, then stopped. What was the point? In a few months' time, if Chase had his way, the shop he was stocking, all the shops and bistros, even the old comic swap store in Pembridge Road she adored browsing in, they would all be gone.

She shivered and bit down into the Christmas muffin, letting the berries and cinnamon and thick custardy syrup coat her teeth and her tongue.

She might have thrown the words 'historic' and 'eclectic' at Chase but she wasn't an idiot. She knew what would happen if these plans were pushed full force. She had been behind similar projects in the past. Granted, she hadn't worked on anything that involved demolishing something the size of Notting Hill, but homes had been bought to make way for roads, shopping centres and park-and-ride schemes. So, did her protest now make her some sort of NIMBY? It was okay working on these proposals as long as they didn't personally affect her? Other places were people's homes too. She hadn't gone on some moral rant on *those* occasions. And she had watched Breekers' clients pay for planning to be granted under the table as well as above it. Everyone knew it was common practice, just part and parcel of the procedure. Rules were well and truly bent, if not completely broken. And Rod Striker's methods were as curved as a Uri Geller spoon.

But what was hurting the most? The fact that the business she worked for was going to build the equivalent of Atlantic City in her neighbourhood or the fact that, like it or not, she had fallen for Chase like she hadn't fallen for anyone in so long ... and he had deceived her. That did more than smart, that tore at her. Because, despite him being her boss, she thought she had been getting to know him on a personal level. He was humorous and challenging and unashamedly obnoxious at times ... and that had been ... well ... hot. Except it had all been a front, a game-plan. She shook her head, snowflakes coming off her hood as she took another bite of muffin. Just how long had he thought he was going to be able to keep the location from her? Just how had he expected her to react when it had eventually come to the table for discussion? Or maybe he would have held off until he was back on the other side of the pond? When there would be no need for personal interaction. When she had laid all the groundwork and he had slithered in like the snake he obviously was. But thinking he was a venomous reptile unsettled her for a few reasons. Firstly, she had seen how he was with his children. He loved them so much. He might be fighting with the work/childcare balance but there was no doubt he was a father who cared deeply about his daughters. And secondly, he had given a ceramic frog the kiss of life just because she wanted to see the fountain in her grandmother's garden working. Who risked frostbite and chapped lips for that? There was nothing to gain from it, and it was a step beyond flattery or intel gathering. He had done it because he had wanted to. To make her happy ... and then he had kissed her.

As she closed her eyes the smell of sweet cinnamon and cedar filled her nostrils, combining with the icy air and fresh snow. His mouth had been that perfect mix of passionate and reassuring, almost asking her lips if this was okay and waiting for her response. And it *had been* okay. It had been *more* than okay. She had got caught up in that moment more than she had been caught up in *any* moment like that. It had been a perfect kiss in Notting Hill ...

She opened her eyes just as a stall holder encouraged visitors to get a closer look at his sausage and fennel-seed slices and she felt sadder than she'd felt for a long time. If she made a stand it would mean leaving the company and maybe becoming intimate with quinoa and sushi at M&S Food. What would life be like without her job at Breekers? She had never known anything else and she had put her all into climbing that ladder. She had been the stable, organised, main breadwinner for so long. She took a deep breath, seeing the tourists with their cameras trained on the galleries, clothing and jewellery shops with their light blue, grey, mint green and baby pink facades. She turned to look down the road and was met with the bright red and gold craziness that was Alice's Portobello, an Aladdin's cave emporium. Outside of it were stands of mismatched teacups, wooden tennis rackets, brass instruments and a black and white plastic pig lined up on the crisp white street outside. It wasn't sleek or fine-lined or futuristic. It was rustic and quaint and ... established in 1887. She sighed. It just didn't seem right and she didn't know what to do. And the very worst fear of all was ... Who exactly was she without this place? Who was she without Notting Hill?

Fifty-One

Breekers London, Canary Wharf

'Oh! Sugar. Honey. Ice Tea!'

It was almost a squeal that had come out of Aaron's mouth as Chase showed him the map for the proposed site of the super-hotel and complex.

'You want some water?' Chase asked him.

'No … I …' Aaron looked up from where he was leaning over the plan and met his gaze. 'Maybe an espresso, actually … a triple shot.'

'Whoa, don't hold back,' Chase said. 'D'you want me to get out the bourbon?'

'You have some?' Aaron asked.

He allowed his eyes to do the answering and then he let out a sigh. This reaction was from someone who had actually lapped up the idea of the super-hotel only a few days ago. What was it with Notting Hill? Everyone seemed to be treating it like consecrated ground.

'Sorry, Mr Bryan, Chase … it's just … I can see why Isla might be finding this a little difficult.' He watched Aaron swallow. 'I mean … it's Notting Hill.'

Again, *Notting Hill* had been said like someone might say *Bethlehem* or *Graceland*. This wasn't boding well and as much as he wanted to feel angry and frustrated that no one wanted to get on with the job, all he actually felt was sickened. At himself. He knew how Isla was going to feel. He knew he *had* deliberately led her away from the whole picture, researched the area with her, just like she said. But that wasn't the entire story. Somewhere along the road lines had got blurry and he couldn't settle right now, wasn't yet able to commit, to anything. Control was slipping away and if he wasn't careful that 'e' word, *emotion*, was going to be knocking on his door and demanding an audience. Perhaps he should change tack for the rest of the day, start by finding out who this Verity and John were and why the hell they had Breekers' top-secret plans. In truth, he wanted to think about anything other than how much he had hurt the woman he had held in his arms last night.

'Aaron,' Chase began. 'Can you do something for me?'

'Of course, that's what I'm here for … now Isla isn't here.' Aaron raised an eyebrow. 'Is she coming back?'

'Sure.' Had he sounded convincing? He really had no idea.

'Today?' Aaron continued.

He ignored the question. 'Hey, Aaron, can you pretend, just for one second, that this plan isn't of Notting Hill.'

'It's not?'

'Just for a second.'

'Where is it then?'

'Does it have to be somewhere else?'

'Well, if it's not Notting Hill then …'

'Okay,' Chase said. 'Let's say it's on the outskirts of Haringey.'

'Oh, yes!' Aaron responded, seeming almost delighted. 'That would be a much better location for a super-village.' He pointed a finger. 'No parking issues there either. And these executives will be car people not Tube people.'

Chase closed his eyes and shook his head. What was it with this firm in London? He had always been of the impression that the British were all about their toeing the line and following rules, but in this office it seemed they didn't want to follow anything.

'Did you enjoy the Electric Cinema?' Aaron asked him. He settled his ass against the table like he was going nowhere. 'The last time I went there I was right at the front on one of those gorgeous giant beds.' His eyes seemed to mist over. 'His name was Justin and he looked just like Will Lexington from *Nashville.*'

Chase swallowed. Yeah, he had enjoyed every second of the bed experience too. That green and black dress smoothing over Isla's curves, her red hair falling on to the deep red velveteen cushions, talking about the places he'd lived and the one place she had lived …

'It was cool,' he replied brusquely. 'They played an old Christmas movie and everyone got a little drunk.' He straightened his tie. 'I met up with Rod Striker.'

'Ugh, that rogue,' Aaron said, raising his eyes to the level of the sparkling pompoms on the ceiling. 'Nothing good comes from anything he's involved with.'

'He's head of planning in this locale though, right?'

'Oh yes, and he will do *anything* to line his pockets,' Aaron stated. 'Isla avoids him at all costs unless it's absolutely necessary.'

'And how does she do that if she has a project within his area?' Now he was intrigued.

'You'll have to ask her about that,' Aaron said, finally standing back up. 'So,' he began, looking back to the plan. 'Now that we're pretending this is in Haringey, what would you like me to do?'

What did he want him to do? He didn't know. The only thing he *did* know was he needed to find Isla.

The boardroom door flew open and Maddie rushed in, white creamy froth all over a red tear-stained face. 'Daddy! Brooke made the coffee machine explode.' She gulped back tears. 'And she posted it on Instagram saying I looked like Santa, only my stomach was fatter.' She sniffed. 'And then Mom commented and she's real mad!'

'Goodness,' Aaron remarked. 'It sounds like you're about to have quite the afternoon.' He put a hand on Chase's shoulder. 'I'll go out for espressos. Triple shot?'

Chase let out a breath. 'Make it four.'

Fifty-Two

Portobello Flowers, Portobello Road, Notting Hill

There were no buckets of flowers outside the shop today, but there were miniature spruces. Some were completely bare of decoration, just a few hours' worth of snow that had accumulated on their evergreen branches; others were sporting baubles of pillar-box red, forest green and frosted silver. As she stood outside, Isla looked through the partial glass door to the interior and her sister at work.

Hannah was plucking blooms from buckets, collating them together as if it was the easiest skill in the world. Isla knew different. And she knew that because she was the worst flower arranger ever. Hannah had always been good with colour, that was why she was the chief Christmas decorator in their home. Instinctively perhaps, or learned through her work in the florists, she could put purple with crimson and gold, wind through some gypsophila and create the perfect display.

Isla sighed, still watching Hannah choosing flowers, pressing them together, pausing, then selecting another stem. This was where she excelled. This was where her disability didn't seem to matter. Here she was the mistress of her domain. The unrivalled expert – even Claudia said so.

She pushed open the door and the bell above tinkled, signalling her arrival. Stepping in she was hit with fragrance. Rich velvety roses, flowering heather and yellow star-shaped winter jasmine. The air was also thick with Christmas – pine cones and the glitter spray Hannah used to coat Yuletide logs.

Hannah looked over and an expression of almost horror coated her face. 'Oh shit, what are you doing here?!'

'Well,' Isla began. 'That's not the best welcome I've ever had.'

Discarding the flowers to the counter, hands on the grips above Ronnie's wheels, Hannah manoeuvred herself towards her, half tentatively, half like a chess grandmaster ready to checkmate. 'You found something out at work, didn't you? That's why you're here … when you should be at work.'

When Isla had pushed open the door to the florists she had been ready to breeze in here, tell Hannah the truth of what was going on with the Breekers project, secret or not, and tell her that whatever happened they were going to get through it. Now, though, with her sister's ashen face, the flash of alarm in her eyes, Isla's conviction was slipping away like Christmas cards badly Sellotaped to a wall.

'No,' she said, swallowing away any doubts.

Hannah didn't respond. She just crept nearer and nearer, one centimetre of rubber at a time, eyes fixed on her. 'Why aren't you at work, Isla?'

Why wasn't she at work? Why wasn't she at work? Think, Isla, think! 'Oh, Chase sent me out here to get … cakes from Sugar High for Maddie and Brooke.' She rolled her eyes. 'Those girls do love the cake there.'

Hannah didn't look convinced and the wrapper from her muffin was practically burning a hole in the pocket of her coat.

'But you came here first?' Hannah queried, still edging forward.

Isla nodded. 'Well, if I can't drop in on my sister while I'm over here and … I wanted to know if you wanted a cake … and Claudia too, obviously.'

'Claudia's out,' Hannah said. 'She's had to do some deliveries this afternoon.'

'What?' Isla exclaimed. 'So, you're on your own here?'

'Yep,' Hannah answered. 'Completely in charge.'

'But, Han …'

'Ugh! Don't start! I went for a wee before she left and there's a baseball bat underneath the counter should all those flower-loving robbers thunder in.'

'They don't have to love flowers, Hannah, they will be after the cash.'

'I'm not stupid … and I'm fine. I've done it before,' she admitted. 'Loads of times before.'

Isla swallowed. Of course she had. Why wouldn't she? And she hadn't told her because Hannah knew she would worry. And, of course, she was right.

'But never mind that,' Hannah said. 'Did you ask Chase about the map of Notting Hill and the plans for that giant hotel resort?'

What to say? This was killing her and, put on the spot, right at that moment, she couldn't do it. She couldn't tell Hannah it was real, that Notting Hill *was* Breakers' plan. She was still, somehow, hoping that even Rod Striker couldn't do something this grotesque, that maybe there was still a chance it might all go away … or go *far enough* away … perhaps Essex.

'Oh yes,' Isla said, flapping her hand like it hadn't even been a concern at all. 'Chase laughed.'

'He laughed,' Hannah said, her face completely straight.

'Yes,' she swallowed. Why had she said that? 'I mean, it's ludicrous really, isn't it? Someone knocking down Notting Hill and building something so ... so ...'

'Huge and ugly?' Hannah offered.

'Practically a glass and steel troll,' Isla agreed.

'So, it's a fake map?'

Isla nodded. 'Yes.'

'Well, who made it?'

'Who made it?'

'The fake map.'

Isla really felt sick now. The custardy syrup that had tasted so sweet and comforting half an hour ago was beginning to curdle. 'Breekers,' she forced out. 'To leak to rivals ... to throw them off the scent of the real project.'

'Which is?' Hannah asked.

'What?'

'What's the real project?'

Hannah wasn't letting this go. Because she wasn't an idiot like Isla. 'I can't tell you that.' She put a finger to the edge of her nose. 'It's top secret.'

And then something wonderful happened. Something wonderful yet equally unsettling. Hannah seemed to let go of a whole world's weight of tension, her body releasing a long, deep sigh, her shoulders slackening, her hands moving from the wheels of Ronnie to her lap. 'Thank God! I haven't been able to think of anything else all morning and I couldn't say anything to Claudia.' She sighed again. 'She kept asking me what was wrong and didn't really want to leave me while she made the deliveries but I threatened to run over her toes and she went in the end but ... oh, Isla, aren't you relieved.'

No. No, she wasn't. Because she had lied. And when Hannah found out she was never going to trust her again. She nodded, forcing a wide smile on to her lips. 'Of course. Not that it was ever in doubt,' she said. 'I mean, seriously, that super-village here? Pah!'

'So, who were Verity and John? And can we please *not* invite them for dinner? I don't want them taking my water glass and fingerprinting it or something.'

Isla shrugged. 'I don't know yet. Competitors like I suggested, maybe. Being fed false information.' She smiled. 'And yes, we don't have to invite them for dinner. I wouldn't want them to try and get real information from me over Mum's special béchamel sauce, which they totally do not deserve.'

'Oh, I'm so pleased, Isla, so pleased,' Hannah continued. 'I thought we were going to have to tell everyone at the wine and cheese night tonight and get some sort of Save Our Suburb rally going.'

Wine and cheese night! Was that tonight? She really needed to get her head back in the game. Everything she was always on top of, always enjoyed organising and attending at this time of year, had been overshadowed by the arrival of Chase. It was her job to buy their wine and cheese. She couldn't let Hannah know she'd forgotten.

'So, what wine and cheese have we got this year? A dark, mysterious Merlot? With a cave-aged Cheddar?' Hannah asked.

'I … think I got Shiraz.' Isla put a hand to her head feigning ditziness.

Hannah smiled. 'Your head is stuck into the Breekers' Christmas party, I know! Still not giving up the theme?'

She shook her head. She didn't even know whether she still had catering. 'You know the rules. A week before the event to add to the surprise.' No food or props would be a surprise for everyone, perhaps she could call it minimalist chic. She smiled. 'I'd better get back.'

'To work?' Hannah queried. 'I thought you said you were going to Sugar High.'

Shit. First rule of lying, remember your lies. 'Yes, on my way.'

'I'll have a Christmas muffin, no, cancel that, I'll have a slice of carrot cake.' Hannah's cheeks began to flush. 'Raj is coming to the wine and cheese night and I want to wear something fitted.'

Isla studied her sister. Eyes now shining bright, bossing her job, looking forward to a night with a guy she really liked, waiting for Christmas and that longed-for kiss in Notting Hill. Perhaps this situation wasn't hopeless. Maybe corporate might winning wasn't the definite outcome. Perhaps it was time she took back control – of her projects, the Christmas party and the destiny of her home. She was, by nature, one of life's survivors … just like her sister. It was time she started fighting back a little.

'I think this year we'll go Australian with the cheese.' She smiled at Hannah. 'Didn't Mr Edwards bring one called Holy Goat last year?'

'He did,' Hannah said, clapping her hands to her cheeks. 'Do you think it might be too soon, to remind Mrs Edwards?'

'Not Australian then … how about Mexican?'

'Perfect,' Hannah said.

Isla smiled. She really didn't care what nationality the cheese was as long as it wasn't American. 'Okay,' she said, heading toward the door. 'I'll be back with carrot cake.'

'So, is Chase coming to the wine and cheese night?'

Isla stopped in her tracks, turning back to Hannah, determined to show no reaction. 'No,' she answered. 'He's got work to do and … he's got the girls so …'

'They could come too,' Hannah said. 'They would love it. Geeta and Iqbal are bringing onion bhajis and chickpea dhal and you know Mrs Edwards always makes that spicy chutney to go with the cheese ...'

'I should go,' Isla said, checking her watch.

'Ask him,' Hannah said. 'He's so hot and you're so ... single.'

'Thanks!'

'Maybe ... not at a work thing, you could relax, have some Mexican cheese and a few glasses of Shiraz and who knows?' Hannah laughed. 'Plus it's almost Christmas and Notting Hill isn't going to be bulldozed. Life's good right now.'

Isla swallowed and gave a requisite nod. The only real truth in her sister's statement was the fact that nothing was stopping Christmas arriving.

'We'll see,' she answered like she had when Hannah was fifteen. 'Now let me get you some carrot cake.'

'I've changed my mind,' Hannah said. 'Get me a Christmas muffin. I can always put my day bag on my lap if my top feels too snug.'

'Okay, one Christmas muffin coming up.'

Isla stepped out of the shop on to Portobello Road and took an agitated breath of snowy air, hoping, for all her lies, the Christmas angels weren't going to drop one of their golden trumpets right on her head.

Fifty-Three

Westminster Bridge

'Is this where all the politicians live, Daddy?'

Maddie's voice drew Chase back from his thoughts about the conversation he had had an hour ago with Breekers New York. What he had been told had forced him from the office looking for some breathing space.

'No one lives here, dummy,' Brooke snapped.

'But it's called the Houses of Parliament,' Maddie pointed out.

Chase stopped walking, coming to a complete halt on the snow-coated bridge and took in the site in front of them. Gothic architecture skimmed the side of the Thames, the ornate towers and slender, wafer-like façade holding Britain's parliament so striking, even against the cloud-filled sky. It was a true icon of this city. And at the back of his mind another thought came quickly. So was Notting Hill. He had seen it first-hand.

'Dur!' Brooke said. 'It doesn't mean it's their homes.'

'Hey,' Chase said, re-joining the moment. 'Don't speak to your sister that way.'

'Come on,' Brooke exclaimed. 'She thought Theresa May had a bed in there. It's funny.'

Chase put an arm around Maddie's shoulder and directed her to look across at the building. He pointed. 'So, if the Prime

Minister goes to sleep in there, look at the size of her alarm clock.'

Maddie sniggered. 'It's called Big Ben.'

'I know,' Chase answered. 'But did you know that Big Ben is not the name of the actual clock?'

'It's not?' Maddie queried.

He shook his head. 'No. Big Ben is the name of the bell.'

Out of the corner of his eye he saw Brooke look at him as if interested in this fact. He wished he had more … where was Isla when he needed her London knowledge? Mad as hell and cursing him every which way she knew he didn't doubt.

'The London Eye needs a better name,' Brooke announced, her gaze moving across the water from where they had just walked.

'Ooo, can we think of one?' Maddie asked, jumping up and down. 'When was the London Eye made, Daddy?'

'I really don't know.'

'I bet Isla would know. Can we call her and ask?' Maddie suggested.

He shook his head and snapped a reply. 'No.'

'Why not?' This came from Brooke.

'Because she's real busy and …'

'Pissed at you for something,' Brooke broke in.

'Brooke!'

'Well, she is, isn't she?' Brooke said. 'That's why you wanted the room when we made coffee earlier.'

'We saw her leave the office, Daddy,' Maddie admitted. 'And it looked like she'd been crying.'

He blew out a breath, his insides reacting to his younger daughter's words. He had hurt her. He had made her cry. What sort of a person was he? And why did he care so much?

'Why was she crying, Daddy?' Maddie asked.

'Because …' He didn't really know what to say. This wasn't something his daughters should get caught up in. There was *nothing* to be caught up in. *But he'd kissed a frog.* He swallowed. He was here to do a job for a few weeks and then they'd all be back in America. He'd conduct everything via Skype and email. The London team would give him progress reports. He'd be back in his penthouse and Isla and Hannah would be … finding somewhere new to live. That's just how things were. How they had to be. They had known each other a few days. Surely that was no way near long enough to make an impact. Although his gut seemed to be telling him otherwise.

He sunk down on to his haunches so his face was level with Maddie's. 'Sometimes business is hard, Pumpkin. Sometimes, Daddy has to make decisions that aren't liked by everyone.'

'What decision made Isla cry?' Maddie asked, batting her eyelashes.

'Yeah,' Brooke commented. 'I think I wanna hear the answer to that one.'

'It's not something for you to worry about,' Chase said, reaching out to stroke Maddie's hair.

'Are you gonna fix it, Daddy? So she's not sad any more?'

'I'm not sure that I can,' he admitted.

'But that isn't what you say in your videos,' Maddie reminded him harshly. 'You tell people that nothing's broken, just temporarily timed-out.'

God, his youngest daughter remembered some of his mantras. How had that happened? And why did that make him slightly fearful? He still believed, didn't he? In what had saved him? The new path that had been a rescue in so many ways ... Until Colt had come back into their lives. It hadn't felt like a temporary time-out then. *He* had *definitely* been broken.

He quickly nodded. 'That's right.'

'So, you can make Isla happy again,' Maddie announced like she was decreeing it. 'And she can come out with us and we can see more of London.' She gasped. 'I want to go see 10 Downing Street and St Paul's Cathedral.'

'It sounds like we have a lot of sightseeing to do,' Chase said, slipping his hand into hers.

'What about what I wanna do?' Brooke queried.

'I haven't had any luck finding tickets to see Skin 'n' Bone Man.'

'It's Rag 'n' Bone Man!' Brooke exclaimed in horror.

'Sorry,' Chase said. 'But I'll work on it and, I promise, I'll find us something really cool to do together.' He nudged Brooke's arm. 'How about it?'

'Whatever,' Brooke replied with disinterest.

'Daddy!' Maddie remarked. 'Can we call the London Eye the I-Circle.'

'The what?' Brooke spluttered. 'That's so lame.'

'Circle, you know, like a wheel and it sounds a bit like icicle, doesn't it?' Maddie shivered. 'And it *is* real cold in London.'

'It is,' Chase replied, squeezing her hand. 'Say, how about we get hot chocolate.'

Maddie whooped and Brooke didn't scowl at the suggestion. The truth was he needed a few more minutes away from the office to get his head around the fact that Breekers *had* employed people to scope out the proposed sites, just like Isla had accused him of, and they hadn't told him until an hour ago ... and only when he'd *asked* the question. What did that say about their faith in him? This hotel plan was his baby. The company hadn't even thought of going in that direction until he had suggested it.

'Bye, I-Circle,' Maddie called, waving a hand.

'Totally lame,' Brooke repeated.

Fifty-Four

Beaumont Square, Notting Hill

Isla just had to keep calm and carry on. That's what Londoners did in a crisis and that's exactly what Isla was going to do now. The Beaumont Square Christmas Wine and Cheese evening was one of Hannah's highlights of the year and Isla was going to make sure it was a night to remember. Wearing a little black dress with boots to stave off the cold, Isla prepared their smorgasbord of delights in the kitchen.

'Load me up!' Hannah held out her arms. 'I can carry the tray of cheeses and I slipped the very last bottle of Nan's sloe-gin into my bag when you weren't looking. It was a bit of a stretch but I managed.'

Their nan. Her bench in Larkspur Gardens she had taken Chase to. She couldn't tell Hannah about that. What a terrible error of judgement. Why had she shared something so close to her with him? 'Han, that bottle was right at the back of the worktop.'

Hannah waved her away. 'Load me up,' she repeated. 'I'm actually Hank Marvin. I hope we don't have to wait until Martin Ayres has given a speech like we did last year.'

'He does love a speech,' Isla said with a grin.

'And do you remember the year he sang "Twelve Days of Christmas" with all religious connotations.'

'Seven sacraments, wasn't it?'

'Three wise men, two testaments and a …'

'Baby Jesus laying in the hay,' the women completed together, falling into a fit of laughter.

'Cheeses,' Isla said, passing Hannah the wooden board she had carefully clingfilm wrapped.

'Cheeses.' Hannah took hold of the board.

'Pickled onions. Can you fit those somewhere on Ronnie?' She held the jar out. 'If not I can put them in my bag.'

'Pass them over,' Hannah said, putting the board on her lap. 'The one advantage of having a wheelchair is its ability to suck up stuff like a well-packed Easyjet case.' She shoved the pickles down the side of her chair.

'Goats cheese and beetroot crisps,' Isla continued, passing them to Hannah.

'Brilliant!'

'And I have cranberry and caramelised onion too.'

'I do love a festive crisp. I'm bringing festive crisps to the Life Start party.'

'So, is Raj meeting you in the square?' Isla asked, putting the bag for life over her arm and facing her sister.

'Oh, you know, it's quite casual.' Hannah sounded anything but and now she was shifting a little in her wheelchair, fingers moving from the cheeseboard to pull down the hot pink top she was wearing. It was long-sleeved with a small embellishment of two glittery cherries on the left breast pocket. Isla had helped her sister put on the fitted skirt, tights and boots she was wearing but the upper wear was definitely new. Possibly another Claudia TK Maxx outing purchase.

'I love your top,' Isla said.

'Do you?' Hannah asked. 'You don't think it's too much?'

'Han, this is the Beaumont Square Christmas Wine and Cheese Night?' Isla said. 'How could it possibly be too much?

Mrs Edwards usually comes in something that looks like it belongs in a ballroom in the 1930s.'

'I don't look like that, do I?' Hannah asked with a gasp.

'No! Of course not. You look … lovely.' Isla could feel emotion welling up and it wasn't just because her sister was making an effort for a boy and seemed to be getting more and more independent every day. It was all this stuff with Breekers' foray into the world of hotels, the plan that spelled disaster … and Chase. Months and months of not finding anyone remotely attractive whether she was really actively looking or not, and now, within days of meeting someone hot and interesting, he had turned into a fiend.

'So, did you ask the gorgeous Chase to come tonight?' Hannah asked, as if reading Isla's mind.

She shook her head. 'He has something on, I think.'

'You think? Or you didn't ask?' Hannah queried.

She swallowed. 'I didn't ask.'

'But why not?' Hannah said, a frown on her face. 'I told you he's off my radar. I told you you've been desperately date-less for too long. I also told you I think he likes you. What's the problem?'

Where did she start? There were more reasons for that than uses for an umbrella. 'Well, because he's my boss and …' She looked at her watch. 'Gosh, is that the time? We'd better get into the square before we miss the complimentary Baileys.' Isla made for the door, bag swinging from one hand, the other clasped around a bottle of Shiraz.

'That was the worst attempt at changing the subject ever,' Hannah moaned. 'And it won't stop me asking. I might have decided he's not right for *my* Christmas kiss in Notting Hill but he's so fit … fitter than anyone else around here … even the window cleaner we used to stare at.' She wheeled herself behind Isla. 'And he seems nice too. And a gentleman. He topped up glasses at dinner, he wiped Maddie's mouth when she got lasagne sauce all over it, he ...'

Isla had heard enough. 'He lives in New York, he's freshly divorced and his ex-wife is living with his brother.' She hadn't meant to say the last bit. She wished she could retract it. Despite Chase being the Demon Demolisher she had sensed it had taken a lot for him to tell her that and it maybe wasn't common knowledge.

'Whoa! Really!' Hannah exclaimed. 'That's Jerry Springer stuff!'

'So, you see, it's best to leave the wine and cheese to us.' Isla smiled. 'Besides you know I don't want anyone to get between me and a slab of Holy Goat.'

'I'm totally with you on that,' Hannah agreed.

Fifty-Five

With the snow having eased up that afternoon and the members of the Beaumont Square Committee creating their usual display of patio heater and chiminea-warmed pergolas, Isla thought that the square looked as beautiful as it always did at this time of year.

There was already a gathering around trestle tables filled with treats, residents dressed in finery underneath their coats and hats. It was a tradition. You dressed for a cocktail party on the inside and the Arctic on the outside.

'Mrs Webley is hogging the free Baileys section,' Hannah muttered. 'No change there.'

'Come on,' Isla said, taking hold of her sister's wheelchair and bumping her up the kerb before swinging into the garden. 'Let's muscle in for our free glasses.'

Christmas had definitely arrived in Beaumont Square. The colourful lights intertwined around the metal railings, the fibreglass Nativity scene set around the biggest fir tree – Baby Jesus's left eye still notably absent – more lights and metallic strings of bunting circa Woolworths 1980. It was odd, maybe a little dated, but also charming and it never failed to make Isla feel warm inside.

Leafless trees were hung with strings of rainbow-coloured, teardrop-shaped lights and a small amplifier sat on the pathway playing Frank Sinatra and Dean Martin. The choice of music catered for the average age of the residents of the surrounding houses. That was another almost unique thing about Beaumont Square: this was a place where people stayed. It hadn't been bought up by young professionals looking for a slice of trendy Kensington. For most it was a forever home. The retro music had provided Isla with the inspiration for the theme of this year's Breekers' Christmas party and, as she looked at the cinnamon biscuits, cheese and chive roulade and indistinguishable things marinating in old jam jars, she knew, no matter what happened with this monster village, she owed it to her colleagues to put on a good party for all their hard work this year. And nothing was going to stop that. Perhaps it might even be the last thing she ever did there. She swallowed. She couldn't think that.

'Good evening, Mrs Webley,' Hannah greeted their neighbour. Isla smiled to herself as she watched her sister position Ronnie as close to the sixty-something vice-chair of the committee as she could without running over her rather jazzy-looking tangerine-coloured ECCOs. The woman's brunette hair had been hairsprayed to within an inch of its life and she was wearing her trademark fluorescent pink lipstick.

'Good evening, Hannah,' Mrs Webley shouted. She then lowered her voice. 'Good evening, Isla.' Why she thought Hannah being in a wheelchair meant she was deaf too no one had really worked out.

'A good turn-out already,' Hannah remarked, then sniffed the freezing air. 'Is that Mr Webley's prize-winning sausages I can smell?'

'Well I never!' Mrs Webley exclaimed, blustering with pride. 'You really are coming along in leaps and bounds. Yes! There are some pork, venison and nutmeg on the griddle along with a new chicken and artichoke he's been trialling at autumn food fairs.' The whole sentence was bellowed like she was standing with a megaphone in Hyde Park's Speakers' Corner.

'Gosh, chicken and artichoke sounds—' Hannah started.

'Divine,' Isla finished. 'Utterly divine.' She hadn't quite been sure what her sister was going to say.

'Is that the complementary Baileys?' Hannah asked, pointing to the large bottles and small plastic glasses.

'Yes. Would you like one?'

'Please,' Hannah stated, reaching for a glass. Mrs Webley swiftly took it from her.

'Let me do that for you. We don't want to spill it, do we?'

Isla took a step towards Hannah, knowing how that comment would have gone down. She put a hand on her sister's knee. 'Shall we take the pickles and the sloe-gin over to the other tables?'

'Yes,' Hannah said breezily. 'I'm sure I can manage that without causing a gin-cident.'

Isla took the two poured glasses of Baileys from Mrs Webley and gave her a smile before whispering to Hannah. 'Mrs Webley thinks all people in wheelchairs are like Clara from *Heidi*.'

'What was wrong with Clara from *Heidi*?' Hannah protested. 'She was really clever. I always liked her better than Heidi even *before* I got into this mess.'

'But back then, people considered ...' She swallowed. 'People considered the less able unable to do *anything* for themselves.'

'I could barbecue her husband's pork any day of the week.'

'You know that and I know that but she's never going to believe that even if you show her,' Isla said. 'It's a mindset thing.'

'Well,' Hannah began, sipping at her Baileys. 'Perhaps her mindset needs to change.'

'I don't disagree,' Isla said. 'But you're not really a girl who loves change, are you, Hannah?' She smiled.

Hannah gave her the benefit of one of her bolshie looks and suddenly someone else came to mind. *Brooke*. Yes, she could definitely get the feel of a teenaged Hannah in Chase's elder daughter. Not that she was thinking about Chase and his family ...

'*I* don't need to change though,' Hannah reminded Isla. 'And, actually, in this new top I'm pretty much perfect no matter what Mrs Webley thinks.' Hannah grunted. 'I bet she even does thinking too loudly.'

Isla clunked her plastic glass against her sister's. 'I am in full agreement.' She took a sip of the creamy liqueur that never failed to make her feel Christmassy.

'Oh my God,' Hannah exclaimed, Baileys drizzling out of her mouth. She leaned forward in her chair to avoid spilling it on her top, hand furiously wiping the remnants away.

'What is it?' Isla asked.

'It's Raj!' Hannah exclaimed, thrusting her plastic glass at Isla. 'Don't let him see me like this. I've got whatever the deeply mysterious ingredients of Baileys are all over my face.'

Isla instinctively moved to shield her sister as Hannah flapped around, reaching backwards rather awkwardly into the day bag hanging on her wheelchair.

'Do you need a wipe?' Isla asked. 'There are some in your bag.'

'I know!' Hannah exclaimed. 'I hate that I carry them around like a big, fat baby.'

'It's not because you're a baby,' Isla said. 'It's because you're exceedingly clumsy when it comes to food ... and drink ... and any liquids really.'

'Thanks for that. I feel so much better.' Hannah grunted and pulled out the pack of wipes. 'Don't look at me! Look at him! Tell me if he's coming and … what's he wearing?'

Isla turned away from Hannah now and observed the ruggedly handsome Asian youth who was standing next to Mr Edwards' rose bush. Were they flowers he was holding in his hands? Isla swallowed. It was romantic. It was like … *suckering up to a frog*. She shuddered.

'Isla! What's he got on?'

'Clothes,' Isla blurted out. 'Nice clothes, from what I can see.'

'He isn't wearing jeans, is he?' Hannah asked. 'I told him it was a smart casual affair and even if it was bitterly cold he still had to forgo a jumper.'

'Dark trousers and proper shoes I think,' Isla said as Raj noticed her and waved a hand. 'He's coming over.'

'Ah! Not yet! Not yet!' Hannah shrieked. 'Look at *me* now. Tell me I don't have anything brown on my chin.'

Isla turned her head again, facing her sister. Hannah was glowing. Her skin wasn't covered in anything but a flush of youthful excitement, her eyes alive, because she was about to spend an evening in one of her favourite places with someone she liked so much. A bubble of sisterly pride coated with a hint of concern floated up in Isla's belly. She whispered. 'You look beautiful.'

'Hey, yous two,' Raj's voice greeted.

'Hello, Raj,' Isla said, turning to face him.

'Hello,' Hannah stated coyly.

'These are for you,' Raj said, proffering the blooms in his hands. 'They're not from your shop, though, 'cause you would be there and …' He offered them further forward until Hannah took them.

Isla watched her sister's face flame with delight. 'Thank you, Raj. They're beautiful.'

'I dunno what they are but they looked cool.' He put a hand through his hair. 'I bet you know what they are.'

'Yes,' Hannah said. 'I do.' She blushed again.

'This is well good, innit,' he said. 'All the lights and the burgers ... and stuff I don't know even what they is.'

'Oh yes,' Hannah replied. 'There are lots of things like that tonight.'

'Would you like some wine and cheese, Raj?' Isla offered. 'Shall I get you both a plate?'

'I dare you to try an artichoke sausage,' Hannah said, beaming at him. 'They're not pork, they're chicken.'

'Are they halal?' Raj asked.

'We can find out,' Hannah replied.

Isla stepped away from Hannah, ready to make herself scarce. She hadn't seen her sister quite this happy in a long time. But when she looked across the fairy-lit park she was instantly reminded of the peril Notting Hill faced, the harsh reality that they might lose their beloved home. And then her eyes fell on someone she hadn't been expecting at all. Chase.

Fifty-Six

This had seemed like such a great idea to Chase in the hotel room, with Maddie egging him on and getting crazy excited about an evening of cheese but now he was back here, in this syrup-sweet, cosy nook of a place, he was having second (and third) thoughts. Plus, he'd had another text from Colt. *Come on, man, this is stupid. We need to talk.* He'd ignored it just like the previous one.

'This square is so dreamy!' Maddie exclaimed, spinning around arms outstretched, hair flying behind her. 'It's so sweet, and British and I want to smell all the cheese.' She licked her lips then faced Chase. 'Why don't we have great cheese at home? Why don't we have wine and cheese evenings?'

'We have mac 'n' cheese and you love that,' Chase pointed out.

'But it's not like this, all twinkly and sparkly and … Christmassy.' Maddie breathed in then released the air into the dark sky above her.

'God, will you shut up? You're like an advert for Hallmark Christmas movies,' Brooke bit. 'Will they? Won't they? Will the injured dog survive? Will the grandmother's secrets die with her?'

Chase looked to Brooke. 'You know, I had no idea how much you loved Hallmark movies.'

Brooke put her fingers to her earbuds. 'Not even listening.'

'Look, Daddy,' Maddie said, slipping her arm through his. 'There's Isla.'

He knew she would be here. It was the whole point of them being here, but having her announced like that triggered a drawing in of his core. He turned his head and, as Maddie had announced, there was Isla.

She was wearing knee-length black boots, a black skirt or dress just visible under a bright red coat that highlighted the beauty of that ginger hair. He took a breath. She moved him, there was no doubt about that, and that terrified him. Because he was making her life difficult and he didn't know how to stop it and because he had cut himself off from any kind of dating opportunity since the break-up of his marriage. He was so scarred by love, by life. He didn't even know where to start in picking up the pieces, let alone putting any back together again. The moment they had shared on her grandmother's special bench, it really had been something to him. It had been him thinking about something other than crisis and catastrophe. Just being him. Just enjoying the now. With her.

'Aren't we gonna say hello?' Maddie asked, shaking his arm.

'Or is she *that* pissed with you she isn't gonna talk to us at all?' Brooke suggested.

Chase turned to his elder daughter. 'I thought you said you weren't listening.'

'Just saying,' Brooke answered with a scowl.

He could do this. He was the business coach after all. He just needed to smooth things over. He took a first step.

Isla felt sick to the stomach. What was Chase doing here with Maddie and Brooke too? How did he know about the wine and cheese evening? Her eyes went to where Hannah and Raj were laughing together as Hannah named all the flowers in her bouquet. Was her sister somehow involved in this?

She looked around the square for somewhere appropriate to hide. Mrs Edwards had arrived, Purdy on a lead by her side. The woman was dressed in what-looked-like vintage Chanel and was smoking a cigarette from an ivory-coloured holder, blowing rings into the air while Mrs Webley poured her the smallest measure of Baileys possible. Supplies were obviously running low already.

At the next trestle table Geeta and Iqbal were setting up their Asian fayre. Iqbal was moving everything Geeta put down from one position to another. She could help them. She looked back to Chase and the children and saw they were moving towards her. There was no escape now.

'Hi, Isla,' Maddie broke away from her father and ran towards her.

Isla, almost knocked over by the force of her arrival, smiled at the girl. She was caught between putting her arms around her and patting her on the head.

'Hello, Maddie.' She swallowed then looked up to Chase as he and Brooke caught up. 'What are you … all doing here?'

'We've come to see your wine and cheese evening,' Maddie announced.

'Well, it's not mine, it's …' Isla began. She was trying to look anywhere but into those gorgeous eyes. 'It's the whole square's and it's really for residents only.'

'Oh!' Maddie exclaimed, hands to her mouth and looking mightily disappointed. 'Are we not permitted to be here?'

'No, I didn't mean that,' Isla said quickly. 'Of course you're very welcome.'

'Can we eat the cheese?' Maddie queried.

'How about the wine?' Brooke added. 'Aaron said there's a lot of wine.'

Aaron. She should have guessed. She might just have to turn him into a gelding.

'Why don't you take Maddie to go get some cheese and I'll join you in a minute,' Chase suggested.

Maddie caught hold of Chase's arm. 'Don't forget to say sorry.'

'O ... kay ...,' Chase answered.

This couldn't feel more awkward but Isla was a little relieved that his body language seemed to be telling her he was feeling it in some way too. As the children left them she suddenly found her boots intensely interesting.

'So,' Chase began. 'I guess I'll start with what Maddie suggested.' He took a breath. 'Isla, I'm sorry.'

She held her stomach in, bracing herself, knowing she would have to look up sooner rather than later. She raised her head. 'But what are you sorry for? When last we spoke you didn't think you had done anything wrong.'

'I've hurt you, I know,' Chase stated. 'And I'm sorry for that.'

He couldn't be apologetic for anything else because this was a business transaction, nothing more. His soul wasn't deeply embedded in this area of London like hers was. And right now that made her exceedingly poor at her job. She had never been cut-throat, her ladder-climbing had all been to do with survival, but she had always been professional, level-headed ... however, this was just too close.

'I apologise for leaving the office today. I will contact HR and make sure my pay is docked appropriately.'

'There's no need for that,' Chase said. 'We could all do with some time-out now and then.'

'I wouldn't feel right,' Isla spoke.

'*I* won't feel right until we're talking again,' he admitted. 'Genuinely. *Properly*,' he said in British tones. 'Like we did last night.'

Last night. Those two words brought back all the delicious memories and seemed to diminish everything else for a moment. His lips on hers, warming her completely as they sat on the snow-strewn bench. She didn't know what to say. What was there to say?

'Listen, I spoke to New York today and they told me there have been employees here in London for a few weeks now,' Chase started. 'In Notting Hill and around the other two sites.'

'Employees,' Isla said. It couldn't be true, could it? That Verity and John worked for Breekers!

'Yeah,' he breathed. 'It was a shock to me too. Believe me, I had no idea.'

'But—' Isla began. 'You're the CEO.'

He nodded. 'Yeah. Go figure.'

'So, Verity and John, who moved into my square *do* work for Breekers.' She shook her head. Everything Mrs Edwards had said about measuring sticks and spying had been true. The elderly lady wasn't going senile. She was more astute than any of them.

'Yeah,' Chase said. 'There's also Richard in the Essex location and Ffion in North London.'

'And you didn't know,' Isla continued.

'No,' Chase said. 'I swear to you. I came over here to tell London about the project and to satisfy myself about the location and to make initial progress.'

'Satisfy yourself.'

'Yeah.'

'And are you satisfied?' Isla queried.

'No, Isla. I'm not.'

'Why not?'

'Because I'm feeling a little like the whole world is conspiring against me right now.'

'Wow, for someone so upbeat and preachy about self-improvement that must be hard.'

'Yeah, Isla, it is.'

'Well, boo hoo.'

She wanted to stuff her mouth with tinsel and sew her lips together. What sort of person was she turning into? *Boo hoo*!

'Listen, just hear me out.' He slipped his hands into the pockets of his leather jacket. 'I came here tonight for two reasons. The first was to say I'm sorry for not being upfront with you about the location of choice for the super-village. I should have done that the moment I knew it meant something to you.'

She sniffed. 'What was the second reason?'

'To ask you to come back to work on Monday.'

'So, I can help you order the right-sized wrecking ball?'

'No,' Chase answered softly. 'I thought we'd take a trip out to the other two sites, maybe meet with the two employees there.' He let out a breath. 'I don't know if that's the right thing to do for the business or not but, considering everything, I think I would be a fool not to look at it. Get some sort of grass roots perspective.' He looked to her. 'Maybe we could see if we can find some USPs that might change the board's mind about Notting Hill.'

Hope invaded her, sparking and fluttering around like a firefly. 'Really?'

'I can't make any promises. I might have the three big letters and the best chair in the boardroom but I'm really not the decision-maker.'

'But they value your opinion or they wouldn't have given you the job after Big Bill, or tasked you with coming here.'

'I hope so.' He smiled. 'At least I wanna believe that.' He shook his head. 'Big Bill, huh? Why don't I have a cool nickname?'

Isla smiled. 'Well, I think I'd quite like to do that,' she said. 'See the other sites, I mean.' She swallowed, trying to still everything inside her that was erupting with sheer joy that there might be a way out of this for Notting Hill. 'And I promise I will act completely professionally and if we come to the conclusion that neither of the areas is right for the village vision then ...'

'Then?' Chase queried, raising an eyebrow as if he was suspicious of what she was about to say next.

'Then I still have the option of lying in front of the bull-dozers.' She smiled.

'I really hope it doesn't come to that,' he answered, looking directly at her.

She swallowed, the sound of Bing Crosby floating through the night, the pop of corks and chatter over cheese and sausages that smelled so tasty ... and here she was again, alone with Chase, outside in the cold, yet feeling hotter than she'd ever felt. She regrouped, clearing her throat. 'Would you like some cheese?' It sounded like the most pathetic sentence in the world and she knew, the way her cheeks felt, Mr Webley could probably grill his venison and nutmeg on them.

'I would like that very much,' he agreed. 'I also wanna meet this Verity and John who work for our company. I'm interested to know what they found out about the area.'

'I'm not sure they're going to be coming,' Isla said, moving. 'And one thing I've learned is you can never trust anyone who turns down lasagne.'

'Absolutely, Miss Winters. That's good judgement right there.'

Fifty-Seven

'Good evening, my name is Gladys Edwards.'

Isla watched as Mrs Edwards stuck out a silk-gloved hand towards Chase, looking every inch an extra from *Mr Selfridge*. Maddie and Brooke were across the square loading themselves up with food and Raj was watching Hannah sample the sloe-gin.

'Good evening,' Chase answered.

Mrs Edwards let out a gasp. 'You are practically a G.I.'

'Well, I wouldn't go quite that far but—'

'Mrs Edwards, this is Mr Bryan,' Isla introduced. 'Chase Bryan. He's from New York.'

'Dan Reed,' Mrs Edwards continued, poking her cigarette holder into the air, her other hand holding the lead Purdy was attached to. 'That was the name of my G.I. Oh, he was a dish. Jet black hair and that uniform ... there is something about that uniform. We danced all night to Glenn Miller.' She stopped talking and looked back to Chase and then to Isla. 'Is this your young man?'

'No,' Isla said quickly. 'No, Chase is my—'

'I'm a colleague, ma'am,' Chase interrupted. 'I'm over here for a few weeks working with Isla.'

'I see,' Mrs Edwards stated. 'I see.'

Isla had no idea what her neighbour could see but she wasn't sure she wanted her seeing anything. Despite her being spot on about Verity and John, there were still occasions where random things came out of her mouth.

Mrs Edwards leaned forward, her slight body invading Chase's personal space. 'She's single you know. Hasn't been on a date since a rather unfortunately dressed boy six months or so ago. Had an odd name and a lisp.'

'Okay,' Isla said, taking hold of Chase's arm. 'I think we need to go and see Hannah.'

'I don't know,' Chase replied. 'I'm kinda enjoying my chat with Mrs Edwards right now.'

'Oh, please, call me Gladys,' Mrs Edwards said, false and slightly wonky eyelashes batting up and down.

'Goodness, I think Hannah might fall out of her wheelchair. We should really go … quickly.' Isla tugged at Chase's sleeve, pulling him away from her neighbour.

'It was nice talking to you,' Chase said, waving a hand at the grey-haired lady.

Isla closed her eyes and half-staggered away from the situation. She did love her tight community, apart from when they told *everybody* everything about your life.

'You know I'm gonna ask what his name was, right?' Chase said.

Isla practically heard the smirk in his tone. 'Not in a million years.'

'And I wanna know what he was wearing to be described as "unfortunately dressed".'

'I believe it was an ice hockey uniform.'

'Very good, Miss Winters, you got me.' He nodded. 'Okay, I can hold off knowing his name as long as you keep holding on to my arm like that.'

Isla suddenly came-to and dropped her hand away. She *had* been holding his arm, like it was perfectly natural, just like the way they had walked through Kensington last night.

'Sorry, I was just—'

'Eager for me not to know about the last guy you dated.'

Chase watched her cheeks go crimson again, clashing a little with that auburn hair. He was glad things between them were like this again. He swallowed. He had no real idea if the location for the village could change, he wasn't even sure he should *want* it to change, but the fact of the matter was he needed to do something. He needed to give something else a chance. He had spent a good period of his life being blindsided. What if this hotel was another example of that? A blinkered view never led to success or harmony. He was absolute living proof of that.

'Come on, Miss Winters, you know all about my messed-up personal life.'

'I know. I just ... have nothing much to say on the subject.' She cleared her throat in that oh-so-British and endearing way. 'Hannah, on the other hand, is doing extraordinarily well on the personal front with Raj.'

Chase stopped walking just short of the amplifier where Nat King Cole was now emanating from the speakers. 'Cute couple.'

'Well, not quite a couple ... not yet, anyway.'

'No?'

'Well, Hannah worries, you know, about being in her chair and although, ordinarily, she's the most confident person I know, it's a bit different when it comes to boys.' She paused. 'I mean, men.'

'He bought her flowers?' Chase asked, observing a bouquet nestled on Hannah's lap.

'Yes,' Isla answered.

'Then she has nothing to worry about,' he assured her. 'And, all the body language is looking good.'

Isla turned her body towards him and he smiled, turning a little too.

'I suppose you're an expert in that too,' she remarked.

'It comes as part of the whole self-improvement package, I'm afraid.'

She nodded. 'So you know that if someone looks to the left they're telling you a lie.'

He met her gaze, ensuring his eyes stayed exactly front and centre. 'I do know that,' he answered. 'But I also know there are techniques you can learn to train yourself not to do that.'

'There are?' she inquired. 'Damn.'

'Although I can't imagine you ever needing to use any of them. You did promise me honesty, remember?'

'I remember,' she answered.

'So,' Chase said. 'Let's put it to the test.'

'I don't know about that,' Isla said with a nervous laugh.

'What are you afraid I'm going to ask?'

Isla's stupid eyes were already frisking all over the place not knowing what they were doing or where to settle. Why had she brought that stupid lie-detecting thing up?

'Nothing,' she replied quickly, attempting to steady her gaze. Never had she needed Optrex more.

'Well, what I wanna know is ...' Chase began.

Her eyes seemed to be locked to his now ... and his were so beguiling. She needed an interruption ... maybe even for Mrs Edwards to come back.

'Have you kissed anyone else in Larkspur Gardens?'

Isla's throat felt dry, like someone had made her eat a whole box of Ritz biscuits ... in a desert.

'Well ... I ... that wasn't anything like the question I was expecting,' she rushed out.

'No?' he queried, eyes still holding hers.

'No, I mean, I was expecting you to ask me something about my work at Breekers or ask when they open all the ridiculous things in jam jars we're all meant to try before the wine and cheese night is out.'

'Isla,' Chase whispered.

'Yes?'

'You haven't answered my question.'

'No,' she blurted out.

'No?' he queried. 'No you haven't answered or no you haven't—'

'I haven't kissed anyone else in Larkspur Gardens.'

She suddenly remembered this had been meant to be a test of her eyes not going to the left if she lied. She hadn't lied. She hadn't needed to lie. She had never kissed anyone in any square. Not even in Beaumont Square. The rare dates she had had were all wrapped up at a pizzeria or the theatre.

'Okay,' Chase replied.

'Okay?' Isla said. Her heart was thumping in her chest and now it wasn't his eyes she was staring at, it was his full lips and that hint of stubble on his firm jawline.

'Okay,' he said. 'We can go open some jam jars now.'

'Well ... what about my question?'

'Your question?'

'Don't I get a question?' Isla swallowed down a barrel-load of nervousness.

He smiled then, opening his arms. 'Shoot.'

She knew then exactly what she was going to ask him. 'Do you think we have a chance, even a tiny, small chance of changing the board's mind about Notting Hill?'

There was no hesitation in his reply. 'Yes.'

Isla nodded.

'Now can we go open jam jars?' Chase asked her.

'Of course,' she replied, smiling.

'Daddy!' Maddie called across the square. 'Raj is teaching me how to rap!'

'Goodness,' Isla said. 'You'd better hurry over there. As much as I like Raj he does have some flavoursome language.'

'Are you coming with?' Chase asked.

'I just need to find Mrs Webley. Talk through arrangements for the Christmas Fayre.'

'Can I get you another drink?'

'I'm fine,' she answered. 'I'll be there in a tick.'

He turned his back and, as he began to walk back to his children, Isla let out a breath. He might have answered yes to her question but, whether he knew tricks and techniques or not, his eyes had shifted just slightly and when they had moved they had moved westwards. To his left.

Fifty-Eight

Isla had eaten three gherkins, two chunks of Seckel pear and a Harukei turnip. Despite almost completing her five-a-day in one foul swoop she was worried, given the pickling process, that she might well have undone all the good with salt and sugar absorption.

'Pah! Pah! Ugh! What the hell is the purple one?' Hannah's tongue was lolling out of her mouth as she looked to Isla for some sort of help.

'I'm not sure. I haven't eaten anything since I ate some of the orange one.' She hadn't been sure what the orange one was. It had tasted of candied jelly and not in a good way.

'Has my tongue gone purple?' Hannah questioned. 'Tell me now, while Raj is in our house using the loo.' She poked her tongue out. 'Is it aubergine? I hate aubergine! Pah! Pah!'

Isla passed Hannah a napkin and then her eyes went to the other side of the square and two figures coming across the road to join the festivities. No. They wouldn't, would they?

'Han,' Isla said as her sister spat into the tissue. 'Is that Verity and John?'

'What? Ugh, this stuff! I can't get it out of my mouth! I think I need to down the Baileys.'

As the couple got nearer, Isla could see it *was* Verity and she could only presume the man next to her was her husband, John. She swallowed. These people allegedly worked for Breekers. They had moved into Beaumont Square with the sole purpose of working out how viable building a super-village in the area was. And they had done all that under the radar. And even, if she really did believe Chase, under the CEO's radar.

'Yes,' Hannah finally answered. 'They've come. How hilarious! All that measuring for a fake plan. I almost feel sorry for them.'

Isla swallowed. None of what Hannah thought she knew about the situation was true. How was she going to handle that?

'Daddy, this cheese is soooo good!'

Chase looked at Maddie. She had a chunk of green-looking cheese in her fingers, speckles of it over her lips. This was one of the strangest yet best nights he had had in so long. It was like a throwback to how life used to be. At the weekends, when he was a kid, his parents had thrown parties by whatever lake in whichever town they were living at the time. Barbecues with new-found friends, swimming, tailgates of trucks down, music up, smiles, laughter and lights just like the ones strung up around the gardens. That's the kind of life he wanted for Brooke and Maddie. Happy, simple yet strong in its lucidity. That wasn't New York … but it was Montgomery. Except their life, far, far away in Montgomery, was without him.

'The drinks are good too,' Brooke answered.

His eyes went to his elder daughter whose earbuds had been out of her ears for the entire evening so far. Was she actually, genuinely, smiling?

'Chase.'

It was Isla at his shoulder, a worried expression on her face.

'Hey, what's up?' he asked.

'Verity and John are here,' she said. 'The colleagues ...' She lowered her voice. 'Who we didn't know were colleagues.'

'Awesome,' he responded. 'Let's go meet them.'

'What? No, I can't ...' Isla began.

'Why not? We need to find out what they've been finding out, right?'

He watched her look to Hannah and almost instantaneously he knew what this was about. He knew how much she cared for her sister, how important she was in Isla's life. As much as the news about the proposal for the area had scared the life out of *her*, she had thought about protecting her sister first. Protecting her sister from *his* plan.

'You didn't tell Hannah about Notting Hill, did you?'

She shook her head. 'I couldn't.'

'No problem,' Chase replied. 'We can be discreet.' He turned to his children. 'Brooke, Maddie, you stay right here and I'll be back in a New York minute.'

'Can we have some more to eat?' Maddie questioned, popping the last remnants of the cheese in her hand into her mouth.

'Nothing you don't know the origin of,' Chase stated. 'I wouldn't recommend the orange or purple things in the jars.'

Isla felt awkward and she wasn't sure why. Why should *she* feel out of sorts when these two people had been in her midst so secretively?

'Are you gonna introduce me?' Chase asked her.

Verity and John were right there, loitering by Mr Edwards' rose bush, dressed completely inappropriately for the event. Verity was wearing worn-down Ugg boots and John was in jeans. It appeared no one had told them about the need for a little sparkle at the wine and cheese night. But ... Isla could do this. She was professional. She was not going to talk to them as if they were the construction equivalent of Fred and Rose West.

'Hello, Verity,' she called out, waving a hand and stepping forward. 'How nice of you to come.'

'Hello,' Verity replied. 'It's Lucy, isn't it?'

'Isla, actually,' she answered. She put out a hand towards the dark-haired man. 'And you must be John.'

'Hello,' the man said, shaking Isla's hand.

'Gosh,' Isla said. 'Well, this is so exciting because I just found out that we actually work for the same company.'

'We do?' Verity responded. Did she look suitably concerned? Isla studied the movement of her eyes.

'We do,' Chase said, holding out his hand. 'My name is Chase Bryan. I'm the CEO of Breekers International and Isla here is my esteemed colleague.'

It sounded so much more of an enviable position than Go-To Girl and Isla smiled at her two neighbours.

It was John who reacted first. 'Wow, that is rather unbelievable.' He shook Chase's hand. 'But it's so good to meet you. And the project ... wow ... it's such an incredible idea.'

'Thank you,' Chase said. 'Well, now we're all acquainted I'm hoping you're gonna get me up to speed with what you've been working on over here.'

'Yes, of course. We've actually been Skyping quite a lot with the New York office this week ... until we had the break-in,' Verity said.

'Break-in?' Chase queried.

Isla swallowed. She had never told Chase exactly how she had come into possession of the map and her gut was telling her now wasn't the time to come clean either.

'Yes, our house was burgled, paperwork taken and before that … our cat.'

Oh God! So Mrs Edwards *did* have their pet. How had that happened? And 'Purdy' was here tonight, on a lead just a few snow-topped bushes away.

'Your cat?' Chase queried.

'I'm sure it can't have gone far,' Isla jumped in. 'It's such a lovely, friendly community.'

'Goodness,' Verity said, hands going to her mouth. 'How are you feeling about these plans? It must be a bit of a conflict of interest for you, no?'

That was a real understatement if ever there was one but she had to hide it. She smiled. 'Business is business.'

'And it's not a done deal yet,' Chase added. 'There are other areas in the running.'

'Really?' John questioned. 'I was under the impression that our task here was more underpinning than anything else.'

'Nothing in business is quite that straightforward,' Chase replied. 'Isla and I are gonna check out those other locations first thing on Monday.'

'The north of the city is ripe for some greater rejuvenation in my opinion,' Isla added.

Chase clapped his hands together, his breath cold in the air. 'Shall we talk?' he asked. 'Tell me what you've found.'

'Excuse me,' Verity said, eyes moving over the Christmas lights towards the trestle tables the rest of the neighbourhood were gathered around. 'I'm just completely convinced I saw my cat.'

Isla reached out and took hold of Verity's arm, directing her, and hopefully her gaze, away from Mrs Edwards. 'So,

Verity, you really must try some of Mr Webley's sausage later. It's always the talk of the town at this time of year.'

'John,' Chase said. 'Tell me how long have you worked for the company?'

Isla smiled as they moved towards an unoccupied table set with more filled jam jars. She had to believe that where there was some sort of company tag-team there had to be hope.

Fifty-Nine

'We need to move the cat,' Isla hissed in Hannah's ear.

She had spent thirty minutes or more hearing about how John and Verity had been scouring the area, learning all there was to know about the businesses and homes in the proposed Notting Hill area as well as performing market research which Isla thought was seriously jumping the gun. Each part of her beloved home they had visited with their 'looking to re-establish' heads on stung like a hornet's barb. But she had maintained her cool, letting them continue, letting Chase soak it all up, secretly hoping there was something, anything planning-wise she could leap on to discredit the area.

'What cat?' Hannah asked.

'Mrs Edwards's cat-that-isn't-Mrs-Edwards's-cat,' Isla replied. 'It's John and Verity's.'

'Is it really?!' Hannah exclaimed, mouth falling open to display a severely purple tongue. 'I really thought I'd got that wrong. I never had Mrs E down as a thief.'

'And she did it all without the aid of skeleton keys,' Isla added.

'What?'

'Never mind. Let's do something,' Isla said, putting her hands to Ronnie's handles.

'She loves that cat,' Hannah remarked. 'And Verity and John turned down lasagne and are spying for your competitor. Is that why Chase is talking to them now?'

'Hmm,' Isla replied. What else could she say?

'And how is the gorgeous CEO?' Hannah asked. 'I did notice your little tête-a-tête seemed to be going well.'

'How about you and Raj?' Isla countered. 'What lovely flowers.'

'That's where he is,' Hannah responded, glowing. 'In our house putting the flowers in some water. They are lovely, aren't they?'

The subject of Chase had been successfully avoided. Now she just had to stop their neighbour being accused of cat theft. Isla's gaze went from Mrs Edwards and Purdy to Brooke and Maddie, who were sitting on the bench dedicated to Edith Rose Winters. Brooke looked decidedly rosy-cheeked and Maddie seemed concerned, nudging her sister's arm and flapping her gloved hands in front of her sister's face. Isla's eyes then found the rather empty-looking bottle on the floor next to Brooke's buckle-clad boots. Not making any assumption, but fearing the worst, she pushed Hannah towards the girls.

'What are you doing? I thought we were on a mission to hide Purdy,' Hannah said, hands going to her wheels as she took back control of Ronnie.

'I think there's a more urgent issue here,' Isla said. She breezed forward to Chase's children. 'Hello, you two. How are you enjoying the evening?'

'Hey, Isla,' Brooke announced, slurring her words and trying to get up from the bench. She was a little wobbly and smiling like a creepy clown. 'Cool party with even cooler food and drinks. Did you know you could put cranberries in a jar and eat them with a spoon?'

'Shit,' Hannah remarked. 'She's drunk.'

'Yes,' Isla responded, bending to pick up the empty bottle of what looked like homemade wine.

'Is that "Sip Me Baby One More Time"?' Hannah queried, trying to look at the label.

'I fear it is,' Isla responded. She turned to the younger girl. 'Maddie, I want you to go over to Mrs Webley ...'

'She's the one with all the hair and the orange shoes,' Hannah added.

'And go and ask her for some water. A large glass, or a bottle, whatever she has.'

'Who's drinking water?' Brooke drawled. 'Water sucks.' She began looking about her person, hands raising up then slapping down on to her lap, eyes rolling, lips in a permanent grin.

'I didn't know she was drinking wine until she started singing. She never sings out loud, only in her head,' Maddie said, bottom lip beginning to tremble as she observed her sister.

'It's okay, Maddie,' Isla said, reaching out and rubbing the little girl's shoulder.

'Is she gonna be okay?' Maddie asked.

'Yes,' Isla said. 'Absolutely.'

'Eat these,' Hannah said to Brooke. She passed her a packet of Kettle Chips she had reached into her day bag for. Isla didn't remember packing those in there earlier.

'What are they?' Brooke asked, staring at the item as if it was something she had never encountered in her life before.

'Crisps,' Hannah stated.

'What are crisps?' Brooke queried.

'God, Isla, she really is drunk if she doesn't know what a crisp is. Perhaps we should get Chase and call an ambulance or something.'

'Chips,' Maddie said. 'In America we call them chips.'

'Okay, Hannah, you go with Maddie and get water from Mrs Webley and I'll go and get your dad in a second,' Isla said.

'Can we put some other music on? All this sounds so the same and, like, really old,' Brooke said, trying to stand up again.

'Just stay sitting down for now,' Isla said. She hurried to sit down next to her and took hold of one of the girl's arms as Maddie and Hannah made their way across the gardens.

'So,' Isla began, trying to engage Brooke, focus her brain and body. 'You like music a lot, don't you?'

'Yeah,' she replied, hiccupping.

'Who's your favourite singer?'

'I like bands,' Brooke continued. 'Loud bands my mom hates and Colt wants to join.' She laughed, then fixed a hard gaze on Isla. 'I really, really hate Colt.'

Isla swallowed. These two children had obviously been through one heck of an upheaval in their short lives.

'I hate him for doing what he did to Mom and Dad.' There was white-hot emotion in her voice now. 'He made Dad sick again and I know Mom is gonna let him move in soon and we'll be meant to play freakin' happy families.' Her voice raised. 'Well I don't wanna!'

Isla squeezed Brooke's arm. 'Listen, Brooke, let's get you some water and some coffee and later, when you're feeling better, you can talk to your dad about it all.' She didn't know what to do. She had no experience in this department. And this was way outside the remit of a Go-To Girl.

'Dad's the only one who talks in our family,' Brooke said. 'The rest of them shout. But he closes up and pretends to us that everything is okay. But it isn't okay.'

'I—'

'So I put my headphones in and I listen to bands,' Brooke informed sadly. Then, with a sudden injection of adrenalin and a change of subject she asked, 'Do you like Rag 'n' Bone Man?'

'I do,' Isla responded.

'You don't know who he is, do you?'

'I do know who he is,' Isla said. 'Hannah played "Human" to death.'

'He's cool, isn't he? His voice speaks to you and I love how it's old and new all at the same time,' Brooke stated.

'Do you study music at school?' Isla asked.

'Not really. Only in class and it's all about dead composers and concertos and boring, ancient stuff no one cares about.'

Hannah rolled up. 'Water. And coffee is on its way. I caught Raj on his way out of the house and he's making some at ours.'

Isla looked up and nodded at Hannah. 'Why don't you take Maddie back to the house to warm up and Brooke and I will follow.' She passed Brooke the bottle of water. 'Drink this.'

The teenager took the bottle with shaking hands. 'If I drink all this can I have some more wine?'

'No,' Isla and Hannah said together.

'Hey,' Chase greeted, arriving at the bench.

'Oh, Daddy!' Maddie exclaimed, throwing herself at him. 'Brooke's drunk on wine that's named after a Britney Spears song and I was so scared.'

Isla looked to Chase and watched anxiety flood his handsome features as he comforted Maddie. She quickly stood up, putting a hand to his shoulder. 'She's going to be fine. We've got coffee being made.'

'Brooke?' Chase said, the situation not seeming to sink in very quickly.

'Hey, Dad!' Brooke responded, waving a hand from left to right with very little in the way of coordination. She pointed a finger as if admonishing him. 'You should be working.' Giggling, she started to sing like Rihanna. 'Work, work, work work work …'

Isla swallowed, looking at her boss's concerned expression. 'Now might be a good time to focus on the fact she's going to be fine. We've all done it. We all learned our lesson—'

'Yeah, Isla, that might be the British keep calm and carry on attitude, but you're not the one with an ex-wife watching your every move and waiting for an excuse to stop access,' Chase snapped.

'I …' Isla began. She closed her mouth again. There wasn't anything she could say to make this situation any better.

'Come on, Brooke. Let's get you back to the hotel.' Chase took hold of his daughter's arm and gently pulled her from the bench.

'Raj is making coffee,' Hannah said. 'I'm sure if she has a cup or three of that before you leave it might save on an unfortunate incident in a taxi.'

'Can we get McDonald's?' Brooke asked, swaying hard. 'Or English pie? I'm real hungry.'

'Here,' Hannah said, reaching back into her bag again. 'I've got some sausage rolls right here.' She passed them over to Brooke.

'Cool,' the teenager answered, cradling the snack like it was a baby.

'I'll go and tell Raj to adios the coffees,' Hannah said, preparing to wheel away.

'Well, I should really find Mrs Edwards,' Isla said, making to leave too.

'Wait, Isla,' Chase said, catching her arm. He blew out an awkward breath, his hands going into the pockets of his leather jacket. 'Listen, I'm sorry … again,' Chase started. 'I shouldn't have snapped at you. I just—'

'You're worried about Brooke,' Isla said. 'It's okay. I get it.'

He smiled. 'She's a challenge, right?'

'She's thirteen,' Isla answered. 'When Hannah was thirteen she drank two bottles of our grandmother's sloe-gin and was sick in our dad's briefcase.'

'O ... kay ...' Chase answered. 'So, any tips? Or do I just put her to bed and hope for the best?'

'Just hold her up,' Isla replied, watching Brooke grabbing on to the back of the bench. 'Support her, and tell her you love her before she goes to sleep.'

'Thank you,' he replied.

And there were those coppery eyes holding hers captive, the faint buzz of Dean Martin coming from the speaker and the scent of pine, mulled wine and peppered meats filled Isla's nose. There was definitely something between them, popping and fizzing like electricity, but it was just so wholly inappropriate. Wasn't it? Isla swallowed.

'So, I will see you on Monday morning,' Chase spoke softly.

'Yes,' she replied. 'Monday.'

He reached for her hand then, gently lifting it to his lips and dropping a kiss on the skin. At that moment her insides started to fall away like a paraglider taking that first leap from a cliff face. All the memories of their kiss the night before came hammering back to her.

'Goodnight, Miss Winters,' Chase whispered.

'Goodnight,' she answered.

Sixty

Breekers London, Canary Wharf

'Good morning, Aaron,' Isla greeted her colleague as she arrived at her desk on Monday morning. It had been a good weekend. She and Hannah had finally, almost, completely got their Christmas decorations nailed. There were all manner of scented candles around the fireplace – marshmallow, pumpkin, spruce – a number of reindeer ornaments Isla didn't even remember owning and strings of garish tinsel in every room. The only thing missing was the tree, and she was determined that this afternoon the white feather one would be theirs.

'Is it a good morning?' Aaron responded. 'Is it really?' He lifted his head from his desk and Isla let out a gasp. His eyes had thick dark circles underneath them like he hadn't slept in weeks.

'What happened? You look terrible!'

'Oh, make me feel better, why don't you?' Aaron exclaimed. 'And truly, darling, this is actually all *your* fault.'

'*My* fault?' Isla queried. She put her handbag down under her desk and paid Aaron her full attention.

'When you handed some of the reins of the Ridgepoint Hospital project over to me was there anything you neglected to tell me?'

Isla was thinking that there obviously had been something she had omitted or Aaron wouldn't be looking at her like a furious drag queen who had had his make-up stolen.

'I'm not sure?' she offered.

'Hilda Stewart perhaps?' Aaron suggested.

'Oh,' Isla said, immediately understanding.

'"Oh"? Is that all you can say?' Aaron exclaimed.

'I owe you something, obviously,' Isla began. 'Mexican beer and ... Mexican food too. We'll put something in the diary for January.'

'Hilda Stewart is a professional speaker,' Aaron continued, almost as if Isla hadn't said a thing.

'I think you'll find that's someone from the House of Commons not from the NHS Trust.'

'The woman does not stop,' Aaron said. 'Not even to draw breath. It's like rapid machine-gun fire ...' He did all the noises, his head bobbing and jerking like he was playing a game of *Battlefield 4*. 'At first I thought she was talking Dutch, then, when I realised it *was* English, I was convinced she was slipping in and out of a Zimbabwean accent ...'

'Aaron,' Isla broke in.

'Do not stop me! I need to get this all out now!'

'Well, I really need to talk to you about why you told Chase about the Beaumont Square wine and cheese night,' Isla countered.

'Oh,' Aaron replied, his bluster seeming to blow out.

'Yes, so, what do you have to say about that?'

'Well, I just thought it might smooth things over a little,' Aaron said. 'And I don't want to see you working at Waterloo Station or selling the *Big Issue*.'

'But you know Notting Hill is where Breekers want to build this hotel,' Isla said, sighing. She lowered herself to her chair. She hated even saying the words.

'Yes,' Aaron answered. 'I stuck my neck out and suggested Haringey. There's that big parcel of land that was cleared for something else a while back and I'm pretty sure I heard the developer went bankrupt.'

'Chase and I are going to look at the two other sites today.'

'You're back being the Go-To Girl then?' Aaron asked with a grin. 'Saddled on up again?' He winked.

'I'm not letting emotion cloud my business judgement, and secretly hoping that we can convince Breekers International that a site outside of Notting Hill would be preferable.'

'Do you think that's possible?'

'Anything's possible at this time of year, isn't it?' Isla asked. She breathed out. 'It's almost Christmas.' Her mind was then spiked with the reminder of the social event of the year she was not in control of. 'Aaron, actually, could you do something for me while I'm out?' She pulled her iPad from her bag and tapped the home button.

'Please do not make me speak to Hilda Stewart today. We've got a Skype call scheduled for tomorrow.'

'No,' Isla said. 'Can you call the caterers about the Christmas party?'

Aaron put his hands to his face and looked practically giddy with shock. 'No! You're not really going to let me be involved with the Christmas party are you?' He breathed in like he had just been given the lead role in *Hairspray*. 'All these years I've waited for this chance.'

'Could you just call them? Ask them if they got my emails and give them my mobile number?' Isla asked. 'I tried them about twenty minutes ago but it's probably a bit early for them to be open.' That was what she was hoping anyway.

'I will do that … on one condition,' Aaron stood up and head-butted one of Ethel's glittery pompoms.

'What?'

'Tell me the theme!'

'Not a chance,' Isla answered.

Chase pushed open the door to Breekers London and stepped in out of the cold. It was snowing again after a freezing night that had left frost on cars, lampposts and letterboxes. Maddie had skipped the whole way from the Tube, delighting in every Christmas element – an organist playing 'White Christmas' in pan-pipe mode, flashing Christmas puddings outside a cooking store, the scent of caramel and buttered bagels … Brooke, on the other hand, was still recovering from Friday night's alcoholic episode. Chase had looked after her, held her hair back while she barfed, gave her water and some painkillers until finally she fell asleep. Then he had called Leanna and come clean, told her about Brooke's drinking episode and sucked up a whole lot of hysteria until his head hurt. Finally, yesterday, they had managed a civilised conversation not a blame game, and he had read the riot act to Brooke about the perils of drinking. He knew it was another attempt at seeking attention and he acknowledged that, understood how serious it was, but he just wasn't in a position to make changes he knew were needed yet. He was caught between trying to get his professional life on an even keel for financial reasons and for his own sanity and being the father his kids deserved. He wanted that more than anything but if he took his foot off the gas …

'Daddy, I'm going to look at the Christmas tree!' Maddie announced, running off towards the tree in the lobby and greeting it like an old friend. He watched his daughter sniff at the branches and finger a small red-and-gold star adornment.

'Mom's messaged me again,' Brooke griped. 'She's asking what I had for breakfast.' She looked up from her phone screen. 'Shall I say vodka?'

Chase reached out and took the phone from Brooke's hand. 'Are you trying to kill me right now?'

'What?' Brooke questioned. 'She asked me what I had for breakfast, that's all.'

'Then tell her,' Chase answered. 'The truth, maybe? Or you might find yourself back in Montgomery early.'

'Why?' Brooke snapped. 'Because you're sick of me too?'

'I'm not sick of you Brooke,' Chase said, his tone a little calmer. 'You're my daughter and I love you—'

'But? 'Cause there's gonna be a "but" coming.'

'I'm worried about you,' Chase said.

'Whatever.'

'Your mom is worried about you too.'

'She's too busy worrying about Colt to be worrying about anyone else.'

What did he say to that? The adult him should tell Brooke that wasn't the case. And it *wasn't* the case. Leanna had always put their children before anything else. It was their marriage she hadn't been so committed to.

'You mom loves you and Maddie so much, Brooke.'

'If she really loved us she wouldn't have made us move to Montgomery.'

He had no answer. He knew Brooke had hated leaving New York as much as he had hated them both going. He should be ready with one of his cheery inspirational quotes right now. *Change is never easy but it always provides new opportunity*. He just wasn't so sure it was what a hormonal thirteen-year-old wanted to hear.

He put an arm around her shoulders. 'Listen, I'm out of the office for a couple hours this morning. I'll set you up with Internet and movies and you can ask Denise to get you anything you want,' Chase said, holding on to Brooke's shoulders as she attempted to dodge the affection. 'Starbucks, fast food ...'

'A hoverboard?' Brooke queried.

'After Friday night I really wouldn't push it,' Chase replied.

Sixty-One

Enfield

Isla stepped down from the people carrier, her boots squelching into snow-covered mud. It seemed that this area on the outskirts of London had resisted the hard frost of the night before or had certainly been on a quick defrost this morning.

'God! This is like quicksand!' Chase remarked, his shoes almost disappearing into the brown mush.

'I'm guessing you don't have boots,' Isla said.

'You guessed right, Miss Winters. To be honest, I had my role here down to meetings … inside.'

'Well, that isn't how we do things at Breekers London.' Isla breathed in the fresh air and observed the view ahead of them. It wasn't a naturally flat space and it was on an incline, mainly fields and wasteland but with an industrial park to the left. Today everything was coated with a dusting of white like someone had shaken a bag of icing sugar over it.

'The reason this site was kinda discounted was because of the road,' Chase stood next to her, indicating the busy A-road a few hundred yards to their right.

'Yes, we don't tend to move main roads in England,' Isla said. 'Adding roads, yes, moving them, not really.'

'Is that something to do with the history dating back eons?' Chase asked.

'There's that jealousy of our heritage again.'

'No, I'm just trying to play devil's advocate,' Chase said. 'If I'm gonna go to the board and try to get them to choose another location I need to have real reasons and solutions to everything they throw at me.'

'And you're really going to do that?' Isla asked. 'Try and get the board to change their mind?'

'I'm gonna make sure other opportunities aren't overlooked,' he answered. 'I can't give you more than that.'

She nodded. She knew that. And, as much as she wanted to save Notting Hill, she knew a business decision was about a lot more than the say-so of one employee who happened to live in the area.

'We would have to lose that industrial park entirely,' Chase said.

'Not necessarily,' Isla replied. She took her iPad from her bag and began tapping the screen. 'If the size of the hotel were reduced or—'

'Isla, it's a super-hotel and village. It has to be super if it's gonna be stand-out different.'

'Does it have to be "stand-out different" in that way?'

'It's Breekers' new arm of the business. It has to make an impact.'

'Well, how about it makes an impact in another way?' Isla suggested.

'What sort of way?'

'Well,' she said. 'Don't they always say that size isn't everything?'

God, now the heat of his ardour was out-battling the biting wind whipping around them. And that was another thing about this trip: Isla Winters. Despite having so much on his plate with his work and broken-home life, she just kept enticing a rather needy libido.

'What if Breekers' new hotels were stand-out because of their attention to detail, to customer service, to people.'

What? Was she serious? Not content with not wanting the hotel where it was she now wanted to change the whole concept?

'Isla ...'

'No, please, hear me out,' Isla walked a couple of steps into the mud in front of him and spread her hands out. 'Look at the city, Chase. Look at the sprawling, grey, chrome and steel ... all the things Breekers have been working with for all these years.' She smiled. 'I was thinking about this over the weekend: how about giving something back?'

'You've totally lost me.' But she was animated, alive and just watching her tell him whatever she was about to tell him was compelling.

'How about Breekers make the hotel idea more boutique?' She slipped her iPad back into her bag.

He shook his head. 'You know "boutique" is just another word for small, right?'

'Well, in the UK, it's another word for "exclusive" and "special".' She sniffed. 'Isn't that what you said you wanted the hotel to be?'

Was she really throwing some of his boardroom talk back at him? He slipped his hands into the pockets of his jacket, keeping his eyes on her.

'My idea is for Breekers to find the right locations for a series of smaller boutique hotels that complement the environment they're built in and that are constructed with the most environmentally friendly materials.' She took a breath. 'They would be relaxed places, not full of hectic circuses and casinos but calm, stress-free habitations that encourage well-being for body and mind.' Her eyes met his then. 'A glorious little haven in the middle of the city.'

He had no idea what to say. Right now he was floored. Somehow she had touched him, wholly, completely like no one had touched him before. It was like, without knowing it, she had reached inside of him and stroked his soul. Right now, there was nothing more he wanted to do than take her mouth with his again—

'You hate the idea,' Isla said.

He took a step towards her, uncaring that his shoes and the hems of his pants were getting spattered in mud.

'Why aren't you saying anything?' Isla asked him. 'Are you going to fire me? It was just an idea and I know you and the board probably won't—'

He stopped walking when he was right in front of her, the wind whipping her red hair around her face, her full lips trembling a little.

'What are you doing?' Isla asked him.

He couldn't answer her. He just had to act now, while this mix of adrenalin and joy and desire was pumping through his veins. He took her face in his hands and drew her towards him, his mouth connecting with hers.

Isla was shaking. From her freezing feet in her muddy boots to the very ends of her hair as Chase's lips held hers captive. It was divine, it was sexy, and she did not want it to end. She deepened the kiss, edging her body closer to his, and letting out an audible sigh of pleasure. How was it they seemed to end up this way despite all their differences?

'God, Isla, stop,' Chase said, breaking contact. 'We have to stop.'

'Yes,' Isla replied. She made to step back until he put an arm around her and drew her back into him.

'No, not like that,' he spoke. 'I meant, we just have to ease up a little because otherwise I'm not gonna be able to stop myself from taking off that very British, very sexy red coat of yours ...' He kissed again. 'And then, once the coat is off I would have to find the zipper on that pantsuit and ...'

'Where would we be then?' Isla asked, her lips finding his.

'In trouble,' Chase answered. 'In a whole lot of trouble.'

She wanted to give in to this so much, just like she had in the sanctuary of the private garden. To hold on to this moment of pure adult indulgence and just let go for once. But what happened after that? Consequence always had a way of catching up with you.

'Chase,' Isla breathed, breaking lip contact and looking deep into those brown eyes.

'No,' he whispered, putting a finger to her lips. 'Let me speak first.'

'Why?' Isla asked, blinking, the touch of his finger on her mouth another sizzling sensation.

'Cause I don't want you to say you want to take this back,' he answered.

She swallowed. She didn't want to take it back. Not really. But taking it back would be the least complicated scenario. He had so much going on with his family. She had so much going on with the threat of everything she knew being uprooted. And, as much as she found him utterly gorgeous, delightfully complex and totally engaging, he was at the core of all those impediments.

'Let me take you out,' Chase whispered, his fingers moving to the ends of her hair.

'Take me out?' Isla repeated.

He nodded. 'Yeah. But not to discuss building hotels or Christmas networking with business owners ... just us,' he stated.

'Just us?' Isla repeated.

'Now who's answering questions with questions?' He smiled.

'Sorry,' Isla said.

'I promised the girls I'd take them out this afternoon but, if you're free, how about tonight?'

'Tonight?' That was soon. That was mere hours away. She usually needed at least a week's worth of notice to prepare for a date. She had nothing decent to wear, she couldn't wear her mother's best dress again ...

'But, if you're busy we could take a rain check and—' Chase began.

Damn it. Why was she hesitating? Hannah would be wheeling into her so hard if she was listening in.

'No,' Isla jumped in. 'I'm not busy.' Was that too keen? Should she try to at least pretend she had a hectic social calendar and lots of interesting things planned apart from community Christmas festivities?

'I'm glad,' Chase replied. 'I'll pick you up at seven thirty.'

She nodded. 'Okay.'

'Okay,' he answered. His fingers moved from her hair to her hand, his digits grazing her skin.

'Okay, so we should take some photos and meet up with Ffion.' She plucked her iPad from her bag.

'We should,' Chase agreed. 'And on the drive you can tell me more about the boutique idea.'

She looked up at him, daring to hope that something she had said had struck a chord.

He smiled at her. 'You're good, Miss Winters. Really good.'

Sixty-Two

Life Start Community Centre, Notting Hill

There were the remnants of broken bottles, cigarette butts and a suspicious-looking yellow puddle outside of the community centre when Isla arrived. Two youths on bikes were also using the large pebble-dash concrete flower tub as a jump, skidding across the snow-speckled concrete, coming close to colliding with anything and anyone who dared to be in their vicinity. If only this little patch of the suburb could be nurtured like the rest of the area. She knew the answer was because there wasn't enough funding and that the community centre's paid workers and volunteers were focused on what went on *inside* the building, not how it looked on the outside. And that *was* the most important thing.

She shot the youths a disdainful glance as one of them careered into a metal bin no one appeared to be using. Isla was here because she was going to surprise Hannah with a visit to the shop to get the white feather Christmas tree. It was just starting to get dark, she had spent the whole afternoon hammering down notes on the Enfield and Essex sites, and she was trying to batter down the excited yet apprehensive feelings about her date with Chase in a few hours. She needed a different focus. One that wasn't blighted by worry about the future, one that involved her sister and their mutual love of this season. She turned away from the front door of the centre and looked up the road towards her grandmother's house and the beautiful garden. Right now it was all still here.

'Oi! Piss off!'

Isla turned back at the sound of Hannah's voice and watched her sister wheel herself across the pavement towards the teenagers.

'Fuck off! You're not the police!'

Isla took quick steps forward as the youths seemed to turn aggressive.

'No, I'm not the police,' Hannah bit back, still moving closer to them. 'But my wheels are a whole lot bigger than yours and I know exactly how to use this Taser.'

She struck out and Isla watched the lads recoil swiftly like they'd been electrocuted.

'Hannah,' Isla said, going up to her as the teenagers retreated, heading up the road.

'God, what are you doing here? First turning up at work and now here,' Hannah said. 'Are you stalking me?'

'That isn't really a Taser, is it?'

Hannah laughed. 'No, of course not. It's an old Remington shaver that looks just like one. It was Poppy's dad's. She gave it to me last year. She's got one too.'

Isla shook her head, her mind boggling.

'So, what are you doing here? We always meet at Sugar High on a Monday and I've usually had time to find out all about Mrs Smith's latest illness or Rolo's latest vet's bill *and* eaten a slice of millionaire's cheesecake before you turn up.'

Isla smiled. 'We're going to visit Nan's bench and then we're going shopping.'

'Have you brought food because I'm starving?' Hannah said, wheeling on. 'Margaret baked again today – cinnamon biscuits – but I'm pretty convinced she used garam marsala instead of cinnamon.'

Isla opened her handbag and shook a bright pink paper bag. 'Christmas muffins from Sugar High.'

Hannah smiled. 'Well, in that case, it's definitely Father Christmas's Nice List for you this year.'

Sixty-Three

Oxford Street

Of all the Christmas displays Chase had seen while he'd been in the city, Oxford Street was head and shoulders above the rest. Lining the entire length of the street was a dazzling light show of neon blue, ice white and gold. Bright globes in orange and silver seemed to float untethered above them and the bustle of shoppers, workers and traffic on the road. Large stars, glistening gold, hung from shops and Christmas carols filled the air together with the scent of pastries and hot turkey being sold by a street vendor.

He had had a great afternoon with Brooke and Maddie. They had visited the Science Museum, where they had learned everything there was to know about robots, aeroplanes and space. Brooke had looked particularly interested in space. Especially when he had shared some of what he had learned when he thought space had been his future. She needed a focus like that. Something to get her excited about something. When this trip was over he would have a meaningful discussion with Leanna about it. After all, they both wanted what was best for Brooke and Maddie.

'Daddy,' Maddie said, squeezing his hand. 'Can we get Mommy a Christmas present in London?'

'Sure, Pumpkin,' Chase replied. 'What did you have in mind?'

'She would love one of those real trashy bags with "I Love London" written on them,' Brooke remarked. She pointed to a stall ahead of them.

Maddie laughed. 'She really would.'

'I remember your mom having a bit more of an expensive taste.'

Brooke shook her head. 'Her favourite things are still anything purple.'

'For real?' Chase asked.

'Yes, Colt won her this ring at the country fair,' Maddie said. 'It's plastic but she loves it and never takes it off.'

'Shut up, dummy!' Brooke exclaimed.

'Hey,' Chase said, turning to face Brooke. 'It's okay.' He let out a sigh. 'Listen, I know all this is weird for you, your mom dating your Uncle Colt ... it's kinda weird for me too, but ...' He took another breath, trying to strengthen himself with an ingestion of air. 'I don't want you to think there are things you can't talk with me about. Because I miss out on so much that's going on with you guys when I'm all the way over in New York.' He stopped walking and looked to them in turn. 'And I don't wanna miss out on anything.'

'We just ... we just don't want you to feel lonely, Daddy,' Maddie told him.

'And I hate him,' Brooke added.

'Hate's a very strong word, Brooke. And he is your uncle before anything else.' He swallowed. 'And nothing can change blood.'

'But you're not talking to each other,' Maddie said.

'Yeah,' Chase said. 'I know. But I'm hoping that isn't gonna be a forever thing.' Was that what he really hoped? He had ignored all his brother's attempts at reconciliation so far. Was he going to start trying to build bridges?

'Are you still mad at Mommy?' Maddie questioned. Those big concerned eyes killed him every time.

He shook his head. 'No, Pumpkin. I was never really mad at Mommy. Things just didn't work out for us, that's all and when things don't work out sometimes people get sad.' He squeezed her hand. 'And when I was sad it made me sick and that was hard for everyone.' He smiled. 'But I'm better now and once we've worked out how to see each other a lot more often we are all gonna be a whole lot happier. I promise.'

'I miss you, Dad.'

It was Brooke. And her four words clawed at his heart.

'I miss you too.' He looked at his eldest daughter and all of a sudden her bravado and rage at the world and their situation seemed to fall away. She was just his baby, still as assailable as she had ever been. He put his arms around her and drew her close, not caring if she pulled away or shirked his attempt at affection. He needed the connection and he wanted her to know she was loved.

He felt two hands hold on tight, her long hair brush against his cheek, and something inside of him sighed with relief and then glowed, the feeling getting bigger and brighter with every passing second.

Finally, Brooke let him go and adopted the uncaring expression that he'd noticed often seemed to appear on girls around the age of twelve.

'Can we shop now?' Brooke asked, smoothing back her hair.

'Daddy, can I get another JoJo bow for my hair?' Maddie asked, flicking the rainbow one on her head.

'Well, I would kinda like your help with something first, if that's okay,' Chase said.

'What sort of help?' Brooke queried.

'Fashion help,' Chase replied.

'Oh, man, you're kidding, right?' Brooke exclaimed, half-laughing.

'No, I'm dead serious,' Chase said. 'I'm going out tonight.' He swallowed. 'With Isla.'

'Another work thing?' Maddie asked him, folding her arms across her chest.

'No,' Chase said definitely. 'No, it's not a work thing.' He felt that kick of thrill in his gut. 'It's a date.'

He looked to both of his children, not knowing what reaction he expected to get. Perhaps this was too much for them to take on. But he wanted to be honest. So much of their lives lately had been heated arguments and hearsay.

'Oh, Daddy!' Maddie exclaimed, sounding as excited as on Christmas morning. 'I really like Isla.'

'Yeah,' Chase said, swallowing. 'Me too.'

'I like her too,' Brooke said. 'She's pretty cool.'

'Yeah,' Chase agreed. 'She is pretty cool.'

'And beautiful,' Maddie added. 'And smart. She told me all about the changing of the guard at Buckingham Palace at the wine and cheese night. Can we go see it while we're here?'

'Sure,' Chase agreed. 'But right now, your dad needs that fashion help.' He looked to Brooke. 'I need to look hot like Rag 'n' Bone Man, right?'

'God, Dad, no, stop!' Brooke said putting her hands over her ears.

'We'll find you something real good,' Maddie said, linking her arm through his. 'I'm thinking stripes and maybe red 'cause it's almost Christmas.'

'Red stripes?' Brooke exclaimed in horror. 'Are you kidding me? He wants a second date, Maddie!' She took his arm, pulling him a little away from her sister. 'I'm thinking grey pants with a blue shirt and maybe braces ... braces are really in right now.'

Chase smiled at his daughters. Right now, with them both animated and involved in lively debate, he couldn't care less if they dressed him as Borat.

Sixty-Four

Larkspur Gardens

'I can still feel her here, you know,' Hannah stated through a mouthful of Christmas muffin.

Isla nodded. She knew exactly what Hannah meant. They had spent so many wonderful times as small children in this place with Edith. Simple things like weeding the flowerbeds in spring, picking up different kinds of leaves in the autumn to form collages that Edith would stick on her kitchen tiles, and picnics on the grass in summer, spraying each other with water from the frog fountain. It was spurting this evening, not blocked with ice, and the Christmas lights all around were just starting to illuminate as the night arrived.

'I know,' Isla said. 'But it's a happy feeling, isn't it? Like we know she's at peace.'

'She would totally love these Christmas muffins,' Hannah said, wiping her face with the back of her hand.

It was now or never if she was going to share this with her sister. And she wanted to. Because she usually shared everything. Except everything was ordinarily nothing spectacular in her ordered world.

'I brought Chase here.' Isla held her breath. The words were out.

'You did?' Hannah queried.

Isla nodded, unable to direct her gaze at the frog. 'And we sat on this bench.'

'Uh-huh,' Hannah said, as if somehow knowing there was more.

'We kissed,' Isla said. She shut her eyes and all the feelings came rushing back including how out of control she'd felt earlier today in Enfield. Chase's mouth against hers, the way she had pressed herself to him ... 'And I kissed him again today and ... he's taking me out on a date tonight.'

The last words had taken all her energy and she looked to Hannah, waiting for the shock, surprise and perhaps a little anger at being kept in the dark. Instead what she got was a smile as wide as the plans for the super-hotel taking over her sister's face.

'I knew it!' Hannah exclaimed. 'I knew there was no way that a: he could resist your red hair and that pantsuit and b: how you could seriously not be hot under the pantsuit over someone as smoking as him!'

'Well,' Isla began. 'I don't know what to say about either of those things.' But in truth she hoped this wasn't just based on hot hair or flaming pantsuits. Or did that really matter? It was a nice development, this passion around the planning, but anything more than a pre-Christmas flirtation wasn't on either of their agendas.

'God!' Hannah exclaimed. 'What's he like? Does he kiss as amazing as those lips look? Is he all about the tongue?'

'Hannah!'

'Sorry, it's just ... wow, I mean, wow, Isla, he's so ... right for you.'

'Right for me?' Isla queried. How could her sister claim that someone she had barely known five minutes be 'right for her'?

'Yeah, I mean he's gorgeous, as previously discussed, he's clever and he's funny and he wears seriously nice suits and yeah, he has kids, which could be a complication, but they're great. Maddie is cute and Brooke, well, she reminds me a little of me.'

Isla smiled. 'Yes, it's funny you say that. I thought the same thing.'

'Oh you did, did you?' Hannah said, stuffing the last bit of muffin into her mouth. 'I don't know how I feel about that.'

'So,' Isla said. 'Do you think I should go on the date tonight?'

'Is that really a question? Of course you have to go on the date,' Hannah said. 'Why wouldn't you?'

'A hundred reasons.' Isla sighed. 'He's my boss. He lives in America.' She swallowed. 'He's my boss.'

'I hate to diss your maths skills but that isn't a hundred reasons,' Hannah replied. 'And so what to the boss thing and the U.S. thing? As always you're looking at the big, giant picture and missing the fun you would be having if you weren't worrying your pantsuit off over everything.'

'I don't see why my pantsuits need to be brought into this.'

'Go on the date, Isla. Have some fun. Kiss the face off the gorgeous Chase.'

'And you'll be all right tonight?' Isla asked.

'I'll be all right even if you don't come home tonight. I can sleep on the sofa or ...'

'No,' Isla said. 'No, there won't be any need for that.'

'Why not?' Hannah asked. 'You've kissed him twice. Surely you're going to be moving on to taking items of clothing off next?'

Isla's cheeks began to heat up. Just thinking about Chase shirtless, let alone trouserless, made her stomach coil with excitement, longing and nervous fear.

'Wear your best knickers,' Hannah stated. 'Not the boy shorts. The black lacy ones you hand wash.'

'I now feel violated,' Isla said. 'How do you know what I hand wash?'

'There are no secrets between sisters, right?'

Apart from the large one she was keeping about Breekers' plans for Notting Hill. Isla settled for nodding her head. 'So … how are things with Raj?'

'Well,' Hannah said. 'I've come to the conclusion that he's a slow-burner.' She crumpled up the paper bag in her hand. 'At first I thought he might be like an advent candle, but I'm now thinking he might be more of one of those big Jo Malone ones that take weeks to burn a couple of inches.'

'He did buy you some lovely flowers,' Isla pointed out.

'But he didn't snog my face off either.' Hannah tutted. 'Beaten to my Notting Hill kiss by my sister.'

'Well I am that much older,' Isla said. 'And it really isn't a competition.'

'I know.' She sighed. 'And I get the feeling he *does* like me he just … needs to be sure and there's nothing wrong with that,' Hannah admitted.

'Gosh, Hannah Winters, that isn't some sort of patience I detect, is it?'

'Don't tell anyone.'

From her handbag Isla's phone dinged loudly signifying a new text message.

'Ooo,' Hannah exclaimed. 'A message from the sexy New Yorker?'

Isla couldn't help a smile but then immediately she wondered if it was perhaps Chase thinking better of his invitation or, worse still, he was cancelling because something was wrong with one of the children. She rushed to get the phone from her bag.

'What does he say?' Hannah asked. 'Are there lots of love heart emojis?'

Isla swallowed as she read the text. It wasn't from Chase. It was from Aaron.

No answer from the caterers so I went to their premises. No easy way to say this. They're gone. The place is more deserted than the England football team's trophy cabinet.

Sixty-Five

Beaumont Square, Notting Hill

The Breekers' Christmas party was done for. In all the years Isla had been in charge of organising it, it had never failed to impress. Now, unless she could find a decent caterer who wasn't booked solid on the run up to Christmas she was either going to have to cancel or make canapés herself. What was she going to say to everyone? She was Miss Super-Organised. It was almost all her worst fears come true.

But, for the time being, as she had done with the super-hotel project, the impending disaster was shallow-grave buried for her own temporary sanity as well as for Hannah. She had decided to focus on something she *could* manage. When Isla had shown her sister the white feather Christmas tree she had made a noise like a squealing firework and declared it the most beautiful thing she had ever seen. Right now, in their close-to-Christmas-grotto living room, Hannah was busy reaching out and positioning all the branches with the utmost care and deciding which ornament belonged where. Isla was looking in the mirror above the fireplace wondering whether she needed to upgrade her current moisturiser as this one wasn't making her quite as youthful as it claimed.

'Have I said how gorgeous this is?' Hannah asked, popping a diamante teardrop on one of the slender arms of the tree.

'Yes, you did,' Isla replied.

'Well it really is,' Hannah repeated. 'And I'm sorry about being a pain in the arse when I kept asking about the tree. I know you've been busy and you've probably got mammoth amounts of work going on with the CEO, not to mention the Christmas party.'

Oh God. She really didn't want the Christmas party mentioned. Any more comments and the earth would start to fall away and the spectre of the problem would start filtering into everything. She nodded quickly and changed the subject. 'Well, Christmas isn't Christmas without a tree, is it?'

'I guess that's one thing that's going to be difficult with me and Raj,' Hannah said.

'What?'

'That he doesn't celebrate Christmas.' Hannah sighed. 'It is my favourite time of the year.'

Isla turned away from the mirror then and looked at her sister. 'Well, we're not exactly big church-goers, are we? And I always thought your favourite parts of Christmas were the decorating and the eating.'

'How very dare you!' Hannah exclaimed. 'I also enjoy watching re-runs of *Dirty Dancing* and *Annie* and getting up early for the Next sale.' She grinned. 'It's surprising how far a wheelchair can get you up the queue if you groan like your injured legs are actually going to drop off.'

'Well Iqbal and Geeta don't celebrate Christmas and they still decorate,' Isla pointed out. 'And you can always get Raj a present just because it's nice, not because it's religious.'

The doorbell rang before Hannah could answer and instead she let out: 'Wooo, your escort is here.'

Her date. She needed to concentrate on that. On grabbing a little bit of down time with someone who made her insides fizz like Christmas party prosecco.

'Are you excited?' Hannah asked her.

She was. Despite everything, she really was. She just wished there wasn't a whole mound of disaster loitering in the background. She should push the party woes a little deeper, maybe a good six feet … inside a sealed box.

'What's wrong?' Hannah asked, turning away from her new best friend, the Christmas tree.

'Nothing,' Isla answered, smoothing her hands down the front of a midnight blue dress she had worn the night of the Breekers' James Bond themed Christmas party. At the time she had hoped it had looked a little like Jane Seymour's Solitaire. Now she just hoped there were no weak seams or missing buttons on the detail she hadn't seen.

'Relax,' Hannah said, wheeling herself towards her sister. 'You're going to have a great time. Where's he taking you?'

She gasped. Hands shooting towards her mouth. 'I don't know. I don't know anything,' she said. 'I didn't even ask if he meant dinner or what I should wear.' She had a sudden thought. 'What if he's taking me … bowling or something.' She looked at her dress. 'Americans love bowling.' There was no way she could bowl in this dress. Loose seams or not there was very little in the way of give.

'Stop panicking,' Hannah ordered. 'And go and answer the door before he thinks you've changed your mind.'

'Yes,' Isla said. 'Yes, I should do that.' She took a breath and rushed from the room.

Chase blew out a breath that formed a white rush in front of him as he stood at the top of the concrete ramp outside Isla and Hannah's home. There was a cranberry-coloured circular wreath on the front of the door that hadn't been there on his last visit. There was also light coming from inside the house and the sound of voices. God, he was nervous. When was the last time he had dated? There had been no one since his break-up with Leanna. He hadn't even thought about it. He hadn't had the time and he hadn't wanted to. This connection with Isla was just so … different. Unexpected but undeniably something he wanted to pursue.

Slipping his hands into the pockets of the new pants his children had made him buy he shifted his feet. Brooke seemed to have a good eye for fashion and everything she had picked up he had liked too, and it all suited him. As well as the grey pants, he was wearing a dark teal shirt, tucked in, with a brown belt Maddie had chosen. It wasn't his usual style but he felt good and the girls had got a lot of pleasure out of adorning him. They had worked together like Team Sister, picking things up, holding them up to him then putting them back on the rack if they had sniffed and shaken their heads too much.

The door opened and his adrenalin shifted into another gear, as if he hadn't been expecting it to happen. There Isla was, looking absolutely incredible.

'Hey,' he breathed, almost too tight to say the one word. He needed to temper his enthusiasm just a little bit. 'I mean, hi …' That was no better. 'Good evening.'

'Hello,' Isla greeted.

'You look amazing,' Chase said, swallowing.

'I like your shirt,' Isla remarked. 'Is it new?'

'Yeah,' he replied. 'Brooke kinda said I'd be "lame" if I didn't buy it so I did the Dad thing and … gave in.'

Isla smiled. 'It's very nice.'

'Haven't you two gone already?'

Chase waved a hand at Hannah who had appeared behind Isla in the hall. 'Hi, Hannah.'

'Hi,' she replied quickly. 'So, where are you taking my sister tonight?'

'Han!' Isla exclaimed, cheeks already halfway on their way to a blush.

'You want to know for … security reasons?' Chase inquired. 'I thought we had established I was not a paedophile or creepy in any way that very first time we met.'

'Very amusing,' Hannah answered. 'No … Isla is worried you're going to take her bowling. And, I think, seeing as she looks like a star of London Fashion Week tonight, taking her up an alley isn't really going to cut it.'

'Hannah! Please, can you just ignore my sister,' Isla begged. 'I like bowling. If we are going bowling then bowling is just fine with me.'

Chase smiled and nodded. 'I thought we'd go bowling then to a diner where we can eat hot dogs, buffalo wings and biscuits with gravy. Plus, you already told me you have a soft spot for grits.'

He looked at each of the women in turn, neither of them making any comment.

'I'm kidding,' he replied. 'No bowling and no American food.'

'Good,' Hannah answered. 'Now, get out of here and let me finish decorating my fabulous feathered friend.'

Chase had no idea what she was talking about.

'It's our Christmas tree,' Isla elaborated. 'Okay, so you're all right for everything?'

'Yes, shove off,' Hannah ordered.

'I will have her home by midnight, I promise,' Chase said as Isla stepped out and joined him.

'You bloody well won't,' Hannah retorted.

Chase smiled at Isla, getting a little lost in her eyes. 'Shall we?' He indicated the waiting car and offered her his arm.

'Yes,' she answered.

Sixty-Six

London Eye, Westminster Bridge Road

'Honestly, you need to excuse Hannah, bowling would have been fine ... and fun,' Isla said as the car stopped at traffic lights. 'I might have needed to change my dress but—'

'Miss Winters, bowling was never a possibility,' Chase said. He couldn't keep his eyes off her. Like before, on their trip to the Electric Cinema, she had pointed out all the tourist landmarks. Plus she had told him stories about other off-the-guidebook places he suddenly craved to know everything about. Apparently there was a pub in Soho that still resembled an old-fashioned drinking den and a club called The Nightjar in Blackfriars that was dark and mysterious with live jazz and swing music going on until three in the morning. Now he literally ached to go there.

'It wasn't?' she asked, turning to him.

'No,' he answered. 'Because as well as taking my girls out this afternoon I also planned our evening together.'

'You did?'

He nodded. 'And I emailed Breekers New York.' He sucked in a breath. 'Isla, I wanna get this out there and then I think we should leave work behind for tonight.'

He saw an almost fearful expression cross her face in anticipation of what he was about to say.

'Okay,' was all she answered.

'I emailed the board and I told them my opinion, taking into account everything I've experienced, heard and thought about while I've been here.' He took a breath. 'I explained what Verity and John told us, what Ffion presented and what Richard showed me over email earlier ... I concluded to the board that I didn't think Notting Hill was the right location for the super-hotel after all. I told them I thought the parcel of land in Enfield was a better fit.'

Isla's stomach danced. It *actually* danced like Aljaž Škorjanec doing a jive at the Blackpool Tower ballroom. She couldn't believe what she was hearing. What she had said to him about her home, all the places she adored, *had* made a real difference.

'Isla, I can't promise they are gonna go with my suggestion this time,' Chase spoke. 'I was the one so invested in Notting Hill after all. I just ...'

'But you tried,' Isla said softly. 'You went out on a limb and I am so, so grateful for that.'

'I think I really needed the reality check you gave me,' he admitted. 'I was blinkered by wanting to create the kind of stir I thought the project needed, but I hadn't taken into account anything but the end-game.' He sighed. 'I skipped over community feeling, pretended it didn't exist at all, I guess, and that was wrong.'

He was looking at her now, his body so close on the back seat of the Breekers' car that if she moved even a centimetre, contact would be made. Her heart was beating hard and the overwhelming feelings – lust, and perhaps more than that – were sweeping right the way through her.

'So, we have to wait,' Chase said. 'See what they come back with and hope they're gonna listen.'

She swallowed. 'How long do we have, do you think? Before they reply.'

He shook his head. 'I don't know. I'd like to think tomorrow, maybe, to at least have a discussion about it.'

Tomorrow. Notting Hill could be saved as soon as tomorrow. She would never have to tell her sister that all she treasured might have once been turned to dust. She felt the car draw to a halt and out of the window she saw the bright blue glow of the London Eye. The avenue of trees were sparkling with white lights like someone had sprinkled diamonds on all the branches. It was beautiful and immediately there was that buoyant buzz about the season starting to grow inside her.

'May I introduce the iCircle?' Chase commented.

'What?' Isla asked with a laugh.

'That's Maddie's new name for it. I really think she's on to something if they can get a sponsorship with Apple.'

Isla smiled. 'I think Coca-Cola might have something to say about that.'

He took her hand in his, lacing their fingers together and the merry, festive feeling turned into something even more delicious.

'Come on,' Chase said. 'I've booked a private capsule.'

Sixty-Seven

This London Eye – or iCircle – was a very different looking landmark tonight. Isla's previous visit with Hannah had been in the daytime and it had been summer. Then there had been warm sunshine and tourists taking photos of everything as they queued to get on board. Now the Thames reflected the lights from the wheel and the nearby pontoon, the pavement was frosted and everyone around them was wrapped up for winter. There was no queuing though. They were called forward immediately, stepping into the glass egg-shaped pod.

'Gosh!' Isla exclaimed. Inside the capsule wasn't the usual oval-shaped bench for sitting on she had expected but a table set for two, a solitary candle burning at its centre.

'No bowling,' Chase remarked, stepping up close behind her. His timbre immediately set in motion a shiver that rolled down her back.

'So I notice,' Isla replied.

'And,' he continued. 'No one in the pods next to us either.'

Isla looked to the glass to confirm what he had said. This really was going to be a private experience. And that notion thrilled her to the core. She turned to face him. 'You seem to have gone to a lot of trouble for a meal we're going to have to eat in the thirty minutes it takes to rotate.'

'Well,' Chase answered. 'We Americans may have invented fast food but that wasn't what I had in mind for tonight.'

'It wasn't?'

'No, Miss Winters. We have a whole evening of slowly circling the London skyline to enjoy.'

She couldn't believe it. They were going to spend the whole evening eating together, the city's night time beauty as a dramatic backdrop just for them. She couldn't hide her delight, almost feeling her body and soul come alive at the prospect.

'Wow,' Chase said, as if taken aback. 'The way you look right now ...' He seemed to pause. 'I take it I've done good.'

'Yes.' She nodded. 'You've done wonderfully.'

As the wheel slowly, silently, began to shift gracefully from its position at the embarkation point, Chase pulled out a chair. 'Ma'am,' he said.

'Thank you,' Isla answered, stepping forward and slipping her slim frame on to the seat. She smelled so good. She *always* smelled so good. It was distinctively Isla, a mix of something fresh like cool mountain air and something effervescent like sweet club soda.

His libido was already waking up and he took his seat opposite, plucking up the bottle of wine from the table.

He poured some of the red liquid into Isla's glass, releasing the deep berry aromas into the air. Then he looked to her, knowing realisation would shortly set in.

'Is that—?' Isla asked. 'Is that Colin Matthews' mulled wine?'

He smiled. 'Yes it is. And this one is vintage. A 2013 he told me.'

She shook her head. 'I don't believe you managed to prise his prized wine out of him.'

'Well, we might have had a brief discussion about his affordable housing projects. As you know, Breekers is looking to raise its profile in new ways.'

Another smile crossed her perfect features. He had come over here so fixed and set, so tight, his true self and feelings all knotted up. Now things seemed different, looser. Perhaps even *lucid*. He hadn't felt that way in such a long time.

He watched her take her first sip of mulled wine. Isla savoured things, that was something else he had noticed about her. Everything was enjoyed so thoroughly. She contemplated, took her sweet time, nothing ever rushed. A life that hadn't existed for him since he was a kid ... and that was wrong. He used to tell his clients how wrong that was. Now he realised she was looking at him so he took a sip of his wine. God, this stuff was good.

The wine was tickling parts of Isla that seemed to need very little other encouragement as it was. Although Chase had had such little time to put something together, he had gone to an incredible effort with the private capsule and the special drink ... what was coming next? And where was the food coming from? They were just about to be metres up in the air. Chefs and waiters didn't just drop from the sky like herald angels.

'I know what you're thinking,' Chase said.

He seemed to do that a lot. How did he know what she was thinking?

'You do?' she asked.

'You're wondering how our food is going to get here.'

'Well ...' Perhaps he *was* a mind-reader. Maybe there was something in his mentalist and mentoring skills after all ...

'Like the best boy scout I'm fully prepared,' Chase said.

Now she was completely intrigued. She couldn't help her eyes moving around the glass pod, looking for culinary evidence.

And there it was, in the corner – well, capsules didn't really have corners – a large bag she was presuming was meant to be there and not a cause for a security alert.

'Hungry?' Chase asked, getting to his feet again. 'Wait, don't answer that, because if you're not it only means I'm gonna have two more-than-happy daughters willing to scoop up the leftovers.'

'I'm quite hungry,' she admitted as her stomach spun with anticipation for everything this night seemed to be offering.

'Close your eyes,' he whispered.

She swallowed, a shiver running through her. 'Not more trying to charm with talk of luxury and quality?'

'I don't need to talk about charming you,' Chase said confidently. 'This food is gonna work its magic, I have no doubt.'

With her eyes closed, Isla's smell senses moved to another level and within seconds she knew what was coming. It was a food she adored but hadn't tasted in so long. The buttery garlic-tinged aroma filled the air and her tongue moved involuntarily almost already tasting the soft cheesy dough.

'How did you know?' she whispered, eyes still closed, ears picking up signals that told her that her plate was being filled.

'How did I know what?' Chase asked. 'You already know what this is?' She could tell from the tone of his voice that he was smiling.

'You've been to Alberto's,' Isla answered. 'It's my absolute favourite Italian restaurant in Notting Hill and … I haven't shown you it.'

'Open your eyes,' Chase ordered.

She did. And there it was. Beautiful little parcels of gnocchi in Alberto's signature sauce sprinkled simply with a little rocket. It smelled divine and it was still hot, steam rising up and bringing all that wonderful scent to her senses again.

'I'm guessing Aaron,' Isla responded. 'We went there together, a while ago now, and he ordered risotto but ended up pinching my gnocchi and being a bit vocal about its quality.' 'A bit vocal' was an understatement. Aaron had sighed and squealed like he had been on the receiving end of a very dirty Thai massage.

'It wasn't Aaron,' Chase admitted, sitting down again.

'It wasn't?'

'I love Italian food and I found Alberto's all by myself,' he said. 'I was gonna order some bruschetta and then I saw something on the wall behind the counter at the back.'

She knew what was coming and put a hand over her eyes as if that would somehow stop the embarrassment.

'There's a photograph of you and ... is it Lord Sugar?'

Isla shook her head. 'I can't believe Alberto still has that photo up.' The photo on her own mantelpiece at home had also made the paper. Hannah had fanned it out proudly every chance she got. Alberto had heralded her as a local celebrity and pinned a copy next to his selfie with John Bishop.

'Well,' Chase said. 'It was my golden opportunity. He knows the girl I'm planning on wowing with food, he's gonna know exactly what you like, right?'

'So, he told you all about my gnocchi obsession,' Isla said with a smile.

'He said he hasn't seen you in a while,' Chase teased. 'I told him I'd tell you. He showed me a rather extensive festive menu.'

She laughed. 'I can just imagine. I'm surprised he didn't soak up your whole afternoon.'

'He did make me sample his grandmother's semifreddo. Which was great, by the way.'

'Thank you,' Isla said. 'For all of this.'

Chase smiled. 'Hey, let's eat it before it gets cold. I'm not sure how much faith I have in those thermo bags.'

Sixty-Eight

After the gnocchi was a chicken dish she hadn't tasted before but it had come straight from Diwali. Chase had visited Geeta and Iqbal too, asking for suggestions on Isla's favourite dishes. And she had definitely liked it. The spice was more chilli than curry and the meat was cooked to perfection, the dish infused with everything she loved about Asian food – cumin, a tang of lemon and a deep, warming piquancy.

And now they were on to dessert … from Sugar High. A spin on their Christmas muffin. It was a glorious, deliberate mess of a cake filled with all kinds of crimes against dieting – a drizzle of white icing on top, syrup-coated sponge and inside a chocolate and sultana ganache. It was heavenly. As had been the conversation between them. It had flowed so effortlessly, so naturally, nothing stilted or awkward. It was the first-ever first date that had felt that way to Isla. And then there was the perfect setting. Gracefully slipping up into the dark above London, the beautiful city spread out like an eiderdown of twinkling lights. Once or twice she had looked out into the inky landscape, eyes seeking familiar landmarks, then her gaze had come back to Chase and the cosy, sparkling dining experience. She wanted to pinch herself. This was already a night she would remember forever.

'Wow,' Chase exclaimed, putting his fork to the plate. 'I am done. Finished.' He stretched his arms. 'Completely beaten.'

Isla wiped her lips with her napkin and nodded. 'Me too. My lips might want to continue the tasting because it's so good but my stomach is definitely telling me it's time to stop.'

'It was great though, right?' Chase asked, grinning.

'It was great,' she agreed.

He filled her glass with more of the wine then did the same to his.

'I have to tell you,' Chase began. 'It feels so good to do this.'

'Do what?' Isla asked. 'Eat dinner in the London Eye?'

'Wow, yes, that obviously.' He cleared his throat. 'But really I meant, being here. Just spending time with someone again.' He met her eyes. 'Spending time with you.'

'For me too,' Isla responded. Her eyes went from his to where his hand was resting on the table. Those strong, tanned hands were toying with the edge of his dessert plate and she willed them closer. Was she brave enough to make the first move?

'Isla,' he said softly. 'There's something I have to tell you.' He paused as if gathering his thoughts. 'Something I haven't been able to tell anyone before.' He took another moment. 'And I just feel, if I don't tell you, that I'm holding out and … I don't want to hold out with you.'

Suddenly she was terrified. She wasn't sure she wanted to hear it. She swallowed, trying to still her immediate reaction, which was to panic. She didn't want the shine to be taken from the night.

'And I really, really need to be honest in my life if I'm gonna be able to own my future.' He shook his head. 'I'm sorry. That sounded like the business speak you hate and I didn't want it to.'

She knew what this was. He was going to go back to his wife. They were going to reconcile. She shook her head. No, that was ridiculous. They had shared so much, were sharing this absolutely perfect night together. She tried to swallow her doubts away but she couldn't help having the feeling that whatever he was about to say was going to devastate her thoroughly.

'Okay,' Chase began. 'Here goes.'

He could do this. He could do this. He *had* to do this. He owed it to Isla and he owed it to himself. And he needed to stop being so ashamed. Hiding it away and trying to bury what was going on had only ever made things worse. Facing up. Facing off. Looking fear in the eye. O-Y-F. *Come on, Chase, man up.*

'Isla, a few years ago ... I had a breakdown,' he said. 'It was when I discovered that Colt and Leanna were still a thing.' He blew out a breath. 'Things weren't going so well after the hockey, financially too, and I lost it.' He ran a finger around the lip of his wineglass. 'I was a mess. I went to hospital for eight weeks and it took months before I felt anywhere near human again.'

His words seemed to fill the capsule, almost as if he could see them, life-size. Already, he had never been so honest and he didn't know quite how it felt. Scary. Freeing. Both of those and more, all at once.

'Chase, I—'

He interrupted, not sure that if he stopped he would be able to continue. 'But, when I started to feel better I met with a private doctor called David Stretton and he changed my life.' He felt the growing ball of confidence begin to ferment in his gut as he remembered his good friend and confidante. The man who had taught him his Own Your Future mantra. 'That's when I discovered self-improvement and knew that I could make a difference to other people who might be feeling the same way as I did.'

And he had been great at it. He had found something he enjoyed, that was personally helping him re-establish his life *and* he was aiding other people to grow themselves and their businesses.

'For a long time, when I was focused and successful, when money was no longer an issue and Leanna and I decided to give things another chance, and the girls were thriving, everything seemed brighter, almost untouchable ... I was owning my own future ...' He stopped talking, the confident feeling dropping away and being replaced by something darker.

'What happened?' Isla asked.

'Colt and Leanna happened ... again.' He shook his head. 'I don't know if they ever stopped. I mean, I must have been blind, or stupid, or both.' He sighed. 'And that was it. That was the end of my marriage right there and it threw me again, right back down to rock bottom.'

He hadn't ended up in hospital that time but those desperate feelings had again overshadowed absolutely everything else.

'I couldn't run a business teaching people how to improve themselves when it was the last thing I was capable of,' he admitted. 'So, when I was ready again, I had to use those skills in a different way. I had to diversify. That's why I took the job at Breekers.' He smiled at Isla. 'Believe it not they wanted someone recognisable from a sporting background who had gone on to run his own business. They were also keen on being seen as a company that prides itself in looking after its staff, so employing a life coach and game-changer was gonna look excellent in their press releases.'

'We never got any of those memos,' Isla admitted. 'I didn't even know Big Bill had left.'

'I'm beginning to think you and he were tight.'

She smiled. 'Unfortunately we never met and I do feel the poorer for it.'

Chase smiled and picked up his napkin, squeezing it in his hand. 'So, for all those aforementioned reasons, that's why I'm constantly focused on work and everything and anything, because if I have too much alone time to think ... it scares the crap out of me.'

There. It was all out and he felt a mixture of relief and anticipation. Whatever happened, whatever Isla thought about it, thought of him, he had done the right thing. The only thing.

'God,' he exhaled the longest breath. 'I'm sorry. That was all way too emotional and I really don't do emotion very well.'

His heart was pounding so hard and Isla had yet to react. But then he felt her fingers slide between his, her hand folding around his. He didn't know how to react. He wanted to tighten the hold and cling on but ...

'When you said you had something to tell me I thought it was going to be something else ... something much worse,' Isla stated.

'For real?' Chase asked. 'There's worse?' He blew out a breath.

'Chase, you were honest. And open. And I can only imagine how hard that was.'

'No kidding.'

'But, all you've just told me is that you're human. That you're fallible and vulnerable. Just like the rest of us.'

'I have?.'

'Were you expecting me to feel a tinge of disappointment? Maybe regret that the man I've fallen for in so short a time, so utterly unexpectedly, isn't quite as perfect as I thought?'

Fallen for. Did he dare to have heard that right? 'I don't know. I guess I just wanted you to know and however you felt about it I'd deal with it.' He took a breath. 'Everything with Leanna and Colt, it's been going on so long, even before I knew it was going on, and I didn't deal with it very well. I lost my focus ... I lost me ... and that was pretty terrifying. For everyone.'

'I can only imagine.' She squeezed his hand. 'But no one is made galvanised. Everyone has a breaking point.'

'But, you told me about how you've coped losing your parents and with Hannah's disability and I just feel like the biggest loser for not being able to just ... what is it you say? Keep calm and carry on?'

'But you did! You built a business and then you picked yourself up a second time and got the CEO position with one of the biggest construction companies in the world. *And* you've designed the idea for a vacation and habitation village.'

'Hey, don't pretend you like that now,' Chase said.

'I'm not pretending I like it, I'm just trying to tell you that dusting yourself off and getting back on the ... horse ...' She cleared her throat. 'It's sometimes even more satisfying than getting things right at the first attempt. Because you worked for it and you fought for it and you survived. You did it.' She smiled. 'And if you don't think that then you really are a ... jackass.'

'Whoa! Hold on right there! You cannot say jackass in that British accent.'

'Why not?' Isla asked. 'What should I say then?'

'I don't know ... maybe a British equivalent.'

'Nitwit?'

'There's no way that's a word.'

'How about nincompoop?' Isla offered.

'You have got to be kidding me.'

'Chase,' she said, her tone a little more serious.

'Yeah.'

'I'm enjoying the man who laughed hard at the Crown Jewels and posed with Nelson Mandela at Madame Tussauds.' She took a breath, her fingers gently caressing the skin on his hand. 'The man who kissed a frog for me.'

He swallowed. 'The guy who came here to demolish your town?'

Isla shook her head. 'I don't think the guy I've been getting to know ever really thought that was a good idea. Although his corporate side did do a pretty excellent job of telling him different.'

'Isla,' Chase breathed. 'I just don't want to let you down.'

'Stop,' she begged. 'The decision about Notting Hill isn't on you. I know that. And I think you need to realise that one person can't shoulder the world's burdens alone.' She smiled. 'That goes for life as a whole, not just the world of construction.'

He smiled then. 'I'm not quite sure I believe that sentiment coming from you, Miss Winters. Aren't you the single-handed trouble-shooter of the business? Then it's on to whipping up a Christmas party to end all Christmas parties every year without any assistance?'

She was just so beautiful and she was still here, holding his hand, not clawing at the glass exit doors looking for an escape. He wanted to hold her. He wanted to kiss her. But he didn't want to pressure her in any way. 'So, what happens now?' he asked tentatively.

She smiled. 'I think I'd like the would-be astronaut in the room to show me the stars.'

Sixty-Nine

Chase was standing behind her, *close* behind her, one arm wrapped around her waist, the other pointing into the ebony sky.

'At night there's only a few planets you can really see without a telescope,' he whispered, his breath in her ear sending pinpricks all over her body.

'You can really see planets just with the naked eye?'

'God, Isla, please do not say the word "naked" again like that. Let's focus on the planets.'

'Planets. Okay.'

'So,' he said, his tone verging on professional. 'Jupiter rules the night time but you can see Saturn too.' He paused. 'Give me a second … okay, look, right there, right there, look.'

He was shaking his finger at the glass as they moved up and over Big Ben and the Thames. His excitement was compelling. She wondered just how disappointed he must have felt knowing he would never captain a spaceship. He had made sacrifices just like she had with Hannah. Family had come first. That was the man she was enjoying having revealed to her, little by little. Then, looking out at the night, she gasped. 'I see it!' She laughed. 'I didn't think for a minute I would see it but, I do! I really do!'

'Atta girl,' Chase stated. 'By the time we disembark the SS *London Eye* you're gonna become a real astrophysicist.'

'Oh, I don't know about that,' she replied, turning her body away from the window in one quick move and facing him.

'Why not?' he asked, looking back at her.

He was so handsome, she had thought that from the moment they met, but now she felt so much more than physical attraction. It was a combination of many things over the short time he had been here. They had laughed, they had fought, they had devoured all her favourite foods, Hannah liked him … and now he had shared something so intimate with her. His fears. His vulnerability. His truth.

'Naked,' she said almost defiantly.

'Miss Winters, I think I warned you that—'

'Naked,' she repeated, moving a little bit closer into his personal space.

'Jeez, I swear, if you say that one more time I will not be responsible for my actions.'

'Nak—'

The end of the word she was more than determined to say again was lost in the force of his mouth on hers. Never had she felt more wanton, more out of control, but completely *wanting* to be out of control in this moment. This wasn't the time for thinking about tomorrows. This was a time for action, for grabbing life and love and thinking about any complications later.

She felt Chase's fingers work the fabric of her dress, slipping it from one of her shoulders as his lips traced the skin. Every subtle action just ignited more of her desire.

'Is this okay?' he whispered, his lips leaving her.

'Yes,' she answered. 'More than okay. Don't stop.'

He kissed her mouth again, moving her away from the windows, edging her downwards with him until she felt the solidity of the floor. Lying back she looked up at him, shifting in response to everything she was feeling, almost waiting for him to honour her body with his.

This meant everything to Chase. The fact he was even here in this moment ... he had never thought it was going to happen again. That he would find someone he wanted to be close to in every single way. And Isla was just coming undone right before his eyes, that beautifully British, somewhat restrained exterior was falling away like melting snow. She was opening up to him, revealing herself just like he had done with her. That mutual sharing of things they hadn't shared before was the biggest turn-on of all.

Without any more hesitation he unbuttoned his shirt, discarded it and unfastened the belt and button on his pants. Her hands met his then, circling the pads on his fingers and thumb as he drew down his zipper. Then, as he relieved himself of his pants, she began smoothing her hands over the flat of his stomach, then upwards, fingers grazing his abs as if imprinting their make-up on to her own.

Reaching out for her, Chase drew her dress down her body, not stopping until he was able to remove it entirely and she bucked then, the reveal of hot black lingerie adding to his fire.

'God, Isla, you're so beautiful,' he whispered.

'Beautiful sounds too good,' she moaned. 'I don't want to be good tonight.'

God, she was literally killing him right now.

'I want to be sexy.' She hit him with those eyes, an alluring look from under long lashes.

'You are sexy, Isla. So goddamn sexy.'

His breathing harried, he unlatched her bra, flipping it away from her body. Taking a second he just looked at her, admiring what he saw, then, unable to hold off, he dropped his head, kissing her breasts, tongue teasing, mouth exploring. She drew his head away, catching his mouth with hers before he felt her hand move lower, slipping over his hips, altering its path and arriving front and centre.

He closed his eyes and held his breath. 'Isla, if you touch me ...'

'What?' she asked, her voice low with lust. 'What's going to happen if I touch you?'

Her fingers made contact, slow, soft, a whisper of a contact that shot his nerve-endings. He couldn't deal with that for too long. It was all too much, too good. He had to distract her.

Shifting a little he wound his fingers around the hem of the lace of her panties and without any hesitation, pulled them away from her body. He actually felt her gasp.

She was going to come and he hadn't even so much as touched her. She could feel the spiralling effect beginning to happen. It was spinning around inside of her just waiting for the moment she let it take over. Well, she wasn't done yet. And she didn't want to be done without Chase.

She pulled at his hips, urging him towards her, making it plain that she was ready. This wasn't the time for foreplay and slow indulgence. This was about connecting, fast and urgent, hot and amorous.

'Isla,' he whispered, holding back.

'Don't say anything,' she begged. 'Just ... show me the stars.'

She looked up at him, seeing every kind of emotion cross his face and then all her breath left her. Picking her up he carried her to the glass and she gasped as the metal framework met her bare back. Her bottom settled on the curvature of the rail, she held on to Chase's shoulders, feeling that athletic strength and wanting it at closer quarters.

'What are you waiting for?' she whispered.

He kissed her mouth, so urgently and then she felt him. Her mouth opened in response to that sweet, deep, hot feeling and she moved against it, encouraging, urging, demanding more. It was so good, so utterly perfect it was bringing tears to her eyes. She clung to him, moving in unison with him, wanting it to last but equally craving the freefall of the culmination. And then Isla felt like she was moving out of herself. Chase's hands held her hips and her eyes found the London skyline, the beautiful winter night and those stars and planets just visible above them. She was gliding through that night, like a celestial being, falling in love for the very first time. Then, he called her name, and her heart soared even higher.

Seventy

Beaumont Square, Notting Hill

'Do you think they knew?' Isla giggled, her hand in Chase's as they walked towards her house. Getting out of the Breekers' car at Portobello Road, they had strolled through her neighbourhood, taking in all the sights and sounds and stopping to visit Edith's bench. Tonight the frog had been spouting a spray of freezing water without the need for mouth to mouth, so Chase had used his skills in the lip department a little more on her instead.

'Do I think who knew what?' he asked.

'The people, in charge, you know, of the London Eye.'

He grinned then. 'Do I think they knew we made love in capsule number fourteen?'

She blushed. Why she was blushing now she didn't know. It was a little after the fact. And she didn't really want to lose any of the girl she had just rediscovered. The girl who wanted a man to share her life as much as she wanted to involve gnocchi and macchiato in her future. But not any man, this man. Despite him living a world away ... in so many respects.

'Well,' Chase said. 'Not to take the shine off what was the most incredible sexual moment of my life ... once we were at the top we had a whole thirty minutes before we travelled down again and ... you know I haven't dated in a while.'

She doffed his arm with a punch and he laughed.

'I promise you,' he said, pulling her close. 'The next time we won't even think in minutes.' He kissed her lightly on the lips. 'We'll be talking hours … maybe even days.'

She wrapped her arms around him as he kissed her again, snowflakes starting to descend around them.

'Isla, dear, they've gone and I'm sure they've taken Purdy.'

Isla broke away from Chase at the sound of Mrs Edwards' voice. There was the little old lady dressed in Pokémon pyjamas and Wellington boots.

'Goodness, Mrs Edwards, what are you doing out here at this time of night? And it's cold,' Isla said. 'You need a coat on.'

'Hello again, handsome,' Mrs Edwards said, her attention now very much on Chase.

'Hello there,' Chase answered, flashing the old lady a smile.

'Who's gone?' Isla asked.

'Verity and John,' Mrs Edwards continued. 'Left in a removal van about nine o'clock. I know it was nine o'clock because that new crime drama on ITV had started. That very talented actress but terrible, terrible hair.'

Isla looked to Chase as if to ask what that meant. Was it good news because Notting Hill had been discarded as a viable option? Or was it just that their work here was done? Hadn't Ffion and Richard said they were getting ready to leave their locations soon too?

'And I haven't been able to find Purdy since. She always likes a bit of kipper for her tea and you know how that smells. If she was here, in the square, she would come.'

'Listen, it's late, Mrs Edwards, why don't I take you back home and we can have a look for Purdy in the daylight?'

'Hey, let me escort this beautiful lady home, won't you?' Chase asked.

'Oh! Lovely!' Mrs Edwards exclaimed.

'Are you sure?' Isla asked Chase.

'Sure. You get back to Hannah,' he said, holding her hands.

Isla swallowed. She really didn't want this night to end. She had hoped for a goodbye kiss on the doorstep but in their crazy community nothing was ever that straightforward. 'Thank you so much for a wonderful night.'

'Right back at you, Miss Winters.' He kissed her lips then moved his mouth to her ear. 'You are incredible.'

'Would you like some kipper, dear?' Mrs Edwards called.

Chase smiled at Isla. 'I really don't know what a kipper is,' he admitted.

'Don't try it,' she responded.

'I'll see you tomorrow,' he said.

'Bye,' Isla replied.

Chase turned to Mrs Edwards then, offering her his arm. 'Now, why don't you and I take a turn around the square and look for Purdy while you tell me all about that G.I. you fell for.'

'Oh, that would be lovely, dear,' Mrs Edwards replied. 'Do you sing too? I've been longing to hear a good rendition of the "Chattanooga Choo-Choo" for years.'

Seventy-One

Breekers London, Canary Wharf

'Okay, let's stop before we go inside,' Chase said, coming to a halt outside the office doors. 'Now, take a breath, a deep one.' He closed his eyes, and through his nose drew in the biting cold air and the scent of everything around him. There was definitely the hint of cinnamon bagels, hot, dark coffee and fir trees. Was he really getting sentimental about the season?

'God, this isn't gonna turn in to one of your motivational lectures, is it?' Brooke asked.

'You're listening to me,' Chase said, delighted. 'Not to Cut to the Bone Man.'

'Dad! You're saying the wrong name again!'

'I can smell chocolate,' Maddie announced.

He looked at his younger daughter, chin tilted up, eyes closed, so trusting and innocent. He always wanted her to keep at least some of that naivety.

'Well,' he said. 'I can definitely smell Christmas.'

'That's so lame,' Brooke said. 'Christmas isn't something you can smell.'

'Perhaps it's the aroma of Santa himself,' Chase suggested. 'Or his reindeer.'

Maddie laughed.

'You are both nuts,' Brooke said.

'So, have you guys thought about what you might wanna do for Christmas?' Chase asked.

'We get to choose?' Maddie said, eyes on stalks.

'No, well, yes … maybe. I mean, I'll talk to your mom but I'd love it if you could spend at least some of the vacation with me … if you'd like that too.' He didn't want to force anything on them, but he wasn't going to step completely aside and give Leanna all of the important times without a discussion about it. There had to be a work around, despite the distance. They were his kids too, and he missed them. And he was feeling stronger, so much stronger, enough to know he didn't want to let himself be brushed aside.

'Yes, Daddy!' Maddie said excitedly. 'Can we go eat in Roxy's Diner on New Year? And go ice-skating in Central Park too and, if I get a hover board, can we take *that* to the park?'

'You don't want everything then,' Brooke teased.

'Brooke?' Chase asked, nudging his daughter's elbow. 'Wanna spend some time in New York over vacation?'

'Do I get to see my friends?'

'I can't see a problem with that.'

'Can they stay over and eat pizza and pretzels?'

'We'll discuss it.'

Brooke shrugged. 'Then sure.'

'Cool,' Chase answered. 'I'll call your mom and we'll fix something up.'

From inside his jacket pocket his cell phone began to ring and he reached to pull it out. *Breekers Int. Dan Germano.*

He swallowed. This wasn't an email in response to his proposal yesterday. It was a phone call. And in New York right now it was 4 a.m. He wasn't sure how to read that.

'Hey, Dan, good morning,' he answered.

'Han, I don't know why we're doing this,' Isla said, speed walking along the snow-covered pavement, Breekers just in sight ahead.

'Because you're giving me a little more freedom, because Lesley from the centre lives right around the corner from here and she's going to take me to the party in her car and ...' Hannah took a breath. 'You haven't told me nearly enough about your date with Chase yet.'

No, she hadn't, because, as seemed to be the norm in their lives, they hadn't *had* a moment. Another early morning wake-up call from Raj had resulted in Purdy, mewing with discomfort, fur dishevelled, bright tinsel wrapped tight around her tail, being laid out on the coffee table to have a decoration cutting almost akin to a veterinary procedure. Then it was a reuniting with Mrs Edwards, a quick shower and change for work, helping Hannah and then out the door.

'You were in bed when I got in,' Isla said. 'And I almost woke you up to shout at you for even attempting to make it from downstairs to upstairs and into bed on your own without anyone in the house!'

'Blah blah blah. Change the download,' Hannah said, waving her away and pumping Ronnie's wheels with one hand. 'I take it there were no spares or strikes involved with the date.'

Not in the bowling context. She couldn't stop the heat reaching her cheeks despite the chill from the wind this morning. 'We went to the London Eye,' Isla informed. 'For dinner.'

'Oh my God,' Hannah stated. 'A private capsule.' She stopped wheeling and put both hands to her mouth, skidding to a halt just before tyres met the road.

'Han, be careful,' Isla said, grabbing the wheelchair.

'Oh my God!' Hannah said again. 'You did it, didn't you?!' Her voice seemed to suddenly get really loud. 'You did it on the London Eye!'

'Hannah, please, people are listening and I work just over there.'

'Isla! You are a legend! I mean, forget the Mile High Club, you've had sex at four hundred and forty three feet in the middle of London, on a freaking wheel encased in glass, looking out over the Thames … under the stars …' Hannah let out a heavy sigh. 'It makes my wish for a Christmas kiss in Notting Hill pale into insignificance.'

'Don't be silly,' Isla replied. She couldn't say anything else. The words her sister had used to describe last night had brought all the tantalising memories flooding back.

'So, is he as hot without his clothes on as the fine cut of that suit would lead us to believe?' Hannah asked with a grin. 'Or did you keep your clothes on? Although if you couldn't bowl in your dress I'm not sure how you would manage to—'

'I need to get to work,' Isla reminded her, beginning to walk again.

'So what happens now?' Hannah asked. 'Are you "in a relationship"? Or is it "it's complicated"?'

'I'm … not sure.' They hadn't talked about it. It hadn't seemed necessary. But today was a new day and they were working together. Professionalism had to be maintained, she really needed to get to grips with this Christmas party, and there was nothing they could do about Notting Hill until they heard from New York. But what did she want going forward? A relationship? Was it even possible?

'Well, right now, I like him,' Hannah admitted with a sniff. 'But, believe me, he treats you in any way less than a princess I can turn … and I can turn quickly.'

Isla smiled at her sister. 'I know.'

'So, I'm the only lonely singleton around here again ... apart from Mrs Edwards and at least she has a slightly crumpled cat for company.'

'No more dates planned with Raj yet?'

'I think it's his turn to ask me,' Hannah said defiantly.

'So, what time does your party at the centre start today?'

'Twelve thirty. But we're decorating the place this morning.' Hannah sighed. 'I say "decorating"; there's only so much you can do with paper chains, two wise men and a rubber turkey.'

From inside her handbag Isla's phone began to ring. 'Sorry, Han, give me a second.' She pulled it out and looked at the display. It was the Warlock Centre, the lovely renovated chapel she had booked for the Breekers' Christmas party.

'Hello,' Isla answered the phone, smiling at Hannah. 'Yes, this is Isla Winters. Yes, that's right.' The very next words made the smile fall from her face. She wanted to drop to the frosty ground. 'Oh, I ... don't know what to say ... that's terrible ... I'm so sorry but of course I understand ...' She wanted to cry, in fact, she could feel the tears building. 'Thank you for letting me know. Goodbye.' She ended the call, dropping the phone into her bag and putting a hand to the back of her hair, pulling at a section in frustration.

'Who was that?' Hannah asked. 'It sounded a bit dramatic.'

Isla nodded. 'You could say that.' She took a deep breath. 'That was the venue for the Breekers' Christmas party. A water pipe's burst and it's completely flooded. They've had to cancel our booking.'

Seventy-Two

'Aaron, I need your help,' Isla stated. Adrenalin pumping furiously, she had run up the stairs to their floor determined to take action.

'Undressing Chase Bryan? Telling Ethel not to make any more of these bloody pompoms that seem to get lower and lower as advent progresses?' He lifted himself up from his chair and headed one of them like a pro-footballer. 'Or is it ... the super-hotel?' He grinned then, almost manically. 'You need ideas for glitz and glamour, don't you?'

'What I need,' Isla said, 'is for you to think.'

'This early?' Aaron asked, checking his watch. 'Darling, I can't work miracles.'

'It's not funny, Aaron.' She was not going to panic. She was panicking! Argh! 'I need you to think of any venue you know that can hold three hundred people that's available on the evening of eighteenth December.'

'Eighteenth December?' he queried. 'But isn't that the date of the Breekers' Christmas party?'

She nodded as calmly as she could manage. Inside it felt like she was being feasted on by cockroaches, tiny little mouths chewing away at her resolve.

Aaron slapped his face with both hands. 'Oh Sugar. Honey. Ice Tea. You've lost the venue somehow, haven't you?'

'Let's not focus on the negative,' Isla said, taking her iPad from her bag. 'Let's focus on finding an alternative.'

'But the caterer ...' Aaron exclaimed, eyes aghast. 'You've lost the caterer too. You did get my message, didn't you?'

'I did,' Isla replied.

'Then, what are we going to do? No food! No venue! This is an *actual* disaster!'

Isla smiled, flipping her hair and trying to dislodge the parasites intent on gnawing out her insides. 'I still have a vocal trio and a band – unless the drummer has a present-wrapping accident or the vocalists wear themselves out carol-singing.'

'How can you be so calm about this?' Aaron was out of his chair flapping his arms now, head bumping into scores of pompoms, setting them off like a woollen Newton's Cradle. 'First Notting Hill and then the Christmas party? What's next? Is the Queen going to team up with Gary Barlow and produce a Christmas album?' He stopped himself. 'Actually, that's not a disaster, that might do quite well—'

'Aaron,' Isla broke in. 'Focus. Help me find an alternative venue and some catering. Please.'

'Yes,' Aaron agreed. 'Yes, I can do that.' He smiled then, the lightbulb flashing on in his head almost visible. 'Does this mean I get to cancel my next Skype call with Hilda?'

'No,' Isla replied. 'Absolutely not.

She took a breath, then her eyes went to the doors of the lift as they opened and Chase, Brooke and Maddie appeared. She hadn't seen him since he had waltzed Mrs Edwards around Beaumont Square. She had watched from her bedroom window, the two of them dancing and laughing in the dark, under the lights of the Christmas tree, until Chase had escorted the elderly lady back home again. There was so much more to him than met the eye and she was so glad she was getting to discover that.

She smiled and waved a hand and the three of them made a beeline for her desk.

'So,' Aaron said, moving into Isla's circle. 'Back in the saddle yet?'

Quick as a flash she turned to her friend and smiled. 'Absolutely,' she replied. 'And completely no need for a farrier. Who would have believed it?' She took a step towards Chase and his girls. 'Good morning.'

Isla looked so good. Her red hair was a little wild from the weather, she was wearing a knee-length skirt and a sheer blouse you could almost – but not quite – see through. If his children weren't right here, if he wasn't in the centre of this office, he would want to take her into the boardroom and re-enact their time on the iCircle. But, for those reasons, and the whole ranch of feeling that was weighing down on his shoulders right now, he didn't know what to do.

'How do you do, Isla,' Maddie greeted, putting out a hand and sounding her consonants.

'Beautiful British diction,' Isla replied. 'How do you do.' She shook Maddie's hand then looked to Brooke. 'How do you do, Brooke?'

''Sup,' Brooke answered.

'Good morning, everyone,' Aaron chipped in. 'Take a pompom if you like.' He jazz-handed the air. 'Better than a Christmas tree ... no annoying pine needles just a few strands of glitter to Dyson up.'

'Please ignore Aaron,' Isla said. 'He's not had enough coffee this morning.'

'Hey,' Chase said. 'Can we talk?'

'Of course,' Isla said. 'The boardroom?'

'Sure.' He turned to his daughters. 'Can you hang here, just for a half hour or so?'

'Aaron, can you introduce the girls to whatever games you play when you're supposed to be working?' Isla suggested. 'Not the poker ones.'

'Ha ha, very amusing.' He looked to Brooke and Maddie and winked. 'I only ever play Blackjack.'

Chase led the way, taking a deep breath, unable to look Isla in the eye. He pushed open the boardroom door and moved to the part of the room with obscured glass, so they wouldn't be looked over like goldfish in a bowl.

He turned around, watching her as she closed the door behind them, all fresh-faced and seemingly as full of joy as he had been after their date together.

'Come over here,' he beckoned.

'Over there?' she asked quizzically. 'Right over there?'

'Right over here,' he said.

She stepped forward, her stride a little unsettled, until she was directly opposite him, a mere six inches or so apart. He took her in his arms, wrapping her up tight, pulling her close, his head next to hers. But it wasn't a display of passion, it was a desire to hold her, to comfort her when he said the next words.

He almost couldn't say it, but he had to. 'They won't go back on Notting Hill, and it's final.'

He held on tight and waited to feel her body react like he knew it would. And it did. Within a second she was poker-straight as if she had been struck by lightning, then she was trembling as the news hit home.

Finally, she spoke. One word: 'No.'

'I know,' Chase said. 'I know it isn't at all what we wanted to hear. I can hardly believe it but—'

'No,' Isla said again. 'They can't.'

'This decision is out of my hands, Isla. I was outside on the street just now for thirty minutes trying to reason with someone who was up all night with the board going through the plans and making it final.' He still gripped on to her. 'They've left me completely out of the loop on so many things because I'm not a player to them. I'm just the figurehead they hired to make them look better. I thought I may have some sway, as after all they took on my hotel concept as the future of Breekers, but I guess that's as far as it goes.'

'Chase, we can't let them do this. It just doesn't make sense.'

'You know they wanted to make a splash.'

'I know but Notting Hill, it's iconic. They can't tear it down. I really don't think they're going to get permission.' He could hear the tears in her voice. 'All those houses, all those people and the history.'

'You know money talks. My bet is they will pledge to make investment in a poorer area as compensation, something to settle the conscience of those who aren't immediately on board.'

'Let me go,' Isla begged, shifting in his arms now, fear, hurt and pain all emanating from her.

'No,' he replied.

'Chase, let me go,' she ordered.

'I can't do that,' he said. 'Not yet.'

A sob left her then and he held on, feeling her drop her head to his shoulder as some of the immediate tension finally left her body.

'So that's it,' she sobbed. 'That's really it?'

'No,' he answered. 'That isn't it.'

'But you said—'

'They may have made their final decision but while we're still working the project nothing is set in stone, or concrete. Not for me.'

He loosened his hold, waiting for what he hoped was coming. He wasn't trying to give her false hope. He just wanted her to know that while he was still here in London he intended to work on finding something to delay the inevitable, maybe long enough for him to come up with some kind of work-around. It was his livelihood, the children's too, and he would be a fool to think of sabotage, but if there was a compromise, something that didn't end up costing her the part of London she adored, then he was going to give it his all.

Isla raised her head, slowly but surely, and he saw that spark of interest back in her eyes. 'What can we do?'

He smiled at her, lightly kissing her lips. 'I have a plan.'

Seventy-Three

Life Start Community Centre

Today, even though the temperatures had barely got above minus figures, there were three shabbily dressed men outside Hannah's centre. Sitting on the ground, legs outstretched like it was summer, backs against the wall, taking it in turns to sip from a bottle of vodka.

Isla checked her watch then looked to the door as it began to swing open. And there was Hannah, being helped by Lesley, wheeling through the door, her face painted completely white with silver and gold glitter on her cheeks. Was she really going to be able to tell her about Breekers' plans for Notting Hill after a Christmas party, when her face was wearing artwork? She swallowed. She had to. The sooner it was all out in the open the sooner they could start thinking about how to stop it.

'What are you doing here?' Hannah greeted roughly, her smile dropping as Lesley let go of the wheelchair and, waving a hand at Isla, the woman left.

'Well, that's a nice welcome I have to say.'

'Did you think I wouldn't get home? I thought we agreed I needed a little more space.'

Isla hadn't agreed, she had just known that fighting it now Hannah was twenty was too difficult, and she did need to embrace independence.

'I love the face paint,' Isla deflected.

Hannah grimaced. 'We had to put on a stupid nativity for the children from Pembridge Middle. I was the Angel Gabriel but the bloody net curtain I had to use as my angel clothes kept getting caught in Ronnie's wheels.'

'Oh dear,' Isla said, stifling a laugh.

'It's not funny! Anyway, why are you here? I was going to wheel past the sorting office and see if Raj was there.'

'Well, he isn't there,' Isla said.

'What?'

'He's meeting us at home,' Isla said. 'With Mrs Edwards and Aaron … Chase and Maddie and Brooke.'

She swallowed, watching confusion cover her sister's face.

'Are we having a party?' Hannah queried.

Isla shook her head. 'No. But we will definitely need some drinks and snacks. We can pick them up on our way.'

'Isla, what's going on?' Hannah asked again.

Yes, she just needed to spit it out. Tell her she had lied about the plans. That Breekers wanted to break up Notting Hill. But there was still hope. She had already considered trying to blackmail Rod Striker to turn down the planning consent, no matter what carrot Breekers dangled in front of him. She was sure there must be someone from the golf club who had something on him. She didn't do underhand ordinarily but the stakes were so high now and there was so much she wanted to protect.

'Isla,' Hannah snapped. The angel paint wasn't looking quite so angelic now her sister's expression was pure devil.

'The plans of Notting Hill you took from Verity and John's house,' Isla began. 'They were real.' She swallowed, trying to press on quickly. 'Breekers wants to build a super-hotel, well, a large village with circuses and zoos and a megabowl, and they want to build it over Notting Hill.'

Isla hadn't thought, given the nativity make-up, that Hannah could look any paler, but she seemed to blanch and somehow shrink. She needed to keep talking, focus on those positives.

'But you don't need to worry,' Isla stated, reaching out to touch Hannah's arm. 'Because it's not going to happen. We're going to make sure it doesn't. That's why we're getting together to brainstorm … to think, all of us together, of all the reasons why this can't happen and how we can stop it.'

Hannah didn't say anything. She was just looking tiny and vulnerable and not twenty but twelve, or fifteen, like she had been straight after the accident when her world was crumbling.

'Hannah,' Isla said. 'It's going to be all right.'

Now there was a reaction, as a tear snaked down her sister's cheek and, as well as looking deflated, she also looked beaten.

'Hannah, we are going to do everything we can to fight this. I promise.'

'Oh, you promise do you?' Hannah growled. 'Just like you promised the plans weren't real in the first place?'

Isla had known that was coming and it was well deserved. She shouldn't have lied but it had only been about protecting Hannah, until now, when the ultimate decision had been made and all she could do now was react to it.

'I know I did,' Isla said. 'And perhaps I shouldn't have. But I was angry with Chase when I found out about it and I had to get through that before I could prioritise trying to change it. And that's what we're planning to do. Because nothing is hopeless. Both of us believe that, don't we?'

Hannah shook Isla's hand off. 'I believed I had a sister who didn't lie to me.'

'I'm sorry, Han, I'm really sorry, I just didn't want you to worry or get upset.'

'What? Because I'm a pathetic baby? A pathetic baby in a wheelchair?'

'Don't be silly.'

'There we go! Straightaway, "don't be silly", like I'm not going to be anything else!'

Isla stood back for a moment, her attention going to the drunks who were now starting to sing a rendition of 'Fairytale of New York' and laughing hysterically at the line about the drunk tank. Hannah needed to express her anger and frustration, whether Isla liked it or not.

'So, you knew Verity and John then! It was all a pretence inviting them for lasagne?'

'No.' Isla shook her head. 'I didn't know them. They were brought on board for this project by Breekers International.'

'And Chase is over here to tear down our home.'

'Yes,' Isla replied. 'But also no, not now.'

'Well, that sounds confident,' Hannah continued. 'Has he changed his mind about it now he's got in your knickers?' She took a breath then blasted, 'I'd be careful about that if I was you. Who knows what he could really be doing. I hope you didn't give him any information ... like the square meterage of Sugar High ... or our house!'

And then Hannah burst into a torrent of tears, folding into herself, hugging her useless knees and putting her hands over her face as she sobbed.

Isla went to her then, bending over her, rubbing her back and trying her very best to console her sister. She had had this news for a while. It was all new to Hannah and it was going to come as a massive shock. But she really did need her sister to be the raging force of nature that she was.

'Hannah, I promise you, faithfully and sincerely, that we are going to do everything we can to stop this happening.' She stroked Hannah's short crop of hair. 'Chase is breaching all sorts of protocol letting anyone outside of Breekers know about the super-hotel, but he wants to find another site for it just as much as I do.'

Hannah slowly raised herself up until she was able to look Isla in the eye. Her make-up was streaked all across her face and her lips were still trembling.

'You think we have a chance of fighting an international company on this?' Hannah asked. 'The company *you* work for.'

'I know it's going to be tough, but they are business people. We just have to find a way to make another site much more appealing, or we have to make Notting Hill much more unappealing.'

'And how are we going to do that?' Hannah asked with a sniff.

'I don't know yet,' Isla admitted. 'But I do know I'm going to need your help.' She smiled. 'You're the ideas girl. I've always just been the implementer.'

'That is true,' Hannah admitted, softening a little.

'So, concentrate, let's save our corner of London,' Isla said, clapping her gloved hands together.

'Not yet,' Hannah said, turning her wheelchair around to face the centre door. 'There's no way I can see Raj looking like Harley Quinn's eviler twin.'

Seventy-Four

Beaumont Square, Notting Hill

Isla and Hannah's living room was as festive as it could get – the decorated white feather Christmas tree, the numerous greetings cards Sellotaped on walls and mantelpiece, the fir cone and holly displays just like Hannah made in the florists – but the people sitting in it, poring over the giant plan Chase had pinned over the bay window, looked like funeral guests. Only Maddie seemed happy, playing on the floor with Hannah's old Barbie dolls that Isla had claimed from the chest of old things in her sister's room.

'I don't get it though,' Raj said, sipping at the cup of peppermint tea Isla had made him. 'How they gonna fit all these things 'round Portobello Road, man?'

'Raj, that's the whole point!' Hannah exclaimed. 'There won't be a Portobello Road. There won't be a Beaumont Square either, or a Larkspur Gardens. This thing would be just built right on top of it.' At the end of her sentence was a sign of hyperventilation and Isla passed her a glass of water.

'I do like a zoo,' Mrs Edwards remarked. She stroked Purdy who was nestled into her lap looking more comfortable than she had that morning.

'Me too,' Maddie piped up. 'Brooke likes them as well. One time she had a face-off with a real grumpy camel.' She nudged her sister's foot.

'Hey! Get off!' Brooke exclaimed.

'Guess who won?' Maddie answered, grinning.

'We all like the concept of the zoo,' Chase broke in. 'But I'm now of the mind that it needs to be somewhere else.' Isla studied him. He was standing by the plan, brow furrowed and despite the cold and heating-on-a-budget control he was perspiring a little.

'Haringey, I told you,' Aaron announced. 'Big parcel of land there was bought by someone called … Solloway Limited and they've gone bankrupt. It's ripe for development. They were going to build houses on it I believe, so consent has been given for that. Perhaps it's worth a discussion about adapting that idea, maybe building some of those needed houses in exchange for the hotel going right next door.'

'Enfield was good too,' Chase replied. 'It was good, right?' He looked to Isla.

'Yes,' she agreed. 'Enfield was a great alternative. But that's what you pitched to the board already.' She swallowed. 'And they didn't go for it.'

They seemed to just be going round in circles and it was as frustrating as it was terrifying.

'I had a beau from Enfield,' Mrs Edwards told them. 'He used to take me up the Pally.'

Aaron coughed.

'Where?' Maddie inquired.

'The Palladium, dear. All the great variety acts performed there. Such class. I used to dress up in my Sunday clothes and when the show was over we would go dancing.'

'What if we did something about the fire routes?' Chase spoke suddenly.

'What?' Isla asked. 'You told me that had been thoroughly considered.'

'It has ... I just mean ... maybe we could suggest to the planning department that it hadn't.'

Chase swallowed as he looked to Isla. Right now he was all out of ideas. He had told her he had a plan but this was it, asking for help, brainstorming, trying to think of anything that would work to hold this project off. He needed more than that. He needed to give her security, hope, assurance. But could he really cripple an idea he himself had brought to the table?

'Chase,' Isla said. 'We can't scupper this plan completely. It's your plan. It might be off the wall and not to my taste but if it makes business sense ... if Breekers want to run hotels ...'

'Yeah,' he breathed, hands going to his head. 'Yeah, you're right.'

'You need a dead body.'

Everyone in the room looked to Brooke then; even Purdy seemed to suddenly take a keen interest, her furry face perking up.

'What did you say?' Chase asked.

'I said you need a dead body,' Brooke repeated. 'You find a body hidden in one of the areas they're planning to build on and they're gonna change their minds pretty quick about digging up a whole serial killer's collection of skin and bone.'

'God, she's right!' Aaron exclaimed. 'Where can we get one from?'

'Well, I know someone who—' Raj began.

Hannah reached out and thumped his chest, shaking her head.

'I had a friend who worked in the mortuary,' Mrs Edwards stated. 'Lovely girl but she did look quite grey after a while. I think that misery rubbed off on her.'

'This is insanity,' Chase remarked. 'You know that right?'

'So is sabotaging the planned-for fire exits,' Isla replied.

'Come on,' he responded. 'That was a better idea than burying a body.' He shook his head. 'And I'm starting to wonder about what my teenage daughter is watching on TV.' He still needed to take Colt to task about the NC-17 movie.

Mrs Edwards suddenly let out a sob. 'And to think, at the beginning, I thought we were going to get a visit from *Time Team*.'

Chase watched Isla leap to her feet, like someone had just given her a caffeine shot. Hands to her mouth she exclaimed, almost a whoop, eyes bright, looking at everyone then looking at him.

'Chase,' she said. 'That's it!'

He was none the wiser but he just wanted to carry on seeing her lit up like this, twinkling like the Christmas tree in Trafalgar Square.

'What's it though?' Raj asked.

'I know,' Hannah said, wheeling herself towards her sister. 'I know exactly what she means.'

'Well, please, enlighten us because I was all ready to head down the cemetery,' Aaron said, biting at his nails.

'Old things,' Isla said.

'Ancient relics,' Hannah added.

'Still not getting it,' Aaron replied. 'Are we going to suggest a Notting Hill episode of *Antiques Roadshow*?'

'We might not be able to get an ancient Roman body but I think we can get the next best thing,' Isla said, grinning.

'Mrs E,' Hannah began, addressing the old lady. 'How many old coins and artefacts have you got left from Mr E's collection?'

'Oh,' Mrs Edwards began. 'I've got lots of the rubbish, tonnes of it, in the cupboard under the stairs. It's mainly Roman coins although there is some earthenware and a few axes and anvils. He used to work for a museum, you see, but it closed down, no one came and the things they couldn't relocate were just left.'

Chase couldn't believe this. He was absolutely dumbstruck. This was something tangible to hold on to. A real, bona fide reason for development not to happen. The British loved their history and a find like that, *several* finds would make the press here and over the pond. If they could make it work. If experts were convinced enough.

'That is genius!' Aaron exclaimed. 'Most developers run a mile in the other direction as soon as the words *medieval* or *neolithic* are mentioned.'

'Breekers won't want the delay while an archaeological dig is undertaken. Time is money, right?' Chase stated.

'This is it, isn't it?' Hannah said, excitedly. 'This is how we are all going to come together and save Notting Hill.'

'I think it is,' Isla said, looking to Chase. Did she want his confirmation?

He nodded, a smile crossing his face before he turned to Mrs Edwards. 'So, Mrs Edwards, can we go see what your husband left us as his legacy?'

Scooping Purdy up, Mrs Edwards got to her feet. 'Anything for you, young man, you know that.'

Seventy-Five

There were two chipped earthenware pots, three broken pieces of what looked like an ancient jug, two bits of wood that could pass for olden-day spoons, a rustic makeshift axe and a whole bag full of terribly old-looking coins. Some of them were almost paper thin, but there was a head of a man and an uneven band of trim, a couple even said the word 'Caesar'. They were the real deal and Isla was sure, if Mr Edwards was looking down upon them, he wouldn't mind his precious treasure being used to save his wife's home and the area in which they had spent their entire lives together.

Isla took a breath as she observed the items on her dining table, hoping with all her heart that this plan was going to come off.

And then she felt a reassuring pair of arms go around her waist and she relaxed a little, settling into Chase's body.

'God, I've been wanting to hold you all night,' he whispered.

'Where are the children?' she asked as his fingers toyed with her hair.

'Trying to beat the ass off of Raj at *MarioKart* in the garden. He's got some hand-held Nintendo they're all wowing over,' Chase informed.

'They're not too cold out there?' Isla asked.

'Hey, they're fine,' he said, turning her around to face him. 'And I'm here, not feeling cold at all.' He kissed her lips and she felt herself slip into that twenty-five-year-old-with-no-responsibilities Isla. 'In fact,' he continued. 'I think I'm getting a fever.'

She blushed as his lips trailed a path to her shoulder then they returned to her mouth for one more, long, lingering kiss. She smiled at him then plucked one of the coins from the table.

'It feels almost ironic that the British history you disparaged so readily when you first arrived here might just help us save Notting Hill.'

He shook his head, a wry grin forming. 'I knew that would come back to bite me,' he admitted. 'But right now I am so cool with that.'

'Do you think it's going to work?' Isla asked him. 'I mean, really. Or are we going to get caught out, then fired and make things utterly worse?'

'I can't answer that,' Chase replied. 'But I do know we're all gonna give it our best shot.'

'Tomorrow night,' Isla said.

'Tomorrow night,' he agreed. 'Dressed in the black hoodies Raj is getting.'

Isla smiled. 'It's best not to ask where they're coming from. He's a good person but I think he has friends who run with the wrong crowd.'

'Hey,' Chase replied. 'I have a brother just like that.' She watched his eyes cloud over for just a second and then the look was gone again.

'So, Holland Park,' Isla said. 'You're sure that's the best place?'

'It's right on the edge of the boundary of the map and Raj said they're in the middle of constructing a new monument so they're doing groundwork already. We can't just dig up a patch of grass and throw this stuff in there. It has to look real.'

Isla nodded. 'Yes. It does.'

Almost all her worries seemed to be subsiding. Apart from the Breekers' Christmas Party. Aaron had had no luck finding alternative catering arrangements or a venue. But now the weight of the super-hotel was relenting a little she was going to put her all back into it tomorrow.

'What's on your mind?' Chase asked, reaching for her hand.

'Nothing,' she answered.

'Come on, Isla, I can read you,' Chase said.

She shook her head. 'Poppycock.'

'Poppy what now?'

'You know I don't believe in all this telepathy nonsense.'

'Hey, it made me a living and it's not telepathy. It's knowing people's "tell".'

Isla smirked. 'I don't have a tell.'

'You do,' Chase answered.

'Really, I don't.' She was the one who had googled it in order to read him. She tried to solidify her face.

'Really, you totally do.'

She swallowed, immediately thinking of the horror of the mess of the organisation of the Christmas party and trying desperately not to let that seep into her expression.

'You're worried about something,' Chase continued. 'Something other than planting ancient artefacts in Holland Park.'

Now he was just annoying. But perhaps she should share her woes. She had never had anyone to share anything with like this. As close as she was to Hannah, she had always shielded her from anything too contentious. And it was her baby, this party, the given-success, the ultimate annual zenith.

'It's the Christmas party.' Her voice was barely a whisper.

'Ah,' Chase said, smoothing his hands down her arms. 'This amazing festive fiesta people can't stop talking about.' He smiled. 'Three women were discussing nail polish in the office kitchen yesterday as if the wrong shade could destroy their whole night.'

She closed her eyes and let out a shaky breath.

'Isla, tell me,' he urged. 'Whatever it is can't be unfixable.' He locked eyes with her, those warm, hazel coloured eyes. 'We're about to outplay the international company we work for, remember?'

'I have no venue,' she stated calmly, almost as if it was someone else talking. 'There was a flood, a burst pipe, and they had to cancel.'

'O ... kay ...' Chase said. 'We'll find somewhere else.'

She ignored him and continued, 'I have no caterer. By all accounts they've gone bust and run off with the deposit.'

'I see,' Chase answered.

'So, no venue, no food or drink ... and I have a band and a vast array of decorations coming and I don't know where they're coming to, or if I even need them at all, and it's just days away, days.' Now she was starting to lose control. Now she was finally giving in to the fear that had taken it in turns with the Notting Hill issue to permeate her nightmares.

'Hey, stop,' he ordered, tightening his hold on her arms. His strength seemed to still her for just a moment. 'Take a breath.'

She shook her head. 'The "taking a breath" trick doesn't work for me.'

'It works for everyone,' he reassured.

'I can't fail at this,' Isla admitted. 'I might not win every contract or solve every problem completely to my satisfaction and that's okay, but the Christmas party … it's faultless. It's always faultless and the staff here who have worked so hard all year round, they deserve faultless.'

Chase nodded. 'I agree. So what's the problem?'

'Chase, I don't know anything about New York during the run-up to Christmas but venues have to be booked months in advance, years sometimes, so there isn't going to be anywhere big enough to hold all the guests that's available.' She let out an anxious sigh. 'And the same goes for the catering. Everyone is booked solid.'

'Everyone?'

'Everyone I've had a chance to contact. I started with everyone I used before, then went through Yell.com.'

'Okay,' Chase said. 'So, it's gonna be a challenge.'

'It's going to be a disaster!'

'How can you say that?' Chase asked her. 'You're my Go-To Girl,' he reminded her. 'The London office's trouble-shooter. You get things done, Miss Winters. That's who you are.'

It was a pep talk. She knew that. It was close to being something a business coach might say … but it was true. She was always calm in the face of adversity. But it was just so personal. Notting Hill *and* the party. It seemed to be a direct hit on the things she held dearest, all at once.

'Do you want my help?' Chase asked her.

Did she? The answer she wanted to give was no. This was *hers*. She didn't let anyone in on the theme, she didn't let anyone help. And it was her success to revel in afterwards. But the real answer had to be yes, didn't it? Because if she didn't have some sort of assistance then this party wasn't going to happen at all. The fact that the CEO of Breekers International was offering the aid still seemed bizarre, coupled with the fact she had seen him naked …

'Yes,' she whispered finally. 'But you can't know the theme.'

'I'm sorry. I didn't quite catch that.'

'Please don't make me say it again,' she begged.

He leant forward and kissed her. 'I'll get you a venue,' he promised.

Seventy-Six

The Royale, Hyde Park

Chase concentrated on the MacBook on the breakfast table in front of him. He was reading through an email from James, a board member, about their plans going forward for the super-village. There were a list of things they wanted him to kick-start in the time he had left in the UK. He had no intention of doing any of them, but he had to think up some sort of reply because going a whole day without a response was going to look suspect and that was the last thing he wanted before tonight's burial. What had happened with his life that he was even thinking the word 'burial'?

'Can I get a Nintendo Switch?' Brooke was pulling apart a croissant and stuffing large pieces of it into her mouth.

'I have no idea what that is,' Chase replied, eyes fixed on the screen.

'It's what Raj had last night,' Maddie added. 'We played MarioKart8 and I got a blister on my thumb.'

'And that's a reason for me to buy it? To help you get skin issues?'

'It's F-U-N,' Brooke said. 'You know, that thing we used to have when I was about eight.'

Chase looked away from his laptop. 'Well, Christmas is coming.'

'Ugh!' Brooke exclaimed. 'People say that when you have no chance of getting what you want but they want you to shut the hell up.'

'That isn't true,' Chase answered.

'Mom said "Christmas is coming" last year when I asked for a puppy,' Maddie chimed in.

'I think she knew by then we'd have to get rid of the cat so a dog had no chance,' Brooke bit.

Chase folded his arms across his chest and looked at his daughter. 'So, how much do you want this Nintendo Switch?'

He watched her lean forward, the croissant dropping to her plate. She was definitely interested.

'I can smell bribery and corruption,' Brooke stated. 'You do know that isn't something you should involve your children in?'

'Oh, like NC-17 movies?' Chase queried.

Brooke's front seemed to diminish quite substantially then. He continued, 'Okay, so, when we get into the office I need you to do something for me.'

'Hold someone hostage?' Brooke asked, almost excitedly.

He frowned. 'Last night it was "let's find a body" and today you're talking about hostage-taking?'

'Steal something?' Brooke suggested.

'No! Nothing like that.' Well, it was a little bit criminal but for a good cause.

'Is it something to do with those Roman coins, Daddy?' Maddie asked.

'Shh!' Chase said, putting his finger to his lips and giving the hotel restaurant a surreptitious glance. The less they mentioned anything about those rarities in public the better.

'Sorry, Daddy,' Maddie replied, looking a little sad.

'It's okay, Pumpkin,' he whispered. 'We just have to keep that on the down-low right now.'

'Boost a car?' Brooke continued.

'Whoa!' Chase exclaimed. 'Stop. Enough.'

'Well, what *do* you want me to do?' Brooke inquired, still sounding eager.

'I just …' Was this right? And to get his daughter to do it? Aaron had already had no luck. He'd got a text an hour ago.

'Jeez, Dad,' Brooke said. 'Tell me!'

'Can you hack into people's laptops?' he blurted out. 'I'm not sure I really want to know the answer to that but I really need to get into someone's laptop – for good reasons, not bad – but I have no idea where to start.'

Brooke yawned, then stretched out her arms, hands laced together, cracking her knuckles. 'So, if I do this, I'll be saying a sweet hello to a Nintendo Switch for Christmas, right?'

Chase took a breath and gave a slight nod. 'I will do my very best to pass that memo on to the man in red.'

'Okay then,' Brooke said, getting to her boot-clad feet. 'We need to get into the office because I have work to do.'

Seventy-Seven

Breekers London, Canary Wharf

Isla rubbed at her eyes as she sat at her desk. Earlier, at home, she had composed a text to Poppy saying if she didn't turn up to walk Hannah to work she was going to come round her house and break her box set of *Game of Thrones*. Then she thought better of sending it and instead thanked her for helping Hannah but, going forward, Hannah would be getting herself to work. It had hurt to press send. She still wasn't completely confident in letting go when it came to her sister, but she needed to have faith and she had promised Hannah more freedom in exchange for being super-vigilant at the horrible four-way crossing and messaging her as soon as she got to Portobello Flowers. And she had. It had been very tongue-in-cheek, she hoped. *Hannah Winters marks herself safe in the ongoing Wheeling To Work Situation.*

It had been an hour since Isla arrived at work and she had been emailing and calling potential caterers in the hope someone, *anyone*, was going to be able to provide *anything*. Gone were the days back in October when she was perusing menus almost tasting the sweet salmon and chive parcels and grazing on online photos of large spreads of olive-topped water biscuits with cool Saint Agur. Now she would be happy if a hot dog van could make it. She'd fit it into the theme ... somehow.

'You have to help!' Aaron was panting like a dog who'd been trapped in a car in a heatwave. His head dislodged a pompom and it fell to Isla's desk.

'What's the matter?' Isla asked.

'It's Hilda. She's going to kill me!' Aaron exclaimed. He let out a blood-curdling screech then clutched at his throat, turning himself backwards and almost lying across Isla's desk.

'She isn't here, is she?' Isla asked.

'She's always here,' Aaron answered, getting himself back up. 'Can't you feel her? And smell her? There's essence of lily of the valley everywhere.'

'Aaron, what do you want me to do?' Isla asked.

'Can you take her Skype call this morning?' He started blinking his eyelashes like he was auditioning for a Revlon commercial. 'She misses you. I can tell.'

'Oh, Aaron, I really can't,' Isla said. She needed to find a caterer and be at her desk the minute any emails came in from the ones she had contacted already.

'Isla, purlease! I wouldn't ask if I wasn't desperate. I've got Martin Quigg coming in at eleven and if I get caught up with Hilda I'll be late for him and you know I—'

'Fancy him,' Isla filled in.

'Yes, well, he hasn't taken my not-so-subtle hints about hooking up for drinks *yet* but I do believe he's toying with me.' He inhaled. 'Some men like to do it slow.'

'What time is Hilda skyping?' Isla asked.

'In ten minutes,' Aaron stated quickly, taking off his jacket and putting it round his chair.

'Ten minutes! Aaron!'

'Not my idea,' he said quickly. 'She has some other meeting with the Forestry Commission at twelve, so you see my dilemma,' Aaron began. 'She's earmarked from now until twelve to talk *at* me!'

Isla clicked her mouse on to her screen, opening up the Ridgepoint Hospital file. 'Well, you'd better catch me up quickly. What's been progressed since I handed it over?'

'Oh, so, so much,' Aaron answered, sitting on the edge of Isla's desk. 'I even know her aunt Amy's special recipe for dumplings.'

'Come on! Come on!' Aaron said, waggling his arms around like an excited French traffic policeman. 'Hilda talks to me for hours but Isla is adept at being concise. We might have thirty minutes if we're lucky.'

Chase, Brooke and Maddie rushed into the space behind Isla's desk, Brooke leaping on the chair.

'The file is called …' Aaron began.

'Breekers' Christmas Party 2017? Got it,' Brooke said, seemingly navigating the system like a programmer navigates code.

'No!' Aaron screeched. 'That's a dummy file.' He shook his head. 'Don't you know how big a thing this is? Staff have been trying to get the heads up on the Christmas party ever since Isla's very first extravaganza.' He put a hand to his chest and looked like he was about to reminisce. 'It was all *The Wizard of Oz* meets *Disney on Ice*.'

'Goddamn,' Chase said. 'Now I'm concerned about my promise to make good on a venue.'

'I've got it,' Brooke said. 'Boulder Cooper Parker 2017.' She nodded like she was satisfied. 'She used the initials of Breekers' Christmas Party and it's the only one that's password protected.' Brooke pulled her phone out of her bag and plugged it into the PC. 'Give me a couple minutes.'

'This is so exciting,' Maddie said, giggling gleefully.

It didn't feel exciting to Chase. It felt like a breach of trust and he really wanted Isla to trust him now. But he needed all the information he could get if he was going to come through for her with the party. He didn't want to take over, but he didn't want her usual flawless night to be marred because he had come to London and turned her life upside down.

'I've got this, Dad,' Brooke said, taking it in turns to look from her phone to the computer.

'Is that binary?' Aaron asked, leaning over and staring at the flashing icons on the screen of Brooke's phone.

'It's something I got from a friend,' Brooke answered. She tapped her nose with her finger.

'Do I need to review this list of friends?' Chase asked.

'Hey, I'm helping you out here,' Brooke said.

'Can you teach me?' Maddie asked.

'No,' Brooke and Chase replied simultaneously.

Brooke's phone made a bleeping sound and she looked at the screen triumphantly, the folder opening at the click of a mouse.

'Okay, we are in,' Brooke announced.

'Oh my!' Aaron exclaimed as the first document revealed itself.

'Is that a Jeep?' Chase inquired, edging nearer to the screen.

'It's a very old British Land Rover,' Aaron answered. He made another exclamation as Brooke opened a second document. 'Oh, would you look at that? It's wonderful! So romantic!' He smiled at Chase. 'It's the perfect theme.'

Maddie turned her head almost upside down, as if doing that would make her see more clearly. Chase watched her blink, then blink again. 'What's that rubber mask?'

'Okay,' Chase said, putting his hand on Brooke's shoulder. 'Close it down. Do whatever you have to do to make sure Isla doesn't know we've looked.'

'So, now we know,' Aaron stated. 'What are we going to do?'

'Well, I'd like you to find us a real old British Jeep ...' Chase began.

'Land Rover,' Aaron interrupted.

'Yes, that,' Chase agreed. 'And we are going to visit Portobello Flowers. I think someone there might be able to help us out.'

Seventy-Eight

Holland Park

It was the dead of night, pitch black and freezing cold. The worst thing about the sub-zero temperatures, apart from feeling like your limbs might seize up completely if you stayed still, was that the earth they were going to disturb was now going to be less child's sandpit and more rock solid.

Isla had fortified the troops with hot chocolate and warm mince pies before they had set off, dressed in matching black hoodies that had a rather alarming logo of a vengeful-looking snake on the breast. No one had asked Raj what it meant or where he had got them. Not even inquisitive Maddie.

With the large, ornate gate at the entrance locked, scaling it had been the only option and that was never going to happen for Hannah and Ronnie. Disappointed but practical, Hannah and Raj had decided to maintain a watch while the group of four – Isla, Chase, Brooke and Maddie – went over the top. Now, trudging over the crunchy white layer of snow on the ground they were trying to muffle every footstep.

'Are we breaking the law?' Brooke questioned, with a hint of too much glee.

'Yes,' Chase answered. 'We are trespassing.'

'Cool,' Brooke said.

'Listen,' Chase said. 'It's not cool, okay. What we're doing is wrong and I am not an advocate for law-breaking.'

'So, this is a "do as I say not as I do" kinda scenario?' Brooke asked. 'Just so we're clear.'

'Something like that,' Chase agreed.

'In the daytime,' Isla whispered, her hand wrapped around the bag-for-life filled with artefacts, 'this is a lovely place to visit. There are two wonderful Japanese gardens and a wild area with peacocks and squirrels.'

'Really?' Maddie exclaimed. 'Do you think we're gonna see them tonight?'

'Shh! We're meant to be in stealth mode,' Brooke said.

'Do you have any idea where we're going?' Chase asked. 'Because I've seen more with a match than I can see with this flashlight.' He waved it around as if to prove a point.

'We don't want to attract any attention,' Isla reminded him. 'It's just over here.' She headed east, knowing exactly where Raj had said the works were taking place.

She still couldn't believe they were doing this. What had her neatly ordered life come to? The run-up to Christmas had always been about preparation, *relaxed* preparation. Parties, prosecco, present-buying ... not planning the plantation of pre-modern-day pots!

'God, I hope this works,' Chase announced into the dark. Isla turned her head towards him. He looked different dressed all in black, the hood over his tawny hair, jeans and Caterpillar boots on his feet, but still so handsome. Her stomach really did flip every time she looked at him.

'Did you speak to New York today?' Isla asked.

'Yeah,' he answered. 'I replied to their email. Just kept it vague, light, nothing controversial. You know, very inspirationally evasive.'

'I can imagine you did that very well,' Isla answered.

'And I am taking that as a compliment.'

'Wow!' It was Maddie with the 'wow'.

'Sshh!' Brooke ordered.

'But, look!'

There ahead of them, now they had turned a corner, was a towering Christmas tree covered in bright white Christmas lights, a star at its tip There were so many lights it looked as though a long, illuminated cloak of lustre had been draped over it.

'That's one great tree,' Chase agreed. He put the barrel of the torch in his mouth, adjusted his hold on the black sack containing the axe heads, then put a hand on Maddie's shoulder.

'Have you got a tree yet, Daddy?'

'In my place in New York?'

Maddie nodded, the hood falling over her face a little.

'No, not yet,' he admitted. 'I've been busy here and—'

'Can we get one together?' Maddie asked. 'When we go back?'

'Sure, Pumpkin,' he answered.

Isla swallowed. Yes, Christmas was coming and no matter what happened with Notting Hill after tonight, Chase was going back to the U.S. She had always known that. But what she hadn't always known was that she was going to fall for him. She needed more time ... just to think.

'We should hurry a little,' she said, quickening her pace. She really didn't have time to be incarcerated if she was going to meet the only catering company who had replied in the affirmative to that day's pleas. They might only offer a dozen different turkey options but turkey was the food of the season and she was sure turkey curry, turkey meatballs and turkey and aubergine rolls would suffice if she sold it to staff as part of the night's theme.

'Let's get this done,' Chase agreed.

'So cool,' Brooke replied.

Chase looked down into the pit of soil in front of them and made a wish. *He made a wish.* Someone who believed you could only make change yourself. He couldn't remember wanting something to succeed as much as this in quite some time. There seemed to be so much at stake. His job. His relationship with his children. This whole area of London. Isla. Being here had changed him in so many ways in such a short space of time. When he'd arrived, he had been the consummate businessman, the Mr Corporate he had to be to fill the role Breekers needed him to fill and to get himself better, back into life. But he had ignored the person he was at his heart. The man who cared. The man who had been too scared to care this past twelve months. He needed to find a way to redress that balance. Because he wanted in on emotion again. And he wanted in on Isla.

'I can't see any of the Roman stuff from here,' Brooke announced, staring into the hole. 'If I can't see it and I *know* it's there, how are we expecting the workers to find it tomorrow?'

'It can't look too obvious, Brooke,' Chase reminded her. 'That's also why we haven't put it all in the one place.'

'But what if they don't find it at all?' Maddie wailed. 'What if they come here with the big digger and just break it all up and, even if they find it, what if they just throw it in the garbage?'

'Well,' Isla said, straightening Maddie's hood so she could see out of it better. 'That's where Mrs Edwards comes in.'

'She does?' Maddie queried.

'She's going to come here first thing in the morning and "stumble over" a Roman coin and "see" the edge of one of the axe heads in the hole,' Isla informed.

'And Raj is gonna be right there, calling all the press I gave him the numbers for tonight,' Chase said.

Brooke grinned. 'So cool.'

'So your dad is cool now, yeah?' Chase checked.

'A little,' Brooke admitted. 'Sometimes.'

'We'd better go,' Isla said, checking her watch. 'I'm surprised Hannah hasn't called me yet.'

'I can't wait for tomorrow,' Brooke said. 'I wish I could see their faces when they find the stuff.'

'I know,' Chase agreed. 'But we can't be here. Isla and I are too close to the situation. If we were here it would look suss and the whole plan might fall apart.' He looked at Brooke seriously. 'Then we might have to go looking for that cadaver.'

'I think that's enough about that,' Isla said, putting an arm around Maddie's shoulders.

'Can we go eat?' Brooke asked as they began to head back in the direction of the gate, breath clouding the air.

'Seriously, Brooke? You're still hungry?' Chase exclaimed.

'Diwali might still be open,' Isla informed.

'Oh, Daddy, yes, Asian food.'

'I feel like I'm being taken for a ride here,' Chase replied.

'Please, Daddy,' Maddie answered.

'Okay! Okay!' He held his hands up in surrender.

'Come on, Maddie,' Brooke said. 'I'll race you to the gate.'

The two girls set off, feet pumping at the ground, hard snow spitting from the soles of their feet and into the blackness.

'So,' Chase said, walking closer to Isla. 'We committed how many felonies tonight?'

'Not being utterly up to speed with criminology of any kind I don't have an exact figure but, without any doubt, enough.' She shot him a tentative smile. 'Probably enough for my whole lifetime.'

'You're acting like you didn't enjoy it at all,' Chase answered.

She let a breath go. 'I'm just hoping that it works.'

'Yeah,' he said. 'Me too.'

He reached for her hand then, holding on to it, wanting to feel her touch. He relaxed a little when he felt her moulding her hand to his.

'But, if it doesn't work, it isn't the end,' Isla said. 'Not for me. Because I live here and I can't give up on it.'

'Hey,' Chase said. 'I'm no quitter either and, being here, seeing all this ...' He took a breath. 'Meeting you.' He stopped walking, and looked into her eyes. 'Notting Hill isn't right for this project. I can see that now.' He reached under the rim of her hood to touch her hair. 'Because Notting Hill is pretty much perfect exactly how it is.'

And so was she. She was perfect too. But he didn't want to scare her saying too much too soon. They needed time. And time was the only thing they didn't seem to have when they were about to be separated by an ocean. But he had to say something.

'Isla ...'

'Yes?'

'Whatever happens after tonight ... will you come visit me in New York?'

He wanted her to say yes. He wanted her to throw her arms around him and kiss him for the longest time.

She smiled and squeezed his hand before letting go. 'We should really catch up with Brooke and Maddie.'

And that felt like as good as a no. 'Yeah,' he answered. 'Sure.'

Seventy-Nine

Beaumont Square, Notting Hill

'Stuffed ... to the brim ... no room for anything else. Can I take this hoodie off now?'

In the middle of the living room, Isla watched Hannah shift and struggle to get the pullover top up and over her shoulders. She stepped in to help, taking hold of the top and edging it upwards and off.

'In this weather, I didn't imagine I'd ever feel hot,' Hannah puffed. 'But who knows what those hoodies were made out of or who they pledge their allegiance to.'

'I think it's best not to think about it,' Isla responded, dropping into the armchair.

'No,' Hannah agreed. 'Let's just remember that Raj provided adequate coverage for undercover operations no matter where they originated from.'

'Yes,' Isla said. She couldn't respond properly. Her brain was fried with thoughts about the morning – what would happen when Mrs Edwards turned up at Holland Park and 'discovered' the history hidden in the hole – and what Chase had said tonight. He had asked her to come and visit him in New York. But how could she? She had Hannah. Hannah liked home and Hannah was part of the reason home had to be saved. New York was a long, difficult flight away. It didn't make sense.

She swallowed. Except what she felt *did* make sense. Somehow it felt, with Chase, that finally all the pieces of her life were starting to fit together at the very moment everything else seemed to be falling apart.

'So, we couldn't really talk much at Diwali with Maddie and Brooke wowing over the poppadoms but the "disposal" went okay?' Hannah asked.

Isla nodded. 'Yes. We did what we talked about. Buried everything, not too obvious, in a few different areas.'

'Then we just have to wait,' Hannah breathed. 'And rely on Mrs E to put on a good show.'

Isla smiled. 'I think if there's anyone we can rely on to put on a good show it's Mrs Edwards.'

Hannah laughed. 'She did look a little too invested in her character when I spoke to her earlier.'

'I have every faith in her performing the role perfectly,' Isla said.

'But is it going to work?' Hannah breathed. 'Is it going to be enough?'

Isla looked at her sister, the lights on the feathered Christmas tree reflecting off her cropped hair. She still looked so young. She was still too vulnerable to let go of completely.

'I don't know,' Isla admitted. 'But we have a good chance.'

'Do you think so?' Hannah asked.

'Well, I wouldn't have scaled a gate and carried around some ancient broken pots if I didn't think it was worth it,' Isla said.

'No,' Hannah agreed. 'I guess not.'

'So, how are things with Raj?' Isla asked. 'Anything to report while you were keeping watch?'

Hannah shook her head. 'We talked. You know, about this and that ... or rather dis 'n' dat ... and it was nice but ... I just don't know how he feels.' She sighed. 'Sometimes I think things are building up to something, you know, and then he almost retreats.'

'You could ask him,' Isla suggested. 'Or tell him how *you* feel.'

'I don't know,' Hannah said straightaway. 'I don't know if I have the guts to do that.' She looked up. 'What about you and Chase?'

Isla swallowed. What could she say? That she had never felt this way about a guy, but she was too scared to believe it could be real? That she was terrified to accept love in case it didn't last or wasn't somehow as genuine as she needed it to be?

'He asked me to visit him in New York,' Isla blurted out.

'Wow!' Hannah said. 'Really?!'

Isla nodded.

'That's amazing, Isla. I mean, it means he must, I don't know, kind of ... love you.'

It couldn't mean that, could it? It was all too soon. He was not long divorced and he had Brooke and Maddie. She swallowed. But she loved kids. She had always wanted kids and Brooke and Maddie were great. Brooke was obviously struggling a little but Isla believed her heart was true ...

'I can't go, though, obviously,' Isla said.

'What?' Hannah asked.

'I can't go to New York.'

'Well, why not?' Hannah queried.

Her sister's gaze was heavy and Isla suddenly felt under scrutiny. What could she say?

'Well, I've got too much going on here with work—'

'He's your boss,' Hannah interrupted. 'Surely he can smooth that over if it's to his advantage?'

'Well, there's the … the … house.'

'Which might end up being demolished,' Hannah said.

'Don't say that!'

'Well, why don't we cut to the chase, so to speak?' Hannah snapped. 'You don't think you can go to New York because of me.'

'No,' Isla said. 'Not at all.' She sounded so unconvincing it was pathetic.

Hannah shook her head. 'You have got to stop doing that!'

'Doing what?' Isla asked.

'Not living your life because of me.'

Isla held her breath. She had never wanted Hannah to think that. She hated herself for causing Hannah to even think that.

'I know that's what you do, Isla,' Hannah continued. 'And, at first, when Mum and Dad were newly dead, I couldn't have gone on without you.' She paused. 'You were … you *are* … everything to me, and I can't imagine what my life would have been without you in it, without you supporting me so wholly and thoroughly, no matter what kind of bitch I was to you.'

'You weren't—' Isla started.

'Yes, I was,' Hannah said. 'And deliberately so some of the time.'

'Well, you had good reason,' Isla said.

'No, I didn't.' Hannah sniffed almost indignant. 'I was just a bitch. But I'm over it now, most of the time. And I'm over you dipping out on stuff and using me as an excuse.' She directed a killer glance at Isla. 'Because that's what you do, you know. You use me as an excuse when you're too scared to do something.'

Isla shifted uncomfortably in her chair, and suddenly found the Christmas cards on the wall exceedingly interesting. It wasn't true. She didn't avoid anything deliberately, just maybe a few things that she considered might be too much for Hannah, or prove difficult.

'Don't try and deny it,' Hannah said. 'I can give you countless examples and I *am* to blame because I let you do it for the most part. But that was wrong. I shouldn't have let you. And I don't want to let you any more.'

'I don't know what you're talking about,' Isla began. 'I don't—'

'You need to start living *your* life, Isla. Yours,' Hannah reiterated. 'First and foremost yours, not yours as a sister to little ol' invalid me.'

'I do.'

'You don't,' Hannah countered. 'And it's not up for discussion or a debate or argument, I'm telling you. I don't need you under my wheels all the time. I need you to be happy. Find someone. Chase Chase,' Hannah ordered. 'You tell him you'll go to New York to visit him. I mean for God's sake, Isla, look at the guy, he's as hot as Jamie Dornan … in fact, from what I've seen, his arse is actually better.'

Isla swallowed. He did have a good arse. She could totally vouch for that. *Focus on what your sister is saying.* Could this work? Could she let go a little? It was one thing agreeing to Hannah wheeling to work on her own but another to spend a few days, a week, out of the country.

'I'll get someone to stay with me,' Hannah said quickly. 'I'm sure Claudia or maybe Valerie would be able to come over and help if I asked them to.' She swallowed. 'I'm not irresponsible or being short-sighted. I know I can't manage completely on my own. But I don't necessarily need *you*,' Hannah concluded. 'And I don't care if that makes you feel redundant, but your supervision is easily replaced.' Hannah smiled. 'And the sister stuff that can't be replicated by anyone else can take place on FaceTime ... from the top of the Empire State Building if needed.'

'I don't know,' Isla breathed.

'Yes you do,' Hannah stated boldly. 'You do know. I've seen the way you look at him and the way he looks at you. *I* freaking know! *Aaron* freaking knows! Don't mess this up!' Hannah ordered. 'I mean what other guy would be working his hot arse off sorting the venue for the Breekers' Christmas Party.' Hannah stopped talking quickly, clamping both hands over her mouth. 'Ignore that. I didn't say anything.'

'Has Chase found a venue?' Isla asked.

'Not saying anything more,' Hannah mumbled through a tightly closed mouth.

'Hannah, just tell me if he's found somewhere, please, I'm going out of my mind worrying about everything. I need to know!'

'I can't. I promised.'

'Hannah, I'm your sister.'

'Argh! Don't play the family card, it's not fair. And basically, if you get married one day, he's going to be my brother-in-law so that would make him family.'

'Hannah!'

'Yes, he's found a venue,' Hannah stated finally. 'And that's all I'm saying.'

Isla smiled. With a venue and catering coming together was it possible that the Christmas party was really going to happen?

'Promise me you won't tell him I told you,' Hannah said.

'I promise,' Isla replied.

'And promise me something else too,' Hannah begged.

'What?'

'Promise me you'll think about New York.'

Isla looked at her sister. She didn't look as young and vulnerable now that determined expression was set on her face. She smiled. 'I promise.'

Eighty

Sugar High, Portobello Road

'Get down, Rolo,' Mrs Smith said, berating her dog that was trying to jump up on Maddie's lap.

Vicky had gone to town with the Christmas decorations in the café now the big day was getting closer. Spirals of glitter hung down from the ceiling, interspersed with stars and little glowing Christmas puddings. There were gingerbread men in holding-hands chains across the window panes and the aroma from the kitchen was constant pumpkin and thick, fragrant cinnamon and nutmeg. Chatter from the customers was all to-do lists of what they had to accomplish before Christmas Day and the background music was Bublé, Sinatra with a dash of Tony Bennett, and Wham!.

'He's so cute,' Maddie announced, eyes on Rolo. 'I wish I had a little dog like that.'

'This one would eat you out of house and home,' Vicky announced, putting hot chocolates and the Mulled Christmas Muffin in front of everyone in turn. 'And then eat *you* probably.'

'I thought he was on a special diet,' Isla commented, moving her cup to make space on the table.

'So did I,' Vicky remarked. 'But it doesn't seem to be enough for him. Yesterday I found him out the back dragging leftovers from the bins.'

Isla looked to Chase. He had been juddering his leg up and down ever since they had sat down, his phone clutched in his hand, looking so tense. Her stomach was revolving too. So much was at stake. Her whole life up in the air like juggling balls being tossed by a novice. The only thing keeping her externally calm was Maddie and Brooke. Neither of them could know just how important this was to their dad and to her. And they really shouldn't need to know.

'May we start?' Maddie asked with perfect British undertones.

'Yes,' Isla said. 'Of course. Eat.' She smiled. 'What are you listening to, Brooke?'

Brooke was nodding her head up and down in appreciation of something and Isla had no idea if she had heard her or not.

Maddie answered. 'It's Rag 'n' Bone Man. She's a lot obsessed.'

'She told me,' Isla replied.

Chase's phone suddenly erupted into life and he looked at it, as if not knowing how to answer.

It was Raj. He should answer it. He was *going to* answer it. Looking up he took in the three expectant faces: Maddie with a slick of custard at the corner of her lips, Brooke popping out her earbuds to engage and Isla … she was toying with her fingers as her hands rested on her lap, trying to remain still and stoic and in control, but he knew how she would be feeling on the inside.

He stood up quickly, shifting past tables, nudging Rolo, and making for the door that led outside.

'Chase!' He heard Isla call out after him.

He stepped out on to the street, somehow needing to be right in the thick of Notting Hill life when he heard whatever he was going to hear. Could the plan have worked? Or was Mrs Edwards being hauled away and dismissed as crazy?

'Hey, Raj,' he greeted.

'Chase, man, it's all kicking off, innit?'

'Kicking off?' Chase queried. He looked across the street to the retro T-shirt store, bright multicoloured tinsel wound around the rails that held every rock-band top you could imagine.

'We's got the police and an ITV camera crew now, man. It's kicking.'

Chase frowned. 'So, is it kicking? Or kicking off?'

'Put it on speaker phone.'

Isla was at his shoulder now, her tension palpable. They were in this together. He shouldn't have run out here. He pressed the appropriate button.

'Mrs E, she played it so good, man,' Raj continued. 'At first they didn't listen … I think they thought she is nuts … but she kept it on going, pointing and saying what she can see and then she reaches down, so low down I think she is gonna fall into the hole, man and she pretends to scrabble a bit in the dirt. I think she was making that coin she kept last night all muddy for the ageing effect and she shows it to the guy and she says …' Raj cleared his throat. '"This is a Roman coin. This could be an ancient burial site. You have to call the authorities". Then, get this, she says "And you have to call *Time Team*".'

Chase looked at Isla and she looked back at him. Hope was growing, he could feel it, like a bulb in spring. But nothing was certain yet.

'Raj,' Isla said. 'What's happening there now?'

'Everything, Isla. It's like the centre of the universe in Holland Park. All the press guys I called are gonna come down here. There is people taking photos and there's tweets about it already, man … and they've stopped digging.'

'Is Mrs Edwards okay?' Isla asked. She was still looking at Chase, a smile spreading over her face.

'She is banging, bro,' Raj replied. 'Everyone is making a real show around her, man, and she is getting free tea and cakes and all that.'

'Raj,' Chase interjected. 'We've gotta go.'

'Sure, man.'

'You've gone a great job, Raj,' Chase told him.

'Phone Hannah,' Isla said. 'She'll be dying to hear.'

There was silence.

'Raj?' Isla queried. 'Could you call Hannah? She'll be waiting to find out and—'

'See, I know I was supposed to call you first, innit, but—'

Isla smiled. 'You've already told Hannah, haven't you?' She laughed. 'Bye, Raj.'

'See ya.'

Chase ended the call and slipped his cell phone back into his pocket. There was only one thing he wanted to do now. 'Isla.'

He waited for her gaze to connect with his and then, when it did, he moved his body forward, capturing her lips with a full open-mouthed kiss, his arm circling her waist and drawing her closer. He felt her respond to his ardour, tongue teasing, almost begging for more. A glance to the left and the frosted, decorated window of Sugar High and he saw Maddie and Brooke, both looking at him and Isla. Maddie was bumping up and down in her seat, a delighted expression on her face and Brooke was shaking her head as if embarrassed, but there was a hint of a smile on her lips. He drew back, brushing a hand through the tendrils of Isla's sexy red hair.

'God, you are so beautiful,' he whispered. Never, when he first arrived here, did he even consider the possibility of finding these feelings, of finding someone like her.

Isla blinked heavy lashes over those blue eyes and looked back at him. 'Chase.'

'Yeah,' he replied.

'I have a confession to make.'

He swallowed, dreading what was to come.

'I've never been to Las Vegas,' Isla blurted out.

He smiled then, continuing to touch her hair. 'I know that. You have a tell, remember.'

'I didn't mean to lie,' Isla began. 'You were just being all bossy and boardroom and I needed something to convince you I wasn't unadventurous.'

'After our trip on the London Eye I can definitely vouch for your adventurousness,' Chase stated.

He watched her cheeks pink up a little in that cute way they always did when she was a little embarrassed. It only made him adore her more.

'But,' Isla began. 'I would quite like to see New York some time, you know, if the offer is still open.'

And there went his heart. Thumping triumphantly and filling him with pure joy he'd never felt before. He wanted to kiss her again … and tell her he loved her. But he didn't want to scare her. And it was so new. Was it too new to be sure?

'But I understand if you might have changed your mind and …'

He kissed her lips again, hard first and then softly, their mouths barely making any contact at all. 'I haven't changed my mind,' he whispered. 'The offer is still very much on the table.'

'Okay,' Isla said.

'Okay,' he replied. Taking hold of her hands he squeezed them in his. 'So, how about now we go eat highly calorific muffins and tell Breekers International the bad news about the Roman artefacts.'

'Yes,' Isla said. 'I think we should definitely do that.'

Eighty-One

Beaumont Square

Standing in the middle of her and Hannah's corner of London on this crisp and wondrous night, Isla was soaking in every subtle nuance about the place. The streetlamp that always flickered on and off no matter how many times it was repaired, Mrs Webley's ugly angel ornament that gurned out every year in front of her equally awful net curtain, Mr Edwards' rose bush ... Isla breathed out into the cold and took a step towards the bare shrubbery. It was thanks to this soft-natured, unassuming man who had had a love of cheese and history, that generations to come were going to be able to enjoy all that Notting Hill had to offer. Eyes glossy she blinked at the rose bush, narrowing her vision and studying it a little closer. Was that? It couldn't be. New buds appearing in December ...

'Coming through!'

It was Hannah, and Isla turned, greeting her sister who was speeding along the path, a pile of paperwork on her lap and Raj, Chase, Brooke and Maddie all behind her, trying to keep up.

'It made the front page of the *Evening Standard*!' Hannah yelled, gasping for breath as Ronnie skidded to a halt by Isla's feet.

'No!' Isla gasped. 'Did it really!'

'Not just that,' Raj interrupted. 'I got all my mates to tweet it and share on Instagram. It's not quite viral yet, but it's getting out there, innit.'

'The New York Rangers shared it too,' Chase informed, moving next to her.

'I asked Rag 'n' Bone man for a retweet,' Brooke said. 'I don't know if he will but ...'

'You should have asked J.K. Rowling,' Hannah suggested. 'She's always on Twitter.'

'Here,' Hannah said, thrusting the newspaper at Isla. 'Some expert has already said it's a—'

'Significant find.' Everyone chorused together.

Isla looked at the article, eyes catching the headline then skipping through words on the front page. *Historic. Notable artefacts. Roman. Site of an old bath house.* And suddenly she was filled with guilt. They had deceived people for their own agenda.

'Hey,' Chase said, taking hold of her hand. 'Stop that.'

'Stop what?' Isla asked him, swallowing quickly and trying to compose herself.

'This is all gonna come good,' he told her.

'Is it?' Isla asked, a sigh leaving her.

'This wasn't about deceiving anyone permanently,' Chase reminded her. 'This was only ever about making this real enough to buy us some time.'

'I don't know,' Isla breathed. 'I can't help thinking it feels wrong.'

'Pah!' Hannah remarked. 'No one thought about morality when they were drawing up those gross plans.' She looked to Chase. 'No offence.'

'I'm of the opinion now the plans were grossly overrated,' he responded.

'Apart from the zoo,' Maddie said.

'We did the only thing we could do,' Chase reassured Isla. He squeezed her hand tight. 'Look around you,' he urged. 'We all had a hand in saving Notting Hill.'

And, as Isla gazed around the square, the Christmas lights shining bright, the moon above them clear and warm, surrounded by everything she loved, with these people she cared so deeply about, the culpability began to wane. They had done what they had done for the greater good and, as soon as the super-hotel's location was reassigned, she would drop an anonymous email to the council and ensure nothing else was dug up for the sake of a fictitious settlement.

'We saved Notting Hill,' she breathed, letting the words fly from her lips with all the euphoria she felt.

'Whoop!' Hannah exclaimed. 'We saved Notting Hill!'

'Notting Hill! Notting Hill!' Maddie exclaimed, spinning around in a circle, pumping her arm in the air as her hair flew about in the night air.

'Oh my God,' Isla said, the reality of everything setting in as she took Chase by the arms. 'We really saved Notting Hill!'

'Atta girl,' he answered, folding his arms around her. 'Atta girl.'

Eighty-Two

Breekers London Christmas Party, Life Start Community Centre

It was a crisp, clear night, the air frosty and skin-numbing, but all Isla felt was excitement and a sweet relief after the previous days of tension and imbalance. Tonight was one of her favourite nights of the year and despite everything it had come together.

As she and Hannah made their way through the pastel-painted Notting Hill streets, a dark blanket above them, stars bright and twinkling, it was a time to take stock and be thankful. This area of Kensington was still standing and hopefully would be in hundreds of years to come. Christmas was right around the corner now and in almost every window shone bedecked trees, strings of lights and decorations declaring peace and goodwill. There was a sense of calm and a delicate burr of contentment all around.

Isla smiled as she smoothed down the front of her replica Wrens uniform. It was navy blue, the skirt just touching her knee, tan tights covering her legs and Mary Jane shoes on her feet. The matching jacket had bright silver buttons and a one-stripe insignia on the sleeve. Beneath the jacket was a pale shirt and blue tie and on her head was an odd-shaped hat somewhere between a bowler and a Stetson.

Last week, when she had finally let her colleagues know the theme of this year's Christmas party, their office had bubbled with the usual frenzy of excitement. Wartime at Christmas. This was another glorious chance to play dress-up. Everyone had seemed so animated, asking each other about costume shops, sharing outfit suggestions and wondering what was in store for the entertainment. And Isla had just hoped this year's party was going to live up to those high expectations she herself had set.

'Okay, slow down,' Hannah said, wheeling to a halt.

'Why?' Isla asked. 'Are you okay?'

'Yes, I'm fine.'

'Okay, well, it's just that it's almost half past. I can't be late,' Isla said.

'Just humour me,' Hannah said, grinning. 'I want you to be ready for what you're going to see when we get there.'

Isla's stomach revolved. What did that mean? She had only left the venue that morning, after ensuring the tables were all set up – ration books and gas marks for props along with old Tilley lamps as atmospheric and authentic lighting – and the staging company knew exactly where they were putting everything. It was possible, if the cardboard cut-out of Winston Churchill was put in the wrong place, no one would be able to see the stage.

When Chase had told her they were going to use Life Start she hadn't known quite how to react. Yes, it had the kind of space and size needed but it wasn't quite the lovely chapel she had planned for either. But beggars couldn't be choosers and she would have taken anything rather than have to cancel.

'What's going on, Hannah?' Isla asked, slowing her place and fixing her sister with a questioning look. Hannah was dressed as a Land Girl. Beige dungarees, a plain white shirt and a red headscarf over her hair.

'Trust me,' Hannah said. 'You're going to love it.'

When they rounded the corner the scene before Isla stole her breath. The outside of Life Start was not only free from youths on bikes and drunks, it had been entirely transformed. It had been painted, the broken window had been replaced and it was free from rubbish. Parked up outside on the concrete paving was a relic of a Land Rover, draped in camouflage netting, and there were two flaming torches either side of the entrance like beacons. Fairy lights and Union Jack bunting skirted the fresh façade and two rather attractive men in G.I. uniforms 'guarded' the door.

'Bloody hell!' Hannah exclaimed. 'It's even better than I imagined.'

'I don't understand,' Isla said. 'Who ...'

She didn't really know why she had started to ask. She knew exactly who had done this. And there he was ...

As their eyes connected, Chase straightened up and brought his hand to his brow in a salute. Isla shivered, all her senses exploding in appreciation. He was dressed in the light uniform of a 1940s American soldier. Beige shirt with pockets and some military adornments, thigh-tight matching trousers and the peaked cap. He looked every inch the wartime pin-up.

'Would you look at that,' Hannah remarked, mouth dropping open.

'I know,' Isla whispered.

'Not Chase,' Hannah said quickly. 'Raj.'

Isla looked to her sister, following her line of sight. Just a few metres away was their postman, helping himself to a mocktail and looking completely transformed. Raj was wearing the uniform of a British fighter pilot including leather jacket with fleece lining, a cream-coloured scarf and goggles on top of his head.

'I think this year's theme might be the best yet,' Hannah sighed.

'Daddy, is my hair still okay?'

Chase looked to his daughter. Leanna had given them a crash course in 1940s hair and make-up over Skype that afternoon. Both girls had rolled and set their hair, Maddie wearing a floral dress and headscarf over her style. Brooke, still in boots, was rocking khaki dungarees.

'You look beautiful,' Chase told her with a smile. He turned to Brooke. 'You look beautiful too.'

She frowned. 'I'm meant to be a kick-ass Land Girl who drives trucks and tractors.'

'Those girls are beautiful too,' he said.

Chase turned his attention back to Isla and there was that stab of lust combined with a large dart to his heart. She looked incredible in that fitted Navy uniform, her hair just like the girls' under a military hat. This past week had been a complete game-changer for him. Since the British press had reported the Roman findings in Holland Park, Breekers had decided it was a difficulty too far to continue to consider Notting Hill as their prime spot for the super-village. There were always going to be complications to do with planning but this, thankfully, as they had hoped, seemed one hurdle too high. And Chase had never felt happier about having an idea quashed. For now, the entire project was in limbo but, he hoped, with Isla's help, Breekers could still think about branching out into the hotel business. He smiled at her as she approached.

'Good evening, ma'am,' Chase said in full role-play mode. 'Permit this G.I. to escort you to the party of the year?'

Isla exclaimed as she looked to the children, her hands going to her mouth in delighted shock. 'Look at you two! Your hair! It's amazing!'

'Mommy helped us on Skype,' Maddie informed.

'YouTube did most of the work really,' Brooke stated.

'Well, your mum and YouTube both did an excellent job,' Isla told them.

'Where's Hannah?' Maddie inquired.

'Oh,' Isla said, smiling. 'She's talking to a rather handsome fighter pilot over there.'

Everyone looked to where Raj and Hannah were caught up in conversation. Chase shook his head. 'Well, well, well, and I thought *I* had the coolest costume.'

Isla checked her watch. 'I have to go in and check a dozen things before everyone else starts arriving.'

'Sure,' Chase said. 'Just tell me. Are you digging the Jeep?' He turned to face it. It hadn't been easy tracking it down at such short notice but it was completely authentic and it definitely added to the wartime vibe at the entrance.

'It's a Land Rover,' Isla pointed out. 'But yes, I am.'

'And the guys on security?' Chase asked, moving towards the doorway.

'A nice touch.'

'Good,' Chase said. 'Because they're gonna be a permanent fixture around here.'

'What?' Isla asked.

'Hannah and her friends shouldn't have to put up with hobos and delinquents and crap like that going on out here. They've got it tough enough.'

'But ...'

'Just call it a Breekers PR exercise,' Chase answered.

Isla took hold of his arm and gave it a squeeze. 'Well now, you really are a life-improvement guru.'

Eighty-Three

'Sugar. Honey. Ice Tea. This is the best party ever,' Aaron, dressed as Winston Churchill, announced later, un-lit cigar bouncing from his lips.

The turkey canapés were being brought around, drinks were flowing and a trio of female singers – The Miller Sisters – were starting off the music with some 'Boogie Woogie Bugle Boy'. The ceiling had been hung with a large parachute, lights underneath to give it a warm, festive glow, and the walls were decorated with wartime posters – Your Country Needs You, Dig On For Victory, Man The Guns, Join The Navy – together with wreaths of holly, ivy and mistletoe.

'Aaron, you say that every year,' Isla reminded him.

'And I mean it every year,' Aaron said. 'The trouble is, you keep excelling yourself.'

Isla smiled. A week ago she almost considered herself a failure, everything in her neatly ordered life suddenly coming apart at the seams. But, despite it all, somehow she *had* excelled. But she had only been able to do that with help. All of those closest to her had played a part, and for that she was grateful and utterly, utterly proud.

'Hey, Aaron, could I steal this Navy girl away for a while?'

Isla felt an all-over body blush arrive as Chase stepped back into her orbit. All night he had been working the room like a true professional, taking time to chat to everyone who had questions about Breekers' future plans, topping up drinks as much as the hired waitresses and ensuring the staff all let their hair – and wigs – down.

'Of course,' Aaron replied. 'I've got plans on snagging a dance with another red-haired minx over there by munitions.' He sent a coy wave across the room to someone Isla only knew as Milo.

'Shall we?' Chase asked as the tempo of the music shifted to smoochy.

'Let's,' Isla agreed.

Chase took her hand and led her to the centre of the room where other couples were beginning to link up. Underneath the parachute canopy, surrounded by Christmas trees lit up in silver and blue Isla gave a little sigh of pleasure. This *was* the best Christmas party ever, because it meant more to her than any of the ones gone before.

'So,' Chase said, his arms slipping around her.

'So,' Isla replied, smiling.

'We saved Notting Hill,' he reminded her.

'We did,' Isla agreed. 'With a little help from Mrs Edwards and her late, great husband's passion for history.'

'She's a wonderful woman,' Chase remarked.

'If I tell her you said that she'll come over all unnecessary.'

'What if I tell *you* you're wonderful?' His voice was low and sultry and his eyes met hers.

'I think I might get a little bit more than unnecessary,' Isla admitted.

'Is that a fact?' Chase queried, moving closer.

'Yes,' Isla breathed. Her heart was beating that welcome tom-tom that happened whenever he was near her but before she could tune into that feeling any further Chase drew her closer still, his lips making his future intentions as clear as crystal.

She loved how he tasted, how their mouths fitted together so perfectly. He drew away and seemed to admire her. 'One day,' he whispered. 'We are gonna get a room.'

Her body reacted instantaneously, breaking out in goose-bumps of desire. 'Or maybe pod fourteen on the London Eye again.'

'You're killing me now, Isla.' He dropped his mouth to her ear. 'So, right about now I think it's time you and I talked about working on a new project together.'

'It is?' she queried.

'Yes,' Chase said. 'I've heard boutique hotels who sell peace, tranquillity and escape are something to be invested in. Apparently, it's all about the people these days.'

An internal ember began to increase and glow, gently warming at first, then becoming hotter with every passing second. He *had* listened to her.

Chase let a breath go. 'I don't know who I was when I arrived in London, Isla. But I know I wasn't me.' He smiled. 'I want to be me again. And this time I really think I can be.' He breathed out. 'I called Colt today and we talked ... just a little ... and we didn't yell so that's a start.' He took a second. 'And I now know that he definitely did not give permission for Brooke to watch an NC-17 movie.' His gaze went to where Brooke and Maddie were dancing with Aaron and Denise. 'That girl will give me George Clooney hair.'

Isla laughed. 'She just needs your love and attention and ... a focus.' She looked to Brooke, tapping her foot in time to the band as Maddie whirled around her. 'She's completely into music. Is there perhaps a course she could do at school? Or lessons at the weekends? I have a feeling she would be incredibly driven, given the right opportunity.'

'I think you're completely right about that. Thank you,' Chase said, his eyes appraising her. 'Thank you for everything, Miss Winters, my Go-To Girl.' He took her hand in his, still swaying to the Christmassy tune The Miller Sisters were crooning out. 'All this change, this chance to find me again … it's all down to you. And this place.' His eyes roamed to the dressed-up, partying employees. 'And Notting Hill and all its crazy, oddball quirks.'

'I think you meant to say "intricate fabric and singular personality",' Isla corrected.

'Absolutely.'

At that moment Isla turned her head, something in the frame of the window catching her attention. She looked hard, watching, holding her breath. Through the frosted glass, outside, under the moonlit sky, snow gently falling from the dark blanket, a Land Girl and a fighter pilot drew together.

Isla watched as Raj leant forward, his hands gently cupping Hannah's face and slowly, inch by inch, he brought her towards him as his lips descended to hers. They connected in a soft kiss and Isla watched her sister reach up, both arms interlocking around Raj's body.

'Wow.' It was Chase who had spoken.

'Wow indeed,' Isla breathed, her heart swelling with love and happiness for her sister. 'It's been in Hannah's plan for quite some time.' She smiled at Chase. 'One Christmas kiss in Notting Hill.'

'Is that some ye olde Christmas British custom?' Chase queried.

'No,' Isla said. 'It's a very new one.' She smiled. 'But it's definitely catching on. And I am utterly keen to get more practice at it.'

'Is that so?' Chase asked.

'If you have the time,' Isla said, daring to hope.

'Oh, I can guarantee I'm gonna be earning frequent flier kudos on trips to London in the future. Come here.' He drew her towards him. 'I'd quite like to perfect this Christmas kiss in Notting Hill.'

Isla smiled. 'Me too.'

Epilogue

Christmas Day, Beaumont Square, Notting Hill

Isla wiped her brow as she stood over boiling sprouts, the extractor fan on full pelt as it tried to remove the lingering scent of the green vegetable. The whole house was heavy with the fragrance of Christmas – turkey browning in the oven along with rosemary-topped roast potatoes, thick brown gravy simmering and a medley of carrots, peas and broccoli in the steamer.

'You did get caffeine-free Coke, didn't you?' Hannah asked, spinning into the kitchen like Richard Hammond doing some daft stunt.

'Yes, I did,' Isla said. 'It's in the fridge.' She plucked out a Brussels sprout and placed it on the chopping board to detect whether it was still bullet-hard. The fork thankfully slipped in easily.

'And I know I've asked you twenty-five times already but the turkey is …'

'The turkey is halal, I promise,' Isla answered. 'I asked the butcher three times. Once when I ordered it, then when I picked it up and again last night when you yelled at me from the shower.'

'Sorry,' Hannah said.

Isla wasn't cross in the slightest. Raj was coming for Christmas dinner. Despite not celebrating the season, he knew it was important to Hannah so it was being labelled as an All Faiths Winter Dinner.

A noise sounded above the howling extractor fan and Isla made a face at Hannah.

'That's Skype,' she exclaimed. 'But I told Chase not until after three our time.'

'Maybe he got the time difference wrong,' Hannah suggested.

'Well, I can't talk now. Dinner is at a critical stage.' She opened the oven door, stuck her head in a little too far and almost got steam burns from the ensuing fog of heat.

'Get real!' Hannah said. 'This is Chase! Your gorgeous Chase!'

Isla's skin prickled at Hannah's words. Yes. And it had been three whole days since he'd returned to New York. They had spoken each night on Skype or FaceTime and had messaged more often. She wasn't sure how they would work out the location issue but, right now, the distance wasn't proving insurmountable. But it was early days …

'Okay, I'm going,' Isla said, tossing Hannah the oven gloves and running into the lounge as her laptop continued making a sound.

Bounding in, she almost tripped on the edge of the stack of presents under the sparkling white Christmas tree, and the winter forest smells of the candles Hannah had set up filled her nose. Quickly checking her appearance in the mirror, Isla looked to the computer, Chase's contact showing up. She smiled, then dropped to the sofa and pressed to answer as, through the speaker, Bing Crosby started to warble.

'Hello.'

'Merry Christmas!' A trio of voices came forth and there were Chase, Brooke and Maddie huddled close together on the screen.

'Merry Christmas,' Isla said, excitement causing her to shift a little on the sofa, wanting to get close to them all.

'Isla, Dad got me tickets to see Rag 'n' Bone Man,' Brooke called. 'Best freakin' gift ever!'

'Wow! That is amazing!'

'And I'm gonna learn the piano when I get back to school,' Brooke continued. 'I've already written the lyrics to a few songs.'

'That is fantastic, Brooke,' Isla responded.

'I got a dog, Isla!' Maddie shouted. She then held something up to the camera.

Isla twisted her head to get a better look.

'It's not real,' Maddie told her. 'But it barks and goes potty and you have to clean it up like a real dog.'

'I love it,' Isla said.

'It's called Reggie,' Maddie stated. 'Like a brother to Hannah's wheelchair.'

'Oh, goodness,' Isla said with a laugh.

'Hey, can I speak now?' Chase asked his family.

There he was. Gorgeous Chase, dressed in that leather bomber jacket he'd been wearing the very first time they'd met.

'How are you?' Isla asked him.

'Ah, you mean "how do I do"?' he asked, all British.

Isla giggled.

'I'm good,' Chase answered. 'But do me a favour, would you?'

'What?' Isla asked.

'Go open the door,' he breathed, steam obvious in the air. 'We're all freezing out here.'

It took a second for her to register what Chase had said. If couldn't be possible, could it? Isla leapt up, then stopped, looking back to the screen, doubting.

'Isla,' Chase said. 'Come open the door. I've got something for you.'

She didn't hesitate a moment longer. Running, hands pushing at doors and walls and Christmas paraphernalia in her haste to make it down the hallway, she finally wrenched open the door. And there on the step were Chase, Brooke and Maddie. Real. Back in London. In Notting Hill. With her. She almost couldn't take it all in and tears sprung forth that she couldn't control. Her hands went to her mouth as unfettered joy overwhelmed her.

'Merry Christmas,' Brooke and Maddie chorused again.

'This is just such a wonderful, *wonderful* surprise,' Isla cried.

'Can I smell turkey?' Maddie questioned.

'Yes,' Isla replied. 'Please go and help Hannah before she attempts something dangerous with gravy.'

'I love gravy,' Maddie said.

'Me too,' Brooke agreed, giving her sister a playful shove before chasing her up the hallway.

Isla's breath stilled as she was left alone with Chase. She took him in, all of him, framed by the backdrop of a snowy Beaumont Square, lights shining from the large fir tree and all along the ironwork fence like scores of icy fireflies.

'God, I've missed you,' he told her, stepping forward and pressing his lips to hers.

Isla shut her eyes and savoured every delectable second, until finally he let her go.

'Happy holidays,' he said and he produced an envelope from inside his jacket and passed it to her.

'Oh, Chase, but I haven't got you anything,' Isla began to protest. 'We said no gifts until we saw each other again and ... this is such a surprise.'

'Open it,' Chase urged, stepping inside and closing the door on the cold weather and winter scene.

With fingers not working properly, such was the anticipation, Isla ripped at the paper before drawing out a cardboard wallet. 'What is it?' She opened up the sleeve.

'Tickets,' Chase stated. 'The flight leaves in three days.' He took a breath. 'Isla, I would really love you to spend New Year in New York with us.'

She looked down at the paperwork as her heart rose up into her throat. There was also a ticket for Hannah. It was the best present she'd ever been given.

'Listen, I know it's a little presumptuous on my part but I've missed you so much and I wanted you to see New York ... before I think about making my base somewhere else,' he stated.

Making his base somewhere else? Isla was practically floating with a little apprehension but *so* much joy.

'I figured as the girls are so far on the other side of the U.S. it would be just as easy for me to travel a little further.' He cleared his throat. 'Once Breekers start the boutique hotel line it's gonna need a man on the ground here in London.'

Isla couldn't wait any longer. Throwing her arms around him she held on tight. 'Yes!' she said determined. 'Yes to New York. Yes to everything!'

'Who knows,' Chase said, kissing her lips again. 'We might even have time to finally get you to Las Vegas too.'

'Isla!' Hannah's voice called. 'I've dropped the sprouts!'

'Coming!' Isla hollered back. And then she took hold of Chase's hand. 'So, do you think, if you're staying in the UK for a while you might have time to master all one hundred and one uses of an umbrella?'

He smiled. 'Yes, Miss Winters, I'd say that's an absolute guarantee. I'm making time for important stuff now ... more Asian food, definitely more Dobble and I'm hopeful for a great deal of kisses in Notting Hill.' He pressed his lips to hers, soft and gentle with a soupçon of sexy ...

Isla pulled herself away. 'How about halal turkey?'

He kissed her lips again. 'How about the stars?'

On a station platform, with nothing to read,
and a four-hour train journey stretching ahead of him...

That's where the story began for Penguin founder Allen Lane.
With only 'shabby reprints of shoddy novels' on offer,
he resolved to make better books for readers everywhere.

By the time his train pulled into London, the idea was formed.
He would bring the best writing, in stylish and affordable
formats, to everyone. His books would be sold in bookstores,
stationers and tobacconists, for no more than the price
of a ten-pack of cigarettes.

And on every book would be a Penguin, a bird with a certain
'dignified flippancy', and a friendly invitation to anyone who
wished to spend their time reading.

In 1935, the first ten Penguin paperbacks were published.
Just a year later, three million Penguins had made their
way onto our shelves.

Reading was changed forever.

—

A lot has changed since 1935, including Penguin, but in the
most important ways we're still the same. We still believe that
books and reading are for everyone. And we still believe that
whether you're seeking an afternoon's escape, a vigorous debate
or a soothing bedtime story, all possibilities open with a book.

Whoever you are, whatever you're looking for,
you can find it with Penguin.